Carla shivered, not entirely from the cold, for a strange, unnerving sensation began to steal over her – a feeling of *déja vu*. Surely, she had experienced this before – standing here at this same window – her mind full of the same feelings of uncertainty and doubt. Could this really have happened before – even in a dream?

Turning and peering into the shadows behind her, she could just make out the shape of an iron bedstead and next to it, a cane-bottomed chair on which, leaning a little to one side, stood a candle in a metal candlestick. She felt she was no longer Carla – she was Lottie, and that little hump in the bed was Violet crying herself to sleep. From downstairs came the drift of voices. Her mother's. Low, urgent and pleading, and her father's monosyllabic replies . . . The place was playing tricks with her. She felt faint with cold and hunger, and she thought of the warmth and comfort of Thornmere Hall. But still she couldn't drag herself away from the window. Invisible ties seemed to bind her to the past. She was reluctant to leave. Her family's roots were planted deep in this old gatehouse.

House of Birds

ELIZABETH TETTMAR

A Mandarin Paperback
HOUSE OF BIRDS

First published in Great Britain 1992
by William Heinemann Ltd
This edition published 1992
by Mandarin Paperbacks
an imprint of Reed Consumer Books Ltd
Michelin House, 81 Fulham Road, London SW3 6RB
and Auckland, Melbourne, Singapore and Toronto

Reprinted 1993, 1994

Copyright © Elizabeth Tettmar 1992

A CIP catalogue record for this title
is available from the British Library
ISBN 0 7493 1066 9

Phototypeset by Intype, London

Printed and bound in Great Britain
by Cox & Wyman Ltd, Reading, Berks

For all those who share
my happy memories of
the Old Gatehouse

I wish to express my very deep gratitude
to Judith Murdoch for all the help
and encouragement she gave me
during the writing of this book.

ONE | *Carla*
The Present

Lottie was dying. Not willingly. She had never been one to give in without a struggle and now in her ninety-fifth year she was still fighting to keep a hold on life.

Carla kept watch. She had not moved from her place by the bedside since she had relieved the nurse. Daylight was creeping through a gap in the curtains, and through that she could see a part of the sky, flushed with pink. Pink skies in the morning – shepherds' warning. Yet October so far had been promising. Warm and mellow, filled with the scents of autumn: apples and blackberries from the orchard and wood smoke from the bonfire. Lottie had always loved October.

A change began to steal over her great-grandmother's wasted face. Was this the end at last? No, she had just lapsed into sleep again. How much longer, dear Lord, was Lottie going to hang on to a life that could have no meaning? What about my life? That still has meaning, she thought desperately. Lottie, for God's sake let go – for *my* sake, let go. I've given you seven years of my youth already – isn't that enough? Oh Lottie, I love you – but I want you to go now.

It seemed incredible to her that she could wish Lottie dead, but she did. Hours of going without sleep had left her bemused – a prey to morbid ideas. Why should the old live off the young . . . sapping their youth and energy and destroying their own chances of ever having a life of their own? Her thoughts did a sudden about turn. What sort of monster was she to harbour such thoughts against a feeble old woman? No monster really . . . Just someone exhausted and fearful of what the consequences of Lottie's death could mean. Freedom, of course – but what else? For years she had lived without a future, and now it was suddenly upon her. A future all her own – and on her own.

How was it possible for someone so old and so frail to cling so tenaciously to life? What did the present mean to Lottie anyway when she lived so much in the past? What would the doctor write on her death certificate? She was suffering from nothing more than extreme old age, but people weren't allowed to die from anything as simple as old age. There had to be a specific reason. Lottie had always been proud of her health, inclined to boast that she had never taken to her bed in her life, except on the occasion when her daughter Charlotte was born.

Carla rose to her feet. She had been sitting still so long the need to stretch her legs had become acute. All the Foster women had long legs. Lottie, Charlotte, Charley, and herself Carla, were all tall and erect. Even now, a mere shadow of her former self, Lottie was a long straight figure in the bed.

Carla drew back the curtains and opened the window a few more inches. A robin in a nearby beech tree suddenly burst into song, the only sound in that sleeping garden. Wearily, she leant her head against the framework of the window. How many more dawns before her own release finally came?

She turned. In the window recess was the Victorian chest of drawers that Lottie had brought with her from Boot Lane, its top used as a base for the collection of photographs she referred to as her 'rogues' gallery'. Carla knew them by heart. Even if she closed her eyes, she could tell the position of every one of them. They were her family.

There was one of Lottie taken with baby Charlotte during the first world war. Lottie, with her pensive smile and wide dark eyes, and little Charlotte on her lap, staring solemnly at the camera, waiting for the dicky bird to appear. Poor grandma, even at that tender age she had to learn the pain of disappointment.

This photograph, in sepia and pasted on board, was defaced by an ugly crack across the middle. It had been in the breast pocket of Lieutenant Henry Massingham's tunic when he had led a charge at the Battle of the Somme, and it had, so Carla was told, helped to save his life. A piece of shrapnel which would have pierced his heart had been deflected by his wallet and had gone through his arm instead, giving him what was called, a Blighty one. Unfortunately, a year later in 1917, back in Flanders, there had been no keepsake from Lottie to protect him from the mustard gas that filtered across the fields near Passchendaele.

Carla replaced the photograph and picked up one of Charlotte, her grandmother, taken twenty-seven years later and again in a wartime London. She posed, arm in arm with an American serviceman, joyfully laughing into the camera. It was the only photograph in existence of a truly happy looking Charlotte.

Carla found it difficult to connect this image of a laughing girl with the bitter old woman she remembered. She could not think of Charlotte as anything but old. Old and crabby. She wondered what it took to turn a joyful girl into a miserable old woman. Disappointment, frustration, grief? She sighed, thinking of herself – trying not to imagine herself as old. One thing she had vowed to herself during the long, tedious hours of her vigil – she would rather die young than grow old and useless, relying on others to sustain her. She would never be a parasite, living off her children, providing of course, that she ever had children. Not very likely in the circumstances. The Foster women didn't marry.

She put down Charlotte's photo and picked up one of Charley. Charley, her mother, and Charlotte's daughter.

There were many photos of Charley about the house,

but this was Lottie's favourite. For the last few years of her short life, Charley had been a much photographed model, and this particular likeness was a copy of the press photo commissioned by a fashion magazine. It had never been published because the day it was taken Charley was killed in a car crash on her way back to London.

Ironically, so it seemed to Carla, the old gatehouse which had been Lottie's birthplace had been the indirect cause of her mother's death. Charley had read in the *Daily Telegraph*, a British Rail notice, offering for sale the level-crossing cottages recently made redundant by the closure of much of the railway system in rural Norfolk. Among those advertised was Lottie's girlhood home at Thornmere, and Charley had immediately thought of it as the venue for her next modelling session.

'Gimmicks are the order of the day,' she said persuasively, bent on selling her idea to the fashion editor. 'And what could be more gimmicky than a disused railway gatehouse?'

'Your mother had set her heart on being photographed at my old home,' Lottie explained years later, when Carla was old enough to be told the details leading up to the accident. 'Driving back to Wenley that night she killed herself.'

It was strange for Lottie to say that Charley killed herself when the verdict of the coroner's court had been accidental death. Why should Lottie think that Charley had killed herself? Carla stared at the photo as if trying to find the answer. What a beautiful face her mother had. Small, pointed, and expressive. She looked the typical model of those times, hugging her fun furs around her lithe, slim body, her long dark hair streaming in the wind. It was the peak of the mini-skirt era which showed Charley's long shapely legs off to perfection. From whom had she inherited her obvious *joie de vivre*? Certainly not from Charlotte. From her American father more likely. And would anyone expressing such radiance as Charley, later that day deliberately crash her car into a tree? That was something Carla could not accept.

Behind the girlish figure reared the tall, grim-looking building that had been Lottie's home. The gatehouse. Not at all cottagey-looking really though Lottie sometimes referred to it as the cottage. Even then it looked deserted, because British Rail, as a precaution against vandalism had boarded up the windows. It stood amidst a winter landscape of empty fields and bare trees and where the level-crossing gates had been was a notice saying 'TAKE CARE – TRAINS CROSS HERE'. But not for long. The trains were withdrawn a few years later.

The gatehouse. Lottie's roots . . . Charlotte's cross . . . Charley's destiny? Perhaps she was being fanciful, but Carla could not help but believe that in different ways that old house had marred or marked the lives of three generations of Charlotte Fosters.

Why always the name Charlotte? Lottie, by giving her own name to her daughter had started a precedent. But why had she? Was she still clutching to the past, hoping perhaps in an oblique way, to recapture her own childhood? A bleak hope if so, thought Carla wryly, for Charlotte grew up nothing like her mother.

Charlotte hated the gatehouse. It was a place she could not bring herself to mention, and neither would they in her presence, in case it brought on one of her, what Lottie called, 'emotional storms'. But on one occasion, in a moment of overwrought passion, she blurted out its name herself.

At the time Carla was five years old and sitting on Lottie's lap as they watched the news together. A clip was being shown of the outside of a registry office where a much married film-star was about to do a repeat performance.

Carla suddenly piped up; 'When I grow up, I don't want to be married in a shop like that. I want to be married in a church and wear a pretty dress and have lots of bridesmaids.'

Lottie gave an amused chuckle, but Charlotte unaccountably exploded with anger.

'Foster women don't marry, you'll learn that soon enough,' she snapped. And when Carla stared incomprehendingly at her, she added viciously, 'If you want to know why, you can ask your precious Lottie. She set the example for the rest of us.'

Lottie refused to rise to the bait. 'I have many things on my conscience,' she replied calmly. 'But the fact that you are unmarried is not one of them.'

'If you had stayed on at the gatehouse instead of running away, I wouldn't have been born in a brothel . . .'

'Perhaps not.' The skin around Lottie's mouth tightened. 'Most likely you would have been born in a workhouse instead. Would you have preferred that?'

Charlotte could never get the last word with her mother. She had swept out of the room, slamming the door behind her. Carla could feel Lottie trembling, could even feel the vibration of her heartbeat. She timed her question when she sensed that her great-grandmother felt calmer.

'Lottie, what is a brothel?'

There was silence for a moment or two. Lottie always treated Carla as an equal. Now she was carefully considering her answer.

'A brothel is a different thing to different people. To me it was a place of refuge.'

'What's a place of refuge?'

'Something I hope you will never have to find out for yourself, sweetheart. Now be a good girl and get down from my lap. You're giving me pins and needles.'

There was a movement from the bed. Carla turned and saw that Lottie was awake. Her head was turned on the pillow and her faded, sunken, once beautiful eyes stared at Carla with a strange intensity. Carla hurried back to the bedside, and kneeling down, took the paper-thin freckled hand in hers.

'What is it, Lottie?'

Lottie's mouth opened soundlessly. Faintly, like a child's whisper came the one word, 'Norfolk.'

'You want to tell me something about the gatehouse?'

Lottie gave a faint nod.

'Do you want me to find out if it's still standing?'

That wasn't it. Lottie's eyes were still expressive enough to register disappointment.

'You want me to take you back to the gatehouse?'

Yes, that was it surely, for the old twinkle appeared in Lottie's eyes, and she even managed a small wry smile, either at the absurdity of such a notion or from wistfulness. A sudden idea come to Carla.

'I *will* take you back to the gatehouse, I promise,' she said, but this time Lottie made no attempt to answer. The effort seemed beyond her. She closed her eyes and appeared to fall asleep again, but a moment later, she was awake, and she tried to raise her head from the pillow, straining towards Carla.

'Your . . .' she said. 'Your . . .' She tried desperately to finish the sentence but her voice faded. Suddenly, her head fell back and she lay with her eyes wide open, staring fixedly at the ceiling. At first the full significance of this did not register with Carla, but when it did, an illogical panic gripped her. Lottie was dead. She had wanted her dead, but now she wanted her alive again. What had she been trying to tell her? Your . . . your . . . what? Her father?

She didn't hear the door open or know the nurse had entered the room until she spoke. 'I thought it was about time I relieved you. How's our patient? . . . Oh, my dear . . . my dear . . . you should have called me.'

The nurse went up to the bed, felt Lottie's pulse, then gently closed the unseeing eyes with the flat of her hand. She turned to Carla, intent on comforting her. 'Don't cry for her, my dear. You must realise that she is better off where she is.'

'But I wanted her dead,' said Carla in dull self-condemnation. 'I kept wanting her to die. I counted the years I had left to me before I was thirty, dreading the possibility that she might still be living even then – that I could still be tied to her. She never did me any harm in her life except to grow old, and I hated her for it. I'm a monster – I'm not human . . . I'm ashamed . . .'

'I think that just shows how human you really are,' the nurse answered prosaically. She coaxed Carla off her knees and onto a chair. 'How long have you been caring for her? Since your grandmother died, isn't it – seven years? It's a marvel to me you haven't broken down before this. Only someone completely devoid of feeling could have made that sacrifice without giving way to resentment at times. Now, come along – this isn't the time for me to be lecturing you – pull yourself together and put such morbid thoughts behind you. Believe me, you have no reason to feel guilty . . .'

'You don't understand . . . It isn't only remorse. She was trying to tell me something just before she died, and now I shall never know what it was . . .'

The nurse sighed. 'Most people mumble something or other on their death bed. Half the time, they don't know what they're saying – nothing that makes sense, anyway. It's distressing for their relatives who always think it's some important message. It rarely is. Believe me, Carla – I've come up against this, time after time. What you need is a good long sleep. Pop off now, and leave me to clear up everything here . . .'

'No, let me stay. I know I won't be able to sleep – I'd just lie and think about things. I'd be better off doing something to help.'

'Then find me a nice clean nightie, and after that you must notify the doctor and the undertaker. But first of all, you'd better ring round and tell the family. It's a bit early, but they must be informed.'

'There is no family,' said Carla tonelessly. 'Lottie was all the family I had.'

She found what she was looking for in a drawer in

Lottie's wardrobe. A white nightgown with a smocked yoke and lace trimming. Lottie had bought it many years ago, and put it away amid lavender bags and tissue paper with instructions it was to be used as her shroud when the time came.

'It's too pretty be buried in,' Carla protested at the time. 'Nobody will see it.'

'*I* will see it.' A distant look had come and gone in Lottie's dark eyes. 'It reminds me of one I had a long time ago when I was a girl about your age.'

'It was special?'

'Very special.'

'What happened to it?'

Lottie sighed. 'It got destroyed, I'm afraid.'

There is little time for thinking of oneself when a death has to be notified, and certain formalities attended to. Carla soon discovered this in the week that followed. It was three days before she really had a chance to be on her own, and by then she felt drained of any emotion except that of a mixture of guilt and relief. She was pleased when Lottie's solicitor phoned to say he would like to call. Preparing tea for them both gave her something specific to do.

The scholarly-looking Mr Lincoln was a regular visitor to Laburnum Lodge. He had worked for Lottie as long as Carla could remember.

'Did Miss Foster ever discuss her financial affairs with you?'

'Not in any detail. I wasn't that interested really – she never kept me short of money.'

'You never left her, did you? You never felt the urge to go away to college or to travel?'

His polite enquiry met with a cool stare from brilliant violet-blue eyes. He had noticed before that Carla always retreated into herself when some questions were not to her liking. She's touchy, this girl, he thought – a little bit on the defensive side.

'I only mentioned it because now you can afford to go

for a trip round the world if you want to. Your great-grandmother has left you in an extremely comfortable position.'

Carla drew in her breath. 'I didn't know Lottie had money. She wasn't mean, but she didn't throw it about.'

'She sold some property she owned near Cambridge Circus, an extremely valuable site. That was some years ago, before you were born – and she invested the money very wisely. This house, Laburnum Lodge, with its two acres of land, and in such a desirable locality, must be worth at least . . . Well, at a guess, half a million.'

Carla laughed incredulously. 'Lottie told me she paid two thousand pounds for it in 1944 and that was considered a lot of money in those days.'

'I don't suppose you'll want to stay here. It's large and inconvenient.'

Carla didn't want to commit herself. 'I haven't thought as far ahead as that. After the funeral I must make plans. You'll be able to come to the funeral?'

'Naturally. Miss Foster was my very good friend. But is there anything else I can do to help before then? With the arrangements I mean, or has the undertaker seen to everything?'

'That side of things, yes. But there is something I would like your advice about . . .'

Mr Lincoln had been preparing to leave, but at these words he sat down again. 'How can I help you, my dear?'

'I promised Lottie I would take her back to the gatehouse – the old level-crossing cottage in Norfolk where she was born. The only way I can think of keeping that promise is by scattering her ashes in the garden. But if the gatehouse is now private property, the owners might not agree to that, so would it be possible for me to scatter the ashes as near to the gatehouse as possible? In the field alongside, or where the railway track used to be. Could you find out for me?'

Mr Lincoln regarded Carla with concern. Her face was drawn and pale, and her eyes bruised-looking as if she had been going without sleep for a very long time. She's too young to have to shoulder all this responsibility, he thought. He felt it rather strange that she knew nothing about the gatehouse. Quickly, to put her mind at rest, he told her.

Carla stared. 'You mean Lottie actually bought the gatehouse from British Rail in 1967?'

'It was British Railway at the time of the sale. Yes, I have the deeds in my possession. Now, of course, the gatehouse belongs to you. I'm surprised your great-grand-mother didn't inform you of the fact.'

Carla was just as surprised and rather puzzled, considering how much Lottie had already revealed about her past. Why had she bought the gatehouse? Not to live in evidently, or even to use as a holiday cottage. Had she made any improvements to it? Had she let it out to tenants? She fired these questions at Mr Lincoln.

There wasn't much he could tell her, but he thought it possible that she had just left it to go to rack and ruin.

'I got the impression she bought it as a safeguard for her family. There was one brother still living then, and he would have lost his home when the railway line closed.'

Knowing what she did about Lottie's family, Carla did not think this likely. 'I believe she may have bought it as a kind of memorial to my mother,' she said, meditatively. 'I don't suppose she liked the idea of strangers taking possession.' Her expression relaxed. 'Well anyway, it makes my errand that much easier. I won't have to ask anybody's permission.'

'It would be a good idea to have someone look over it for you first. I could contact my opposite number in Beckton Market and get him to arrange it. Would you like me to do that?'

'If you would, Mr Lincoln, I would be very grateful.' Carla rose to her feet and the solicitor followed suit.

'Thank you for taking the time to come and see me and explain Lottie's affairs to me. I've never taken much interest in that sort of thing.'

'Then, on the advice of an old man, start taking an interest – start thinking of yourself. You have a life of your own to lead now and the opportunity to do what you like with it.'

'Yes, I know – and I'm going to take that opportunity, believe me.'

He found her self-assurance touching, for he was inclined to believe it was used to mask a vulnerability Carla would be the last to admit to. How much of her defencelessness was due, he wondered, to being brought up by two old women?

'What a pity,' he said, putting thoughts into words. 'That there isn't a man in your life you could turn to.'

Colour flooded Carla's face, and her eyes flashed. 'There never has, in all my twenty-five years, been a man in my life,' she said decisively. 'We Foster women have always managed quite well without men, and I hope I shall continue to do so . . .'

Mr Lincoln didn't answer, thinking it wiser to keep his thoughts and his conclusions to himself in future. Carla walked with him as far as the gate. The house stood well back from the road and beyond that spread the jealously guarded acres of green belt. That prized barrier of valleys and woodland that kept property developers at bay and sent the price of houses in the area soaring.

'As soon as I have any news regarding the gatehouse I'll write to you,' the solicitor promised, unruffled by her sudden outburst. He shook hands, got into his car, waved, wound up the window and drove off. Carla heard him hoot cautiously as he approached a blind corner.

She stood on the doorstep, biting on her fingernail, her mind in a turmoil. What a stupid thing to do, taking her frustration out on poor Mr Lincoln – giving herself away like that. He, himself was the man in her life at present, wasn't he? One she couldn't very well do without in the circumstances. She thought of another man – a shadowy figure, an unknown quantity – her father. Oh Lottie, why couldn't you have been honest with me . . . ?

She made for the stairs, then for Lottie's room, avoiding looking at the bed which was now stripped and covered with a dust-sheet. She had come, as she had been coming since she was a child, to gain comfort from her mother's portrait. Just a small water-colour sketch of a girl's head and shoulders, a painting of Charley at nineteen. 'A Portrait of a Girl in Love', it was called. Such a very apt title.

Until Charlotte's death, the picture had hung on the wall of her bedroom, opposite the bed so that it was the last thing her grandmother looked at before she went to sleep and the first thing she saw when she opened her eyes each morning. It was the only thing of Charlotte's that Lottie ever coveted, and Carla thought it heartless of Lottie when, soon after Charlotte's death, she had carted it off to her own bedroom. She didn't intend to follow Lottie's example. She'd leave Charley where she belonged.

Ever since, as a small child, she had been told who the smiling girl on the wall was, she had been drawn to the portrait, going secretly into the room whenever Charlotte was absent, to stare up at it until her neck ached, trying to find in the artist's impression, the elusive memory of a laugh and a delicious fragrance that was all she could remember of her mother. My mother . . . that happy girl of nineteen, her dark eyes spilling over with – with what? Love – or was that too simplistic an answer? She had something more – some magic working for her that gave a hint of provocation to her smile. Was the artist trying to create another La Gioconda, or was it just his interpretation of the effect of love? Lucky Charley, to have found a love that could make her feel like that.

For years, she had persuaded herself that the artist was her father. Only someone who had known her mother very intimately could have painted her looking like that. L.M. The artist's signature – an elaborate pattern of an 'L' entwined with an 'M'. An affectation for an unknown painter as Laurence Marsh was then, but now such a signature guaranteed a sure sale. Had Charlotte, or indeed

Lottie, had any conception of what the painting might be worth these days? Not that it would have made any difference. They weren't interested in its monetary value any more than she was.

Laurence Marsh – her father? Mr Lincoln's remark to her about needing a man in her life had been kindly meant, but it had touched her on a raw nerve. From the day she had started school and realised that there were such creatures as 'Daddies', she had felt the lack of one. She was cut off from her playmates – one apart – envious of those others whose lives seemed more rounded off and finished than hers.

When did it first begin to dawn on her that the person who had painted her mother might have been her mother's lover? It was useless to question Charlotte for she had long sensed that though her grandmother loved the painting, she detested the painter. With Lottie, unexpectedly, she came up against a wall of silence.

'But you must have known him!'

'Very briefly.'

'Was he my father?'

Lottie's face became suffused with pain. 'Listen Carla, there's only one thing I am really sure of in connection with Laurence Marsh, and that is . . . That he was a very unhappy episode in your mother's life.' It was the only time, Carla felt, that Lottie had been less than honest with her.

But it didn't stop her believing that he could well be her father. His work inspired her. She admired him as an artist, even if she had some reservations about him as a man. She began to nurture her own flare for painting, trying to adopt his style, trying to capture the enviable quality of his brush-strokes. Gradually, she built up an image of the artist by going to exhibitions and studying his work. His gifted, colourful personality left its stamp on every one of his paintings.

If Charley were alive now, she'd be in her middle forties, so Laurence Marsh was probably about the same age.

And even if she were flying too high and Laurence Marsh was *not* her father, he must surely know who her father was. He must have been one of the group who had lived as a commune in Cornwall in the swinging sixties — otherwise, how would he have met Charley? What was to stop her making herself known to him? She was free to do so now — she had no ties. But freedom was something she had yet to come to terms with.

She didn't see Mr Lincoln again until the funeral and at that time he had no news of the gatehouse, but a week later she received a letter from him together with a copy of Lottie's will in which she had left, with the exception of a gift of three thousand pounds to Mrs Baker, the twice-weekly domestic help, and donations to certain charities, everything to Carla.

'This will post-dates an earlier will,' Mr Lincoln wrote. 'Miss Foster made out a new will, in your favour, following the death of the younger Miss Charlotte Foster in 1982 . . .' His letter continued in the same business-like manner, giving fuller details of the extent of Lottie's estate, but ending on a more personal note. 'The key to the gatehouse is now with Lawson and Grindley of Beckton Market. Mr Grindley kindly arranged for one of his clerks to go out to Thornmere and check up on the gatehouse. He sends this warning. It is in a very derelict condition. There is broken glass everywhere, and he said it would be advisable to take a torch and to wear old clothes . . .'

TWO | *Lottie*
1911–1913

Plainly, across the fields, came the sound of revelry and distant music. Lottie paused to listen as she climbed the stile onto the footpath that led through the woods to Thornmere Park. Above the top of the trees she could see the flags of the Empire straining in the light summer breeze. Great Britain, Canada, Australia, and the Colonies. A tingle of pride and pleasure went over her. She had never experienced such an occasion as this in her life before.

It was 22 June 1911, and King George V's Coronation Day – a day she would remember for the rest of her life. Sir Roger Massingham was giving a fête in Thornmere Park by way of celebration, and what was more – she was part of it. From all the girls in the district who could have been picked to help serve teas, she – the daughter of a signalman – had been one of the lucky ones. 'It'll cost sixpence to speak to her now,' said some disgruntled villagers.

With a little jump, and careful not to snag her gown on the rails, she landed on the footpath, walking decorously until her high-spirits got the better of her. In spite of the fact that her hair was up for the first time that day, and that she was wearing borrowed finery, she lifted her skirts and ran. She just couldn't wait for the fun to start.

At the entrance to the Park, she was greeted by a strident blast of noise. Above the sound of a steam organ came the strains of the village band, and above that came high-pitched excited voices, and screams of laughter from the children having boat rides on the mere. Lottie stared bemused at the crowds milling around the side-shows, chancing their luck and a few hard-earned pennies on hoop-la and skittles and coconut shies, and wondered where they had all come from. From villages, miles around? Holidays were too few and far between to be wasted, especially those with the prospect of a free tea thrown in.

But as she drew nearer to the large red and white striped marquee where the teas were to be served, she felt her excitement giving way to apprehension. Her mother, she knew, had been highly flattered when her daughter was chosen as one of the helpers but now Lottie was beginning to feel the weight of the responsibility.

'Now don't you be doing anything to let me down in front of the gentry,' was her mother's last warning. 'No putting on airs. Just you be your natural self, and you'll come to no harm.'

Lottie had no intention of being other than herself, and she wouldn't know how to put on airs if she tried, but once in the hands of Mrs Osborne, the vicar's wife, her confidence soon returned. She was inspected and approved of, and given a mass of instructions to follow.

It was cool and quiet inside the marquee, and smelled pleasantly of damp earth and roses. Pots of hot-house flowers, grudgingly loaned by the head gardener, were placed at strategic points, and red, white and blue bunting was wound decoratively around the ridge-poles. Along one end of the marquee were trestle tables, on which food hampers were being unpacked by servants from the Hall. Mrs Webster was in charge here; she and her staff had been buttering bread and cutting up cake all morning. Mrs Osborne with Miss Davies, the village school-teacher, and Miss Brookes, the doctor's sister, were busying themselves arranging flowers for the top table which was reserved for the Massingham family and their guests.

Lottie, and Henrietta Cartwright, a local builder's daughter, were allocated the task of serving here. Henrietta, Lottie could tell, was torn between pride at being chosen to wait on the quality, and dismay at the thought of being harnessed to the daughter of a railwayman. She was also full of chagrin because Lottie's dress was more stylish than her own.

Long before the flaps were open to admit the public, Lottie was having trouble with her hair. She had gone off to a quiet corner in an attempt to deal with it, when she was hailed by a breezy but unfamiliar voice. 'Here, let me have a go, you'll never manage that on your own.'

It was the girl with a powerful voice and high colour who Lottie had seen helping to cut sandwiches. She was noticeable on account of her marked London accent, and lazy pale green eyes under extraordinary long white lashes. 'I betcher this is the first day you've had your hair up, ain't it?' she said.

Lottie nodded, silenced by the sudden realisation that the girl's high colour and red lips owed nothing to nature. She had never seen a painted woman before and though she didn't feel as shocked as a decent girl should, she could not avoid staring.

'Have a good look, then you'll be sure to know me again,' the other commented dryly, and Lottie blushed.

'I'm sorry, I didn't mean to be rude. I was wondering if you were new here . . . ?'

'I don't work at the Hall, if that's what you mean. I'm staying on holiday with Cook – she's me aunt. Perhaps you can tell me why everyone calls her missus. She ain't married you know, she's a Miss Webster – not Mrs Webster.'

Lottie explained that all cooks were given the honorary title of Mrs whether they were married or not. The girl was not surprised. To her way of thinking all them that worked up at the Hall didn't own their own souls, let alone their names.

'You in service yourself then?' She looked Lottie up and down. 'You didn't buy that frock outer a servant's wages, I bet.'

Lottie fingered her biscuit-coloured crêpe-de-Chine with a little smirk of pride. 'It belongs to Florence, my sister, she sent it for me to wear today. Her mistress passed it on to her when she was finished with it. We often get clothes come down to us that way. My three eldest sisters are all in service, but I'm – well, I'm a kind of pupil-teacher.'

'That explains it – the way you talk I mean. I can understand you, but I'm blowed if I can understand that lot over there. They jabber away like a lot of foreigners.'

'That's the Norfolk way of speaking. I used to speak that way myself, but Miss Davies, that's my teacher, she ironed it out of me. She said I'd stand a better chance of getting to teachers' training college if I could speak nicely.' Lottie, slightly affronted at what she thought of as a reflection on her people, tossed her head and another lock of hair fell down. 'I'm not ashamed of being Norfolk.'

'Nor should you be, any more than I'm ashamed of being a Londoner.' Aggie started again on Lottie's hair. 'What's your name?'

'Charlotte, though I'm always called Lottie.'

'And I'm Agnes, Agnes Sharpe, but everyone calls me Aggie, even me aunt, but I'm not allowed to call her anything but Mrs Webster, unless we're on our own. She don't like me much,' Aggie added, without rancour. 'She thinks I make myself look common, but I'd rather look common than look like some around here. That Miss Veness, the lady's maid, fr'instance. She's a real stuck-up piece of goods, if you ask me!'

Cook glared in their direction and Aggie lowered her voice, 'I live in West Ham, I don't suppose you've heard of it, it's in East London, and me Dad's a tram driver. What's yours?'

'A signalman. He works for the Eastern and Coastal Railway Company and we live in the level-crossing cottage down the lane.'

Aggie looked impressed. 'We've both got fathers in uniforms, then. That's something to crow about. My Mum sets great store by being married to a someone in uniform. She says that though you'll never be well-off, you'll never be in want neither. I s'pose she's right, though I've never eaten so well in me life as I have this week.' Aggie stepped back to admire her handiwork. 'Well, that's the best I can do for you, I'm afraid. Your hair's too thick for these potty little pins. You tell your ma to get some of them large tortoiseshell ones.'

Someone had opened the flaps of the marquee and the waiting public came surging in, making a beeline for the tables. 'I'd better go and get ready,' Lottie said. 'We've been told we've got to help at the long tables until the party from the Hall arrives. Thank you for doing my hair, it feels much more comfortable like that.'

For the next half-hour Henrietta and Lottie found themselves run off their feet. Mounds of sandwiches disappeared quicker than they could be replenished, gallons of tea were brewed and disposed of, cakes melted away as if by magic. 'Where the dickens do they put it all,' Cook muttered as she refilled the tea urn with boiling water. She was scarlet from the heat of the paraffin stove. The air was becoming oppressive. The tightly-packed bodies at the tables, in stiff, unyielding Sunday clothes were generating waves of heat and bodily odours. Lottie's flannelette bodice was sticking to her skin.

The ladies from the Hall, when they arrived, looked enviably well-groomed and cool. They were led in by Sir Roger and Lady Massingham, the latter a magnificent figure in shot grey taffeta that rustled as she walked. Lottie nervously smoothed her apron. Her hour had come. If she fumbled and dropped a cake in her ladyship's lap or spilt tea over one of the guests, she'd never hear the end of it. The villagers would titter gleefully about it for weeks. The unfortunate Henrietta had already had an accident, spilling a jug of milk down her front and had been sent home to change. Lottie would now have to manage on her own.

The family from the big house were no strangers to her. She had opened the level-crossing gates to all of them in her time. Lady Massingham, straight-backed and aloof in her carriage, or Sir Roger on his sturdy old grey mare. Sometimes Miss Lucy, taking a languid afternoon drive in the pony-cart. Pale and self-absorbed, considered a beauty chiefly on account of her remarkable violet-coloured eyes. Master Henry, always friendly and smiling. Lottie remembered him as a bashful school-boy in a sailor suit. Now he was a pleasant-faced youth about her own age, or perhaps a year older. She noticed, with relief, that Mr Joseph, the elder son, was not one of the party. There was talk that he had been sent on a tour of Europe to avoid a scandal concerning a chorus girl. But her mother had pooh-poohed this story, warning Lottie to pay no heed to gossip. Under no circumstances would Ellen Foster have anything said against the gentry.

The Massinghams had brought a large house-party with them. The men all in light summer suits or blazers, and the ladies in fashionable narrow skirted dresses and balancing wide-brimmed hats on their carefully coiffured hair. For once, Miss Lucy in a white lace dress with trimming that matched her eyes, was without her usual petulant expression.

Lottie found that once she had got over her initial stomach-churning trepidation, her nervousness left her. She was helped, she knew, by the fact that most of the party took no notice of her. She was just a pair of hands that put dishes before them and took them away again. She could have been invisible or deaf. But at the same time, she also knew that two at that table were not entirely oblivious of her presence. Lady Massingham looked her up and down quite openly. Henry was a little more discreet. His shy, admiring glances caused Lottie little flutters of nervous pleasure.

*

That evening Ellen Foster dropped her bombshell.

'I don't understand.' Lottie stared stupidly at her mother. 'What parlour-maid?'

'If you'd only pay attention, I wouldn't have to repeat myself,' Ellen answered sharply. 'As I was saying, Lady Massingham was so impressed by the way you waited at table she told me she would like you to join her staff. As a house-maid at first, until there's an opening for a parlour-maid. She said you would make an admirable parlour-maid, what with your height and the way you carry yourself. It's all been arranged. You're to start at the Hall when the family return from Scotland in October.'

The blood rushed in and out of Lottie's face. Her dreams of going to college – of becoming a teacher – suddenly dispersed like a puff of smoke. She knew it was useless to argue with her mother, but she argued just the same.

'But I could do much better for myself if I had an education – Miss Davies said so. I'd be in a position to help you, and perhaps Violet and Billy too when the time comes.' Lottie knew she was clutching at straws, and not very substantial straws at that, judging by the scepticism on her mother's face.

'Teaching in a village school – like your precious teacher! That won't get you very far. Now, you just listen to me, gel. Most girls your age would give their eye-teeth for such a chance. I told her ladyship how clever you be with your needle, and she said that coming from me was a good enough recommendation, and I thought, if all goes well there's no reason why you shouldn't even finish up as a lady's maid. You speak nicely, and you've got lady-like ways. You'd be no disgrace to Lady Massingham as her personal maid.'

'If I speak nicely, and have lady-like ways, it is all due to Miss Davies,' retorted Lottie with spirit.

Thwack! She felt a blow to her head that nearly set her teeth rattling.

'Don't you ever answer me back like that again,' said

Ellen, crimson with fury. Then as she saw weals rise on her daughter's cheek, her temper died as quickly as it had flared. 'There there, don't cry,' she said, contritely. 'I know you set your heart on going to college, but you must have known it couldn't be, we haven't got that kind of money. You could have been keeping yourself for the past two years if you'd been in service, but we let you stay on at school, costing us more than we can afford . . .'

'I'm earning a shilling a week.'

'A shilling a week! That doesn't even keep you in boot leather. Do grow up, gel.' Ellen's tone softened. 'One thing, you won't be going far from home, you'll be able to pop in and see us on your half-days, which is more than your sisters can. You'll thank me for this one day, Lottie, not that I expect you to believe that now, but you will. Now dry your eyes and go and tell your father that his supper be ready.'

Sidney Foster had loitered over his watering of the vegetable plot, Lottie suspected on purpose, knowing what his wife had in mind. Even so she still harboured hopes when she ran off to appeal to him, for he had given her just as much encouragement as Miss Davies had.

He shook his head even before she opened her mouth, his eyes glancing off the crimson finger marks on her cheek.

'It's no good, lass. I can see what's in your mind, but it's no use – your mother has had the last word. The arguments are all in her favour. Money don't grow on trees . . .'

'Miss Davies did hold out hope of a scholarship . . .'

Her father gave a dejected shake of his head. 'When you're my age, Lottie, you won't set much store on hope. No, it can't be done – it can't be done.' He bent and pulled out a weed from between a row of radishes, then straightened up and stared with a blank expression into the distance. 'Edication ain't for the likes of you and me, gel,' he said dolefully. 'We have to learn to get by without it.'

Lottie had no appetite for supper that night, and no ability to sleep either. Little Vi, dead to the world after the day's excitement, lay curled up beside her. Restless and hot under the covers, Lottie threw them aside, and pattered bare-feet over to the window.

A light shower had fallen earlier, drawing out the sweet elusive scent from the bean flowers in the field alongside the lane. Edward and Alfred, her brothers, would be hoeing that field tomorrow. They wouldn't give a fig for education. At twelve years old they'd been fretting to leave school, anxious to be out in the world, doing a man's work and bringing home a few shillings a week to hand proudly to their mother.

Lottie sighed. Why did she have to be the odd one out in the family? Because, like her father, she loved reading and knew what wonders there were to be discovered between the covers of a book? There would be little opportunity for reading once she went into service – if some of the stories her sisters told were true. All they had energy for when they got to bed was to fall into a dreamless sleep.

She felt a slight tremor beneath her feet – signs that a train was approaching. The last train to Beckton Market went past the gatehouse just before eleven o'clock. She listened for its faraway whistle, then felt the vibrations increasing as it got nearer. Leaning out of the window, she watched the sparks from its fire-box shooting skywards. The rush of air as it flew past, shook the window frames. She drew back as the acrid, sulphurous fumes belched into the room. Trains had been running past the gatehouse for nearly fifty years and likely to run forever. They were part of her life – a life she felt was now drawing away from her.

But by next morning she had made up her mind that she wasn't going to give in so easily. There must be some way she could avoid being sucked into domestic service.

Perhaps Miss Davies could advise her. She arrived at school early, ready to appeal to her.

Miss Davies' pretty, faded face held little hope. 'I can't go against your parents' wishes, Lottie. Things are different now. When your father was backing me, but now . . . I wish I could help you, I really do. Perhaps I could give you some extra coaching in your spare time?'

'I won't have much spare time if I go into service,' said Lottie bitterly.

Her mind ran along desperate channels. She thought of Henrietta Cartwright. She attended a private school in Beckton Market run by a Mr Lee and his middle-aged daughter. Private schools were outside the jurisdiction of the Board of Education, and often employed unqualified teachers. And surely she was qualified enough to teach children younger than herself? She had a sudden vision of leaving home, earning enough to keep herself, and moving into lodgings. What's more, she could rely on Miss Davies to give her a good reference.

It was a three-mile walk to Beckton Market, less across the fields. Lottie went by road. She wished she was wearing her crêpe-de-Chine instead of the navy delaine she always wore for school. She had been wearing it for two years, and had now outgrown it. It felt skimpy and looked it, and was so short it only reached down to the top of her boots. Unfortunately there was no question of going home and changing, not with her mother about.

It was a humid day and Lottie had raised a blister on her heel long before she reached the outskirts of the market town. She had stuffed her long rope of hair under her tammy, hoping she would look more grown-up than leaving it hanging down her back. She was teased by the thought that if Lady Massingham had seen her as she looked now, instead of in her finery, she might have had second thoughts about employing her. It was an afterthought that gave her small comfort, for it didn't say much for her chances at Carisbrooke College.

Carisbrooke College! That proved a disappointment to

start with. The name suggested an imposing school, but it turned out to be a narrow-fronted, semi-detached, Victorian house of gloomy aspect, a gloom that continued inside with even greater oppression. Lottie was shown into a darkened parlour by a small skivvy wearing a cap and apron several times too large for her, who ran off repeating aloud in case she forgot, the message Lottie had given her. 'A Miss Foster to see Mr Lee – a Miss Foster to see Mr Lee – a Miss Foster to see Mr Lee.' Lottie sat down on the edge of a shiny leatherette covered chair and waited, already feeling that she had come on a fool's errand, but determined to see it through.

Twenty minutes later, she was on her way back to Thornmere with tears streaming down her face.

She ploughed across the fields, past caring if her skirt got snagged by brambles or her boots became clogged with soil, carried forward by the impetus of despair. Never as long as she lived, would she forget the look on Miss Lee's face when she had introduced herself.

'I understood you wanted to see my father. What could *you* want with my father, may I ask? I am the one who interviews domestics, and there is no opening for another servant at present.' The woman's indignation matched her contempt.

Lottie, feeling her mind go blank, tried to pull herself together. The other had her at a disadvantage. So very neat, so very precise, with eyes behind pince-nez glasses, like small round pebbles. Miss Lee's mouth slackened with disbelief when she learnt the reason for Lottie's visit.

'You a teacher! What could you possibly teach anybody?'

'I have been working as an assistant to Miss Davies of Thornmere school for the past two years. I teach the infants to read and I help the older ones with their sums . . .'

'Sums! We do not do *sums* here – we teach mathematics.' The scorn in Miss Lee's voice raised goose-pimples on Lottie's arms. 'I'm afraid you have wasted your time coming here, and what is more to the point, you have wasted mine. Now, please leave, and by the tradesmen's entrance, if you do not mind.'

Lottie made one last desperate attempt, and in her anxiety, caught hold of the woman's arm. 'Please give me a try . . . just a few weeks on approval. I promise you, you won't be sorry. I'll work hard . . . I'll do anything . . . anything to make myself useful . . .'

Two hectic spots of colour appeared on Miss Lee's cheeks, her nostrils flared. 'How dare you touch me,' she said, shaking her arm free. 'How dare you put me in this ridiculous position. You must be mad. Go back to your class of clodhoppers. There is nothing you could teach the young ladies here, except perhaps bad manners.' She pointed to the door. 'Now go.'

Lottie drew herself up to her full height, biting back words that would have scorched her tongue. It was vital for her own sake to rescue some little shred of dignity from this sorry situation. She was suddenly fired by an inspiration.

'Miss Lee,' she said quietly, 'You mentioned your young ladies, I think you meant your pupils, for you will never be able to teach your girls how to become ladies – not real ladies, because you would need to be a lady yourself to do that. And you are not a lady, Miss Lee, you are a snob. A small-minded snob, and I'm very relieved you've turned me down, because I would hate to become just like you. I can see my own way out, thank you,' – which she did, and through the front door, with all the hauteur of a Lady Massingham.

But once safely out of sight of the house her hauteur left her, and she broke into a run, not caring who saw her or the state she was in. She ran without stopping until she found herself in a ploughed field, out of breath and now past tears.

She had burnt her boats. Her brief moment of triumph was a poor return for her blighted future. The story would soon be out. No other school would consider her now. And what would Miss Davies think when she heard, as she surely would. Henrietta Cartwright would see to that. And the village folk and her family? They would all have their say, and at her expense.

She was entirely alone in the field. To her right a scarecrow stared at her with a blank turnip-like face. Its empty eye sockets seemed to mock her distress. She looked up to where clouds were sailing like old-time galleons across the sky, and she made her vow.

'I swear, as sure as God is my witness,' she cried aloud. 'I swear that I'll never let anyone else humiliate me. As long as I live, nobody will have the chance to look down on me again, ever!'

If she had expected a sudden flash of lightning or a thunder-bolt, she was disappointed. This was not to be her road to Damascus. It was the footpath that led straight to Thornmere Hall. So be it. She could still dream her dreams. People could order her body about, but they couldn't control her mind. That was still her own.

It was December, and a bitterly cold winter's day just before Christmas, Lottie's first Christmas at Thornmere Hall. She had been a housemaid exactly ten weeks, but it seemed like years.

As always, at this time of the morning she was in the library, and had just finished polishing the grate and re-setting the fire. Sitting back on her heels, she looked about her at the comfort and splendour of the room and compared it, not for the first time, with the freezing attic which she shared with one of the kitchen-maids.

She looked at the clock. Twenty-past six; the only other souls astir in that sleeping house were the kitchen-maids, busily occupied on the other side of the green baize door. Wiping her hands on her apron, she carefully selected the book she had started on yesterday. She had twenty-five precious minutes in which to lose herself in another world.

Sitting absorbed in her reading, she didn't realise some-one had entered the room, until she looked up.

Joseph Massingham towered above her. He was still in evening dress, a well-built handsome man, with pale blue eyes in a face already showing signs of dissipation. He must have travelled down from London on the overnight train. She had not heard the carriage, or the library door opening. Now she was trapped, on her knees, an open book before her. She was too frightened to move.

He was smiling in a way that boded no good. She and Mr Joseph were old adversaries, dating back to the days when she used to help open the gates. She had feared and mistrusted him since, when riding once across the level-crossing, he flicked her with his whip. He didn't intend to hurt, he just wanted the satisfaction of seeing her flinch, and she wouldn't, no matter how many times he tried to make her. It was a battle of wills that only ended when Mr Joseph went off on his first trip to Europe.

But now she couldn't escape him, and she fancied his old grievances flared into life, for there was a malicious glint to his eyes. 'So the pretty little wench can read, can she,' he said mockingly. 'Let's see what takes her fancy.' He took the book from her and flipped through its pages, then laughed. Not a pleasant sound to Lottie's ears. She rose. Being on her knees before him might seem too much like grovelling.

'Ruskin?' he said. 'You admire the works of radical writers, do you? You don't harbour thoughts of equality for the masses, I hope? Or worse still, think of joining the suffragette movement?'

There was a spiteful note in his raillery that jarred her nerves. She said apologetically, 'I have never heard of John Ruskin before. It was the title that attracted me, it sounded so pretty – *Sesame and Lilies* . . .'

He interrupted her with another, harsher laugh. 'There is nothing lily-like about you at the moment. You should see yourself. Smudges on your face, dirty finger prints on your apron – yes, and another on the book!' He lowered his brows, his eyes steely beneath them. 'That deserves punishment in some form, wouldn't you say?'

She felt alarmed, remembering his reputation as a violent man, who once in an ungovernable fit of rage had whipped his horse until it screamed with pain.

'What I was thinking of,' he said, coming nearer and taking her by her wrist. 'Was a little forfeit for being found out. Shall we say a kiss?'

Lottie tried to back away, but he held her firm. 'Please sir, I'll pay for any damage I may have caused,' she pleaded.

He grinned. 'But presumption has no price on it. And don't you think it is presumptuous for a servant to read my father's books without permission? No, a kiss it must be. Nothing else will satisfy me.'

I mustn't lose my temper, thought Lottie, feeling her heart hammering against her ribs. I spoilt my chance with Miss Lee – I can't afford to do that again. But the thought of being kissed by this man filled her with revulsion. She had never been kissed before, and she didn't want her first kiss to be taken by force.

With an effort she twisted her arm free, and stood at bay against the book shelves. 'If you kiss me, I'll scream,' she threatened.

That amused him. His eyes sparkled gleefully. 'Carry on – scream. Who will hear you at this time of the morning? It will be your word against mine, and don't forget you've left your mark on my father's book. He won't like that at all.'

Lottie felt stricken by the futility of her position. What should she do? Let him have a quick kiss and get it over with? No, why should she! Just because he looked upon her as an inferior. She would show him that even a servant knew how to behave correctly.

'Let me go, please,' she said. 'I will tell Sir Roger about the book myself when I take him up his hot water.'

Joseph's expression hardened. 'Forget the book –

don't care a damn about the book, but I do mind being defied by a little slut like you.' Before she could move he had caught her by her shoulders, and pressing her head back he fastened his lips on hers and forced her mouth open.

Before this moment Lottie had thought of a kiss between a man and a woman as something romantic – something infinitely sweet and full of bliss, a sharing of love. But there was nothing loving in this kiss, nothing sweet or romantic about it. It was repulsive and cruel, and when he thrust his tongue into her mouth, she felt her gorge rise. Disgust gave her strength and she broke away from him and stood back panting. He was also panting, out of control, his eyes glaring savagely. He went to make another grab for her but she dodged away. She ran to the door, flung it open, and ran to safety in the servants' quarters. She half expected him to follow, but he didn't. She went into the butler's pantry and sluiced her face and hands at the sink, and then rinsed out her mouth, trying to get rid of the awful feel of his tongue. When she felt calmer, she collected her cleaning materials and went upstairs to turn out the drawing-room. Though Mr Joseph left for another tour abroad shortly after-wards, she never again felt safe in the library. Her clan-destine affair with the books came to an end.

June the 22nd came round again, the anniversary of George V's Coronation and Aggie was back in Norfolk for another brief holiday.

'I'm not staying at the Hall, this time,' she confided to Lottie. 'I'm being boarded out with the under gardener.'

Aggie had changed. She had put on weight and looked older than the twenty years she claimed she was. Her hair had grown many shades lighter and her eye-lashes had miraculously darkened. And she drenched herself in a strong perfume she called Phul Nana. Lady Mas-singham, she claimed, had given orders that she was not to stay at the Hall.

When Lottie asked why, Aggie shrugged her shoulders philosophically. 'A barmaid ain't good enough to breathe the same air as a baronet's wife, I'spect. Anyway, I feel freer staying with the Stoneham's, and young Reuben smuggles me in peaches from the greenhouse.' Aggie threw Lottie a sideways look out of her gooseberry green eyes. 'What do you think of Reuben Stoneham?'

Lottie had difficulty in placing him. Wasn't he the tall, rather spotty youth who helped in the stables? Yes, Reuben Stoneham – she remembered him now, the same age as her brother Alfred.

Aggie tittered. 'Reuben's taken a fancy to you, I reckon. He's always asking after you. What's happened to your other admirer?'

'What admirer?'

'That young bloke with the baby blue eyes who kept ogling you at the fête last summer.'

Lottie gave an embarrassed laugh, looking around to check there was nobody within earshot. 'You mustn't say things like that, you'll get me into trouble. Mr Henry is family and I'm only a servant.'

'Servant or lady – we're all the same under our skins,' Aggie retorted, grinning. 'Where is he then?'

'He's away at school.'

'And what about the other – the one that was always getting himself talked about? The black sheep, they call him.'

Lottie didn't answer immediately and when Aggie glanced at her she saw that Lottie's mouth had tightened into a straight line. 'He's in Kenya, farming. Some scheme to shore up the family fortunes, I believe, though from what I hear, it's a scheme that's costing Sir Roger money.' She shrugged her shoulders and changed the subject. 'Come on, Aggie – tell me more about London. I'm coming to London, one day.'

'I'll believe that when I see it.'

'I am. I'm determined to get to college, somehow.'

Aggie's stay went all too quickly as far as Lottie was

concerned. Lottie knew that the other servants thought Aggie vulgar, and few had a good word to say for her, but Lottie liked her. She saw beneath the strident façade, a warm-hearted generous nature, and a steadfast friend. They promised to write to each other when they said goodbye, and did for a few months, Aggie's letters reeking of Phul Nana. Then suddenly they ceased altogether, and Lottie's letters went unanswered. One day she plucked up courage to approach Cook on the subject, choosing her moment carefully, for that formidable lady could be frighteningly short-tempered at times.

She wasn't in the best of tempers now. 'Don't ask me where that young hussy has gone – I don't know and I don't care! All I do know is that she has left home. Now, get out from under my feet and make yourself useful.'

Lottie felt she had made herself useful to good purpose when she suddenly found herself a parlour-maid. No more carrying scuttles of coals up three flights of stairs. No more blackleading grates and lighting fires. Now one of her duties was to help Cooper the head parlour-maid wait at table under the watchful eye of Mr Thorne, the butler.

Her salary had jumped up from fifteen to twenty pounds a year. She treasured the independence this gave her. Now it was her turn to put a few shillings into her mother's hand occasionally, and a few more shillings into her savings account.

And then her fortune took another turn for the better. Miss Veness retired and Lottie, much to her gratification, was asked to take over the duties of a lady's maid. Lady Massingham had started on another of her economy drives, becoming now more frequent as the farm in Africa became more dependent upon the resources of the Thornmere estate. One of the perks of her new position which pleased Lottie more than any other, was a far more becoming uniform.

It fits perfectly, she thought as she preened herself one

October afternoon in the cheval mirror in the sewing-room. It emphasised her tapering waist and narrow hips, and was short enough to show an inch or two of her slender ankles. Though she was no more vain than any other good-looking girl of eighteen, she did take pride in her appearance. It was her height and her carriage that had brought her to Lady Massingham's notice in the first place. Two years, she thought – two years to the day I started here.

She had come a long way since that first morning at Thornmere Hall. She remembered her misery and despair when she had presented herself at the tradesmen's entrance. I'm too good for this, she thought then. I won't always be a servant – I'll show them.

But who had she shown? Sir Roger and Lady Massingham? They wouldn't believe one of the lower classes capable of such ideas. Mr Joseph? She already knew what he thought of her! Miss Lucy? Lottie doubted whether Miss Lucy ever thought seriously about anything – it would take too much effort. Mr Henry? No, he had never treated her as an inferior – his manner was always courteous. She often bumped into him as he wandered about the grounds, marking time until he went up to Cambridge, and it took her some little time before she suspected that their chance meetings were not entirely accidental.

In September, Lady Massingham had made a sudden decision to go off to Africa and find out for herself why the Kenya venture was failing, taking Miss Brookes with her as a travelling companion. With the absence of his mother, and her authoritative presence, Henry began to take risks. He even gave up the pretence that the meetings were purely accidental. All this Lottie found highly flattering, but as the meetings continued, and the first few shy encounters gave way to an easy friendliness, her misgivings started. But it was so entirely innocent, or so she tried to assure herself.

She didn't flatter herself that Henry sought her out for

any other reason than to fill in his time until he left for college, but this knowledge didn't lessen her own pleasure in his company. And it was at this point in her reflections that she noticed the door handle turning. She hurried back to her chair and picked up the mending she had discarded.

It was Henry. The unexpectedness of his appearance, for he had never sought her in the house before, sent colour to her cheeks. She bent over her sewing, seeking to hide her confusion.

'I hope I am not intruding,' he said. 'I've come to ask a favour. Would you mind sewing this button back for me?'

The third button on his Norfolk jacket was hanging by a thread. 'Do you want me to take it off,' he said, as Lottie rethreaded her needle.

'That won't be necessary, but if you wouldn't mind loosening the belt . . .'

Lottie stood up, her head on the same level as his, acutely aware of his eyes on her as she stitched the button into place. By necessity they were so close she imagined she could hear the beating of his heart. She heard him clear his throat. 'Did you know this room was once the day nursery?' he said.

'Yes, Nanny told me.' Nanny was now retired and lived at the lodge, but sometimes she would return to her one-time kingdom and sit with Lottie, telling her anecdotes about the Massinghams when they were children.

Henry was nineteen, with a sensitive intelligent face, but at that moment he seemed more like an embarrassed schoolboy as he blurted out his confession. 'I loosened the button on purpose. I wanted an excuse to come and see you.'

Lottie's colour heightened. She felt touched but wary, not sure how to handle this. She broke off the thread, returned the needle to a pin-cushion, and went back to her mending before answering.

'You don't have to make excuses to visit your old

nursery, Mr Henry. You have prior claim to it. I'm only here as a needlewoman,' she said reprovingly.

'You misunderstand me. What I was trying to say was . . .'

'Mr Henry – please. You're standing in my light.'

Henry drew back, disconcerted, fastening up his jacket. Lottie concentrated on her mending, but he could see her chest rising and falling, and a tiny drop of blood appeared where she had jabbed her finger. He watched as she sat with her head bent over her sewing, her needle flashing like a moving point of light. Where a ray of sunshine touched her hair, it turned the brown to gold. Her eyes, under their long upcurved lashes, were dark and lustrous. In her modest grey dress, she made him think of a seven-teenth-century Puritan, though there was nothing puritanical in the sweet, promising curve of her lips. The thought of those lips yielding to his gave him a yearning ache. With nervous agitation he reached in his pocket for a book.

'Would you mind if I read something to you?' he said, and Lottie nodded, relieved that the conversation had taken a turn towards discretion.

'It's from a poem by Thomas Hardy . . .'

'Oh. Modern poetry. I won't understand that.'

'I think you will.' Henry opened his book at a page he had already marked. 'It's called "We sat at the window" – very apt under the circumstances . . .

> ' "We sat at the window looking out,
>   And the rain came down like silken strings
>   That Swithin's day . . ." '

Lottie interrupted with a laugh. 'I don't call that apt. It's October not July, and it isn't raining.'

'Let me finish. Listen . . .

> ' "We were irked by the scene, by our own selves; yes,
>   For I did not know, nor did she infer

How much there was to read and guess
By her in me, and to see the crown
    By me in her
Wasted were the two souls in their prime,
And great was the waste, that July time
    When the rain came down." '

This time Lottie did not laugh, but her needle was stilled. 'I don't think that is very apt either,' she said quietly.

'Oh Lottie, don't you see what I'm getting at? Can't you guess – you must realise by now . . .'

Across the park came the sound of guns. A pheasant shoot was under way.

Lottie grabbed at the opportunity this gave her. 'You're not going out with the guns this afternoon, Mr Henry?'

'I don't get any pleasure out of killing,' he said, so vehemently it startled her. 'I prefer reading poetry.'

He waited as for an answer, and when there was none forthcoming, he added challengingly: 'My father's guests despise me, and my father despairs of me. What do you think?'

Lottie thought of the brace of pheasants that was sent down to the gatehouse every Christmas. 'I can appreciate both,' she said, 'In their season.'

'Implying that the season isn't right for poetry?' Then throwing discretion to the winds again: 'Lottie – dear Lottie, don't you see what I'm getting at. Can't you guess? You must realise by now . . .'

In great agitation she rose to her feet and made an imploring gesture towards him. 'Please, Mr Henry, don't you see how embarrassing this is for me?'

'For goodness sake stop calling me Mr Henry . . .' He tried to reach for her, but she backed away, putting the chair between them.

'That's just the point. You *are* Mr Henry – you can never be anything else to me. And you mustn't call me

Lottie. I'm Foster here – to everybody. Mr Henry, if you go on like this you'll lose me my job.'

That sobered him. It was the one plea that could in the heat of that moment. He said earnestly; 'I don't want to do anything to compromise you. I can't bear the thought of you leaving Thornmere Hall. It wouldn't be the same without you.'

His words touched a chord in Lottie's heart. The Hall wouldn't be the same without him either. He had sweetened her life here. Sometimes, just seeing him passing by, exchanging a smile with him, had made a difficult day more bearable. And their clandestine meetings had been something to look forward to, but now the dream was over. Henry had gone too far – It was time to return to reality.

She knew, all her womanly instincts told her so, that though she was younger than Henry by a year, she was much older in perception. The difference between them wasn't just one of class, it was also the difference between the outlook of a boy and the outlook of a woman. She had grown in more than years during her time at the Hall. Listening to the ripe, earthy comments of the older servants had taught her much that was a mystery to her before. By contrast Henry lived a sheltered life – he was what Mrs Webster would call, 'one of life's innocents'. She knew his outlook would change once he went up to college, but until then it was she who would have to do the thinking for both of them.

He paused at the door and looked back at her, his grave young face drawn and troubled. 'I love you,' he said. 'And nothing you can say will ever make me stop loving you.' Then he had gone, taking all her good resolutions with him.

'Foster, what do you think!' For once Miss Lucy looked and sounded quite animated. During her mother's absence she had taken to using her ladyship's sitting-room, and was there now, lolling before a roasting fire. 'I've had a letter from my baby brother, and it is such a very odd letter. Listen to this bit –

' "I quite like it here at Cambridge, it's better than I expected, but I do miss you all. I long for the sights and sounds of those who are dear to me. I think especially of that room at the top of the house that used to be our nursery. Do you remember, Lucy? We were so happy there. I count the days until I'm home again – not so long to wait now." '

Lucy looked up at Lottie with a smug expression. 'I didn't realise Henry was so fond of me, and I certainly can't understand him having such a yearning for that poky old room. Personally, I hated it, it was always so cold. Why, Foster, you have gone quite red – it must be the fire. Move away, you stupid girl.' Lucy read the letter through a second time. 'I can't remember Henry ever writing to me, before,' she mused. 'Poor boy, he must be homesick. Do you know, I am quite looking forward to having him home again – and Mama too, of course,' she added, as an afterthought.

Lottie was both amused and flattered by Henry's coded message. He had banked on his sister reading the letter to her. Clever Henry. But she hoped he wouldn't become too confident and give himself away. She kept a look-out for another letter with a Cambridge postmark, but one from Kenya came instead. Lady Massingham would be back in time for Christmas and was bringing Mr Joseph back with her. Her intention was to stop off in London for a few days to do some Christmas shopping, and it would please her if Henry came straight from Cambridge to join them. Everybody knew that a request from Lady Massingham was an order, but only Lottie felt a pang of disappointment. It meant an extra week's delay before seeing Henry again.

There was a sharp frost on the day of the travellers' expected arrival. Lottie woke up that morning to find that the water in the toilet jug had turned solid and the frozen condensation inside the window had given it the appearance of frosted glass. Ruby, who shared the attic bedroom with her, was already downstairs making tea for Mrs Webster. She smuggled up an extra cup for Lottie.

'Oh, Ruby – you angel. I was just trying to pluck up courage to get dressed. What are the roads like this morning?'

'Very bad Mr Adams said when he brought the milk. He sez there'll be no ploughing this morning because the fields are all friz – an' the points are friz too, so the six-thirty ain't gone through.'

'Oh dear, does that mean the carriage won't be able to get to Norwich?'

'Well, there's a light in the tack-room and the stable boys are already cleaning the 'arness, so I reckon they be going to try. An' Cook's in one of 'er black moods. I think if we want any breakus this morning, we'd better get it ourseln.'

By mid-morning a watery sun had helped dispel the worst of the frost. The stable lads had been out laying straw in the drive so that there was no danger of the horses slipping. Shrouded and hidden away in one of the unused stalls was an object that was causing Beeney, the coachman, a considerable amount of anxiety. A twenty horse-power 1913 Daimler, a combined Christmas and welcome home present from Sir Roger to his wife.

'I don't like the look of that there,' he confided to the groom. 'What do it mean for our future?'

The groom had been out helping with the straw-laying, and his ears were stinging with cold. 'We won't 'ave to do no more of this ole preparing of roads for 'osses,' he said with relish.

Ruby was in a radiant mood. She had been given permission to go home for Christmas, normally a time when none of the servants could be spared. Exception had been made in Ruby's case, as her mother had recently given birth to another baby. She was to have Christmas Eve and Christmas Day off, with orders to be back for Boxing Day. That was a small price to pay for two whole days with her family. It would be the first time, Ruby chirruped, that she would be home for Christmas since she started in service.

Lottie, drooping with weariness after unpacking her ladyship's clothes, pressing and mending, washing and starching, listened to Ruby's tinny little voice coming to her as through a funnel. Fortunately, she had no idea of the far-reaching effects that Ruby's leave of absence was to have on her. The girls undressed and got into bed, fitting into each other like spoons for extra warmth, Ruby still wearing her woollen stockings, and still talking nineteen to the dozen. Eventually they drifted off – Lottie to dream of Henry, and Ruby of her mother's plum pudding.

Early the following afternoon, Lottie was dispatched to the lodge with a message for Nanny. The ground was still frozen, but the sky was a brilliant cloudless arch. Lottie loved days like this when everything stood out crystal clear, and the air felt brittle. The drive was a half-mile long, bordered each side by massive elms which, this morning, threw long dark blue shadows on the ground.

Nanny wanted to detain her, for she was lonely with nobody to talk to, but Lottie made the excuse that her ladyship needed her. She walked back through the tree-lined avenue, keeping a lookout for Henry, one moment fearful of not seeing him, another anxious about the consequences if she did. She was rounding the house, going towards the stable yard when he suddenly appeared before her.

There was a momentary hesitation on both their parts, neither speaking, just searching each other's faces hopefully, then Henry jerked her into his arms and kissed her. Remembering that other bruising kiss in the library, she stiffened at first, then relaxed. This was so different. Henry kissed her gently, and none too expertly. She guessed he hadn't had much experience in kissing, but he was getting better at it by the second. She pulled away from him.

'We mustn't – no, Mr Henry, this is all wrong . . .'

'Lottie, it's been agony seeing you and not having a chance to speak to you. Don't stop me now . . .'

'But it's so open here . . . We might be seen . . .'

'Lottie, please, look at me.' He took her by her chin and looked into her eyes, and whatever he saw there assured him. He cupped her face in his hands, and kissed her again, and she found it impossible not to respond. She felt drunk as if on a heady wine, and it was only when she began to shiver uncontrollably that she came to her senses. 'This is madness – we must stop – we must control ourselves . . .'

Henry opened glazed eyes. She noticed there were beads of sweat on his face. 'Come back to me, Lottie,' he pleaded.

'I can't – I mustn't. In any case, her ladyship is waiting for me. No, Mr Henry, you must be sensible . . .'

'How can I be sensible with you looking at me like that! I've missed you so much . . .'

'I've missed you too.'

'No more nonsense about Mr Henry and Foster?'

She laughed unsteadily. 'I promise. Now will you let me go?'

He looked at her with a sad and cheated expression. In the ten weeks he had been away he seemed to have grown from a boy into a man. 'If I let you go now will you meet me tomorrow? About ten? I'll wait for you in the old coach house – the one they use as a feed store.'

On Christmas Eve, Lottie was given permission to visit the gatehouse in order to take presents to her family. Ellen, knowing she was coming, had a present ready for her in return.

'It's only a bit of cambric I picked up in the market, I wanted to give you something special for Christmas,' she said in an off-hand manner, but couldn't quite mask her satisfaction in her handiwork.

With skill and infinite patience she had turned a piece of plain white cotton into a nightgown as delicate and pretty as anything Miss Lucy possessed. Tears of delight stung Lottie's eyes. 'Oh Mother, I've never had anything so lovely given me before.'

Ellen pleased by Lottie's reaction, smirked a little. 'I wanted you to have something pretty instead of something useful, for a change. We all need a little spoiling once in a while. And you deserve it, Lottie. You're turned out to be a real credit to us.'

'It seems such a pity to hide all that lovely work in bed. Who will see it?'

'You could always put it away for your trousseau,' said Ellen archly, and was surprised at the way her words brought the colour to Lottie's face. Now what was significant about that, she wondered. Was Lottie thinking of anyone in particular? Young Reuben Stoneham? She hoped so. Lottie could do a lot worse.

But Reuben was the last thing on Lottie's mind as she crunched her way back along the deserted lane. She had thought of a plan so daring it made her cheeks tingle. She knew Henry would waylay her somewhere. They had met almost daily, since their rendezvous in the coach-house. These illicit meetings were becoming a sweet torment for them both — aware of the passion that was fuelled by stolen kisses. Endearments that had started innocently were now getting out of hand, but the biggest factor that denied them fulfilment was lack of opportunity.

She climbed the stile, and there was Henry, hurrying towards her along the footpath. He held out his arms and she ran into them, relishing the warmth of his body as he held her close.

'I can't go on like this any more,' he said, his voice low and urgent. 'I want you, Lottie. I can't think of anything else but you and loving you. I've tried to put it out of my mind, but I can't. Please, darling . . . don't deny me.'

Awkwardly, his eager hands began to fumble at the hooks and eyes of her bodice, but she stopped him by putting her hands over his and holding on to them. Her need was as great as his, but she had enough control over her feelings to know that here was no place for the fulfilment of their love. Not in this icy furrow within sight of farm-workers making their way home for tea. She told him of the daring thought that had come to her.

He stood back, staring at her in disbelief. 'You really mean that? I may come to your room tonight?'

'I shall be on my own. Ruby has gone home for Christmas.'

He swept her into his arms again, laughing with school-boyish glee. 'Oh, darling, precious Lottie – what a girl you are.' He grew sober, and frowned as if in doubt. 'I have never, you know,' he stumbled over his words. 'I have never gone the whole way before. I may not – I don't quite know – you will make allowances for me?'

She laughed and reddened at the same time. 'It will be my first time, too. We'll just have to learn from each other, won't we?'

In the attic bedroom, Lottie looked with satisfaction at her reflection in the spotted, yellowing glass. The night-gown was fit for a bride. That thought alleviated any doubts that still lingered. She could pretend this was her wedding night. To her, it was.

She had unpinned her hair and now it fell unhampered to her waist, covering her shoulders like a soft dark mantle. Three candles lit the room which was an extravagance, for usually there was only one. But this was a special occasion.

Yet her mind wasn't completely at ease. Her mother's warning came back to her when she first went into service. 'There will be a lot of temptations facing you up at the Hall, and I hope you will always remember to keep yourself respectable. No man thinks much of a woman who cheapens herself, no matter how much he flatters her.' Would Henry think she was cheap?

Then came a gentle knock on the door followed by Henry's voice: 'Lottie – Lottie – it's me.' He sounded both excited and anxious, and a gush of love that was almost maternal, flowed over her.

She opened the door cautiously, holding it just wide enough for Henry to slip through. The rest of the servants had not yet come to bed. They were having their Christmas dinner tonight as there would be no time for them to indulge on the morrow. It could be hours before any of them made a move.

There was a lamp in the passage, dim but sufficient to light up the attic stairs. It threw long shadows across the landing and against those shadows Henry's face looked like a pale cautious oval. Lottie held out her hand towards him and at that same moment, as quick as a blink of an eye, one of the shadows detached itself, and took on the form of a man. It was Joseph Massingham.

'I guessed something like this was in the wind.' His voice was triumphant and viciously gleeful. 'It's been worth the waiting, skulking in the shadows. You've served your purpose, little brother. You can run away and hang up your stocking now. This is a man's job – leave it to me.'

To Lottie, petrified with fear and shock, Joseph looked like the devil personified. He stood there in the flickering half-light shaking with silent laughter. Suddenly Henry came to as if from a trance and made to lurch at his brother, but Joseph was bigger and stronger. He put the flat of his hand on Henry's chest and pushed so hard that the boy over-balanced and fell flat on his back. Before he had a chance to scramble to his feet again, Joseph had thrust his way into Lottie's room and bolted the door behind him.

He stood swaying slightly, flushed with victory, and breathing heavily. Slowly he undid his tie and peeled off his dinner jacket. 'All ready and waiting, I see.' His calculating glance travelled the length of Lottie's body. 'You look virginal in that, my lovely – but it's wasted on me. Take it off.'

'Sir, please – please . . . leave now or I'll scream . . .'

He laughed. 'I think I've heard that threat from you before. What good would screaming do? I'd say you invited me in. You opened the door yourself, remember. Oh no, my pretty, that won't do. I've seen you two young fools together – I've been watching you for the past few days. Why should brother Henry have all the fun? I've come to finish the job I started in the library. I've waited a long time for this.'

Fear and rage filled Lottie with a kind of madness. He would not humiliate her a second time – she would not let him! She flew at him, clawing his face, leaving the marks of her nails on his cheeks. His reaction was just as swift. He swore at her, and gave her such a blow it knocked her off her feet.

She lay stunned. Blood was oozing from her lip, she could taste its saltiness filling her mouth. Joseph swooped, picked her up, and flung her on the bed. He grinned, his eyes glittered menacingly in the candlelight, then deliberately and with relish, he ripped the nightgown from her body and tore it into shreds.

She moaned. Her anger had gone, only fear remained now. She began to plead, knowing all the time that it was useless. He looked sub-human, she thought, like some mythical beast about to devour its prey. She tried to think of something pleasant, of flowers in spring, of the poetry that Henry loved to quote to her, anything to take her mind off what he was doing, but all she was conscious of was the weight of his heaving body on hers, and the whisky on his breath as he forced her mouth open. This time she bit him, and he began to hit her, and hit her until she felt no more pain, only a sense of blackest, deepest despair as he plunged into her again and again.

THREE | *Lottie*
1913–1914

Lottie stirred, struggling awake from a nightmarish sleep. The only part of her body she could move without feeling pain were her eyes. The room was strangely light, too light for this time of the morning. A clock chiming the hours had aroused her, each vibrating boom pushing her nearer to consciousness. Five. She counted the strokes; she had an hour and a half before anyone stirred. She had to get up. She had to find a way of escape from her shame and anguish.

A feeling of nausea gripped her as she dragged herself out of the bed. There was a slop pail by the washstand, and crouching on the floor she vomited into it. Still on her knees she reached up for a corner of the curtain and pulled it back so that she could see out of the window. Her head came just above the window-sill, and she looked out on acres of moon-whitened virginal landscape. Snow. During the night the temperature had risen and now snow was gently falling, turning the countryside into a Christmas-card picture. How was it possible for such beauty and such ugliness to exist side by side? For what had happened to her was as ugly as sin. Just thinking of it drained her of the will to go on living.

She pulled herself to her feet, stifling a cry of pain. Her jaw felt as if it were broken, but a broken jaw was of no consequence now. She stumbled as something wound itself round her bare ankle. She stooped and pulled at it. Just a piece of rag. Her mind wouldn't function properly. She couldn't think what it was or how it had got there.

She felt for the box of matches, struck one and put it

to the inch left of one of the candles. By the fitful light from the flame she saw that what she was holding was not a rag at all, but a strip torn from her nightgown. It took a moment or two for her senses to register shock, and then the tears spurted to her eyes. She wept for the destruction of the nightgown. For the loss of something that had once been beautiful. For the hours of wasted labour her mother had spent on it. She wept for her own lost innocence.

The water in the toilet jug was covered with a thin layer of ice. She broke it, poured some water into the bowl and first sponged her swollen face, then cleaned the blood stains from her legs. If she was going to her death, she might as well make herself as presentable as possible for the sake of whoever it was who found her body.

Long before dawn on Christmas morning Cook, disturbed by the discomforts of indigestion, reluctantly opened her eyes. Struggling from the depths of her feather mattress into a sitting position, she gave a tremendous belch. She knew the relief that followed would be short-lived, and knew too that before long she would have to brave the cold and go down to the kitchen for some bicarbonate of soda. A pinch of bicarb in warm water would soon settle her stomach. She sighed for the days when she could tuck into roast wild duck and boiled fowl, mince pies and Christmas pudding washed down in the privacy of Mr Thorne's sitting-room with a glass or two of Sir Roger's vintage port, without suffering the consequences. With a little moan she eased her ample bulk from the bed and took a peek out of the window. Snow! Would that alter plans for the day, she wondered? The drive through the park to church or the arrival of guests for dinner? She decided not. It would take more than a few inches of snow to interfere with the Massinghams' traditional Christmas.

Pulling a wrap over her flannel nightgown she creaked her way down the back stairs. It was far too early for anyone to be about, yet as she approached the kitchen she could see a gleam of light showing under the door. She frowned, instantly suspicious. Had one of the kitchen-maids left a burnt pan to soak all night and had now crept down to scour it? It was an unwritten law in her kitchen that no-one went to bed until every utensil was scoured and gleaming clean and back in its rightful place.

But this morning, as it was Christmas, she was prepared to be magnanimous. She opened the door and confronted, not the scared kitchenmaid she had expected, but a girl in an old reefer coat with her bare legs thrust into unlaced boots, and clutching a bottle of carbolic.

Cook and Lottie stared speechlessly at each other. It was Cook who recovered her senses first. 'Dear God in heaven,' she exclaimed. 'Who did that to you?' Lottie's face was swollen and discoloured, and her bottom lip was caked with dried blood.

'I said – *who* did that to you?' But Lottie was in no condition to speak. It was then Cook realised the signifi-cance of the carbolic. For one so large she could move swiftly when the need arose. She grabbed the bottle from Lottie's hand. 'You little fool – that's not the answer. If you wanted to do away with yourself a knife would have been kinder.'

'I did try to stab myself but I couldn't, I was too frightened.' Lottie's voice was barely audible. She grabbed at the table as if suddenly overcome by giddiness.

Mrs Webster helped her to a chair. 'You would prefer to die in agony! Do you know what the disinfectant would have done? Slowly eaten your insides away. Who did this to you?'

Lottie shook her head and Cook didn't press her. She could guess who it was anyway. He had been in a wild mood last night, drinking too freely – bursting into the servants' hall on the pretext of wishing them a Happy Christmas, his feverish eyes roaming around those seated at the table.

Cook felt herself shaking with anger, but what this

child needed now was not sympathy, but a doctor. Could she risk calling a doctor? She thought over the consequences. The perpetrator sent away until the whole sordid affair had blown over. The victim blamed for her part in the affair, for no violated woman was ever regarded as innocent. And what of herself? What would happen to her for bringing something best hidden out in the open? She had an easy, comfortable, well-paid job in the service of the Massinghams, with the chance of a rent-free cottage when she retired. Could she risk all that?

It was a question of putting aside her principles for the sake of expediency and Cook, once her mind was made up, became her no-nonsense, no-time-to-lose self once more. She had an hour before the scullery-maid came down to riddle the kitchen fire, and in that hour there was much to be done.

Submitting to Mrs Webster's ministrations, Lottie thought, was like sinking into some warm comfortable bed. She no longer had to think for herself. Cook helped her upstairs, and into her own large, well-ordered room, giving her hot water to wash in and a clean nightgown to put on – one of Cook's own, as voluminous as a tent and as protective. Cook brushed her hair and braided it and held a damp sponge to her swollen cheek.

'Why are you doing this for me?' Lottie asked her.

'I had a young sister who was treated much the same way, but not knocked about. Why did he do that?'

'I suppose because I fought back – I wanted to kill him.'

'And now you want to kill yourself? You know that's not the answer. You think your life is over. It isn't. One day you'll be glad I came in at the right moment.'

Lottie said, weighing up each word carefully; 'What happened last night was partly my own fault. I brought it on myself. I feel I ought to tell you that. You shouldn't feel too sorry for me.'

Cook looked at the pathetic figure of the girl sitting with her face averted. She had paid a high price for her moment of weakness, too high in Cook's opinion. 'It's time I got you back to your room,' she said.

Lottie flinched. 'I can't go back there . . . not to that bed. Please, Mrs Webster, let me stay here.'

'You can't stay here, child, you know that. Don't worry. I've cleaned the place up and changed the sheets, it's perfectly all right now. I want you to stay in bed until you're fit to be seen. I don't want tongues wagging over this.'

'But what will her ladyship say? I wasn't there to help her undress last night, and if I'm not there this morning . . .'

'What do you think she'll say if she sees you looking like this? She'll ask questions. Is that what you want?'

Lottie didn't know what she wanted at that moment. Only a short while ago she had wanted to die. If she hadn't taken so long over deciding how to do it, she might have been dead by now. Dead, or writhing in agony, screaming with pain. She shuddered and Cook said, 'Come along gel, you're cold, let's get you to bed. And I'll give you something to help you sleep.'

An hour later when Cook looked in again, Lottie was sleeping soundly, lying on her back, snoring slightly. Cook looked down at her pitiful face and her eyes misted over. The poor little fool – what a fine pickle she had got herself into. She squared her shoulders, already concocting in her mind a plausible story for her ladyship.

For the next forty-eight hours Lottie drifted in and out of sleep. She could never be sure if she was awake or dreaming or whether it was day or night, but she was aware of being washed and fed, of hands that cared for her efficiently and kindly, and sometimes of other hands that were small and rough, but in their clumsy way, more gentle. She sometimes imagined her little sister Vi was in the bed with her, cuddling her.

On the third morning she woke up to bright daylight, feeling refreshed and hungry. But it wasn't until she made an attempt to get up that she realised how painful every movement was. Cook was by the bedside.

'So you are awake at last, and about time too. Well now, how do you feel?'

'Weak. I tried to get up, but . . .'

'You need feeding up. You've been living on slops for two days.'

'*Two days*. I can't have been lying here for two whole days!'

'You have, and by the look of it, it's done you the power of good. That's what you needed – a good sleep. Nature's cure.'

Nature's cure, repeated Lottie to herself. How much sleep would it take to cure her of this deep-rooted feeling of guilt and shame? 'What excuses did you make to her ladyship?'

'I told her the truth in as far as it went. I said I had found you in a sorry state in the kitchen. That you felt achy all over as if you were sickening for flu, and in a fit of giddiness you had fallen and banged your face on the fender. I said, I thought it best if you stayed in bed for a day or two.'

'What did she say to that?'

'Not a lot.' An odd reflective look crossed Cook's moon-like face. Lady Massingham had been in an unusually quiescent mood. 'She certainly showed she didn't want you around Miss Lucy if you were sickening for something – especially as there's a lot of flu about in the village. She did say she hoped you'd be better by the New Year. You haven't forgotten the New Year's Eve ball? We've started to prepare for it already, and hardly over Christmas yet.'

Lottie wanted to ask after Henry, but feared that sort of enquiry would raise all sorts of questions in Mrs Webster's mind. She asked after her family instead. Did they know she had been – well, indisposed?

'I sent word down that you had a nasty fall, and was staying in bed for a few days. Now, no more talk. Just put your mind to getting better. I'll send Ruby up with a tray.'

That surprised Lottie. 'Does Ruby know?'

'The little minx slipped up here on Boxing Day when my back was turned, but she's made herself useful. Saved my legs many a time. Don't worry, she doesn't know what happened. I told her the same story I told her ladyship, what I told the rest of the staff, so don't you go and let slip something that could make me out a liar.'

Lottie knew by now Cook's true worth and no longer minded her brusque way of speaking. What would she have done without her support these past few days? What was she going to do in the future? How could she stay at the Hall, knowing that anytime she could come face to face with Henry or . . . But she couldn't bring herself even to think that other name.

''Ere you are then, bacon and sausage and kidneys, toast and tea. It's what's come back from the breakfast-room, an' Cook sez there's plenty more . . .' Ruby placed an enormous tray alongside Lottie on the bed. Her pointed little face was expressive with self-importance as she put a finger to her lips. 'I've got something else for you too. A secret . . . But I'd better bolt the door afore I give it you.'

She returned to the bedside and produced a letter from her pocket. 'I'm sorry it's got crumpled, but I been carrying it around for nearly three days. Mr Henry said not to give it to you unless we was on our own.'

Without a word Lottie took the letter, but did not open it much to Ruby's disappointment. The note had been burning a hole in her pocket, and now with its loss came an acute feeling of anti-climax.

'I expect it's to tell you about the fight he had with his brother.'

Lottie raised startled eyes. 'A fight? Mr Henry?'

'That's what they're saying downstairs. The two brothers were not talking to each other, and on Christmas morning Mr Joseph come down with a great big gash on the side of his head and his face all scratched, so he must have got the worst of it. Anyway, they both left on Boxing Day, but not together. Mr Joseph is on his way back to Africa and Mr Henry's gone to Cambridge. Lady Massingham stayed up in her room all day, never mind it being Boxing Day. It wasn't a bit like Christmas – more like a funeral wake, Cooper said.'

Lottie stared at Ruby with a glazed expression, then slowly her numbness wore off. 'I haven't asked you about your own Christmas. Was it a good one, Ruby?'

'I was home. It's always good, being home. Well, I s'pose I'd better leave you to have your brekkus. There's plenty for me to do downstairs.'

Left on her own, Lottie pushed the tray aside. She had lost her appetite. She turned Henry's letter over, ripped it open, and read:

Dear Lottie,

This letter is nothing but a clumsy excuse for my behaviour. I'm running away because I feel too ashamed to face you. If I could right the wrong that's been done, I'd stay, but there is nothing I can do now. I've left it too late. I should have gone for help at the time. I can't explain why I didn't, except that for a while, I just couldn't come to my senses.

I wanted to kill myself. I didn't know how I could go on living with this on my conscience. Then I thought, the one who deserved to die is my brother. I did try to kill him, but I messed that up too. I got my father's twelve bore from the gun room with the intention of blasting Joseph's head off. I expected him to be asleep – if he had been, I think I could have gone through with it. But he was lying there, wide-awake and laughing at me, and I lost my nerve. I chucked the gun at his head and walked away without saying anything.

I hope to God I never have to see him again. I'm returning to my rooms at Cambridge. I can study there. I want to get my degree, and make something of myself, and then I'll come back for you. That is if you can forgive me. I want to marry you, Lottie. Perhaps we could start a new life somewhere where nobody knows us — abroad even. I hope Ruby is able to give you this letter on the quiet, I don't want to cause you any more trouble. I know I've acted like a worm, and squirm every time I think of it. You couldn't think less of me than I do myself. Please — please write to me. Then I'll know that you have forgiven me.

Ever yours,
Henry.

Ever mine, thought Lottie sadly, staring at the signature until it became an indecipherable blur. She wiped her eyes with her fingers. Did Henry really love her enough to marry her? She doubted it. He was trying to make amends, trying to ease his self-imposed guilt. Marriage between them was out of the question, he must know that. Poor Henry, he was too young to know how to deal with this situation. There had been an innocence about their love that had vanished and she knew, regretfully, that they could never pick up the threads again. She tore the letter into tiny shreds, feeling as she did so that she was destroying part of herself. But it was better that way — a clean cut rather than a long drawn-out withdrawal. She knew what Henry meant by being too ashamed to face her again, for she shared that same feeling. They could never meet as they had before, with a delightful sense of irresponsibility. Joseph had violated more than her body.

Will-power alone got her out of bed to resume her duties, that and the thought that she owed too much to Cook to let her down. Her cuts and bruises did not go unnoticed but the story of her fall was accepted without question, and then, as if to give credence to Cook's story, a mild form of influenza suddenly struck the Hall attacking both staff and family alike. For Lady Massingham it was the last straw. Christmas had been a disaster, now it looked as if she might have to cancel the New Year's Eve ball.

Without the boys and their acquaintances, whose names were on her invitation list, it was likely to be a very watered-down affair anyway. She had pinned her hopes on it as a last opportunity to acquire a husband for Lucy. The girl was twenty-one and chances were passing her by. Three years ago when at eighteen she was due to come out in Society, the death of the late king, Edward VII, had prevented any form of celebration. It wasn't Lucy's fault, of course, but she was the kind of girl that sort of thing happened to.

However, all preparations for the coming ball went ahead in spite of red noses on both sides of the green baize door and Lottie was run off her feet, amply making up for the time she had spent off duty. There were gowns to be altered and pressed, shoes to be cleaned, fans and gloves carefully chosen and left out for inspection. Miss Lucy would change her mind a dozen times a day. Not until the last minute could Lottie be sure which dress to put out for her. Cooper, the head parlour-maid, pressed into helping, complained continuously.

'Don't know why she makes so much fuss, that Miss Lucy. She don't dance – just lolls about on the sofa pretending to be an invalid. She ought to be up and down the stairs umpteen times a day like we do, that would really give her something to moan about.'

Lottie did not answer, she had stopped listening to Cooper's grumbles. The parlour-maid stared at her belligerently. 'You all right?'

'Of course I'm all right.'

'You don't look it – you look different somehow.'

'I'm just tired,' Lottie said. It was her stock answer

when questioned about her health, dismissing in those three words the despair and guilt that still dogged her.

One morning in late March when spring was making a real effort to live up to its name, coaxing celandines into bloom and bringing the newly-born lambs out of the barns and into pasture, and the coots were beginning to nest amid the reeds that lined the mere, Lottie sat by the window in the sewing-room, putting the finishing touches to a baby's gown. Flo, her eldest sister, who just over a year ago had married a man from York, a gardener who worked for the public work's department, had given birth to a son in January. The baby was already eight weeks old, and Lottie was making his christening robe. A garment that would be carefully treasured in that thrifty family, and put away for the other babies who would come along in due course. Lottie put down her sewing and stared out of the window – not seeing the fields or the glint of water through the bare black trees in the park, but staring sightlessly into the future and what it could mean for her.

The door opened suddenly and Ruby looked in, her narrow little face quivering with anxiety. 'Lottie, Cook says please come down at once. There's a message come for you about your little brother. He's had one of his wheezy attacks.'

Lottie knew her mother would not have sent for her unless it was urgent. She dashed down the back stairs and into the kitchen. Cook's expression was grave. 'He's very poorly – the doctor's with him. Reuben has harnessed the pony-trap and is waiting to drive you to the gatehouse.'

With Cook's help Lottie struggled into her coat. Her fingers were all thumbs as she tried to do up the buttons. 'I was only up home two days ago, and Billy was as right as rain then.'

'The croup came on suddenly last night,' Cook said, rebuttoning Lottie's coat for her and straightening the collar. 'Tie this scarf over your head, there's bitter wind out. Hurry gel, don't keep your mother waiting.'

At any other time Lottie would have resented Reuben's intrusion, his unwanted attentions were beginning to cause her irritation, but now as he helped her into the trap she was hardly aware of his presence. He was a tall, thin, gangling young man who blushed easily, and he reddened now with pleasure at having Lottie sitting beside him. She was withdrawn and silent, but that suited Reuben as he never had much to say for himself, either.

As they neared the gatehouse, Dr Brookes driving his high-wheeled gig passed them on his way back to the village. That was a good sign surely, Billy must be better. But the doctor shook his head at her and she was suddenly filled with foreboding.

She hurried into the gatehouse, into a roomful of village women come to comfort her mother who sat putty-faced and straight-backed at the table, staring dry-eyed before her. 'You be too late to see him. He's gone,' she said in a dull voice.

Lottie thought she was referring to the doctor. 'But I did see Dr Brookes, I passed him just now in the lane.'

'I mean your brother.' Her mother's voice was as expressionless as her eyes. 'Billy — little Billy. He's dead, Lottie, he died in my arms.' And then she let herself go, crying in an ugly unrestrained manner. The mourners closed in, kind in their way, but failing to understand that this was a time for mother and daughter to be left together. 'Go you up and see him,' Ellen said when she could speak. 'Mrs Burrell be with him but you go up and say goodbye to him.'

Mrs Burrell looked up as Lottie entered the boys' bedroom. She was a familiar sight at a lying-in or at a death. She had washed Billy and put him into a clean nightshirt, now she was tucking the covers carefully under his chin. 'I don't believe in covering up their faces when they be that young,' she said. 'But I've drawn the curtains out of respect. Do you want me to open them again so that you can see him properly?'

'I can see him well enough.' Lottie bent over the bed and touched Billy's face. It felt unnaturally cold, but then the room was freezing. 'He doesn't look dead – he looks as if he's only sleeping . . .' She caught her breath on a sob.

'At least he bain't suffering anymore. Last night he was fighting for his breath and it was pitiful to listen to him, poor little chap. I'll leave you here with him, and go down and get that bunch of chattering magpies off the premises. They mean well, but they don't know when they've out-stayed their welcome.'

Lottie sat close by the bed, remembering the day Billy was born. She was fourteen then, and a good little mother's help, so Mrs Burrell said. Her eyes filled with tears as she recalled her last visit to the gatehouse. Billy had climbed into her lap and demanded a ride to Banbury Cross. He was too heavy, and she had to refuse. Dear Lord, she had refused him, and now he was dead. Her little brother!

Callers came all day, some walking three miles from the other end of the village to bring little gifts of flowers, a few buns, or a freshly baked loaf. Simple gifts with which to express their feelings. Ted came in for his lunch, silent and awkward, and had quickly gone away again, taking a tearful Violet off to stay with a friend. A house of death was no place for a child. That evening, after supper, Sid Foster took his two sons off to the Ferry Inn. Not because they wanted a drink, or preferred more congenial company, but to give Lottie and her mother a chance to be alone. Before he left, her father told Lottie to sleep with her mother, saying he would kip down in Violet's room that night.

By this time the undertaker had been, and Billy lay in his small coffin propped on two chairs in the parlour with a lighted candle beside him. Because he feared the dark, Ellen said.

Now she sat by the fire, still very pale but calmer as she watched Lottie making cheese sandwiches. 'I can't eat anything,' she said in a monotone.

'You must eat, mother, if only for the family's sake. The girls will be home tomorrow. You must keep up your strength for them. Come, just one sandwich and a cup of cocoa.'

Mrs Foster held the cup in both hands, staring into the fire with sunken, red-rimmed eyes. After a long silence, she said, 'I feel as if I've murdered my Billy.' She placed the untouched cup on the fender. 'Don't be looking at me like that, Lottie, I haven't lost my mind. I did try to murder him. I tried to get rid of him afore he was born.'

'Oh mother . . .'

''Tis true. I didn't want him, I felt I was too old to go through all that agen – I was weary of having children, and I tried all ways of getting rid of him. I dosed myself with castor oil but that only gave me cramps in my insides, and I had so many hot baths my skin went all crêpey.' Ellen made a sudden harsh sound that could have passed for a laugh. 'I reckon I was the cleanest woman in Thornmere, and, God forgive me, I even jumped off the table to try and bring on a miscarriage. But I twisted my ankle so bad I couldn't walk for a week. That brought me to my senses, and when little Billy was born I was so glad I hadn't got rid of him. I loved him so much, my little Lammas lamb, I reckon I loved him more than any of you.' Her voice quivered to a stop, and then she broke down into fresh weeping. 'I was so ashamed of what I did I never told anybody, tried not to think about it 'till now. And then it came to me that I was being punished for what I tried to do then. I wanted to destroy my baby, my little Billy – so God took him from me. Oh Lottie, I'm being punished for my sins and I can't bear it.'

Lottie finally got her mother to bed. She helped her up the stairs, undressed her and washed her and made her a fresh cup of cocoa which she liberally laced with the brandy that was kept for medicinal purposes. She sat by the bed holding her mother's hand until at last she fell asleep, and then in the dark she undressed and got into the bed beside her.

She could not sleep herself. She kept going over in her mind what her mother had told her. Was that what she herself had been doing? Trying to murder her unborn child? She had not thought of it like that. She too had tried all the old country remedies for getting rid of an unwanted pregnancy, like drinking an infusion of pennyroyal and dosing herself with castor oil, but they hadn't worked. She hadn't tried jumping off the table because the idea hadn't occurred to her, and hot baths were out of the question. That meant hauling one of the zinc tubs up three flights of back stairs, followed by the same climb with cans of hot water. Though two bathrooms had been installed at the Hall, they were for the family's use only, and the servants made do with what they called an 'upper and downer' in the privacy of their bedrooms.

Lottie put her hand on her abdomen. Her baby was safe now. She would make no more attempts to get rid of it. Her mother's confession guaranteed that.

Flo stayed on after the funeral with the express purpose, Lottie suspected, of having a private word with her. On her last evening she persuaded Lottie to go for a stroll as far as the Beckton Market road.

'Now tell me true, Lottie – what ails you?' she asked. ''Tis more than grief the matter with you. I don't need eyes to see that.'

Lottie turned her face away. 'I'm upset. We're all upset. Please, Flo, don't keep on at me.'

Flo looked disappointed. 'You're keeping something to yourself. I'm no fool, Lottie, I can tell – and I'll tell you something else – you'll not be able to keep anything to yourself in Thornmere for long, you should know that.' She took her sister's arm in a chummy way.

'Well then, if you ever want to get away for a while you could always stay with me. I'd like you to see my house. It's only small, but it's very modern with tap water in the kitchen, and gas lights, even in the bedrooms. I'd really be glad of your company, Lot, and that's a fact. I get awful homesick for a Norfolk voice, once in a while. And then there's little Tommy. You could help me with him, so what do you say?'

'I'll bear it in mind,' said Lottie, but that sounded churlish which she hadn't intended. 'It's kind of you, Flo, and I'd love to come and stay, perhaps for a holiday . . .' Knowing that a holiday in York was but a pipe dream. 'But Tom might have a say in the matter. He might not like the idea of a sister-in-law for a boarder.'

'Tom would do anything to please me,' said Flo, speaking with more haste than certainty.

Ellen looked at Lottie with eyes dulled by defeat. She tossed a letter on the table. 'I had that from Flo this morning. You'd better read it as that concerns you.'

Lottie removed her hat and loosened her coat and saw her mother's eyes go instinctively to her waistline. Embarrassed she drew her coat together again.

'You don't show yet,' her mother said wearily. 'And for goodness sake do stop fidgeting with your coat and go hang it up.' She waited for Lottie to come back to the table. 'I never thought you'd be the one to let the family down. Rose perhaps, or Annie, they both be flighty girls, but never you.'

Lottie opened Flo's letter. The words on the page danced before her eyes; 'When I saw her at the funeral, I could tell it wasn't just Billy's death on her mind . . . There will always be a place for her here until the talk dies down.' Her hand clenched over the paper.

'This will give them in the village something to talk about, unless he do intend to marry you,' Ellen said.

'Who mother? Who do you think wants to marry me?'

'I didn't say wants – I says intends. That young Reuben, of course.'

'Mother, it is *not* Reuben.'

Something like fear flickered in and out of Ellen's eyes. 'Oh, dear girl,' she said brokenly. 'What have you done – what have you done.' She wouldn't allow Lottie to comfort her, or even to come near her. 'Give me time,' she kept saying. 'Give me time – I've got to get used to the idea. Flo's letter was a shock, but I thought to myself, well, it's not the first time a young couple do anticipate a wedding – and Reuben – I liked the idea of Reuben as a son-in-law.' She dried her eyes. 'You're not going to tell me who the father be, are you?'

She waited, but Lottie remained silent, her chin quivering slightly.

'I'll have to tell your father, or would you rather do that?'

Lottie hesitated, struggling to keep her composure. 'Would you, please.'

'You know you won't be able to stay here, not with all the talk. I couldn't take it, not just now. But Flo suggests you go and stay with her for a few months, just until the fuss blows over ... You never know, Lottie, you might like it up there, settle down even. What do you say?'

'I can't go,' said Lottie firmly, though it cost her something to defy her mother at a time like this. 'I'd hate it there. I'd be made to feel like an unrepentant sinner.'

Ellen's colour rose. 'That's a nice thing to say about your sister, and her going out of her way to help you!'

'I don't mean Flo, I mean Tom. You know what he's like. He'd give me a home to please Flo, but he wouldn't accept me as one of the family, and all the time I'd feel he was praying for me. I wouldn't feel comfortable there.'

'You'd feel a lot less comfortable walking the streets,' Ellen retorted, but her anger didn't last. 'I shouldn't have said that,' she said bleakly. 'There's no question of you being put out on the streets. This is your home and will be your home for as long as you want it. Don't you go worrying yourself, we'll manage somehow.'

Lottie saw her mother as someone torn between dread of a scandal and loyalty to her daughter, and felt a sudden helpless sorrow for her. She had wept so much in the past few weeks she felt she had no more tears to shed but they came readily enough now. She flung herself at her mother's feet and buried her face in her lap. 'I wish I could stay here. This is my home,' she sobbed. 'I feel safer here than anywhere else. But I've got to leave Thornmere and not only because of the talk. There's another reason, a more important reason.'

'I won't waste my breath asking what reason,' Ellen said, despondently. As much as she wanted to take Lottie in her arms and comfort her, she could not bring herself to do so. Her disappointment in her brightest child went too deep. 'If you won't stay here and do refuse to go to your sister's, where will you be going then?'

Lottie sat back on her heels and regarded her mother thoughtfully. Where will I go she asked herself, and out of her desperation came a sudden inspiration.

'I could go to London.'

'*London*! Who do you know in London, for goodness sake?'

'Aggie Sharpe. You remember, Mrs Webster's niece, the one I got friendly with . . .'

'That girl! She'll do you more harm than good, and where would you get her address? You'd told me she'd left home.'

'I'll get it from Cook, I'm sure she knows it. And mother, it would be somewhere for me to go until I decide what to do. Nobody knows me there. I could get a job until my time comes, and I'm sure I could find some place where to have my baby . . .'

Ellen slumped in her chair. She suddenly looked old. 'Yes,' she said in a hollow voice. 'I expect there are workhouses in London the same as anywhere else.'

For her mother, Lottie's decision was the quickest way

to perdition. But her father, once he had got over his bewilderment, was mildly pleased. In his slow-thinking way he assumed Lottie was going off to better herself and hopes revived of her becoming a school-teacher. Hopes that were severely quashed when he was told the truth.

His reaction was to retreat into his shell. He neglected his garden, sitting for hours in his tool-shed, finding solace in his pipe. Lottie had been fearful of her father finding out, dreaded him raising his voice to her, something he had never done yet. But instead he took refuge in silence.

Cook was even more disparaging than her mother. 'What d'you think you'll find in London you can't find here?' she wanted to know.

'A job for one thing. I want to go on working for as long as I can.'

'A job! More likely you'll finish up on the streets – or in one of them sweat-shops where they'll work you until you drop. You won't get back into service, not without a reference.'

'Cook, you originally came from London. You must know of opportunities there – better even than Norwich . . .'

'I haven't been back to London these thirty years and nor I would if someone was to pay me!' retorted Cook emphatically. 'And I refuse to encourage you in such foolishness. You've got a perfectly good home here – you stay in it.'

'I thought perhaps you'd give me Aggie's address.'

'Don't mention that hussy to me!'

Of all her detractors, Lady Massingham proved in the end the most helpful. At first she was outraged that Lottie should have the audacity to leave her service, but as Lottie's last days at the Hall slowly ticked past her attitude changed. On Lottie's last night she was summoned to her ladyship's sitting-room.

'I can't give you a reference under the circumstances,'

she said, and even at her most gracious as she was now, she couldn't quite lose her stiff-necked manner. 'But here is a small parting gift for you. It might tide you over until you get settled somewhere else.'

Lottie opened her gift in Cook's presence. It was a small chain mesh purse containing ten sovereigns. She gasped. That was more money, all at one time, than she had ever seen before. But Mrs Webster was unimpressed.

'Hush money,' she said grimly. 'She suspects or has heard something.'

Lottie stared at the riches lying in the palm of her hand. 'But I don't like taking all this. I haven't earned it . . .'

'Not even on Christmas Eve,' said Cook brutally, her concern making her cruel. 'And you certainly mustn't do her ladyship out of a chance to ease her conscience.' Her manner, just as quickly, mellowed. 'I've got a leaving present for you too, seeing as how I can't talk you into staying.' She gave Lottie a box of scented soap but, far more welcome in Lottie's eyes, also Aggie's present address.

'You and Aggie were good friends once and she'll find you somewhere to live. She don't live at West Ham anymore. She quarrelled with her mother and left home, just after her father died too. I'll never forgive her for that. She's working as a live-in waitress now, in some fancy restaurant near Cambridge Circus. She might be able to help you, but I can't promise. Still, better to have somewhere definite to go to than to land in London at the mercy of any tout.' Cook produced a sheet of paper. 'Here, I've written her address down for you, but don't ask me how to get there. I don't know that part of London. You'd better enquire from someone when you get to Liverpool Street.'

Nearly everyone on the staff gave Lottie something as a farewell present. She had always been popular; most knew or had guessed at her condition, and nobody condemned her for it. Ruby had nothing to give but her love, which she did in a flood of tears, and then dashed off to hide her heart-ache in the cold little attic they had shared together and Ellen produced a parcel of Billy's cast-off baby-clothes. 'I kept them in case they come in useful. I was going to send them on to Flo, but you be more in need of them than she.'

The only person who gave her no parting gift, not even his blessing, was her father. Lottie made one last desperate appeal. He was sitting in the garden on one of the kitchen chairs, smoking his pipe, staring blindly into the distance.

'Father, don't let me go without your good wishes. I've been stupid, and thoughtless, and selfish – but I am not wicked. You know how much my home means to me, I don't really want to leave, and one day I hope to come back again. That's the one thought that keeps me going. Father, please, please say something to me before I go. Anything.'

At first her father made no move – just sat on like a graven image, and she was just thinking that she could more easily have borne his abuse than this chilling silence, when he broke it.

'What do you want me to say? I've kep' silent because I was frightened of what I would say. I've never laid a finger on you, but it's taken all my will-power to keep my hands off you these past few weeks. We set such store by you, your mother and me. We made sacrifices for you – yes we did, my gel. Those last two years when you could have been out in the world earning your own living. We kep' you on at school thinking you would repay us with your learning – make us proud of you.' He spat at her feet. 'Proud of a trollop – a little slut – willing to jump into any man's bed . . .'

'*Father* – it wasn't like that . . .'

'Then why won't you tell us the man's name – why're you keeping it to yourself? Are you protecting somebody? Now, it's you won't answer me. Why? Hev' you got something to hide? Go on – off with you, outer my sight.

Go off to London and mix with your own sort – that's where you belong. You certainly don't belong here. You're no longer a daughter of ours.'

Lottie flew indoors to sob out her heart to her mother. 'I couldn't believe he could say such things. He was like a stranger – his eyes . . . Oh, mother I really believe he hates me . . .'

'It's not you he hates – himself more likely, but he's a proud man – he wouldn't admit it.' Ellen stifled her own ache as she comforted her daughter. 'If it had been one of your sisters, he wouldn't have taken it so hard. But he thought the world of you – you could do no wrong in his eyes, and now he feels you've betrayed him. Don't carry on so, Lottie. He'll come round before you leave. I wouldn't be a bit surprised if he don't be waiting at the station to see you off when the time comes.'

But he wasn't. It was Reuben who was waiting with the pony-trap at the crossroads. Lottie had walked across the fields to avoid going through the village, mindful of watchful faces waiting behind lace curtains or half-drawn blinds. It was early May and the cuckoo had arrived in the land. If she heard the cuckoo now, she thought hopefully, she would be walking this field the same time next year. But though there was bird song all around her, the cuckoo didn't oblige.

Reuben had pulled up beneath a wayside oak. Lottie blushed furiously when she saw him and would have hurried by but he got down and came after her.

'It's another mile to the station,' he said in his slow Norfolk fashion. 'An' that suitcase be too heavy for you to carry any further.' He ignored her protests, took it from her and helped her into the trap. 'I'm on an errand for Mr Beeney an' seeing you acoming thought I could offer you a lift.'

Lottie knew that wasn't true, that he had been lying in wait for her, and wished she could bring herself to feel indebted to him rather than embarrassed. Did he know? Had he been told anything about her?

As if in answer to her thoughts he said, after careful reflection, 'I would've married you, Lottie, if you would 'ave me, but I'm not twenty-one yet an' I can't marry without my folks' consent. But as soon as I'm old enough, you do only 'ave to give the word an' I'll come up to London an' fetch 'ee.'

Lottie felt her throat constrict with tears. 'You're a good boy, Reuben,' she said huskily.

'That's where you be wrong, Lottie, I ain't no boy – I'm a man.'

The train from Thornmere Halt ran on the branch line between Beckton Market and Norwich, there Lottie would have to change for London. She took a corner seat in an empty Ladies Only compartment of a third-class carriage, and Reuben handed in her case. They shook hands and he stood on the platform watching until the train steamed out of sight. It passed landmarks Lottie had known all her life. The pack-horse bridge near the Ferry Inn. The little dell where the juiciest and sweetest blackberries could be found. The windmill in the field at the end of School Lane. And shortly afterwards, the tall chimneys of the Hall glided in and out of sight. Last of all the gatehouse, tall and solid like a fortress, with a homely plume of smoke drifting upwards from its chimney.

Her mother and Violet were waiting by the gates to see her go past. Violet spotted her first and began to wave, then her mother, clutching her throat with her other hand. Lottie leant out of the window to catch a final glimpse of them before the train rounded a curve, and then one long last hungry look at the gatehouse.

The train gained steadily on the signal-box that her father manned, and he was there at the window, staring out as if looking out for her. Lottie waved urgently, putting all her longing into her smile. But he turned away.

She sank back in her seat and stared out at the familiar countryside, seeing not the passing fields and hedges, but her father as he used to be, enthusiastically mapping out her future. It was for her father as much as for anyone that she had kept quiet about that fateful night. Sir Roger was a director of the Eastern and Coastal Railway Company and any scandal caused to his name by a member of the Foster family might well have cost her father his job as well as his home.

And now he had turned away from her, treating her like a stranger. Lottie wiped her eyes on the back of her glove. 'I'll never go back,' she vowed. 'I'd die rather than go back.'

FOUR | *Carla*
The Present

The main road from Beckton Market to Thornmere, which in Lottie's time had been little more than a cart-track, was now a dual carriageway. The windmill, a land-mark Carla had kept a look-out for, was still standing, now minus its sails and converted into a private residence. Though it was her first visit to Norfolk she felt she knew her way to Thornmere as if by instinct. She had been brought up on the rich and varied diet of her great-grandmother's history as other children are brought up on fairy tales, and she carried in her head a detailed picture of Thornmere as it used to be. She accepted the changes as inevitable, but she was pleased to find that the heart of the village remained very much the same as Lottie had described it.

Neither had the river changed. It had escaped the com-mercialisation of other more populated parts of the Broads because of its narrowness. Only the smallest of the pleasure cruisers could negotiate the awkward bends, and there were two now, moored at the staithe by the Ferry Inn. Who took holidays on the Broads in Novem-ber? she wondered. Nature lovers? Honeymooners? – remembering something Lottie had once said.

She drove on through the village street, passing cottages that had once housed agricultural workers but were now the homes, perhaps holiday homes, of a wealthier society. Then the church. The sight of the church saddened her. Its thatched roof needed repair, its fabric was crumbling. Lottie had sung in the choir there. She hurried past, on to her destination, the old railway cottage.

Within a short drive the tall brick chimneys of Thornmere Hall came into view. An imposing mansion, its Georgian façade disguising earlier origins. A large notice board erected at the entrance to the drive caught her eye. Thornmere Hall Hotel – open to non-residents. What a stroke of luck – somewhere to stay the night. An ironic touch that appealed to her. A guest at the place where Lottie had been a servant. There was poetic justice in that, she thought.

But her high spirits didn't last. Only as long as it took her to drive the half-mile or so further on to the gatehouse. She stopped the car, got out and stared. Whatever would Lottie think of this sad, blind, deserted relic? This ruin – this desecrated travesty, of what had once been her home. Thank God she would never know. Or would she?

A great black cloud appeared suddenly out of the cloudless sky, making a sound like the rushing of a train. It wheeled around the roof of the old gatehouse, broke apart, then formed again. It was a flock of starlings, home from a day's foraging in the fields, to roost on any ledge or space available. Once Carla, as a child, had stood in a city square and witnessed the same phenomenon. A susurration of starlings, Lottie who knew so much about birds, told her. Clouds of them, coming into the city for their nightly roost, as these were now.

It was suddenly quiet. The twittering chorus of the roosting birds had ceased. Only the wind, whistling through the loose slates of the old house, made soft plaintive noises. Then across the empty, darkening fields came the evening crow of a cock pheasant. It was the sound of Norfolk.

Well, she had fulfilled her promise to Lottie – she had brought her home. But what a homecoming! Carla drew in her breath on a long disheartened sigh. The pheasant crowed once more, his shrill *kwark – kwark – kwark* rousing her into action. For too long she had been standing there, putting off something she found distasteful. The act in itself was not distasteful, just the idea that all that remained of Lottie was contained in a small black japanned box. She shivered, suddenly feeling a chill as if cold lips had touched her cheek. But it was only her imagination – or possibly the wind. Parchment-like leaves were swirling in the lane.

She opened the lid of the box and tipped the ashes into the wilderness that was once a garden. The fine dust powdered the undergrowth, then was blown away on the next gust of air. Carla felt a rush of tears to her eyes. 'Damn you, Lottie,' she cried aloud. 'Why did you have to leave me? How am I going to cope on my own? I wanted you dead – but I miss you, Lottie. I miss you.'

She pulled herself together. This was ridiculous – madness, even. She brushed her hand across her eyes. The trouble was, she had been Lottie's carer for so many years that now without someone to look after, she felt lost. Useless, even. It would take time to adjust to thinking only of herself.

Stolidly, she stared about her. In the creeping twilight the landscape looked bleak and inhospitable. What was there about this place that had drawn Lottie back, even after death? Was it her youth she had been hankering for rather than her old home? Norfolk had meant so much to her, yet she had spent such a short part of her life there. Most of it had been spent in London, and then in Wenley, a pleasant, leafy suburb. Laburnum Lodge where her granddaughter and great-granddaughter had both been born meant very little to her. 'I can never think of this as my home,' she said once. 'This is just a transit camp.' A transit camp now worth half a million pounds thought Carla wryly.

She was reluctant to go into the gatehouse. The outside was bad enough. There was hardly a window left unbroken; the shutters had long since been wrenched away. But it would be stupid to come all this way and not have a look at it. She had to make a decision about it. Perhaps she could sell the site as a building plot. Nobody would want to buy the house.

She returned the japanned box to the car and took the key of the gatehouse out of the dashboard. A quick look, then off to Thornmere Hall for a hot bath and a meal. Tomorrow, first thing, she would return to Essex and get on with living. She would have done her duty by Lottie. That chapter was now closed.

The door to the kitchen opened with difficulty. Carla paused, feeling in a heart-stopping way that she was stepping into history. But the wave of fetid odour that greeted her soon jolted her back to reality.

The floor was covered with litter. She didn't look too closely, the smell was enough. Her torch picked out mushroom-like growths of fungus on walls and ceiling. The smell of the damp seeped into her lungs and made her cough. The cooking stove was brown with rust, and the hearth, which every morning, Lottie had had to whiten before going to school, was coated with a thick crust of soot and brickdust.

So this was the Fosters' kitchen. The heartland of that long-ago family and the cornerstone of Lottie's young life. Lottie's tales of coming home from school on cold winter afternoons and stepping into a kitchen that was all shining cleanliness, warmth and lamplight and mouth-watering smells seemed hollow now. 'I can see it yet,' she would say, narrowing her eyes as if better to conjure up past images. 'Mother toasting bread by the fire, and the smell of Norfolk buns baking in the oven. And other smells too. Apples and onions from the garden, bunches of herbs drying, and joints of bacon hanging from the ceiling.'

Oh, what was the good of seeing over the rest of the place? It would just be one more illusion blighted. The state of the kitchen was a warning to her. What about the other rooms? The store-room, the parlour, the three bedrooms. Best to think of the cottage as it had been in

Lottie's day. Yet she hated to give in. Lottie had never given in — only at the end, and then only to the last enemy.

She needn't go upstairs — just a quick look at the parlour. The room used only on Sundays and holidays — the Holy of Holies, Lottie's brothers had called it. Gingerly, she pushed the door open. It creaked on rusty hinges. She expected the worst, but it wasn't the worse, in fact it was an improvement on the kitchen. Her spirits rose. The walls were damp with mould, and there was a similar mat of cobwebs as in the kitchen, and more litter and broken glass, but the last of the daylight gave the room a sense of space and light, and it had a fine outlook across the fields.

She trod on something that yielded to her foot, and drew back with distaste, wondering what she had stepped into. It was the dead body of a bird. There were others, scattered about among the litter, mummified by the cold. Where had they come from? Trapped in the gatehouse perhaps and unable to find a way out again? She started for the stairs, unmindful of Mr Grindley's warning, crunching broken glass underfoot, feeling her way up the narrow treads. More dead birds, and she found their source in the main bedroom. A frieze of house-martins' nests ran round the walls like a decoration. Some old, some freshly built that year. Obviously the martins had been coming here for generations, returning each year to repair old nests or build afresh.

She was delighted. The house wasn't dead after all. Every spring it came alive to the sound of twitterings and wing beats and the hungry cries of fledglings. It was a house of birds! Excitedly, she ran to the other rooms. More martins' nests — they were everywhere. How overjoyed Lottie would have been at the thought of house-martins taking over her old home. House-martins were supposed to bring good fortune.

Lottie believed all of the superstitions associated with birds. House-martins and swallows brought good luck.

Magpies brought trouble. And you had to listen for the cuckoo to ensure that you would live long enough to hear it again the following year. For whatever you were doing, or wherever you were, when you heard the first cuckoo call, you would be doing the same thing, in the same place, at the same time the year after.

This solemn warning had given Carla several anxious springs when she was young until it dawned on her that Lottie, being hard of hearing, had not been able to hear the cuckoo call for many years. Yet she had gone on living, with or without its aid.

The smallest bedroom was the one that Lottie had shared with her little sister, Violet. It was just big enough, Lottie had said, to take a double bed jammed against the wall, with a chair beside it. Their clothes had been kept on shelves behind a curtain across one corner. Into the other two rooms were packed the rest of the Foster family. Not all at the same time, of course. The three older girls had left home to go into service before Billy, the baby of the family, was born.

Carla leant on the window-sill and looked out into the gloaming. There was frost in the air and the first star of evening was already gleaming in a pale sky. Had Lottie ever stood at the window like this, worrying about the future? Feeling she had reached a crossroads in her life and not knowing which way to turn?

Carla shivered, not entirely from cold, for a strange, unnerving sensation began to steal over her – a feeling of *déjà vu*. Surely, she had experienced this before – standing here at this same window – her mind full of the same feelings of uncertainty and doubt. Could this really have happened before – even in a dream?

Turning and peering into the shadows behind her, she could just make out the shape of an iron bedstead and next to it, a cane-bottomed chair on which, leaning a little to one side, stood a candle in a metal candlestick. She felt she was no longer Carla – she was Lottie, and that little hump in the bed was Violet crying herself to sleep. From downstairs came the drift of voices. Her mother's. Low, urgent and pleading, and her father's monosyllabic replies.

Carla shook herself free of her fancies. She was allowing her imagination to take hold of her, giving substance to nothing more than Lottie's memories. As she had grown older, Lottie had retreated more and more into the past and Carla had acted as her sounding-board echoing back to her voices long since stilled. Echoes that were still ringing in Carla's ears.

The place was playing tricks with her. She felt faint with cold and hunger, and she thought of the warmth and comfort of Thornmere Hall. But still she couldn't drag herself away from the window. Invisible ties seemed to bind her to the past. She was reluctant to leave. Her family's roots were planted deep in this old gatehouse.

Then she heard it. The sound of a steam train approaching. She knew just what to expect. The hissing of steam, the fumes from the firebox, the sparks flying upwards from the funnel, the trembling of the metals, the vibration of the floor, the house shaking as the train thundered past. Abruptly she came out of her trance. The noise had grown louder, tearing at her ear-drums. An ugly menacing sound – the scream of fighter jets warming up on a nearby RAF airfield. Carla let out her breath in a long shuddering sigh. Like Lottie, she was superstitious about many things. She shared with her a strong belief that fate played a deciding role in one's future. It was meant she should come here. To see the gatehouse, and for a brief moment stay suspended in time, being Lottie, listening to a train go by.

Was Lottie even now beside her, prompting such thoughts? Carla tried to dismiss the idea but it would persist. Lottie had been her guiding influence throughout her lifetime. Wasn't it feasible that that same influence could continue after death?

There had been a time, she thought sadly, when Lottie had had too much influence on her life and she had bitterly resented it. Even now, all these years later, it was still painful to remember that unhappy period just after Charlotte had died. So why remember? The past was finished. The present was for marking time. The future was ahead of her and she must make up her mind what to do.

I could rebuild this old place, she thought on a sudden impulse. Make it how it was in Lottie's time. There was nothing to stop her. She had the money, and she had the time. It would be something to fill in the winter months, and by the spring – who knows, she might have other plans by then.

She wasn't too old to fulfil her old ambition and take up art again. She could study in London – or Paris – or Rome. Or she could stay here in Norfolk. Or – and it was a big 'or' – she could fulfil her old secret desire and make contact with her father. Only the thought that he might reject her as Lottie had been rejected by her father, had prevented her getting in touch with him before this.

She turned from the window, her mind full of ideas. First make the gatehouse habitable. She felt she was destined for that. She would have to contact a builder, a local man if possible. Ideas proliferated. Electricity installed, and a deep bore well sunk in the garden.

Taking on such a task would be a challenge, but like Lottie, she enjoyed a challenge. Charlotte, who mistrusted and disliked anything to do with the world of art had been furious when told of Carla's ambition. 'You draw?' she had scoffed. 'You'll never be able to draw anything but your breath!' Which had made Carla more determined than ever to prove that she could, and she had, in a modest way.

Downstairs, the squalid state of the kitchen no longer worried her. It could be put right. Lottie had trodden this same path before her when in 1944 she had purchased Laburnum Lodge at Wenley. That had been left in a state of disrepair also, though not as bad as the gatehouse. It had been uninhabited since the beginning of war when the owners had left it for the comparative safety of the West Country. In those days, professional help was impossible to come by, so Lottie and Agnes Sharpe had set to work themselves, scrubbing and scraping, washing and scouring and then with buckets of whitewash and distemper, wallpaper in war-time being unobtainable, had brought brightness and freshness to rooms that had been dark and grimy before. It had been a labour of love. Making a home for Charlotte's coming baby.

Had Charlotte appreciated it? No. Years later Carla found herself the unwitting eavesdropper of one of her grandmother's emotional outbursts. 'I don't want another penny of your money. I'd rather starve than be indebted to you any longer,' she screamed at Lottie. 'It's bad enough that I have to live under your roof, so spare me your charity. You can't buy me anymore!'

At nine years old Carla had not understood the meaning behind the words, but she had recognised the ugliness of the tone, and she had crept away bewildered and frightened by the sound of the two old ladies quarrelling. It took her years to understand and sympathise with her grandmother, but she could never forgive her.

Lottie. Every thought she had seemed to bring her back to Lottie. 'You're not going to leave me in peace, are you?' she said out loud, as if expecting Lottie to answer. As long as this gatehouse stands, Lottie will live, she thought, and she wanted Lottie to live now. She needed her strength to sustain her.

'We'll do it, Lottie,' she promised. 'Somehow, between us, we'll bring this old house back to life again.'

Thornmere Hall was lit up like a Christmas tree. The sweep of her headlights picked out the lodge in darkness – then the fine proportions of the Hall came into view. She parked in the forecourt among the other cars, and taking her overnight bag out of the boot, she started up the flight of steps that were guarded on either side by massive stone lions. Lottie had made no mention of stone lions, but then, how often did Lottie use the front entrance?

She was shown into a room on the first floor. A double room, as no single rooms were available. The splendour of her surroundings made her acutely aware that she wasn't exactly dressed for a place like this. Her boots were muddy and her jeans were caked with dirt and cobwebs. Fortunately, she had packed a dress to change into.

The bathroom was even more resplendent than the bedroom. It had gold-plated taps – or what would pass for gold-plate. Remembering Lottie's stories of carrying cans of hot water up to these rooms in the old days, made her smile. Nothing that a guest might require had been overlooked. She would have her bath, then wash her hair.

She turned on the hot tap, poured in a liberal helping of bath oil, and went into the bedroom to undress. A few minutes later, when she returned, she found the bathroom full of steam. A quickly opened window soon cleared it, but the sudden cold draught on her unclothed body took her breath away. What was it Charlotte had said about Norfolk? 'Nothing but pigs, cess-pits, and east winds!' No pigs or cess-pits today, Grandma. Only the east wind.

She luxuriated in the bath, soaking up to her chin in frothy, scented water, then she let out her breath on a long and expressive sigh.

'Oh Lottie,' she said. 'You should see me now!'

She had dined so well the evening before she hadn't expected to manage breakfast. But she did – a full English breakfast – something she hadn't attempted in years. It must be this Norfolk air, she thought appreciatively. She felt relaxed and carefree this morning. She had slept well. Later, she went to the reception desk. 'Could you give me the name of a local builder?' she asked the girl.

The receptionist stared in surprise. It must have seemed

an unusual request. 'I don't come from these parts,' she said. 'But Miss Stoneham, the housekeeper, does. She might be able to help you. At this time of the morning she should be in the linen-room.'

She was, checking off items against a list. She was probably a young-looking sixty, Carla thought. She had a motherly figure and a placid expression on her cheerful face. 'What can I do for you?' she asked with a smile.

That familiar heart-tugging Norfolk accent! Carla immediately warmed to her. 'I wondered if you could recommend a builder, a local man if possible . . .' She hesitated, wondering how to word her request, then decided to be completely frank. 'Do you know that old gatehouse down the lane? I've recently inherited it, and I'd like to have it made habitable . . .'

Carla felt herself being regarded by a pair of shrewd and curious eyes. 'The best man for the job is Fred Cartwright. I can recommend him personally for he's just finished doing some repairs for me. Did you notice the lodge as you came in? That's where I live.'

Carla wrote down the builder's name and phone number. 'You don't seem at all surprised that I intend to do up the old gatehouse,' she said.

The woman's smile broadened. 'My dear, it's your own business what you do with your money. But if it was me, I'd think of a better way of spending it.'

'Hallo. Is that Cartwright and Sons?'

'Fred Cartwright speaking.'

'My name is Carla Foster. I'm staying at Thornmere Hall for the time being, and I would like your advice.' She had some difficulty in finding the right words. Would he laugh at the idea of renovating the old gatehouse? Would he consider it a lost cause? She explained what she wanted. 'If you think it will be money wasted you will tell me, won't you?'

'I have too much respect for money to see it wasted,' came the laconic reply. Carla pictured Mr Cartwright as a man in his fifties, plain spoken and direct. She arranged to meet him at the gatehouse at eleven o'clock.

'How did you know about me?' he asked.

'Miss Stoneham recommended you.'

'That should be good enough. Jessie Stoneham's known me all my life. See you in about forty minutes' time then, Miss – em . . .'

'Foster.'

'Foster? That's a familiar name in these parts.'

In the cold light of morning the gatehouse looked more than ever like a ruin. Goodness knows, it had looked bad enough in the dusk, but there had been something romantic about it – a link with the past. Now with the November sun highlighting its dereliction it just looked pathetic. She could imagine what the forthright Mr Cartwright would say about it.

She had visualised someone short and stocky with the weatherbeaten look of a farmer – that was the image his voice had suggested to her. But he turned out to be a tall, spare man with a humorous face.

'Haven't been down this way for years,' he said. 'Not since old Ted Foster died. He was the last of the gatekeepers.' He eyed her speculatively. 'Any relation of yours?'

Such a question caught her unawares. She didn't want to tell an out-right lie, yet she felt it was too soon to talk about her connection. 'I wouldn't know. Foster is a fairly common name . . .'

'That's true. Well, let's go in and see the damage.'

They stood in the kitchen. Fred Cartwright looked about him with pursed lips. Finally he said, 'It's like a cold storage in here.'

'Do you think it would be safe if I lit a fire?'

He examined the kitchen range. 'Not in here . . . See – the stovepipe is cracked. What's the fireplace like in the other room?'

They went together to find out. The original Victorian

overmantel had been replaced at sometime by an insignificant tiled surround, circa the 1930s.

'The grate looks OK,' was his verdict. 'But before you light your fire, I'd better make sure there isn't a jackdaw's nest in the chimney.' He went out into the garden and came back with a long thin branch of a tree which he poked into the blackened maw.

'Seems clear to me. I think it'll be safe to risk a fire. We'll soon know if there's an obstruction. The smoke will billow back on us.'

'If there isn't a nest up there, it'll be the only place in the house where there isn't one. You should see upstairs.'

'All in good time. I want to have a look round down here, first.'

Carla rooted around for the wherewithal to start a fire. There was no shortage of combustible material. Screwed up old newspapers, fish and chip wrappings, bits of wood and candle-ends along with other debris she had no wish to scrutinise too closely. Mr Cartwright handed her some matches.

'Looks like someone's been using this place as a squat,' he commented. 'On the other hand, it makes a good hide-out for poachers. Pheasants are strutting around here like chickens.'

Surprisingly she got the fire alight first go – the candles helped. The chimney had a good draught, drawing the fire greedily into life, and though the wood was damp it was soon blazing away, snapping and crackling and sending sparks flying. She felt she had achieved something really useful. Even if it only warmed up a few bricks in the chimney it was something towards combating the damp.

Fred Cartwright was now upstairs. She imagined page after page on his clipboard being filled with a never-ending list of defects. She wished there was something she could do to take her mind off the outcome. If she had a broom she could sweep up most of the rubbish. She went in search and was lucky enough to find what

83

she wanted in the little room off the hall she thought was a store-room but which the builder referred to as the pantry.

'I see you've been busy down here.' He was back.

'Yes, I found an old broom and I've been trying to sweep the floors, not very successfully as half its bristles are missing. I've been burning the rubbish. Does it smell?'

'I don't mind the smell. It's the warmth I appreciate.' He held his hands to the blaze, then rubbed them vigorously on his buttocks. He had placed his clipboard on the window-sill and as Carla had suspected, it was filled with small neat writing.

'Don't keep me in suspense. Is there any hope? Can this place be made habitable?'

He cocked one eye at her. 'Depends what you mean by hope. Hope for this old place – or hope for your bank balance?'

She grinned. 'I just want this place restored – I want to make it into a home. Do you think it can be done?'

'Young lady, anything can be done if you've got the money to pay for it. Yes. The structure is sound. The roof is good too, though some of the slates are missing. They could be replaced – taken from that old outhouse at the bottom of the garden. It will be costly, but it's not impossible. And I'll tell you something else ... In my opinion this old house will still be standing when those new houses springing up at the other end of the village have all collapsed like a pack of cards.'

Carla knew his words were prompted by the scorn felt by the small traditional builder towards the nationwide construction companies assembling homes out of prefabricated kits. But she believed him because she wanted to believe him.

'What's the first move?' she said, anxious to get down to details.

'The first thing to do is to nail polyglaze over the windows. That will stop the birds from getting in. It's a wonder to me the starlings haven't taken over. Did you know there's enough guano upstairs to start a small industry? Polyglaze will also help keep the rain out. This place is damp enough as it is. And talking about damp – how does a hot cup of coffee appeal to you?'

'There's nothing I'd like more – but I was hoping to get some matters settled before we go.'

'No problem, we can have coffee, here. I've got a flask in the truck. I'll nip out and fetch it.'

He went off whistling between his teeth, leaving Carla staring thoughtfully into the fire. It was glowing with real heat now, and soon she would have to go scavenging around for something more to use as fuel.

But not just yet. For a few moments she wanted to stay put, musing over ideas that were going round in her mind. She would sell the Wenley house. She would stay at the Hall until the cottage was made ready – that should take until the spring. Then, before she decided what to do next, she would seek out her father.

FIVE | *Lottie*
Spring–Summer, 1914

'Lottie? You can't be Lottie! My gawd girl, I wouldn't have known you.' Aggie stood in the doorway, blinking stupidly into the noon-day sun. She wore slippers and a wrapper, hastily donned by the look of it, and her hair, unkempt, straggled down to her shoulders.

On the doorstep, Lottie wilted. 'Oh Aggie, I'm so tired. I've walked miles. Nobody I asked seemed to have heard of Boot Lane, and then when I finally got here, I walked past this place several times before I noticed the name plate. I've been ringing for ages. I was beginning to think there was nobody in . . .'

Aggie swiftly came to her senses. 'You've caught me on the hop, gel – I was sound asleep. Why didn't you let me know you was coming? No, don't bother to answer that just yet. Let's get you indoors first. You look ready to drop.'

She pulled Lottie into the entrance lobby and closed the door behind her. They stared at each other. Their friendship had been brief, but deep-rooted. Lottie saw Aggie's eyes start to water; she felt near tears herself. Awkwardly, they exchanged kisses, then Aggie threw off all restraint. She hugged Lottie close. 'Crikey, girl, it's good to see you again. Come on in. I want to have a good look at you.'

She saw a girl sagging with exhaustion, and carrying a battered, fibre suitcase. That looked significant, but she made no comment. 'This way,' she said. 'We can talk better in my room; besides, you look as if you could do with a sit.'

Lottie was dimly aware of being led through a long, narrow room, heavy with red plush hangings and redolent with stale cigar smoke and heady perfume. This must be the restaurant she thought, seeing the tables laid for dinner. But it was empty.

'What sort of restaurant is it that closes at lunch-time?' she asked.

'The sort what don't open until eight o'clock in the evening,' Aggie said with one of her explosive laughs.

They passed the kitchen. Its door was ajar, and Lottie saw, amid the disorder, a figure of an elderly woman, sprawling dead to the world at the table. By her elbow was an empty gin bottle.

'It don't look as bad as this all the time,' said Aggie defensively, seeing the kitchen through Lottie's eyes. 'Mary Ann must've gone on a bender last night, that's why she didn't hear the doorbell. She's a good worker when she's sober. The kitchen'll be spick and span before Monsieur Jacques and his staff get here, or there'll be ructions. Mind you, he's no monsieur really, (she pronounced it monsewer) he comes from Whitechapel. But monsieur sounds posher for a chef.'

Lottie was swaying. 'Here, give me that case. Only one more flight of stairs now and we'll be there . . .'

The first thing that Lottie noticed on entering Aggie's room was a pair of black satin corsets draped over the bedpost. Aggie grabbed at them and pushed them under the eiderdown. 'This place don't look no tidier than the kitchen,' she said with a self-conscious titter. 'But I ain't got round to doing it yet. Come on, ducks, it's bed for you . . . I'll just smooth it over first. There you are . . . we can have a jaw later.'

Lottie was quite willing to be helped onto the bed, and have someone minister to her. She felt her boots being removed, her skirt unbuttoned and her stays loosened. She closed her eyes, sinking into a state of blissful unconsciousness.

She slept for two hours, so Aggie told her later. She

awoke refreshed, bewildered until the events of the day came back to her. The room had been tidied, strewn garments removed, curtains drawn, a window opened. And a bunch of sweet williams in a pink china vase had appeared on the mantelpiece.

'So you've woken up at last,' said Aggie, from the foot of the bed. 'I've looked in twice, already. How'dya feel now?'

Lottie pulled herself up to a sitting position. Aggie had changed little in appearance – slightly more matronly-looking perhaps – but the same knowing green eyes, the same broad grin. 'I shouldn't have landed myself on you like this,' Lottie said apologetically. 'Mrs Webster only gave me your address at the last minute ... Oh, Aggie ... dear Aggie, it's so good to see you again.'

'Now – now, don't start blubbing ... I don't want you with red eyes when you go to see Maud ...'

Lottie blew her nose. 'Maud? Is that why this place is called Maudie's? I saw the name on the plaque, and wondered.'

'Yes. Maud is the proprietress – the queen bee. I've just been along to get her up, and I told her about you. She said she'd like to see you.'

'You got her up?' Lottie's mind flew back to Thornmere Hall. 'Are you her personal maid?'

'Me! A lady's maid – blimey, what an idea!' Aggie gave another of her loud laughs. 'No, poor old Maud carries a bit of flesh around if you see what I mean. She likes me to help her out of bed and get her dressed and so on ...'

'You've put on a bit of weight yourself, Aggie. But it suits you.'

'And you've lost weight, especially about the face ... Never mind, you'll soon put it back on again when that bun in your oven begins to swell ...'

Their eyes met. Lottie's were full of shame. Aggie's were tender and mocking at the same time. 'How did you guess?'

'It don't take a Sherlock Holmes to put two and two together, not when a girl from the country turns up unexpectedly, looking washed out, and lugging a bloody big suitcase. Want to tell me about it . . . ?'

'Sit there – where I can have a better look at you.'

Lottie, perched uneasily on the edge of her chair, was acutely aware of Maud's relentless scrutiny. Maud's chest jutted out like a headland, and on this taffeta-encased promontory rested a necklace of jet beads that rose and fell with every breath she took.

'Aggie has told me your story,' she said. 'Also, that you are looking for work. What can you do?'

'I can sew and mend.' Lottie could see that suggestion made no impression. 'I can wait at table. I was trained as a parlour-maid.'

'I have nothing to offer you in the way of mending or sewing, and I certainly don't need a parlour-maid, and waiting at table is out of the question considering your condition. But I could use you in the kitchen. Monsieur Jacques is always complaining that he hasn't enough staff, and Mary Ann isn't getting any younger. She won't like you being there, but you'll just have to put up with her tantrums and not let her brow-beat you. Can you stand up for yourself? You look rather soft to me.'

Lottie coloured up. 'I can learn. There are a lot of things I'll have to learn from now on.'

'You sound bitter. Are you bitter? About what happened to you, I mean?'

'No, I'm not bitter.' Bitter didn't exactly describe her constant warring emotions of anger, guilt, shame and resentment.

'I don't suppose you are. You're still too bewildered, too hurt to feel bitter. An embittered woman is no use to herself or anyone else, and it rubs off on others. This is a happy establishment. I don't want someone coming along and causing trouble.'

'I said I am not bitter,' Lottie repeated, wearily.

'Right then, let's get down to business. First, you'll want some money for clothes. You can't go around looking like a frump, not in this establishment, anyway. Here, take this . . .' Maud pulled her skirts well above her knees, revealing enormous silk-stockinged legs that tapered into surprisingly small feet. Embarrassed, Lottie looked away, as Maud unearthed her purse from somewhere amid her underwear. She counted two sovereigns into Lottie's palm.

'That'll do to be going on with. We'll come to some firmer arrangements later. Your board and lodging will be free of course.'

Lottie's eyes filled with tears at this unexpected generosity. 'I don't want you to think I've come begging. I'll work for my keep . . .'

For the first time Maud smiled, and that smile changed the whole structure of her face, giving her a gentler, more approachable look. 'If you're trying to thank me, save your breath . . . or thank Aggie instead. She's talked me into letting you stay. And don't looked so worried, child. You're among friends here.'

'Why is this restaurant only frequented by men? I've been here nearly four weeks, and except for the staff, I haven't seen a single woman. Why don't the customers ever bring their wives or daughters with them?'

Lottie did not miss the wary look that Aggie shot in her direction. 'Because it's a kind of gentlemen's-only club,' she said.

'Why waitresses and not waiters then?'

'Because waitresses come cheaper.'

'And why don't the waitresses wear anything under their blouses? It's really shocking . . .'

Aggie counter-attacked.

'What do you wear under your blouse, Lottie?'

'A flannel bust-bodice.'

'My gawd! In this weather — no wonder you're always itching.'

After that unflattering remark, Lottie gave up wearing her flannel bodices and bought herself some silk camisoles instead. She could afford it out of the money Maud was paying her. She now received considerably more than she did as a lady's maid, and though she was working harder, in many ways she found life easier. There were no class distinctions at Maudie's – she was one of a team – one of a family. The 'girls', as Maud called the waitresses, were on Christian name terms.

She was happy on a certain level, providing she kept her homesickness under control and stopped watching out for the postman. Her mother was no letter-writer, and her two brothers couldn't spell. Her father was a self-taught scholar, but she knew there was no possibility of hearing from him. So far, her letters home had gone unanswered.

And always that niggling suspicion at the back of her mind that Maudie's was not all it seemed on the surface.

June that year was the hottest Lottie could remember, or was it that she was missing Norfolk's bracing air and shady lanes? On Sunday, 28th June, she read in Maud's paper the news that the heir to the Hapsburg throne, the Archduke Franz Ferdinand and his morganatic wife had been assassinated in Sarajevo, the capital of Bosnia. She read this as if reading about people on another planet, for she had neither heard of Sarajevo nor Bosnia, and had never come across the word morganatic before. She was looking through the paper in the vain hope that she would find some snippets of news about Norfolk. Had she but known it was an event that was to plunge Europe into the bloodiest war of all time, she would not have treated it so lightly.

All that day, she was nagged by a splitting headache. By night-time it was unbearable. She had taken two headache powders without effect, and now clad only in her night-gown, she sat by the open window. There was no fresh air – only coal fumes from nearby chimneys and the odour of horse dung. She knew now that nothing would cure her head but a good night's sleep, and sleep was impossible in such heat. Then she remembered the bottle of eau de Cologne that Aggie kept on her dressing-table. Eau de Cologne was a cooling agent, it was refreshing as well as soothing, and some of that dabbed on her forehead might ease her pain.

Like the other girls, Aggie worked long hours, not getting to bed sometimes until dawn was breaking. Lottie would often awaken, just as it was getting light, to hear the girls go clack-clacking down the street in their high heels. She was so used to the sound now, she didn't give it another thought, except to pity them their hours of work. Then she would turn over to snatch another hour or two of sleep before getting up herself.

She walked cautiously along the narrow passage to Aggie's room, conscious that her nightgown was stretched tightly over her swollen belly. She hoped she wouldn't meet anybody. Not only because of her appearance, but because she was venturing into forbidden territory. Only a door and a shallow flight of stairs separated the domestic quarters of the building from the private rooms above the restaurant from which she was excluded by her condition.

A light hung on a bracket outside Aggie's room. Everywhere was very quiet. No voices from downstairs – no high-pitched laughter – no tinkling music – yet for Maudie's the evening was young. Lottie opened the door, and went in, fully expecting to find the room in darkness.

It was not – neither was it unoccupied. Aggie was very much in evidence and so was her companion, a portly gentleman, both naked and interlocked on the bed. Immobilised by shock, the only thing that really registered with Lottie was that Aggie's nipples were painted a brilliant red. Aggie, feeling a sudden draught, raised her head from the pillow. 'Shut the door after you, duckie,' she said.

Lottie fled. By the time she got back to her own room she had completely forgotten her headache.

'So now you know,' said Maud complacently.

It was the following morning and Lottie had gone to Maud's room to give in her notice. Maud asked her to sit down.

'Why didn't you tell me? Why didn't anyone warn me! Why did you let me have to find out like that!'

Maud did not answer immediately. She took another draw on the long flat Turkish cigarette she was smoking, and squinted narrow-eyed through its aromatic smoke.

'Did I really have to tell you? Be honest. Didn't you suspect anything?'

'Of course I didn't! Not at first anyway . . . Then . . . well, I did start to wonder . . . but I never dreamed . . . not to that extent. But it was cruel of you not to tell me when I first came, that this . . . this place is . . . well . . . a . . .'

'Brothel?' Maud finished for her. Some ash fell on the projection of her chest and she flicked it off.

The heat in the airless room and the strong smell from the cigarette started in Lottie a feeling of nausea. She heaved, and put her handkerchief to her mouth. 'It was cruel of you,' she repeated. 'Why didn't you tell me?'

'Because I wanted you to find out for yourself. Aggie said it would take you months to guess, but I credited you with more intelligence. I wanted to see how you would react when you first suspected. I was prepared for you to sweep out of here in high dudgeon. When you didn't . . . when you hung on, I said to myself . . . She knows which side her bread is buttered on.'

Lottie stared helplessly at her. Again, she heard herself saying, 'Why didn't you tell me?'

'What would you have done that first day, if I had told you? Would you have stayed?'

'No,' said Lottie without hesitation.

Maud shrugged her shoulders. 'Well then . . . That's

why I didn't tell you and wouldn't let Aggie tell you either. Let the girl have a good rest first, I said. Her health needs building up before she's let loose in London. What would happen to you out there – no job, no home, no nothing? I knew the answer well enough, so I decided to let you wait until you found out and see what you did about it. What did you do . . . Nothing!'

'I didn't know for sure until last night,' said Lottie, defensively.

'You are not unhappy here, are you? I've seen you blossom out . . . I've heard you laughing. You were a long way from laughing when you first arrived. You've got a cushy little niche here, Lottie, and you know it.' Maud lent forward and stubbed out her cigarette on a brass ash-tray 'Now that you know the truth about Maudie's, or think you do, has it changed in any way? Does it seem any worse . . . does it look different? Would a stranger going past suddenly stop and ask himself, 'Is that a house of ill-repute?' Do you think you have changed overnight because you live here? Do you yourself feel different?'

'I would be ashamed for anybody to know I work in a – a brothel.' Lottie nearly choked on the word.

'Who is anybody?'

'My family . . . the people of Thornmere.'

'I wouldn't set much score by what *they* think,' Maud said scathingly. 'The only ones you have to consider are yourself and your baby. You've got a good home here and to tell you the truth, I don't really want to lose you. You've worked wonders in the kitchen. Jacques thinks very highly of you. He says you are a born cook and he's prepared to teach you some of the tricks of his trade. Even old Mary Ann has a grudging respect for you now. But I'm not going to beg you to stay if you don't want to. All I ask of you is not to make up your mind in a hurry. Sleep on it. Then come and see me again tomorrow.'

'After . . . after my baby is born . . . you won't expect

me to be like one of your other girls, will you?' It took a lot of courage to say that, but it had to be said. Maud's answer depended on whether she stayed or not.

Maud rose to her feet — four feet six of impassioned outrage. The eyes she turned on Lottie glittered like little pieces of jet.

'You can leave at once,' she cried vehemently. 'I don't want anyone under my roof who can think so ill of me. Go — go now!'

'I'm sorry . . . Maud . . . I'm sorry. I shouldn't have said that . . . I shouldn't even have thought it. Please forgive me.' Lottie suffered agonies of remorse.

'I have never ever asked anybody to do anything they didn't want to. This is a *respectable* establishment — respectable compared with other brothels I could mention. Girls clamour to work for me. They know they'll be treated right by me, and by their clients. I won't allow any funny goings on here. This is no den of vice, and if that's what you think, the sooner you go the better.'

Tears welled into Lottie's eyes. They oozed from beneath her lids and down her cheeks. She groped in her sleeve for the handkerchief again. 'I don't know what I think. I don't know about such places . . . I just don't know . . .' She broke into loud unrestrained sobs.

Maud watched her for a while unmoved, then slowly, unexpectedly her face began to crumple and her own eyes to water. 'There, there, don't take on so, child,' she said. 'Crying like that won't do your baby any good.' She moved in swift, mincing steps to Lottie's side and hugged her, her head barely up to Lottie's shoulder. 'See what you've done . . . you've started me off too.' She blew her nose. 'My gentlemen wouldn't believe it. They've never seen me cry — few people have. Come,' she said. 'Sit down here beside me. There is something I have to tell you.'

'I was fourteen when I had my last good cry. Hollering, actually — hollering at the top of my voice. I was being stitched up after some gentleman had had his way with me. Afterwards I cried . . . and not only because of the pain, either. That was the day it all started.'

'You too, Maud . . . you were raped?'

'Technically, I suppose I was. Actually, I was sold. That shocks you? Three pounds my mother got for me. Three pounds went a long way in the 1860s, and when you're starving, and your family's starving . . .' She shrugged. 'You don't go into the ethics of it. I was sold for a few pounds to a woman calling herself Mrs Constantine. I didn't know the truth of the transaction at the time. I thought I was being apprenticed to a dressmaker – that's what I was told. I remember how delighted I felt . . . getting away from the grinding poverty of Grays Buildings . . . my father's beatings . . . the prospect of learning a trade. The West End was another world as far as I was concerned . . . and Mrs Constantine's house seemed like a palace.'

'Maud, don't go on . . . you're upsetting yourself.'

'I'm just a foolish, sentimental old woman, but I'm all right. Let me tell you . . . It'll be better to get this out in the open. As I said – I was taken to Mrs Constantine's house and given a bath and something to eat and drink. My clothes . . . rags, I should say . . . were taken away from me, and I was put to bed. When I woke up next morning, all I could feel was this dreadful pain, and there was blood all over the sheets.

'Then Mrs Constantine came and told me what had happened. I'd been given what she called a black draught – ginger-beer laced with laudanum – a powerful drug to a half-starved fourteen-year-old, and as soon as it had put me out I was handed over to one of her regular gentlemen. There was quite a demand for virgins by some of her customers, and many were willing to pay up to ten pounds a time. Mrs Constantine wasn't the sort to turn down an offer like that, and there was always girls for the asking in the slums of London. Some went willingly, some were tricked, some like me were sold off.

They had to be young – over thirteen, the age of consent, and under fifteen when they weren't so easily fooled.'

'Don't go on,' pleaded Lottie. She found listening to this too painful.

'I may as well finish now I've started. Mrs Constantine gave me two choices. To stay and work for her, or be paid two pounds and put out on the street. There was no choice really. I couldn't go home so I stayed. And I stayed in that place for three years. Then one of my regulars, a solicitor from Holloway, took me away and set me up in a nice little house in Islington. He said his family was off his hands, and his wife didn't want to have anything more do with that side of marriage. He treated me well, my Mr Hammond. He spoilt me – showered me with presents, gave me everything I wanted. I was a pretty little thing in those days . . . very small . . . very dainty. You wouldn't think so to look at me now, would you?' Maud gave a slight titter, and followed up with a sigh. 'Our relationship lasted until he died – fifteen years. Long before then, we'd stopped sleeping together, and Mr Hammond took it upon himself to educate me instead. He gave me books to read, taught me better manners, even tried to teach me how to speak properly. I think he looked upon me as a kind of pet he was teaching new tricks to.'

Maud paused, her expression reminiscent of happy memories. 'When he died he left me the lease of the Islington house, its furniture, and some pieces of jewellery. I'd already made plans for my future. I knew by now why men such as Mr Hammond felt a need for brothels. Widowers or bachelors, or some with wives like my protector's . . . I saw nothing wrong in supplying their needs. The wrong lay in the evil practices, such as child prostitution, that I had seen at Mrs Constantine's. I began to look around for the right kind of premises, and found this place, which I got cheap, because it was then just a cluster of ramshackle shops. I sold the lease of my house to raise the money to acquire the buildings and have them converted into one establishment and a year later I was in business. I pick my girls carefully, laying down strict rules, and anyone breaking those rules is immediately sacked. They can do what they like in their own time, I tell them, but they don't do it under my roof. Clients come to Maudie's for a satisfying meal, and afterwards good clean sex. Man's two basic needs.'

Lottie who found it hard to equate sex with being either good or clean, listened to Maud's story in stupefaction and despair, and finally a grudging admiration for the unbroken spirit of this indomitable woman. She had run the gamut of emotions, the strongest of which, and in spite of trying to be open-minded, was a niggling disapproval.

'And Aggie? How did she come to be here?'

Maud laughed. 'Aggie's a case on her own. She wasn't a whore, though she did oblige some of the customers at the public house where she worked, from time to time. That was to help her mother after her father died, but when her mother found out she threw her out. Aggie heard of me and came and asked for a job. Best day's work I ever did, taking her on. She's like a daughter to me, now. But that's enough for one morning. I just wanted you to understand that I'm not the wicked old woman you might think me. Go away and think it over, then come and tell me whether you have decided to stay on or not.'

'I'm sorry about last night,' said Lottie, feeling awkward and rather foolish. If Aggie had looked at all humbled or embarrassed, she could have managed a better apology. But Aggie's grin put her off, as did the cynical gleam in her green eyes.

'I wasn't spying on you . . . I was after some of your eau de Cologne for my head. I hope I didn't embarrass your . . . em . . . gentleman.'

Aggie roared with laughter. 'He didn't even notice, poor old sod – he was past it.' She clapped her hand to her mouth. 'Sorry, Lot, that slipped out like. I know you don't like me swearing, and I do try not to. D'you notice I don't say "my gawd," anymore?'

Lottie's eyes watered. 'Oh Aggie, you do make me feel so mean. What a narrow-minded little prig you must think me.'

'I think no such thing. And about last night . . . it don't make any difference to our friendship, do it? I mean, now that you know the sort of person I am.'

Lottie felt too choked to speak coherently. 'I don't deserve you, d'you know that. You're the best friend I've ever had.'

They were in the kitchen, preparing afternoon tea. Enoch, the handyman, was down in the cellar, sleeping off the after-effects of his lunch and Mary Ann had been marched off to confession by two nuns, after another lapse from grace.

'But you're thinking of leaving here. Maud told me.'

'No, I am not. It did cross my mind at first, but I've given it some thought, and I've decided to stay. And not because I've got a cushy little niche, as Maud said. It's because I really want to stay here – you are all my friends, I can't give you up. And I feel at home here – safe.'

She said the same thing to Maud when she took in her tea.

'You won't regret it,' Maud promised, taking genteel bites from a slice of seed cake. 'For sometime I've been looking around for someone suitable I could train as a manageress, someone to take some of the responsibility off my shoulders. I think you're the right person. Your head is screwed on the right way, and you are quick to learn. Time will tell, and it's too soon to think on those lines yet, anyway. Get your baby over first. How are you feeling these days?'

'Considering all things, very well.'

'I think it's time you gave up the marketing side. You can do the bookwork instead. I'm no good at figuring –

never was. That was something my Mr Hammond never could teach me.'

Lottie went to bed that night with her mind going round in circles. The prospects Maud held out to her ensued a settled future – but what about her principles? What would her child think when, as was inevitable, it came out that their comfortable way of life was based on immoral earnings? Yet there were other women, working in the sweat shops of the East End, making shirts at sevenpence a dozen, or stitching furs all day for a paltry five shillings a week. What about their employers? – living off the profits of sweated labour. Did they have any qualms? Moral issues came in many guises.

She rolled over on her back, the only way she could now lie in any comfort. Her baby was very lively tonight. She placed both hands on her abdomen and felt the movements inside her. Her baby – hers alone. Whatever plans she made now were, in the long run, for her child. Her family had deserted her – so in his way, had Henry. She tried not to think of him these days, but in the night, when she couldn't sleep, it was hard to keep him at bay.

He came to her as a shadowy image, sometimes with his gentle smile and wistful blue eyes. At other times, as she had last seen him, with an anguished and demoralised face. Joseph too, came to plague her, and then she would dig her fingers into her eyelids as if to gouge him from her sight. But lately, since her baby had become more active inside her, Joseph ceased to worry her. It was as if the infant when quickening into life had taken over her life also, cancelling out that part of the past that no longer concerned them. If she had to imagine a father for the baby, she preferred to think of him as Henry. It was a harmless fantasy that helped her to cope with day to day reality.

'It's a rum old Bank Holiday, sitting here waiting for war to be declared,' said Maud philosophically. 'But cheer up girls, let's make the most of it. Aggie, go down to the kitchen and get some of that black fruit cake, and you Lottie, you pop along to my office and fetch that special port I keep in the cupboard. We'll drink to good old England and the health of the British Tommy.'

Lottie was gone so long that Maud sent Aggie after her. 'I expect she can't find the bottle. I've hidden it too well from Mary Ann. Go and give her a hand.'

But Lottie had found the port. She was standing by the cupboard, clutching the bottle in both hands, looking both flushed and fearful.

'Aggie, my waters have broken,' she said anxiously.

Aggie caught off guard, came out with, 'Oh, my gawd!' Then, 'I thought the baby wasn't expected for another coupla or more weeks yet. Come along ducks, we'd better get you to bed.'

Charlotte Agnes Foster was born on the 4th August a minute before midday. Her mother was senseless at the time, put out by a whiff of chloroform. Maud and Aggie stood by with their sleeves rolled up above their elbows, their faces streaked with perspiration. It had been the longest twenty-four hours in their lives. The doctor was repacking his bag, carefully wrapping up his forceps.

'Could I give you a drink, doctor,' said Maud, desperately in need of a drink herself. They left the room together. The doctor was an old friend and regular customer.

Aggie untied her soiled apron, screwed it into a ball and threw it in the corner. She sponged her face with cold water, and dried her hands and face on the towel that had been put out for the doctor. The baby, cocooned in a woollen shawl, had been laid to sleep in a wickerwork picnic hamper.

Next, she took the flannel and wiped the sweat from Lottie's face and neck. Poor little devil – it wasn't right the way she had suffered! Her pains hadn't really started until the early hours of Tuesday, then they had come on suddenly. The midwife Maud had booked beforehand refused to come. When Aggie went round to fetch her, she said she wasn't going to budge from her home in case war started. Nobody knew what to expect from them Germans – look what they'd done to the French in 1870. But Aggie didn't know what had happened to the French in 1870, she was more concerned with what was happening to Lottie now. She hurried back to Boot Lane.

When the pains got really bad they couldn't keep Lottie in bed. She preferred to stand, clinging to the bedpost, alternately moaning and weeping. 'She'll have that baby on the floor, if she's not careful' said Maud, by now in need of attention herself. It was Aggie who got Lottie back into bed and tied a roller towel on the bedpost and gave her the other end to pull on.

That seemed to help. Lottie braced herself, straining until her face went scarlet, then relaxing a little between each contraction. It was only when she became too weak to strain anymore, that the others realised the seriousness of the situation. Lottie was mumbling in a semi-delirious manner, calling for her mother and then for Henry.

'Aggie, you'd better go for the doctor,' Maud said. 'My nerves can't stand much more of this.' Agnes wasted no time. She ran into the street, still in her apron and without a hat, pushing her way through the good-humoured crowd who had gathered in wait for the next edition of the papers. There was an air of excitement and jubilation, and a few were singing the National Anthem.

The doctor looked grave as he gave his verdict. 'Pity you didn't send for me sooner. The trouble is, the mother's pelvis is too narrow to allow the infant a normal passage. It's a case of a forceps delivery, I'm afraid.'

'Anything, as long as you get it over quick,' said Maud.

By the evening, all three had recovered. Lottie was pale but composed. She had been washed and dressed in a clean starched nightgown that smelled fragrantly of Norfolk lavender.

'Well, is she worth it?' asked Maud. She was sitting by

Lottie's bedside, marvelling at the smallness of the bundle who had been the cause of all the trouble.

Lottie considered Maud's question. She had paid for that night of conception in months of anguish and guilt, and a sense of loss that nothing could put right. Except now. The baby in her arms nuzzled against her breast, snuffling like a new-born kitten. Lottie lowered her cheek against the downy head. The agony of her labour had given birth to such joy it made her feel light-headed, like having too much to drink. She now had someone of her very own to love. 'Yes, she's worth it,' she said.

It was late at night, and Lottie was wakeful and over-excited — making plans for the baby's future. Charlotte was to have all the chances that she herself never had. There would be no shilling-a-week job as a teacher's apprentice for Charlotte. She was going to college. And for a start, there was that little Catholic school just round the corner. Lottie rather liked the idea of her daughter being taught by nuns. She wanted her to grow up to be a lady. Nothing would be too good for her — no sacrifice too great.

SIX | *Lottie*
1916–1918

Aggie sat at her dressing-table putting the finishing touches to her make-up while Lottie looked on. Lottie herself had taken to using face-powder, carrying a little booklet of *papier-poudré* in her handbag, and dabbing her nose with a leaf whenever it became shiny. Aggie, she thought, looked very stylish in her new sage-green teagown, though one could wish that she wouldn't dye her hair quite such a brassy colour.

Aggie looked over her shoulder. 'Well, here I am, ready and willing to do a little extra war work.' She grinned, knowing that Lottie would neither condone nor approve – but neither would she pass judgement. Some months ago, Aggie, torn between her urge to do something for her country and her loyalty to Maud, had become a conductress on a tram and thereby stirred up a hornet's nest.

'There's men fighting out there old enough to be my father,' she told an outraged Maud. 'The war's been going on nearly two years now, and I feel it's about time I did my bit. Time I did some war work.'

'What do you think you're doing here! This is war work – very essential war work in my opinion!'

'I'll still be able to put in some extra time for you, Maud,' she said, and tonight, not for the first time, she was keeping her promise.

But it wasn't like the old days. As she complained now to Lottie. 'It's lost its dignity – having to sneak up the backstairs so as not to shock the respectable matrons we now have in the dining-room.' She opened her mouth to wipe away an excess of lipstick. 'Upstairs trade is getting slack too, and we can blame the war for that. After all, why should the gents pay for something what they can get free these days.'

'You're becoming very cynical, Aggie.'

'You can blame the war for that too, ducky.'

The character of Maudie's was changing. The shortage of food had boosted the restaurant business, and those places which could still provide good meals in spite of restrictions, were doing a roaring trade. It had been Lottie's suggestion to expand the restaurant and encourage a different type of clientele. The time was ripe, she said, for Maudie's to change its image.

Maud had at first demurred. But before anything else, she was an astute business woman. 'All right,' she had conceded finally. 'If I can't run the classiest brothel this side of Regent Street, then I'll run the classiest restaurant.'

The door opened with a jarring noise, and a disgruntled Mary Ann glared in at Lottie. 'I guessed you'd be up 'ere, jest when you was wanted downstairs. In '*er* office.' She never gave Maud a name if she could avoid it.

In the office? Not in Maud's sitting-room? That sounded ominous. Lottie thought of all the possibilities. A telegram? Someone in the family killed? Her heart was pounding as she hurried downstairs, but it couldn't be bad news after all. Maud would not be sitting at her desk smoking so casually if it were.

'A young soldier has called to see you, and I sent him to wait in my sitting-room. I thought it would be more private for you in there.'

Again Lottie's mind was filled with wild possibilities. One of her brothers? Flo's husband? He had been newly conscripted, and was now stationed at Aldershot. Reuben Stoneham? Any one of them could be passing through London on their way to the docks. She ran her tongue over dry lips, and Maud said, without looking up, 'It's a Lieutenant Massingham.'

Lottie grabbed the back of a chair as the room began

to reel. She felt suddenly very cold. 'L-Lieutenant Massingham?' she repeated feebly, and as if from a distance she heard Maud's answer. 'Yes. Lieutenant Henry Massingham.'

Her colour seeped back, the room steadied, she straightened her back. 'Maud . . . I *can't* see him . . . you should know that.'

'You may regret it if you don't. He told me he hasn't got long – he's on his way to join his unit. Lottie . . . he's going back to the Front . . . it would be cruel not to see him.'

Lottie felt as if a gun was being pointed at her head. Woodenly, she walked to the door. Maud called her back.

'Lottie . . .'

'Yes?'

'Be kind to him.'

He was standing with his back to the door, his hands in his pockets, his shoulders hunched, staring into the empty fireplace. He turned as soon as he heard her. He's still so boyish looking – so fresh-faced – thought Lottie until she looked into his eyes and saw that they were the eyes of someone who had looked on hell. A sudden desire to run to him, to comfort him, to soothe him as she soothed Charlotte when she was crying overcame her, but she fought it back.

'It's been so long,' he said hesitantly.

She found herself quite calm, outwardly at least. 'Why have you come?'

'I had to see you. I wheedled your address out of Ruby . . .' He took a step forward, but stopped as she recoiled.

He stared at her in a crestfallen manner. 'I knew you wouldn't want to see me. Why should you, after the way I acted . . .' He ignored her faint, strangled cry of protest. 'I waited and waited for an answer to my letter . . . then I gave up hope. I took it that you never wanted to see me again.'

She found it hard to meet his gaze. Long dead emotions of grief and shame came back to torment her. And now, an added embarrassment. 'My mother thinks I work at a hotel. You must know differently.' Her tone challenged him to deny it.

His face lit up with relief. 'Is that what's making you so edgy? Dear girl, if you only knew . . . I thought it was because . . . but never mind. I've known about this place since my Cambridge days. Some of the students used to spend the odd night here. Lottie, you don't think I condemn you for working here, do you? It's not as if you were . . . and anyway, who could blame you . . . after what happened.' He saw her flinch, and he reddened at the failure of his clumsy attempt to put her at her ease. He said earnestly, 'I've been in London for three days trying to pluck up courage to call on you, and today is my last chance. I came to plead with you – to ask your forgiveness . . . to beg you to marry me . . . not now . . . after the war. Things will be different then, the old social barriers will be down. Life is never going to be the same again. Lottie, couldn't we try to pick up the pieces and start afresh . . . ?'

In some ways, she thought, Henry was just the same hesitant, anxious suitor for whom she had poured out a mature, and almost maternal love. He had changed much less than she had, and that made her feel sad, and rather worldly. 'Let's not think about after the war,' she said. 'Let's just think about the present. Maud told me you are returning to the Front.'

'Either tonight or tomorrow morning. There's talk of a big push later this month which could turn the tide in our favour. I couldn't go without seeing you again. There was so much I wanted to say to you, but now my mind is just a jumble of thoughts. I want to know how you are, and about your baby. How is your baby? I wish I could see her.'

His simple request made all the difference. Any remaining awkwardness vanished. He spoke as if the baby were

hers only and had no connection with that dreadful night.
Regretfully she had to tell him that Charlotte was asleep
and would only be bad-tempered if woken up. She didn't
want him to see her in one of her paddies.

'But I can show you a photo of her, if you wish.'

On the mantelpiece, among a gallery of Maud's old
girls, was the photograph Lottie had recently given to
her. A photograph of herself with Charlotte. She took it
down.

'This was taken about two weeks ago. Doesn't Charlotte look solemn? The photograper tried so hard to
coax a smile out of her, poor man. She was very crotch-
ety. She was wearing her best velvet frock, and it made
her hot and fidgety. The photographer told her that if
she sat very still and watched the camera, she'd see a
dicky bird pop out.' Lottie laughed, seeing now the funny
side of the occasion which at the time had been so frus-
trating. It was like old times, talking easily to Henry
again. 'She threw such a tantrum when she realised she
had been tricked, I couldn't do anything with her. I had
to force her back into her pram, and she screamed all the
way along Tottenham Court Road. I felt everybody was
looking at us. But it was worth all the trouble. It's a
good photo.'

Henry searched for a likeness to himself in the child's
pretty, chubby face, but was disappointed. 'No . . . she's
all you, Lottie. She even has your beautiful eyes . . .'

'No trace even of . . . your brother . . . ?'

Henry's expression hardened. 'No, thank God . . . she's
been spared that.' A pause, then bitterly, 'He'll come out
of this war unscathed, covered with medals and glory,
you mark my words. He was fêted like a hero for coming
back to fight for his country. The truth was it was a good
time for him to get out of Kenya, he was in some kind
of trouble. He's the kind that can ride roughshod over
everybody and get away with it.' There was a silence
brittle with unspoken feelings. Henry finally broke it. 'I

suppose you wouldn't have one of these photographs to spare for me, would you?'

'I have one in my own little apartment. Come with me, but don't make a noise, I don't want to disturb Charlotte.' She led him along a corridor, down the stairs, through a door, two more steps and another door. 'My front door,' she said with a smile. This was her home, this three-roomed self-contained apartment, which Maud had presented to her soon after Charlotte was born.

'This suite of rooms used to be a barber's shop originally,' she explained as she led Henry into her private living-room. In the room beyond, Charlotte was sleeping. 'Then for years it was used for storage. Maud had it all done up for me – it's cosy, isn't it? The furniture belongs to her, bits she doesn't want, most of it from a little house she once had in Islington. I've even got my own separate entrance onto the street, but I never use it.'

She gave her copy of the photograph to Henry, and watched as he carefully put it in his wallet and then placed the wallet in the breast pocket of his tunic. She thought of what he was going back to and wished she had the confidence to show him how much she still cared. Their eyes met, and recognising the old loving look in hers, he drew her into his arms and kissed her.

'I love you, Lottie . . . I wish I didn't have to leave you, but I'll have to go.'

She gave a teasing laugh. 'You sound just like the song.'

'I'll send you my army address. Promise me you'll write . . . ?'

She promised. They kissed again, this time with more ardour, recapturing the old-remembered passion. Lottie broke free first and showed him to the outer door that led onto a small alley off Boot Lane. This door hadn't been used for years, and, at first, resisted their combined efforts to shift it. They tugged at it together, laughing at their futile attempts, hiding the despair they were both feeling. It gave at last, opening into a small paved area below street level. Henry kissed her once more, a lingering kiss, then mounted the narrow iron steps that led up to street level. She followed him, and stood listening to his footfalls ringing out on the worn cobbles. At the corner of the alley, he turned and saluted, then walked on and out of her sight.

The much looked for letter arrived ten days later. Henry was back in France but couldn't say where. It looked, however, as if he had dropped a hint, for that part of the letter was heavily censored. The quotation from an anonymous 16th-century poet with which he ended his letter, had been left untouched.

> Western wind, when will thou blow,
>   The small rain down can rain?
> Christ, if my love were in my arms
>   And I in my bed again!

Oh Henry, she sighed, why can you only express your feelings in someone else's words?

The Somme. A name that would come unbidden like a spectre to haunt for years those who took part in it. A massacre. A victory only for the angels of death. It began on the first day of July and went on until November. It claimed the life of her brother Alfred. It crippled Ted. It inflicted wounds on Reuben Stoneham which, fortunately, did not prove fatal, and Henry owed his life to a piece of pasteboard in the breast-pocket of his tunic. His prophecy regarding his brother proved correct. Joseph Massingham was awarded the Military Cross for bravery on the field of battle. Otherwise, life went on very much as usual except for those who had lost loved ones, and those so psychologically marked by the battle they would carry invisible scars for the rest of their lives.

Her mother's infrequent letters ceased altogether after the death of Alfred. Lottie knew it was useless to write to her father, so she wrote to Flo, begging for news of the gatehouse. It wasn't good. Ellen had had a heart-attack and the doctor had told her to take things easy in future.

'I can't help out,' wrote Flo. 'I've got little Tommy to care for, and I'm also having to work part-time as my army allowance isn't enough for us both to live on . . .'

She's trying to make me feel guilty, thought Lottie, folding up the letter. But what can I do? Father would shut the door of the gatehouse in my face.

Christmas was something to get through as decently as possible, and then the hope . . . the constant hope . . . that the tide would turn in the Allies' favour by the New Year.

Lottie and Aggie were in the restaurant putting up Christmas decorations, festooning the walls with red and green crêpe paper. Later in the week they would blow up coloured balloons, and then go off to Covent Garden and come back with bundles of greenery.

Lottie, perched on a step-ladder with a tin tack between her teeth and a hammer in her hand, nearly over-balanced when a sharp rat-a-tat-tat sounded on the outer door. Her heart skipped a beat and then started to race. That was the knock of the telegraph boy.

'I'll go,' said Aggie.

Lottie got down from the ladder and waited. It couldn't be Henry. Henry was convalescing in Leicestershire, at his mother's old home. Ted was in a military hospital in Surrey, and Alf was dead. So who could it be?

Aggie came back with a telegram, holding it as if it were something contagious. 'It's for you.'

Lottie tore the buff envelope open with clumsy fingers. It read: 'Mum dead — come at once,' and was signed, 'Father'. An agonising pain shot through her. 'Tell the boy there's no answer,' she said through stiff lips.

When Aggie returned she gently took the telegraph form from Lottie's lifeless fingers. 'Oh Lottie . . . Oh, your poor mother . . . Is there anything I can do?'

Lottie didn't answer. She's too choked, thought Aggie. 'Tell you what,' she said helpfully. 'You go off and pack and I'll find out the times of trains to Norfolk. And don't worry about Charlotte. She'll be all right with us.'

Lottie mechanically went on plaiting ropes of red and green paper as if she had not heard.

'I said leave everything to Maud and me. You just go and get yourself ready.'

'I'm not going anywhere.'

'What d'you mean? Your father'll be expecting you . . .'

'My mother is dead. My going to Norfolk won't bring her back to life again.' Lottie's voice was harsh and unrecognisable. 'Aggie, finish this for me. It's time I put Charlotte to bed.'

Aggie flew off to tell Maud that Lottie was acting queer and looked like death and that she had received a telegram telling her that her mother was dead. 'It's the way the telegram was worded,' she said. 'It could've been put more tactful. It's put her into shock.'

Maud eased herself out of her chair. 'Help me down to her.'

In the living-room of Lottie's apartment was a recess fitted with a sink which when not in use was hidden behind a chenille curtain. The curtain was drawn to one side and they could see Lottie busy bathing little Charlotte.

'We could have done that for you,' said Maud gently. 'If you were to get yourself ready now you'd be in Norfolk by nine o'clock.'

'I'm not going to Norfolk.' Lottie lifted Charlotte out of the sink, wrapped her in a towel and sitting her on her lap, began to rub her dry. She put her in a vest and nightgown and took her off to the ante-room in which she slept. Through the thin partition the other two could hear Charlotte's wails of protest. Maud and Aggie's unexpected visit meant only one thing to her infant mind and that was something nice to eat. A constant source of irritation to her mother was the way kisses were coaxed from Charlotte by bribing her with sweets.

Tonight Lottie closed her ears to her daughter's cries, and shut the door on her. She collected up the discarded garments, and folding them neatly, put them away in the bottom drawer of a rosewood bureau that Maud had given to her.

Maud and Aggie watched her deliberate actions with incredulity. Aggie broke the silence. 'D'you want me to send a telegram to your father to say you can't get to Norfolk 'til tomorrow?'

'I have no intention of going back to Norfolk.'

'It's the shock,' said Maud to Aggie. 'She hasn't come to yet. She'll feel different tomorrow.'

Lottie turned on them an unfamiliar face. 'I will not feel different tomorrow. I am *never* going back to Norfolk. Two years ago, last year even, I would have crawled on my hands and knees to see my father . . . but not now. He's ignored all my pleas for forgiveness. I wrote to him when Charlotte was born – I grovelled to him, and he ignored me. So why do you think he's sent for me now? Because he needs someone to run his house for him, that's why. I haven't had a single word from him since I left home, and now I get an order . . . "Come at once". Well, he can whistle for the moon for all I care, for I am not going back!'

Maud couldn't believe this. 'Do it for your mother then. Do it for her . . .'

Lottie clutched at her throat. They saw her lips whiten in her effort to prevent them trembling. 'I've got to think of Charlotte . . . What sort of a future will she have at Thornmere? She'd be pitied . . . talked about . . . dubbed a bastard. She'd end up in service as I was . . . or in a factory. I've got other plans for her. She's going to have the education I never had. And what about me? What would become of me? I'll tell you. I'd be an unpaid drudge. Working for nothing . . . certainly not for love.'

Lottie couldn't go on. She was suddenly struck by the thought that the biggest drawback in returning to Thornmere was the likelihood of meeting Joseph Massingham. That was unthinkable. Unthinkable too, for him to ever know about Charlotte. She closed her eyes, shutting out the awful possibility. 'I can't go back to Norfolk, ever,' she said.

'You'll regret this one day,' said Maud darkly. 'You'll be sorry. How would you feel if your daughter ever turned on you . . . ?'

'That's my funeral,' said Lottie.

'Yes, it may well be. And what about your mother's funeral? Will you refuse to go to that too?'

Lottie showed signs of cracking. She sat at the table with her head in her hands. 'How can I go to the funeral,' she said tonelessly. 'They'll get at me . . . the family . . . neighbours. I might not be able to hold out, and I can't afford to take that risk.'

Maud and Aggie exchanged unhappy glances. 'I thought I knew you,' Maud said. 'But this is a side of you I've never seen before and I don't much like it. You've turned hard.'

'I'm a quick learner,' Lottie answered unrepentantly, but she was unrepentant only until she went to bed — then she cracked.

Alone in the darkness, images of the past kept appearing before her. Helping her mother with the mangling. Cutting up the candied peel for the Christmas pudding. Sitting on her father's lap and combing his quiff when she was not much older than Charlotte. They had such hopes of her, her mother and her father, and she had denied them both. She started to cry with great gulping sobs that shook her body. She was weeping for her mother, but she knew she was also weeping for the girl she might have been. But in mourning for that was she not now denying Charlotte?

She got out of bed, and barefooted on the cold lino, she went into the slip of a room where Charlotte was sleeping with her thumb still in her mouth. Lottie got in beside her and cuddled her, taking comfort from her small, warm body.

Maud, through sources known only to herself, still maintained a small but good supply of port, and with a glass of this, and in the cosiness of her private sitting-room, she would entertain a few of her erstwhile regulars.

Former clients grumbled at the changes which had taken place at Maudie's. They complained that the old pleasure ground had become so sanitised it looked more like a temperance hotel. They felt uncomfortable eating in the dining-room under the eyes of respectable ladies. They missed the plush curtains and gilt framed mirrors. But mostly they missed the waitresses. Some of the girls couldn't accept the changes and had left to work in other establishments – or do war work – according to their natures. The girls who replaced them were very pleasant and efficient, but they weren't available, and that made all the difference.

But Maud was too loyal to desert her old regulars altogether. Special arrangements had to be made for them, and a glass of port in her private sitting-room acted rather like an aperitif before the main dish. Half an hour in her company, when she was at her most charming, was guaranteed to put anyone in a good humour.

One of her callers was a certain Major Peacock, a veteran from the Boer War who was prone to strut about in uniform, wearing old campaign medals and sporting a monocle. He had a job in the War Office, but nobody knew quite what. Lottie took an instant dislike to him. She resented the way he leered at her with pale protruding eyes. She hated his moist red lips which seemed to her to drool too readily. She detested the very look of him. It stemmed from the time she overheard him say to Maud, 'I like the look of that tall willowy gel with the dark eyes. Who is she?'

And Maud's reply. 'She's not for you, Major. She has nothing to do with that side of the business.'

'And who's that pretty little toddler I sometimes see with her?'

'That's her daughter. Now, would you mind closing the door?'

The rest of the conversation was lost to Lottie. Inside the room, Maud was pouring out two glasses of port.

'I don't want you ogling my Lottie, Major,' she said, handing him a glass. 'She is a very respectable girl, and I wouldn't like to see her upset. As a matter of fact, I think so highly of her, I have just made her my manageress.'

'Well then, that deserves a toast,' said Major Peacock, grinning. He raised his glass. 'Here's to Maud and her charming successor, and may they long continue to give their customers full satisfaction.'

'Don't play games with me, Major.'

Late one afternoon, when Lottie couldn't find Charlotte in her customary place which was in the kitchen under Mary Ann's feet, driving that short-tempered woman mad, she went off to look for her in Aggie's room.

'I 'spect she's with Maud,' said Aggie, stripping off her conductresses uniform. She had just come off the early shift, and a hip bath of hot water was waiting for her.

Maud's room was a treasure trove for a lively, curious child like Charlotte. It held an assortment of interesting knick-knacks on every table and every shelf. Paper fans that opened and shut, china animals, a bird in a glass case, and a bowl of polished fruit which Charlotte discovered, after a stolen nibble, was for show only. But best of all, a big brown box with a pink trumpet which when wound up, played music that she delighted to dance to, watching as she did so, her reflection in the polished front of Maud's piano.

'But I thought Maud was having her rest?'

'Not a hope, ducky. Major preening Peacock just called . . .' But Aggie found she was talking to herself. Lottie had gone.

She burst into Maud's room, and in a flash of an eye took in a picture of Charlotte perched on the Major's broad fat thigh, reaching for a piece of chocolate he was dangling just out of her reach. And Maud was sitting opposite, watching and smiling indulgently.

Ignoring the Major, ignoring Charlotte's howl of protest, Lottie snatched her into her arms and confronted Maud. 'I would prefer it if in future, you did not allow my daughter to come into your room while you are entertaining one of your gentlemen.' She made the word gentlemen sound like something unmentionable. Then she swept out again.

Like a bantam with ruffled feathers, Maud had it out with her later. 'How dare you speak to me in that hoity toity manner in front of one of my guests . . .'

'Charlotte was on his lap . . . *that* man's lap. And he was enticing her with a sweet . . . Maud, how could you let such a thing happen?'

Maud began to bluster. 'What's the matter with you – there was no harm in it. He has a granddaughter the same age – he's fond of children – he told me . . .'

'I don't care if he has sixty granddaughters. I don't want him near my daughter again, ever!'

Maud must have passed this message on for when a week later Lottie came face to face with the Major in a narrow hallway, he blocked her way. 'You've got a mind like a sink,' he said, fixing her with his bulging stare. He looked her slowly up and down and a cold, malicious smile crossed his face. 'I shan't forget this in a hurry,' he said. 'And I shan't forget you. I never forget a face.'

Shaken, Lottie ran off to unburden herself to Aggie. 'There was something menacing about him at that moment – something really evil. I believe he would have killed me if he could.'

Aggie laughed. 'That old turkey cock! He couldn't hurt a fly. "All talk and no do", the girls used to call him. Don't give him another thought. From what Maud says, he won't be coming here again.'

But Lottie couldn't get him out of her mind. His image haunted her for days to come until, at last, she was able to convince herself that the possibility of their paths ever crossing again was a chance in a million.

'Take this five pounds,' said Maud to Aggie. 'And take Lottie off my hands for the day. I want you both out of the way. Go off and have a good time – buy yourselves something nice to wear, and go to a show. Leave Charlotte with me. You can do more without her.'

They went to an afternoon performance of 'Chu Chin Chow', the popular and long-running show in the West End, and afterwards had a meal at the Marble Arch Corner House. Treating themselves to champagne cocktails, and having a fit of giggles. They felt light-hearted and young and for a few brief moments forgot the carnage on the Western Front. But when the orchestra broke into a medley of popular war songs, they grew thoughtful and slightly tearful. For a few short hours that afternoon they had escaped from the reality of war, but now the war was back again in the form of the uniforms dotted at tables all around them.

They lingered in the soft summer twilight, strolling along Oxford Street, window shopping for something to spend the rest of Maud's money on, until Lottie said, 'We'd better get a move on, Aggie. It's long past Charlotte's bedtime. I can't leave everything to Maud.'

They turned the corner of Boot Lane arm in arm, chattering like magpies, and didn't notice anything different about Maudie's until they drew level. Then Lottie stared bewildered, and Aggie began to giggle. 'That Maud – she is a one. So this is what she had in mind.'

For the brass plaque with Maudie's engraved on it had been taken down and in its stead, on the glass panel above the entrance, was painted in gold leaf in large bold letters the word – FOSTERS.

'Aggie! You knew about this . . . !'

'No, I didn't, but I'm not surprised. I guessed Maud was up to something.'

Lottie felt a sudden rush of tears to her eyes. 'But

Maud can't do this — I can't let her . . . Aggie — can it possibly mean . . . ?'

'Better go and ask her.'

Lottie faced Maud across the room, trying, not too successfully, to control her feelings. Such a turmoil of emotion gripped her that she could hardly find her voice.

'Maud, I can't possibly let you do this . . . I can't accept it. But, oh . . . if we could come to some arrangement . . . If I could raise a loan . . . Maud — I'd work like a slave.'

Maud silenced her. 'The place is yours now, Lottie. No talk of arrangements or loan. I told you I'm beginning to feel my age . . . I'm glad to pass on the responsibility. Maudie's — Maudie's that was, I mean — has had its day. Your idea of turning it into a family restaurant was a good one. You're young and with fresh ideas . . . You'll make a success of it, and we'll all benefit . . .' She sighed, just for a moment looking wistfully over her shoulder to the past. 'There's no-one else I can trust the business to. Aggie is no good . . . she'd fill the place with hangers-on in no time. But remember, Lottie, this is her home. I'm making the business over to you on the understanding that you'll always take care of her. That goes for Mary Ann too. I want to make sure that they'll both be provided for after I'm gone.'

'Maud, don't talk like that. You've got years ahead of you yet.'

'No I haven't, Lottie. This dreadful war is taking its toll on me.'

Christmas 1917 — the fourth war-time Christmas. Please God, begged Lottie, please let there be peace by next Christmas.

In spite of shortages and deprivations, in spite of air-raids and the worsening news from the Front, they tried to make the best of it for Charlotte's sake. She was now at an age when undoing presents was a delight to her. They ate royally that day. An old friend sent Maud a brace of pheasants which Lottie plucked and roasted.

They had eaten their dinner with Mary Ann in the kitchen as she refused to join them upstairs, but now they were back in Maud's room, sitting round a banked-up fire, the end result of many weeks of going easy with the coke.

Maud was smoking one of the last of her hoarded Turkish cigarettes and Lottie and Aggie were cracking nuts with their teeth, when the second post of the day arrived. Lottie felt her heart leap at the sound of the postman's knock. A long awaited letter from Henry? She had had no word since he had rejoined his regiment. But it was only a delayed Christmas card from Flo, in which she had enclosed a letter.

Lottie read it quickly, then slipped from the room. Aggie, seeing a glimpse of her face went after her, and found her slumped on her bed in the basement flat, the letter still clutched in her hand.

'Lottie, what's up? I saw you go white.' Aggie sat down beside her. 'Want to tell me?'

Lottie looked up with an anguished, dry-eyed face. 'It's the postscript to Flo's letter, just a casual mention. It's Henry. He took part in the battle at Passchendaele last September. He was gassed . . . that terrible mustard gas. I thought something must have happened to him otherwise I would have heard from him before this. In my worse moments, I feared he might be dead. But gassed! Aggie, that thought never crossed my mind. You know what they say about mustard gas . . . it can destroy the lungs . . . or cause blindness. And this happened in September . . . Aggie . . . three months ago!' Lottie clutched at Aggie's arm. 'Why didn't somebody tell me . . .?' Mercifully, she found relief in tears, and Aggie took her in her arms, rocking her like a child.

'I don't know where he is,' Lottie sobbed. 'I must find out more about him, but I don't know what to do . . .'

'Write to the War Office, lovey. They should be able to help you.'

*

Ruan Park in Kent was not what Lottie had expected. She had pictured it as a place of barracks and army huts and sentries on duty. It was a country house, temporarily being used as a hospital, and the sister in charge of Henry's ward was understanding and very helpful.

'I was told Lieutenant Massingham was transferred here from a military hospital in France,' Lottie explained. 'It's taken me months to get any information.'

'That's just as well . . .' Sister hesitated. 'At first he didn't want visitors. He was very firm about that, but now . . . now, it doesn't matter.'

'You mean . . .' Lottie hesitated. 'He's . . . he's dying?'

'My dear, you wouldn't want it otherwise when you see him. He is blind and his lungs are badly affected. Do you feel brave enough to see him? I warn you, he is not a pretty sight.'

Blind. Those gentle blue eyes . . . Oh Henry. 'I've come a long way to see him. But will *he* want to see me?'

'If you are Lottie, then yes, he will – though see is perhaps not the right word to use. Come this way.'

Lottie found herself at the door of a small side-room, just large enough to take a bed, a locker and a chair. A figure was lying motionless on his side, with his back to the door. Bandages hid his eyes. 'Just for cosmetic purposes,' Sister whispered. 'He is sensitive about the feelings of others.'

Lottie kept her expression fixed, and her self-control rigid. She did not want to expose her inner self before Sister, nor allow Henry to guess at her horror and pity. 'He does have visitors, then?'

'His father visits him regularly. Go on in, dear.' Sister gave her a little push. 'Go and talk to him.'

'Henry . . . I've come . . .'

He turned his ruined face in her direction. 'Lottie . . . my Lottie.' He groped for and found her hand. Every movement he made was a tremendous effort – even talking was too arduous. But now that they were together talking seemed unimportant. She wondered if he was weeping behind the bandages ... or realised that she was crying. She felt as if she had never loved him as much as she loved him now, when he was so helpless. She wanted to take him back to Fosters with her and nurse him back to health ... but he had no health to be nursed back to.

Every minute that ticked away was one minute nearer the end. That evening while he slept she walked down to the village and booked a room at the inn, then she wrote a letter to Maud telling her not to expect her back for the time being. Tomorrow she would send a telegram which would reach Maud before the letter, but at least, writing a letter had taken her mind, for the time being, off other things.

By the third day, even she could see that Henry was considerably weaker, but he still had strength enough to show agitation when she attempted to leave his bedside. Speech was difficult for him, but towards the end he sacrificed all the breath he had left in order to tell her something that was worrying him.

It was a letter – she understood that much. A letter, which after much guesswork on her part, she found in his locker. It was addressed to her, and he seemed relieved when she told him she had found it.

'I'm cold,' he said suddenly, and very clearly. 'Lottie darling ... I feel so cold.'

She lay down on the bed beside him and put her arm around him and gently lifted his head until it rested on her shoulder. Then she lowered her cheek against his, and closed her eyes, feeling for the first time in many days, a sense of peace.

She was awakened by a gentle shake. A young VAD stood over her. Lottie wondered why the girl's eyes were wet ... then realisation came like a cold douche. Henry was dead ... he had drifted away from her even as she had tried to warm him. She stumbled off the bed, not looking round. Not wanting to know. 'He's dead, isn't he?' she said.

Sister was there, taking charge. 'You made him very happy in the end. See for yourself,' she said.

Lottie steeled herself to look. Poor Henry. His poor disfigured face. Who could say he looked happy? She bent and kissed him on the lips. 'Goodbye, my love,' she said.

On the steps as she was going out, she passed Sir Roger Massingham. He had come, she guessed, to take Henry back to Thornmere; to be buried in the family tomb in the same churchyard as little Billy and her mother.

Sir Roger didn't recognise her of course, she doubted whether he even saw her. He had aged. She could have passed him by in a London street without knowing him. On her way to the station she came to a florists and went inside and arranged for a bunch of violets to be sent to Lieutenant Henry Massingham at Ruan Park Hospital.

'Is there a message to go with them?' the assistant asked.

'No . . . no message. He will know who they're from.'

The journey back to London seemed to take forever. She was aching to be home now. Her home, the suite of rooms at the back of the restaurant. She wanted to feel Charlotte's soft, cuddly little body in her arms, to make contact with her living flesh. She stood at the rail of the paddle-boat which ferried between Gravesend and Tilbury, staring into the murky waters of the Thames, torn between grief and a desire to scream with rage against the stupidity of war and the wastage of all those gallant young lives who had gladly answered the summons. A whole generation – Henry's generation – slaughtered.

She opened his letter. She had read it twice already on the journey from Ruan Park to Gravesend, and had memorised whole passages by heart. Now she read it once more, against a background of mewing seagulls and the splash of paddles, and the chill March wind biting at her face.

Henry's light, boyish voice came through to her from the pages; 'I'm sorry I didn't get a chance to see you again before I left for France. My summons came unexpectedly. I want you to know exactly how much you mean to me, my darling. I feel very strongly that I won't survive the next push, and have written this to you in case. But you will only see this letter if the worst happens. I don't want to upset you unnecessarily. I have also written to my solicitor about my will. I have left everything I have to you. It's not much . . . about three thousand pounds all told. I wish it were more. It's for you and Charlotte, Lottie. I think of you as my family — my own little family. God bless you both.'

The package from the solicitor which she received a few weeks later, contained a copy of Henry's will, and what remained of his possessions. A slender volume of poems, and the photograph of Charlotte and herself, cracked across the middle. She banded them together, and put them away in a pigeon hole in the rosewood bureau.

On Armistice day, when Aggie, Maud and Mary Ann went off in a cab to join the revellers in Trafalgar Square, Lottie stayed behind with Charlotte. The narrow streets around the restaurant were deserted. Everyone else had followed the drift to the West End. She dressed Charlotte in her best velvet coat and fur-trimmed bonnet and putting on her own black velour took her daughter by the hand and they walked as far as Cambridge Circus.

The thoroughfare here throbbed with the sound of cheerful singing. Buses passed, packed with soldiers and roisterers — it was a populace hysterical with joy. The noise they made sounded like the rhythmic beat of a heart — the capital's joyful heart-beat. Were they also rejoicing at Thornmere? She thought of those who had been killed or died from the effects of the war: Henry; her brother

Alfred; Louis Barr, Monsieur Jacques' son; her mother. She thought of her youngest sister Violet and Lucy Massingham, early victims of the Spanish 'flu epidemic. Was it worth it? Did all the cheering in the world make up for what was lost?

She turned, and with Charlotte trotting beside her, retraced her steps back to Boot Lane. She paused and looked at her name, gleaming in the dull November light above the entrance to the restaurant. This was now her world, and her independence. She looked down at Charlotte, who stared solemnly back at her, sobered by her mother's brooding silence. Lottie smiled.

'It's just you and me on our own, Charlotte,' she said. 'Just you and me against the world. Together, we'll make Fosters a place to be proud of.'

SEVEN | *Carla*
The Present

As the spire of Norwich Cathedral came into view Carla retrieved her bag from the luggage recess behind the seat. She could hardly restrain herself from opening the door before the train slid into the station, so anxious was she to get back to Thornmere. She had said goodbye to her past life – she had severed all ties with the Wenley house, and though she was glad to be back in Norfolk, of course there were bound to be regrets. One couldn't live twenty-five years in the same house without putting down roots – and being pulled up by the roots had proved painful.

Her taxi swung out of the station yard, taking the road that led towards Broadland. Could it only be three weeks ago since she had left Norwich for Wenley? She had stood on the threshold of Laburnum Lodge listening to the silence. No rustle of movement, no footsteps. The house was empty. Forcefully, the awareness that Lottie was really gone came back to her afresh. For as long as she could remember, Lottie had always been there to welcome her whenever she came home from school or back from a holiday. She had thought of this return as a test – and she had passed it. No rush of tears – no feeling of remorse, for in a way, Lottie was still there. Her imprint was everywhere.

The house felt warm. Mrs Baker had called in earlier to switch on the central heating and re-stock the fridge. Carla put down her bag and went across to the hall table where a pile of letters – mostly junk mail – had been left in a neat pile. She flipped through them – nothing of importance. The personal ones had already been forwarded to her. There was a large jug of winter flowering jasmine in the window recess, and in that shadowy hallway it had the effect of a burst of sunshine. She responded to it with an uplift of spirits. Spring was in the air. Life was being renewed.

Since Christmas, she had been living at the lodge with Jessie Stoneham, a suggestion on the part of that practical-minded lady herself. A suggestion that Carla welcomed, for after a while, even gold-plated taps and an over abundance of rich food could pall.

'I could easily put you up at the lodge for less than half you're paying at the Hall,' Jessie said. 'Though it's not the money, you understand. I'd willingly have you just for your company. Anyone connected with Lottie Foster is always welcome in Ruby Stoneham's old home.'

She had been joyfully surprised when told about the link between Carla and her mother's old friend and fellow-servant. Every hour off duty now, she spent chewing over old times. Seven years of caring for Lottie had made Carla into a good listener.

'I've been hearing tales of Lottie Foster all my life,' Jessie said one January evening, as they scorched their legs by the fire while outside the rain drummed against the windows. 'But I never thought I'd see the day when I'd entertain her great-granddaughter in my living-room.

'How old did you say she was? Ninety-four! That's a good age even for a Norfolk woman. D'you know what they say about the old ones in these parts? They don't die – they have to be culled. Ruby lived 'til she was eighty-six and still doing her own housework and cooking. Did you know my father was sweet on your great-grandmother? Oh yes, he set his cap at Lottie, not that it got him anywhere. I think that's what brought him and my mother together in the first place, talking about Lottie. They both loved her in their different ways. When they finally got around to marrying they moved into this lodge, and here I was born some years later. Before then Mother was cook-general up at the Hall and Dad was Sir Roger's chauffeur. Sir Roger was all on his own — all his family passed on except for that Joseph Massingham, and he was living out in Kenya where he had returned after the war ended. He came back to England when his father died, but not to stay. Just long enough to split up the estate and sell it off. The Hall, the farm, the cottages — all went under the hammer. Sir Joseph had no time for sentiment. Dad thought his job was on the line, but the new owner asked him to stay on, and the same with my mother — her job was secure.

'The new owner of the Hall was what they called in those days one of the *nouveau-riche*. He made his money during the war, the first war, that is. He wasn't liked at first, but Mum always said he was a good employer. He dropped a large sized hint that if my mother and father got married they could have the lodge, and they did.' Jessie's shoulders shook. 'I'm not saying they got married just to get a home, but it jolted my father into doing something positive. They lived there until the Second World War started, then they had to move out. They had no option because the Hall was requisitioned by the army and that included the lodge too.'

She enlarged on this theme another evening, while Carla was doing the ironing.

'I remember when the Yanks came to the village. That was a great day for us kids. We used to follow them everywhere, pestering them for chewing-gum or candy. To us, they were the best thing that had come out of the war, but not everybody in the village felt as we did.

'Some of the lads, the soldiers too, really had it in for them — accusing them of pinching their girls. There were plenty of punch-ups down at the Ferry Inn on a Saturday night. There used to be a big American air-force base on the Beckton Market road. Where that housing estate is now . . .'

Carla recalled that conversation as she mounted the stairs of the Wenley house, thinking of Charlotte in particular. She went to Charlotte's room first, the bedroom that became her studio after Charlotte's death. It was in this room that she had found her grandmother lying dead at the foot of the bed, her eyes wide open and her face contorted with an expression of bitter disappointment. The first time in her eighteen years that Carla had seen a dead body, and the shock had sent her rigid for a moment or two.

Recovering, she flew downstairs to tell Lottie, who, before removing her coat, had gone into the kitchen to put on the kettle for tea. They had just returned from Ilford where they had been to buy Carla some of the things she would need before starting her first term at an art college in Bath. She had chosen Bath because Michael was studying at the university there, and she wanted to be near him.

Carla could still recall the nervousness and yet pride with which she had driven her great-grandmother through the busy streets towards the shopping centre, very much aware that it was the first time she was out without her L-plates. Hitherto Charlotte had been the family chauffeur. Today she had refused to go with them.

'She hasn't enough confidence in me,' said Carla, her pride hurt.

'She was always a nervous driver, and she'd make a worse passenger. You're better off without her,' said Lottie.

'But you are not nervous!'

'At my age, Carla, what is there to be nervous of . . . ?'

From the landing window, Charlotte watched their departure. So now Carla was a fully licensed driver. It was stupid and belittling of her to feel jealous of her granddaughter . . . But no – not jealous – envious. Envious of her youth and energy and an unblemished life. That's what she envied the most.

Would that I could have my life over again, she thought, and know what I know now. I wouldn't have given in to Lottie so easily – I wouldn't have allowed her to tie me to her apron strings. I should have fought for my independence and taken Charley with me. I could have worked. Just after the war there were jobs for the asking. She had no experience except in housekeeping and she was good at that – and housekeepers at that time were in great demand. One only had to browse through the classified ads in periodicals like *The Lady*. She could have branched out on her own – lived anywhere in the country – looked after some elderly lady or gentleman in congenial surroundings. Somewhere like Bath or Cheltenham where life would have been more gracious than in this upstart suburb.

In 1944 Wenley had been a village and she had been happy then. One of the happiest times of her life when she had Charley all to herself. She would put her in the pram and wheel her down to the post-office stores to get her rations. Then back up the hill to the house that smelled deliciously of lavender floor polish, to play with Charley, to bath and feed her and put her to bed, and spend the evenings leisurely, listening to the wireless or reading. She was never lonely.

But that time of contentment didn't last. Lottie had retired, bringing Aggie with her, and after that she never had Charley to herself again. Now Wenley was a sprawling conurbation of executive-type housing, whatever that was supposed to mean, and the post-office stores, where everybody had been known by name, had been swallowed up by a soulless and characterless supermarket.

I'm crabby, she thought, I'm getting crabby – I see nothing to look forward to anymore. It's the pain, I'm always in pain – headaches and now indigestion. She felt in the pocket of her cardigan for one of her bismuth tablets. Lately, she had become a martyr to indigestion. It was all very well for Lottie to say it was all in the mind. Her mother could afford to say that, couldn't she – not having known a day's illness in her life.

She turned from the window and wearily mounted the last few treads of the stairs. The effort increased the pain in her chest, and she decided to lie on her bed until it passed. But once in her room she was side-tracked by the portrait of Charley. Her lovely girl – her darling child – to die so young. Life was beastly unfair. Lottie would go on living forever.

She went to her drawer where she kept an old shoe-box that contained her souvenirs, and took out Charley's school reports to read again. Her marks were average, except for sport. Against that her sports-mistress had written: 'Poor and proud of it.'

Lottie had laughed – Oh, how she had laughed at that, but for her, her mother's pride had been wounded. She wanted Charley to excel in all subjects – to go to college and get a degree. But, all these years later, she could smile, even laugh a little, knowing now that brains and muscle did not measure up to what Charley had . . . A loving heart and an unquenchable spirit and the gift of spreading happiness. Just like Lottie.

It wasn't a blinding revelation. It was something she had known all along, and resented. But not any longer – she was suddenly too tired to be resentful of Lottie any longer. She stood up, knocking the shoe-box off the bed as she did so, gasping in anguish as the pain in her chest gripped suddenly like a vice. She knew immediately that she was dying, and prayed for strength to stay alive just long enough to make her peace with her mother.

My mother. It was years since she had thought of Lottie as that – but now she cried out for her like a child in pain. She didn't want to die – not here on her own. There were so many things she wanted to say to her mother first. But she had left it too late – that was her last coherent thought. And the last thing she saw as her sight slowly dimmed was Charley smiling down from the wall at her.

Even in death Charlotte looked as if someone or something had disappointed her, thought Carla. Poor Charlotte, life for her had been one long disappointment. An old shoe-box she had been carrying had burst open and strewn its contents on the floor. Letters, a baby's shoe, dried flowers, yellowing theatre programmes, railway tickets, school reports – souvenirs of a lifetime. This evidence of a sentimental side to her grandmother's nature came as a complete surprise to Carla, and her eyes welled with tears of pity. Lottie, however, stood dry-eyed beside her, shaken but impassive.

'I never thought she would go before me. I didn't even say goodbye. She was so snappy this morning. Poor Charlotte . . . she was her own worst enemy . . .'

When it was all over – the doctor's visit, the inquest, the funeral, nursing Lottie through her belated grief – the date for starting at college had come and gone. Then came the low-water mark in Carla's life. Even now, all these years later she winced with shame, thinking of her love-hate relationship with Lottie then. Why did Charlotte have to die and leave her this burden, she would ask herself. This legacy of a woman so old and frail she needed someone to care for her. Dear God, she had resented Lottie for just existing.

She had made excuses for herself. She wasn't well. She hadn't got over the shock of finding Charlotte dead. She imagined those staring eyes were still following her – accusing her. Charlotte had not approved of Carla leaving home. She could not understand she argued, why if Carla did have to go to an art college, it couldn't be somewhere within travelling distance.

Well, Charlotte had got her wish. She wouldn't be going to a college anywhere, now. She was stuck here with Lottie, and it was on that thought one afternoon, she lifted her eyes and met those of her great-grandmother across the room, and the gentle compassion she saw in their depths was her undoing. She fell on her knees in a storm of weeping, and buried her face in Lottie's lap.

'You don't have to stay because of me,' said Lottie. 'I'm not completely decrepit yet, and I'm sure I could come to some arrangement with Mrs Baker about the shopping . . .'

But Carla had already put dreams of college behind her, and had closed her mind on thoughts of Michael, her schoolgirl crush. Michael with his dark good looks and easy charm would soon find someone else to take her place.

'Don't make me feel more ashamed of myself than I do already,' she pleaded. 'I can keep up my painting at home. I can attend classes locally. The Institute here has a good reputation . . .'

It was a makeshift policy that worked well on one level, though Carla knew she was only making do with second best. She was learning to paint pretty little pictures suitable for greeting cards or calendars but it wasn't enough. Her frustration at times set her nerves on edge.

Charlotte's room had made an ideal studio with its large north facing windows, and became more than Carla's workshop. It became her escape, her refuge, sometimes her arena when she wrestled with her conscience before putting away her paints and brushes, and going downstairs to keep Lottie company. She had her successes too. The Town Hall exhibition was an example – a small fillip to her vanity, and as Lottie said, at this stage getting known was the important thing, and she had had a good write-up in the local press. Laurence Marsh's name was often in the press – the national press of course, and on the arts page. She cut out and saved any cutting that referred to him.

But now her mind was on another studio. She planned to build one at the bottom of the gatehouse garden. And then she would take up her painting again, and who knows – perhaps one day, her name might also be featured in the national press.

She smiled ruefully. Just wishful thinking. Nothing but daydreams, and she hadn't got time for daydreams. Her Wenley past was over, and a question mark hung over her future, but the present, it seemed, never ceased to make demands on her.

She spent the rest of the day sorting out, salvaging, disposing, choosing which pieces of furniture to take to the cottage and which to send to the sale-rooms. She wanted to keep the rosewood bureau, that was a must, and it would fit nicely into the gatehouse, which the rest of Lottie's furniture, the bulk of which had come from Boot Lane, would not. And the portrait – her mother's portrait. She wouldn't trust that to the removal men – it would travel back with her.

She was reluctant to go into Lottie's room, remembering it as a waiting-room for death, but she need not have feared. Mrs Baker had kept it spotless and unruffled. A pale February sun filtered through the drawn curtains, drawing out a faint smell of lavender furniture polish.

She drew them open, letting in more light. This was no sickroom – no mortuary – this bright, sunny, rather old-fashioned bedroom with its heavy Victorian furniture. It had been her childhood haven – somewhere to run to for comfort after one of Charlotte's scoldings or when she had done badly in an exam or fallen out with her best friend. And a place to share with Lottie, her pride when she had received a good report from school or later, when she sold her first painting. Yes, Lottie, you were always there when I wanted you. But did I always want you?

'I see you arrived safely. I nearly called on you last night, but I thought you might be going off to bed early. I saw your light on through the trees. Did you find the ham I left in the fridge?'

'Mrs Baker, you're an angel – you thought of everything. And thank you for sending on my clothes and the other things I asked for. I see you put some pussy willow in Lottie's room . . . That was a nice thought.'

'I went along the hedges looking for primroses but it's a bit early yet. There's some out in the garden, but I didn't like to touch them. I thought perhaps you'd be digging up a root to take back to Norfolk.'

'The gatehouse garden is full of primroses and snow-drops, coming up through the weeds. That's the next thing on the agenda, finding someone to help me clear the garden.'

'Getting on all right up there, then?'

Mrs Baker didn't waste time when talking. She removed her coat, donned her apron, changed her shoes, put away her basket, and filled the kettle. She didn't waste words either.

'It couldn't be better. The outside work is finished, and by the time I get back I hope to see a difference indoors. We've been lucky with the weather. The men have been able to work right through the winter, it's been so mild. What's your news?'

'Only what I wrote and told you. That last lot of people I showed over were very impressed. I think they're serious – not like some who only come out of curiosity. The Pargeters wanted to know what you mean to do about the furniture. They haven't got any of their own – they've just come back from Hong Kong. I think they'd like to make an offer for the house and the contents. There's no lack of money in that quarter, if you ask me. I said I thought everything not required was going to auction, and they said something about coming to a private arrangement. I hope I did right . . .'

'Yes, you did right, Mrs Baker. You've given me more information than I've managed to get from the agents. I'd better go and see them tomorrow. Oh, please do leave the washing-up and come and sit down. There's so much I want to ask you. Would you like a piece of toast with your cup of tea?'

'No thank you, Carla – or should I call you Miss Foster now that you're the lady of the house?'

'Mrs Baker – are you serious?' She was. Carla could tell that by her expression. Doreen Baker had known her since she was in nappies so why this sudden formality?

Because she was now a householder and because Mrs Baker had some funny old-fashioned notions? She had been born middle-aged, Carla sometimes thought.

'It's Carla, as it always has been, and I'm going to start calling you Doreen,' she said firmly. 'It's about time – goodness knows we've known each other long enough.'

Mrs Baker went pink, but she looked pleased. Flustered, she set about clearing the table.

'And about the furniture. There are one or two little pieces I'd like to keep for myself, I've ear-marked those already. And all the photographs, I'll take those. And that painting of my mother of course, but nothing else. Now Doreen – I want you to take anything from the rest that would be of use to you. Lottie would have wanted that, and it's the least I can do after the way you've looked after this place these past few months. There is that drawn threadwork tablecloth you have always admired, and the ornaments on the drawing-room mantlepiece – those for a start. Just take anything you fancy . . . Oh, Mrs Baker – I mean Doreen – you're not going to cry, are you?'

'Not really.' Sniff. 'I'm just a bit overcome, that's all . . .' Another sniff. 'Carla, I say this from the bottom of my heart: if there is anything more I can do for you, you only have to say . . .'

'There is one favour I wanted to ask of you . . .' Carla hesitated. 'I've got to go through Lottie's personal belongings – her clothes, things like that. And I'm dreading it . . .'

'Say no more. I'll come up and help you as soon as I've finished off down here.'

The rosewood bureau would have to be emptied before the delivery men came for it. That was another job she dreaded, but a job she would have to tackle on her own. The drawers were full of old business papers – agreements and deeds that had long expired. She'd parcel those up and send them off to Mr Lincoln – but Lottie's old cash-box? Would that turn out to be another Pandora's box? Her treasure trove, Lottie called it. A battered old tin box where she kept her souvenirs.

Carla turned the key and lifted the lid and took out a bundle wrapped in tissue paper: greeting cards, old birthday and Christmas cards from herself and from Charley when they were young, their love and kisses sprawled unsteadily across the page in pencil – these she had hoarded. Carla's eyes misted over. Oh Lottie, don't make this too hard for me. She put them aside and took out the remaining contents – so pitifully few. A small record for ninety-four years.

A telegram discoloured with age; some letters; a slim calf-bound book, and a small package. The sum total of Lottie's souvenirs? She had stored the rest in her memory. Carla picked up the telegram and read it: 'Mum dead – come at once.' Ah – *that* telegram. She put it down and picked up the letters – mere fragments of letters really, so fragile they nearly fell to pieces in her hands. They had been read and re-read so many times they were in tatters. Henry's letters. Carefully, she put them away again, feeling that they were sacrosanct. Perhaps one day she would read them, but not now. It was too soon. Only four months ago Lottie had been a living person in that bed.

A Flanders poppy marked a page in the book of poetry. One of the earlier Remembrance Day poppies, surely – for these days no poppy was made of silk with green cloth leaves and black stamens. On the open page a passage had been marked with pencil – just one stanza from a poem by Tennyson.

> O that 'twere possible,
>   After long grief and pain,
> To find the arms of my true-love
>   Round me once again!

Carla sighed. What was it that Lottie had once said? That Henry seemed unable to express his true feelings except in someone else's words. Why, she wondered? Was he just shy or diffident? She didn't know much about him really, apart from the fact that he was fair and had blue eyes like all the Massinghams, though only Lucy Massingham's had that outstanding violet tinge. 'Like yours,' said Lottie. 'And I hope to goodness that's the only trait of hers you have inherited!' Lottie sometimes, could be surprisingly tart.

Carla turned to the package. It had once been sealed with sealing wax, but that had been broken. It was addressed to Miss C. Foster, Boot Lane, London WC2, in neat copperplate handwriting, and inside was a letter, very discoloured, which Carla opened rather gingerly. A small object wrapped in tissue paper fell out.

It was an oval brooch made of a miniature photograph set in pale blue enamel with a gold filigree edging. The head and shoulders of a young soldier in the uniform of a lieutenant of the First World War. Carla turned it over but the back was just plain enamel – no engraving. If there was a clue to the soldier's identity it would be on the back of the photograph, and she could only get to that by breaking open the seal which would be an act of vandalism. She turned to the letter for further clues, and found the heading sufficient.

'Thornmere Hall,
Norfolk,
21st June, 1922

Dear Miss Foster,

I have obtained your address from my son's solicitor. Forgive me for this presumption, but knowing you were Henry's sole legatee, I felt you must be a very close friend, and I wanted you to have this small token in memory of him.

He had this brooch made for his mother on her birthday, sadly, as it turned out, the last before he died. I understood from the Matron at Ruan Park that you visited my son and were with him during his last hours. I wish I had had the opportunity of meeting you. My dear wife died a few weeks ago and I found this brooch among her jewellery. My daughter is no longer living, and I have nobody in the family to give it to. I want you to have it. I think you made my son's last days very happy, and for that I am very much indebted to you . . .'

Why did Lottie never wear the brooch? Why did she tell no-one about it? Did she value it too much to flaunt it? Lottie had once described Henry as having sensitive features – the face of a poet. Carla stared tearfully at the miniature. Yes, Lottie was right about that, but had she not also noticed he had a weak chin? Oh, poor Henry.

She put the contents back in the cash-box, shut the lid, and paused, thinking, with her hand upon it. No, this was no Pandora's box, but just a repository for an old woman's most treasured memories. She thought it sad that there was no memento of Charlotte among them.

She turned to her mother's portrait and found as she always did, comfort in its perfection. She took it down from the wall and blew from it a light covering of dust that had gathered. Henry and Charley, she thought. Two of life's victims, both cut down in their youth. She placed the picture on the bed and going to the top of the stairs she called down to Mrs Baker. Back to earth now, and the task of sorting through Lottie's personal belongings.

The taxi had turned into the lane that led to the gatehouse and was nearing the lodge where Carla could see Jessie's washing straining on the line. The driver nodded with his head towards the Hall.

'I remember that place when it was a posh girls' school,' he volunteered. 'Now it's a posh hotel. There's a woman works there called Jessie Stoneham. She used to be a matron at the school, then when the hotel people took over, she stayed on and worked for them as a housekeeper. Did all right for herself, by all accounts.

Lives at the lodge, and I heard that she's taken in a lodger . . .'

'That's me,' said Carla promptly, to save the man any further indiscretions.

He was quite unabashed. 'You don't say.' He laughed, then braked. 'D'you want to be put down here, then?'

'No, take me on a bit further – as far as the old gatehouse. Do you know it?'

'Oh yes, I know it. It's being done up, innit. Heard some nutter plans to live there . . .'

Even in three weeks the landscape had changed. The fields had greened over with a faint flush of winter-sown barley, and rooks were nesting. She saw them flopping like black rags on to the bare branches of the trees behind the cottage, cawing loud enough to drown the purring of the taxi's engine.

She paid the driver off and tipped him generously, though he didn't deserve it after that last remark. A cock pheasant dived for cover as the taxi turned. Pheasants were everywhere, safe to come out of cover now that February had come. In the field opposite, the last of the sugar beet was being harvested. One of the men loading the beet lorry recognised her and gave her a cheery wave. She was accepted now. This was her home.

Since she had been away, the outside of the gatehouse had been painted with white emulsion, and the woodwork picked out in dove grey gloss. It had lost its old image as a fortress, standing four-square to the elements, but it was still very much a landmark, tall and distinctive in a green and brown landscape.

There were no builder's vans outside the gatehouse today. When she had phoned Mr Cartwright before leaving Wenley, he said there was a delay with the delivery of the bathroom fittings, and he had sent his men on another job. She wasn't sorry of this chance for a more private homecoming. She put her key in the lock of the back door and turned it, and stepped into the kitchen no longer fetid with the odour of decay, but smelling of fresh paint and sawdust.

She was delighted to see that the kitchen units were now in place and a vitreous enamel cooker where the rusty kitchener had stood. The new cooker was fitted with a back boiler for heating water, and the central heating would run off that once water was obtainable.

Every room had the same pristine freshness, and the throat-grabbing smell of damp had at last been mastered. The only thing she regretted was the loss of the birds. Where their nests had been was now a painted cove. They had had a problem with the starlings at first, for even after polyglaze had been fitted over the empty window frames, they had pecked their way through it to get into the house. She didn't mind foiling the starlings and sparrows, but she hoped the house martins would return in the spring. She was superstitious enough to believe that if they did not she would run out of luck.

She wished she had thought to pack a tape measure. She had a notebook and pencil with her, and she could have spent the time here measuring the windows. She begrudged every minute wasted now. The curtains were her contribution towards the metamorphosis of the cottage. Jessie had offered her the use of her sewing-machine.

When she had seen all she wanted for the present, she closed the kitchen door behind her and locked it. She stepped back to take one last proprietorial look around, and just then a jackdaw alighted on the chimney-pot carrying a beakful of twigs. He cocked his head and stared down at her with a wary, beady eye.

'You just dare,' she threatened laughingly.

She had left her car in the multi-storey car-park at St Andrews and was making her way back there now through a maze of narrow medieval streets which, in her opinion, was one of the more fascinating parts of the city. She had bought some maize-coloured linen, sufficient to make curtains for the whole of the cottage, and had shopped at Sainsbury's for Jessie. She would have liked to browse in Marks and Spencer, but her parcels were heavy, and she wished now she had arranged to have the curtaining delivered. She suddenly thought of a café somewhere around here that Jessie said was renowned for its cappuccino and chocolate fudge cake and decided to treat herself.

This was how she came upon Rendall's Gallery, in a pedestrian street that was new to her. She stopped short, staring into the window where a collection of the work of East Anglian painters was on display. She recognised it at once. The gatehouse. *Her* gatehouse. She read the signature – L M, and the date – 1968; about a year after her mother's death? Was that significant? A painting of the gatehouse shuttered and already beginning to show signs of neglect, and titled: *Redundant*. Without hesitation, she opened the door of the gallery and went in.

'May I know the price of that Laurence Marsh that you have in the window? The one of the old gatehouse?' she asked of a portly gentleman who came forward, smiling urbanely.

She took him to be Mr Rendall himself, he had an air of authority. 'I'm afraid that is not for sale,' he said. 'It is only on loan for as long as the exhibition lasts. I have an earlier painting by the same artist which I may be able to let you have, but . . .' he hesitated, discreetly ascertaining her worth, Carla guessed. Not many young women her age could afford a Laurence Marsh.

She shook her head. 'No, it's only that particular painting I'm interested in. Could you – I mean would you give me the name and address of the owner? It might be possible to make a deal . . .'

He shook his head though still retaining his professional smile. 'I wouldn't want you to waste your time, and I can assure you that painting is not for sale – has never been for sale. I even had great difficulty in persuading the artist to loan it to me. He told me it means too much to him to part with it. Has some sentimental attachment, I believe . . .'

Carla felt as if the floor beneath her feet trembled very slightly, then realised that her own suppressed excitement had run like a tremor through her body.

She tried to appear cool but her voice betrayed her. 'Could you tell me where he lives? I didn't know Laurence Marsh was an East Anglian painter until I saw your display in the window. I had the idea he lived in Cornwall. The reason I'm so interested in the painting is – well . . . I . . . I actually own that gatehouse – Thornmere gatehouse. It was left to me as part of a legacy – a ruin then, but it's being done up, and I hope to live there eventually. You do understand now, don't you, my interest in the picture? I would like to know why the artist chose that particular gatehouse for his subject. And whether he could tell me anything about it as it was then.'

It was to Mr Rendall's credit that he did not doubt her story even for a moment. 'My dear young lady, this is the most incredible coincidence I have ever heard of! So you know the gatehouse – you *own* the gatehouse. It's unbelievable. Larry will certainly want to know about this. You are right though – he did live in Cornwall for a time. He's lived in many places. Born in London, I believe. Let me see now . . . how long has he lived in Norfolk? Just over twenty years, I think. He came up here on a Broads holiday, fell in love with the place, and stayed.'

In good spirits Mr Rendall fetched a sheet of paper and wrote down an address and telephone number. 'He doesn't do much painting these days. He says he's reached the time in his life when he can afford to rest back on his laurels. Such a pity – perhaps you could persuade him differently. Perhaps you could get him to do another painting of the gatehouse – as it is now? I have an American client drooling for another Laurence Marsh, but don't tell him that – it might put him off. He's a contrary sort of chap.'

He handed her the slip of paper. 'Perhaps you'd let me know how you get on if or when you contact him – I'd be very interested to know the outcome.'

Carla promised. They shook hands. She had the impression that he stood watching from the back of the window as she made her progress along the paved walkway. Out of sight she read the address again, savouring every word.

The Thatched House, Station Road, Beckton Market. A coincidence, Mr Rendall had called it. She thought it more than that. Is this all part of your scheme of things, Lottie? Is this what you were trying so hard to tell me on your death-bed? Is that the reason you wanted me to come to Norfolk?

EIGHT | *Charlotte Winter 1930*

That year, Armistice Day fell on a Tuesday. It didn't matter which day it happened to fall on – a weekday or a Saturday or a Sunday – everything came to a stop at eleven o'clock on the eleventh day of the eleventh month. People put down their pens or their tools; shoppers paused; motor cars and horse and carts came to a halt as a nation kept a two-minute silence, paying homage to their dead.

In the chapel of St Faith's Convent School, Charlotte stood among the serried rows of girls, all in their best navy pleated skirts and clean white blouses, happy in the knowledge that on this one day in the year, she attained real importance in the eyes of her peers.

The teaching sisters in the choir stalls, looked, she thought, like hooded statues. Not by a tremor, did they show any movement. Neither did the awe-inspiring figure of Mother Superior, standing at the lectern, ready to give the signal for silence. From the lay sisters standing humbly at the back of the chapel to the apprehensive eight-year-olds in the front pews, all felt chastened by the solemnity of the occasion.

When the boom of a distant maroon sounded, Mother Superior lifted a warning finger – an unnecessary precaution, for some of the younger pupils were too nervous even to swallow. Thoughts make no sound, which was just as well, for Charlotte's thoughts were rampant. This was the day above all others when she stood tall among her fellow scholars. For had not her father been awarded for his bravery at the Battle of the Somme, and had he not a year or two later died a hero's death — his sight and lungs destroyed by mustard gas?

She swelled with pride. No other girl at the school could claim such distinction. Many had fathers who had fought in the war, and some had been wounded — but nothing to the extent of Henry's sacrifice. She was conscious of surreptitious glances aimed in her direction, and felt the girls' sympathy coming towards her in waves of friendliness, and it was this feeling of being treated with a kind of reverence that caused her eyes to water.

She was not the only one in tears. Many of the more susceptible girls were sobbing quietly into their handkerchiefs, but the thoughts of those less sensitive were dwelling on the hot milk and currant buns waiting in the refectory. The girls were chilled to the bone, for the chapel was unheated. But as it was Tuesday, there would be no more lessons that morning. Hockey practice instead — a cheering thought for the majority of them.

Over buns and milk, a few of the senior girls gathered around Charlotte to pay their annual tribute, among them Frances Peacock, a self-imposed leader of a set who considered themselves the élite of the school. Normally she had little to say to Charlotte, except when she wanted to borrow something — for didn't Mrs Foster run a restaurant or something in London? Which made her nothing more than a shopkeeper really. Frances looked down her nose at any girl whose family was connected with trade.

Obviously though, there were advantages in having a restaurateur for a mother, for Charlotte was never short of money, and her tuck-boxes came from Fortnum and Mason. Even so, it would not do to give her any encouragement — she boasted enough as it was. However, today was different. The simple ceremony in the chapel had united them all in a glowing pride in their country. And Henry Foster had been one of their country's heroes.

'Pity you haven't got a photograph of your father in his uniform,' said a girl called Enid, not a remark to be taken seriously, for Enid trotted it out every Armistice Day. But it was a sore point with Charlotte that she had no photograph of her father. She cherished her mother's memory of him – slightly built with the face of a poet, and gentle blue eyes. Still, a photograph of him in his uniform would have done much to boost her rating.

'What was his rank?' said Frances, smothering a yawn. Her father, now deceased, had made a lot of money out of the war, mostly through commerce, but that wasn't counted against him, mainly because his mother had been the granddaughter of an earl.

'Major, I think,' said Charlotte, unconversant with the rank and file of the British Army. She blamed her mother's reticence for her lack of knowledge. If pressed too much on the subject of her father, Lottie was inclined to become distraught, which, Charlotte thought, was taking grief a bit too far. After all, she had been a widow now for twelve years.

'I thought, last year, that he was a first lieutenant. Has he been promoted since?' The girls sniggered at this example of Frances' wit, but Charlotte quailed. She had the feeling that the truce would be shorter than ever this year, and then the sniping would begin all over again.

'Lieutenant or Major, does it matter! All I know is that he was in the Royal Artillery.'

Frances' bulging eyes, bulged more so. 'Does it matter! Of course it matters – it is all to do with superiority. It's a good thing my Grandpop didn't hear you say that, it would give him apoplexy. He was a Major in the Boer War, and very proud of his rank too.' Her mood changed suddenly. 'Oh, I'm sick to death of all this war-talk. It's all I ever hear at home when my mother's friends visit. War – war – war – and the shortages and the air raids. The Zeppelins and the Gothas bombing London. It's all so tedious. Well, I'm off to change for hockey. Anyone else coming?'

Charlotte was left on her own. Because of a slight heart murmur, a legacy from the rheumatic fever she contracted as a child, she was excused all strenuous exercise. Not that she minded, she disliked exertion in any form.

Frances returned unexpectedly, smiling sycophantically, which Charlotte knew could only mean one thing – she was on the cadge. Being short of ready cash was a chronic condition with Frances, not only because she was a compulsive spender, but since her father's death her mother had kept a tight hold on the family purse-strings.

'I hate to ask you so soon after last week, but could you lend me another half-crown?' she said silkily. 'You are a good sport,' – as Charlotte brought out her purse. 'I shan't forget to repay you – and also what I already owe you ... as soon as my postal order arrives. And, by the way ... Mama says I can ask a friend to spend Christmas with me, to make up another girl. Two of my boy cousins are coming. I've haven't decided whom to ask yet ...' Her smile was obliquely calculating.

Charlotte took the bait and produced another half-crown. Another five shillings down the drain, she thought crossly as Frances went off with her spoils. She wasn't very hopeful about the invitation, and she certainly didn't expect to see her money again. The only time she had made a tentative suggestion to Frances about paying back, Frances had withered her with a look.

'You'll get your filthy lucre, and with added interest, if that's what's worrying you,' she said. Empty words but wounding, nevertheless.

In her heart, Charlotte despised Frances, but despised herself even more for toadying to her. She desperately wanted to be accepted by Frances and her clique – to be counted as one of them – the group of girls from families on the fringe of the upper classes. She felt in her bones she was just as good as they were, and certainly more clever. But her accent gave her away. At least, it did when, at the age of eleven, she first arrived at St Faith's.

Frances picked on her one day after a geography lesson. 'When you say Wows,' Frances said, grinning across her at a crony, 'do you mean dogs barking, or do you mean

Wales? The country, you know. It does look a bit like a dog, come to think of it.' There were screams of laughter from the rest of the class.

Charlotte called it Wows because the only time she heard it pronounced was when Aggie said it. Aggie had a cousin living in Wows. Why hadn't her mother corrected her and saved her this embarrassment? Perhaps because her mother hadn't noticed. Lottie didn't speak English all that well herself. She still had a trace of a Norfolk accent, and often lapsed back into dialect, Charlotte thought expressly to annoy her. Only at Prizegiving and on Sports' days, was she really proud of her mother.

Lottie had not followed the fashion for bobbed hair. It was still long and plentiful, worn in a burnished fat bun at the nape of her slender neck. 'Who is that distinguished looking woman, in the tailored suit with the lace jabot?' she overheard one of the fathers ask on one occasion.

'Where? Oh, there . . . That's Mrs Foster . . . Charlotte Foster's mother. The girl I told you about . . .'

'The one you don't like? The one who's always boasting about her father? From what I can see, it's her mother she should be boasting about.'

'I thought I would find you here Charlotte – hiding yourself away in the dormitory.' It was Sister Teresa, the youngest sister on the teaching staff . . . very popular with the girls, for it was not long since she was a girl herself. It was she who had taken hockey practice, joining in the game with her skirts tucked up. Her face had an habitual shining look about it – round cheeks and round laughing eyes behind round glasses. To Charlotte, she was the embodiment of inner grace, the only true friend she had at school.

'Because you have been excused games is no reason you should skip exercise,' Sister admonished gently. 'Fetch your coat – we will take a walk in the grounds.'

The day was cloaked in November gloom. Moisture dropped like raindrops from the trees, pattering on the fallen leaves below. It was damp, but not cold. There was a stillness – an uneasy tranquillity in the atmosphere that was in tune with the melancholy mood of the day. The grounds of the school were extensive, with tennis courts, and playing fields, and a large vegetable garden where the lay sisters worked like navvies. Three of them were working now, in boots and sacking aprons over their coarse linen habits, turning over the soil with large, heavy forks.

The lay sisters reminded Charlotte of pale blue moths as they flitted silently along the corridors of the school, usually carrying cleaning utensils. To them fell all the unpleasant tasks in the smooth running of the convent. The laundering and starching and ironing; the cooking and housework; the cleaning and the gardening. They must be doing all this work to assure themselves a place in Heaven, Charlotte thought, for she could not see how they would get their reward on earth. She thought them more saintly than the teaching nuns, who with the exception of Sister Teresa and Sister Regis, the elderly nun who taught needlework, put the fear of God into her.

Unlike the little Roman Catholic day school she had attended as a child where she had been the only non-Catholic pupil, here she was in the majority, for most of the girls were Church of England. They were the daughters of serving officers, or had fathers in the colonial service, domiciled overseas. St Faith's excelled in teaching girls to become young ladies: it was not their aim to prepare them for higher education, for the taking of exams was not mandatory, and it was to discuss this matter that Sister Teresa had sought her out.

'I understand that your mother would like you to begin studying for your matriculation, Charlotte. If that is so, we'd better arrange some extra tuition. How do you feel about it?'

'She wants me to go to college and then to take a diploma in education. But Sister . . . I'm not cut out to be a teacher . . . I haven't got the patience . . .'

'Then what do *you* want to do?'

Charlotte had often pondered this, but so far she had come up with only one answer. She wanted to stay on at the convent – not as a religious, she had no vocation to be a nun, but she felt she would give anything to stay put in this cloistered and sheltered life. She had never told anyone, though she thought Sister Teresa guessed, how much she dreaded going back to the noise and claustrophobia of the place she called her home. Every holiday, the dread got worse.

After every absence, she felt herself more and more distanced from her mother. They lived in different worlds – one so small and frenetic – the other spacious, quiet and orderly. It amazed Charlotte that in a school of more than a hundred girls the predominant atmosphere was one of peace and quiet.

Once, long ago it seemed now, when she attended day school, how she had longed to get home to fling herself into her mother's arms and to be smothered in kisses. Things had changed – or had she changed?

Until she started at St Faith's she hadn't noticed the noise or the smell of the restaurant – or the way the staff shouted at one another, just in ordinary conversation. Aggie for instance, always talked at the top of her voice . . . and as for that laugh of hers! The smell of the restaurant – that was another thing Charlotte hated about it. A smell compounded of years of rich food, and cigar and cigarette smoke, and larded with the sickly odour of Aggie's scent. Old Maud had contributed to it too by leaving her own smell of strong cigarettes and stale clothes behind. A smell that caused the young Charlotte to hold her breath every time she was obliged to climb into the massive black-taffetaed lap, to give a goodnight kiss.

To get away from all that she had turned to fantasies of her father. Out there, somewhere, was a family she had never met. The only bit of information she had wrestled out of Lottie so far was that he was a Norfolk man.

One day, she vowed, she would go to Norfolk and trace the family tree of the Foster family, for she was sure that somewhere in the past, she would come across a granddaughter of an earl.

But that didn't solve her present problem – what to do with herself on holiday? Lottie had little time to spare her, and in any case, she didn't find it easy confiding in her mother. What she needed, Charlotte told herself, was someone of her own generation to chew problems over with.

There were so many things she had only a sketchy idea about – sexual matters for instance. The garbled half-truths she heard at school alarmed and disgusted her. And it was only during the last eighteen months she had finally discovered the actual mechanics of childbirth. Before then, the general belief among the convent girls was that, at the appropriate time, the mother's belly would split open like a ripe plum, and the baby pop out. This idea was based on the fact that one girl had seen a scar on her mother's abdomen that ran from her navel to that part of her anatomy nobody knew the right word for. The Catholic girls, they felt, should be able to enlighten them because childbirth was a recurring theme in their households, but any hint of a subject that touched on sex, and they shied away. Not from reasons of delicacy, but from fear of the Confessional.

Her mother, sensing her frustration and loneliness during the holidays, once suggested she had a school-friend to stay, but Charlotte had no intention of bringing that disaster upon herself. She could imagine the titters at her expense, at school, later. She had boosted the importance of her mother's business as something on a par with the Café Royal: sumptuous salons and dining halls; lavish furnishings. Fosters, in her eyes and therefore their eyes – was paltry by any standards. Never mind its reputation as being one of the best eating places in London, and known for the warm welcome of the *maître d'* as much as the quality of the food – look at its image!

Not even a foyer. No banks of flowers or gentle fountains, no palm court – nothing but a mezzanine floor where a quartet played for the newly introduced *thé dansant*.

And the biggest drawback of all – Aggie Sharpe. Charlotte's toes curled at the mere thought of Aggie meeting anyone from the convent. Aggie with her peroxided hair and short skirts, and the danger of a knees-up, if she'd had a drink too many. Charlotte went cold at the thought.

She was thankful that those other two encumbrances, Maud and Mary Ann were no longer with them. She could still remember Maud – a solid ball of flesh with a suety face. The relief to her six-year-old sensitivities when Maud died, and she was released from the distasteful duty of kissing her, knew no bounds. The other old woman, shrivelled and bent and minus her teeth, lived on for several more years.

'She'll live for ever,' said Aggie. 'She can't die – she's pickled in gin,' and the prophecy might well have come true, Charlotte feared, if one night, coming out of the George and Dragon, Mary Ann hadn't stepped out from behind a stationary bus right into the path of another. She was buried in the double grave with Maud, and her name added to the headstone – 'MAUD VICTORIA SPICER and MARY ANN WHITE – Friends in Death as in Life' the epitaph read.

'What a hope,' said Aggie. 'They never stopped bickering.'

'You've been miles away,' said Sister Teresa. 'In what my mother would have called a brown study.' It always surprised Charlotte to think that Sister Teresa had had a life outside the convent, with a mother and father and brother and sister, and a sweetheart too, she had once confided in a moment of frankness. 'What were you thinking about, Charlotte? Something serious, obviously.'

'I was thinking how much I'd like to stay on here.'

'You will, until you have taken your matriculation.'

Charlotte looked from Sister to the horizon beyond.

The mist had lifted, and there was a rim of gold marking the division of sea and sky, both pale and grey like long smooth slabs of slate. Give up all this – the Sussex Downs, school trips to the Brighton Pavilion and Arundel Castle – for Boot Lane and the choking, dirty atmosphere of London? To exchange the convent with its fragrance of sanctity for the poky little hot-bed of a restaurant. And Aggie and her mother, as close as thieves, making her feel like an outsider?

'I'll get my matric,' she said, looking inwards to invisible horizons. 'And then I'm going to travel – to see the world. But first I want to make a pilgrimage to Norfolk.'

'To Great Walsingham?' said Sister Teresa, her face lighting up like a holy picture.

'No – somewhere personal.'

Moreton-in-Marsh, when they arrived, was shrouded in mist – a chilling damp mist that crept insidiously into their bones. Charlotte, here as Frances' guest, pulled the collar of her coat tighter. London was never as cold as this.

In the station yard waited an ancient carriage and between its shafts, an equally ancient horse, who stood patiently blowing into its nosebag, while the driver snoozed under his waterproof cape. There was no sign of a limousine with liveried chauffeur which Charlotte had conjured up in her mind, only a post office van collecting the mail bags from the London train, and some coal carts.

The tip of Frances' nose was red. 'There's usually a taxi waiting, but somebody must have beaten us to it,' she said crossly. 'It's your fault – you took such a time to get your things together.' She stared at the ancient carriage. 'Shall we risk taking that fly, or had I better ask a porter to phone for another taxi?'

'Is it too far to walk?'

'Of course it's too far to walk! And what about the luggage? This is not London, you know. There's no trams or buses or taxicabs passing every other second. Come along, let's find the waiting-room.'

The waiting-room was empty and warm. They sat on a shiny leather bench by the fire, but neither felt up to making conversation. They were tired and hungry and bored with each other's company. And Charlotte suspected that Frances was already regretting her invitation.

It had come to Mother Superior's attention that one of her pupils was regularly borrowing money from one of her school-fellows, and forgetting to honour her debt. Shock waves swept through the school in consequence, and with quaking hearts the girls obeyed the summons to attend assembly. More than one girl was guilty of this crime, but none felt as guilty as Frances. She flung Charlotte a look of fury.

'I will not tolerate such heinous practices in my school.' Mother Superior on the dais, her hands tucked into her sleeves, her eyes steely behind her spectacles, searched the faces of the girls aligned before her for signs of stricken consciences. She saw only fear. Even those girls whose only crime was to borrow a penny for the Ladies wondered if they had been guilty of a heinous practice.

'I know I have never encouraged tale-bearing,' she said. 'But this is something far more serious. I will give whoever is guilty until the rest of the day to come to my study and confess. If no-one is forthcoming, there will be no more half-holidays for the rest of the term. Dismiss.'

There was a smothered concerted groan as the girls formed a line and silently filed away. They relied on their half-holidays for shopping and other forms of recreation. Charlotte felt that all eyes were upon her – she was the only one with money to spare. She managed to dodge Frances until the prep hour, then Frances ran her to earth in the library. She was alone except for the Sister in charge.

'It wasn't me,' she whispered fiercely, as Frances took a seat beside her. 'I didn't sneak on you.'

'I know that now,' Frances answered just as fiercely. 'It was that little worm Enid Butler. Sister Regis is selling rosaries to raise money for the Overseas League of Pity. Ninepence if the rosary is blessed and threepence if it isn't blessed. Enid could only afford an unblessed one and she told Sister it was because another girl had borrowed all her money. *All* her money. It was only a shilling . . .'

'Ninepence for a blessed rosary! What did Enid want a blessed rosary for? She's not even a Catholic . . .'

'Just to be in the swim, I suppose. You know Enid.' The eyes of the two girls met, and a flash of genuine humour passed between them. It was their undoing.

The library Sister looked sternly in their direction. 'This is a place for study, not for amusement. Will you please go and do your sniggering somewhere else.'

'Yes, Sister.'

Outside the library, Charlotte said; 'But Enid didn't give your name?'

'She would have been lynched if she had, and well she knew it. But now she's had the bally cheek to deliver an ultimatum. Either I pay her back what I owe her or she'll go to Mother Superior. She feels very brave all of a sudden . . .'

'How much do you owe her, Frances?'

'Nearly seven shillings . . . I don't suppose you could see your way . . . ?'

'I haven't got that much on me, but if I can get permission to go to the post office, I could draw it out of my savings account . . .'

'I won't forget this, Charlotte.'

A few days later, Charlotte received from Mrs Edmond Peacock a formal invitation to stay at Holbrook House, Moreton-in-Marsh, for the Christmas holiday. She considered it was worth every penny of seven shillings.

When they heard the sound of a car drawing up outside, Charlotte was the first to jump to her feet, but Frances said, 'Sit down and wait for the driver to collect our cases – that's what he's paid for.'

Their taxi turned left at the top of the station approach, and Charlotte's first impression of Moreton was of a large rectangular market place with wide tree-lined roads, and buildings of mellowed stone. Shops, houses and inns – all the same attractive honey colour. It made a pleasant contrast to the soot-encrusted streets of London.

The mist grew thinner as they laboured up the long hill out of town, giving Charlotte a clearer sight of the Cotswold uplands which Frances had lauded so often. In places, groups of trees overlapped the dry stone walls that sectioned the rising meadows, and similar walls braided the sides of the road, stretching like a sandstone ribbon, out of sight over the rim of the hill. Charlotte had to concede that in this instance Frances had not exaggerated. Even on a day like this, the Cotswolds had a charm that was unique.

'At the top here, on the left. Holbrook House,' Frances instructed the driver.

'I know it well, miss.'

The dim outline of a house appeared, not as large as Charlotte had been led to believe, but imposing nevertheless. Like the houses in the town, it was built of stone and in the same architectural design, with mullioned windows and tall cylindrical chimneys. The furnishings inside were even more impressive. There was nothing new or brash, everything was old and in keeping with the period of the house which was late eighteenth century, so Frances said. Shabbiness, and there was that too, was respectable in such a setting.

Charlotte had dreaded her encounter with Frances' mother, imagining her to be another Mother Superior but in different attire. Instead she was introduced to a rather timid-looking lady, who apologised for the smokiness of the fire, but told them tea was ready. Hot buttered muffins arrived in a silver dish, and tea the colour of pale amber smelling faintly of verbena.

There was just one muffin each. Charlotte who was hungry enough to eat the lot, wondered how long she would have to wait before dinner. Meanwhile, Mrs Peacock put her through a gentle cross-examination.

'I understand your mother is a very successful business woman. I do so admire clever women, though they do make one feel rather inadequate.' Was she being sarcastic? Charlotte looked into child-like, but faded eyes and decided not. If Mrs Peacock had a mistaken idea of her mother's importance, who was to blame? Herself or Frances? And did it really matter? She settled down more comfortably to listen to Mrs Peacock's genteel but monotonous voice.

'The women in our family have never been encouraged to use their brains. The gentlemen didn't approve. My late husband was the exception. He wanted Frances to go to a public school, and she would have done so, had he lived. But I didn't like the idea – turning girls all out to the same pattern – as if they'd been made in a mould.' She gave a tiny shudder. 'And as for examinations . . . well, how do examinations help a girl to find a suitable husband? I thought a convent school so much more suitable, though we are not Roman Catholics, you understand. I am delighted with St Faith's – so very *civilised*, I think. And you, my dear . . . why did your mother select St Faith's for you?'

'I suppose because my first school was a convent. It was the nearest school to where I lived.'

'Really . . . how interesting. And whereabouts was that? I don't think I know of any Catholic prep schools for girls . . .'

'Oh, it wasn't only for girls – it was for boys too. They were mostly French and Italian,' said Charlotte, so carried away that she was unaware of the trap she was setting for herself. 'There's quite a colony of Italians and French in that part of Soho.'

'*Soho!*' said Mrs Peacock in a faint voice. 'How . . . how very cosmopolitan.'

An uncomfortable awareness of not fitting in worried Charlotte for the first few days. She was so frightened of putting a foot wrong, that she couldn't be her natural self. It was not that she was made to feel unwelcome; her hostess was cordiality itself when they met, which was usually only at meal times, for Mrs Peacock spent her time either in her room writing letters, or working in the garden. She was an indefatigable gardener and Charlotte felt that if she herself had had any knowledge of gardening it would have made a common ground between them, but the only garden she knew about was Covent Garden, and she didn't think that would count with Mrs Peacock.

Frances made no attempt to entertain her – quite the opposite. She saddled up her piebald pony every morning, and went off to visit friends, looking for all the world, thought Charlotte sourly, as if she were mounted on a cow. After all, the invitation to spend Christmas at Holbrook House, had come from Frances in the first place, so why show her dissatisfaction now?

Another bigger worry, was that of her constant, gnawing hunger. Though she had no regrets about not going home for Christmas, she couldn't stop thinking of Fosters, and the generous supplies of delicious food readily available there. The meals at Holbrook House, though beautifully cooked, and served at a table laid with silver and cut glass, lacked in substance what they made up for in presentation. Either Mrs Peacock considered that large helpings were common, like licking one's fingers or sucking fruit stones – or else Frances and she had very small appetites. Unfortunately, Charlotte had not.

She often wondered how the buxom Mrs Mason, who ran the house with the help of a daily woman, managed to appease her hunger. Sometimes, mouth-watering smells of freshly baked bread came wafting from the kitchen. Was that how Mrs Mason filled in her corners? New bread never appeared at tea time. It came wafer-thin and sometimes rolled. Charlotte devoutly hoped that the larder would be restocked before the rest of the guests arrived, otherwise Christmas would be a very lean time indeed.

On the Tuesday before Christmas, finding herself with nothing to do as usual, she decided to walk to Moreton to finish her Christmas shopping. She didn't relish the walk, but it was downhill all the way, and she could have a taxi back. The day was crisp and clear, bringing into sharpened relief the contours of the Cotswold uplands. Its tranquil beauty was nearly enough to appease her hunger.

This was sheep country, hence the walls, instead of hedges. Sheep could so easily snag their fleeces on thorn or bramble. In this clear light it was easy to trace the line of the walls as they trailed off into the horizon, dividing the fields into a patchwork of muted colours. How did Norfolk compare with this, she wondered? But Norfolk was flat, so there could be no real comparison. One day, she would go and see for herself.

Nobody had told her that Tuesday was Moreton's market day. She loved a market, and her spirits soared at the sight of the well-stocked stalls that jammed the square. She spent an hour just browsing, thinking of all the purchases she could have made but for the thought of lugging them all back to school at the end of the holiday.

She soon found something for Frances – a leather pencil-case; decided on stockings for Mrs Mason, not very original but always welcome, but couldn't think of anything suitable for her hostess. Then quite by chance, she stumbled on a secondhand book shop. An historic gem, much older than the next-door premises, and inside, she found something she thought just the thing. A calf-bound edition of *Elizabeth and her German Garden*.

Now nearly out of money, she went in search of a post office to draw on her savings account, and it was as she was walking back to the square that her eye was caught by a promising looking café.

With the walls of her stomach sticking together, she didn't hesitate. She crossed the road and went in, but took care to choose a table at the back in case she was seen by anyone passing by. Her school uniform was conspicuous, and someone might recognise it as being similar to the one worn by Frances, though never on holiday. Charlotte was made to feel she had committed a *faux pas* by doing so.

She ordered beefsteak pudding and chips, with rhubarb tart to follow, and the minute her knife cut into the thick suety crust, releasing a gush of thick brown gravy as well as the delicious aroma of steak and kidney, she began to drool. There was to be another time when the same mouth-watering smell of meat pudding would make her feel faint with hunger and then she would look back on this occasion, when her only worry was how to satisfy a healthy appetite.

On the morning of Christmas Eve there was delivered from Fortnum and Mason an enormous hamper, which contained, among other things, a twenty-pound turkey. 'Such a generous man, the Major,' cooed Mrs Peacock. 'Is there a cooked ham also, Mrs Mason?'

'Yes m'm. I've just come to it,' said Mrs Mason, on her knees, before the hamper.

The Major and his grandsons were not expected until late that evening. Charlotte and Frances were in bed, but not asleep when they heard the sound of wheels on gravel, the banging on the outer door, bolts being released, loud greetings, laughter. A barking welcome from the dogs. 'At last,' said Frances, petulantly. 'Some stimulating company, for a change.' She missed no opportunity, Charlotte thought, to aim her little darts of poison.

On Christmas morning, Mrs Peacock, Frances and the two cousins went off to church in the Major's Wolseley, driven by Anthony Peacock, the elder of the two brothers. Charlotte declined an invitation to join them, not because she didn't want to, (she would have loved to) but because she wasn't conversant enough with the Book of Common Prayer. The thought of standing up or sitting down in the wrong place during the service, or not standing up or not sitting down at the right time, was too much for her. She didn't want to make a fool of herself in front of Anthony, who was tall and good-looking and had given her several provocative glances across the breakfast table.

Among Frances' small stock of books, Charlotte had found an old favourite, *Anne of Green Gables*, which she had read many times, and looked forward to reading again. She was curled up in a deep leather chair in the morning-room, her hair falling forward as she bent over her book, when the door suddenly opened, and the Major entered, taking her by surprise. She had thought he was out walking the dogs.

'No . . . No, stay there,' he said, as she made to rise. 'You don't bother me. Will it bother you if I smoke my cigar?'

Charlotte shook her head, her mouth suddenly dry. She had avoided the Major so far, as he made her feel very uneasy. It was the way he scrutinised her with those pale, prominent eyes.

He had stared at her all through breakfast, not even shifting his gaze when her eye inadvertently caught his. She had the feeling he had already quizzed Mrs Peacock or Frances, or both, on her credentials, and that they didn't come up to expectations. Were her table manners letting her down? She found she couldn't eat another mouthful with him watching her.

She felt obliged to straighten her legs and smooth her crumpled skirts. Had she committed another *faux pas* by putting on her party dress too early in the day? She had been dying to see how it went with her new silver kid pumps – the shot silk dress her mother had sent her for Christmas. The Major was dressed in casual tweeds and gaiters, and now at ease in the opposite chair, was puffing at his cigar. He smiled across at her, and that gave her a little comfort, though there seemed no corresponding smile in his bulging eyes.

She guessed he intended to probe into her background, and was terrified that the dreaded subject of trade might be touched upon, but what he actually said completely floored her.

'Are you anything like your mother to look at?'

'Do – do you know my mother?' she stammered.

'I think I may have done so once' He flicked some ash into a convenient ash-tray, then resumed his pose, leaning back in his chair, finger tips together. Across his paunch, the gold chain of his pocket-watch caught the dancing lights of the fire.

'Tell me,' he said conversationally. 'Is my daughter-in-law correct in telling me that your mother owns a restaurant in London? In Soho, she thinks, as you attended a school close by.'

This is it, thought Charlotte with sinking heart, he can see the word trade written all over me.

'Would that restaurant at anytime have been known as Maudie's?'

Her mouth dropped open. 'You knew Maudie's? You knew Auntie Maud?' The question came out spontaneously.

'Very well at one time. Yes indeed – we were very good friends.' He drew contemplatively on his cigar. Charlotte could have wept with relief. He knew Maud – they had once been friends – and she had worked herself into a state for nothing. 'Auntie Maud?' he queried. 'You were related?'

'Oh no, we weren't related. Auntie was just something I called her. But she was very close to my mother, and treated her like a daughter, so my mother always said.' Charlotte thought it might be helpful to cash in on the Major's friendship with Maud. 'As a matter of fact, my mother took the business over when Auntie Maud died.'

'So I heard.' He smiled again . . . just a show of teeth, yellow against the white of his whiskers. 'Ah, I believe I hear the church party returning. Shall we go and meet them?' He stubbed out his cigar and rose. Charlotte followed his example, and stood awkwardly, looking down on him.

'You are very tall for your age,' he said, 'Tall like your mother, and your eyes are very similar. That was the first thing I noticed about you.'

'You knew my mother very well, then?'

'I only met her once, but then I never forget a face.' He said this matter-of-factly. 'I believe I knew you too, as a toddler, but of course, you wouldn't remember. You were very fond of sweets, I seem to recall.'

Charlotte followed him in a sort of daze. What a fortuitous coincidence. Christmas now, could only get better.

Sitting at the table in a state of bliss with David, the shy younger brother beside her, and exchanging glances with Anthony sitting opposite, next to Frances, Mrs Peacock at the foot of the table and the Major at the top, Charlotte had never in her wildest dreams expected Christmas to be like this.

It had all been perfect – every minute of it, even her early discomfiture hadn't lasted after talking to the Major. Luncheon was an informal affair, and in the afternoon, the presents were given out and then games were played. Simple games which she hadn't played since a child, but now imbued with extra liveliness by the antics of the brothers. Was it just by chance, she wondered, that no matter what they played – she was either caught by Anthony, or found herself on his lap, or outside the door with him? Whatsoever, he always managed to give her a squeeze before they were interrupted, and once even a dodgy kiss. In all her imaginings, Christmas had never been as promising as this.

They sat down to dine at seven o'clock, and nearly two hours later, were still sitting there talking amid the ruins of a most stupendous feast, when the Major, with some difficulty, rose to his feet – to give another toast, they thought. In the light of the candelabra, his eyes looked as glassy and as hard as marbles.

He steadied himself. 'It is my painful duty to inform you,' he said, 'That we have been harbouring a snake in the grass ...' He paused and looked pointedly at Charlotte. 'There is somebody here, who is not fit to be under the same roof as you other decent young people. I could have warned you about this sooner, but I didn't want to spoil your Christmas dinner ...'

'He's drunk ...' Charlotte heard David mutter above the roaring in her ears. 'He's the same every Christmas ...'

'*Miss Foster*!' Charlotte jumped at the ring of command in his voice. 'You know to whom I'm referring. Will you please oblige me by going to your room, and start packing. I shall be taking you back to your school first thing tomorrow.'

She couldn't stop trembling. She sat huddled on the bed with the eiderdown around her shoulders, but she still felt cold. What had she done? What unmentionable crime had she committed, to be sent up to the bedroom in disgrace like this, and then to be left alone with no explanation. She had cried so relentlessly that her swollen eyes now refused to focus properly and she saw everything through a blur. She could cry no longer – she could only tremble.

It was still too early for bed. In any case, if she did get undressed and into bed, she wouldn't sleep – not with this hanging over her. She was determined to sit up and wait for Frances. Bully her, if necessary, to make her explain what had gone wrong.

She must have dozed a little, for she came to with a frightened start when the door handle rattled. It was Frances, pale-faced and subdued, who kept her distance as if suspecting Charlotte of being infectious.

'I've only come to collect my night things,' she said. 'I've been told I must sleep in mummy's room tonight,

165

and that's all I'm allowed to say. Grandpop said on no account must I speak to you.'

Charlotte was off the bed in an instant, and guarding the door. 'I'm not letting you out of this room until you tell me what's going on . . .'

Frances at that moment, showed a distinctive likeness to her grandfather. The same pale and glassy eyes. 'I don't know – I really don't know . . . But you must have done something really dreadful to make Grandpop blast off like that.' Her expression grew crafty. She's relishing this, thought Charlotte. What a story to tell at school. 'You were alone with him this morning . . . you must have said something to upset him. Can't you remember?'

Charlotte racked her brains. 'We talked about someone he used to know – a friend of my mother's. You don't think it's because my mother has to earn her living . . . ?'

'Of course not, stupid. I've got lots of aunts who earn their living. It's how they earn it, that counts.'

'Perhaps he thinks running a restaurant is not respectable . . . But why didn't he say so at the time and spare me all . . . all this. It was such a cruel, heartless thing to do . . .' Her tears began afresh.

Frances watched her without a shred of pity. 'You needn't feel so sorry for yourself. This wouldn't have happened if you hadn't wheedled an invitation out of me. You came here and spoilt our Christmas. Mummy can't stop crying, and the boys are sulking, and Grandpop's in a furious temper because he wanted to go out with the hunt tomorrow – and now he's got to take you back to the convent instead. Oh, why did you have to ruin everything . . . this is the worst Christmas of my life.'

Out of that welter of words, only one phrase impinged itself on Charlotte's mind. 'What do you mean – I wheedled an invitation out of you! You asked me to come here for Christmas. The idea never crossed my mind until you mentioned it . . .'

'That's a lie – you schemed it – that's why you lent me that money. If I hadn't got the invitation in first, you would have blackmailed one out of me . . .' Frances' flow of words petered to a halt. The look on Charlotte's face frightened her. She was frightened even further when Charlotte made a grab at her, opened the door, and thrust her out with such violence, that she nearly over-balanced. Her nightgown and towel and sponge bag followed in quick succession. Then the door was slammed shut.

When, a few minutes later, Charlotte heard a soft tap-tap on the door panel, the wildly improbable idea that Anthony had sneaked upstairs to comfort her, crossed her mind. However, it was only Frances' mother. She gave Charlotte a weak smile. She wouldn't come in.

'I've come to say goodbye as I won't see you in the morning. My father-in-law insists on making an early start as it is a long drive to Sussex. I couldn't go to bed without seeing you. I am sorry it has ended like this. I don't know what you've done, but I do not think it can be all that terrible. Frances' grandfather is a man of unpredictable moods. If he has a grievance it smoulders inside him until he suddenly erupts . . .' She makes him sound like a volcano, thought Charlotte, hearing the genteel monotonous voice fading away, leaving with her instead, an image of the Major with red hot lava gushing from the top of his head. She wanted to laugh, but it wasn't funny.

'What I am trying to say, dear,' Mrs Peacock's voice came to her as from a distance, 'Is that when this all blows over, and Frances and I are on our own again, you must come and visit us. Sometime in the spring, perhaps . . .'

Both knew there was no possibility of that. But conventions had been satisfied, and they parted civilly, Mrs Peacock again thanking Charlotte for her delightful present. Charlotte bolted the bedroom door after her, not wanting any more interruptions, undressed, and crept shivering into bed. In spite of her fears to the contrary she did sleep, but only fitfully, and she was up and dressed long before Mrs Mason came to call her.

*

They arrived at St Faiths late morning, keeping up a steady speed the whole way. There was very little traffic on the road, and the Major had no need to stop to look for a garage, as he had a spare can of petrol clamped to the running board. Not a word passed between them. Charlotte sat in the back, clutching her case and the presents she had been given. David had got up early to say goodbye, but the Major, with a sharp reprimand had told him to go back to his room. Looking through the rear window, as they drove off, Charlotte could see David standing on the steps, staring after them with a mulish expression. At least, she thought, someone in that sleeping house had put himself out for her.

Mother Superior must have been advised of their coming, for she was awaiting them in the hall. She told Charlotte to go up to her dormitory, and she took the Major into her office. Charlotte took off her hat and coat and sat on a bed waiting for the summons she knew must come. The heating had been turned off in the bedrooms, but she no longer felt the cold. She was numb right through to her marrow.

Charlotte didn't know for certain how much time had elapsed before she heard the Wolseley drive away. It could have been minutes but it seemed more like hours. She passed the time thinking of ways to put a curse on the Major. She hoped he would have an accident on the way home and suffer the most appalling injuries – though nothing that happened to him could possibly equal her suffering. She had started to make a figure of him out of her handkerchief and some paper, but gave up because she had no pins to stick in it. In any case, she felt that practising black magic in a convent had little chance of succeeding.

One of the lay Sisters, sweet-faced and with eyes full of compassion, brought her the summons from Mother Superior. She dreaded the interview, but at least she might learn what charges the Major had brought against her.

Mother motioned her to sit down, which she would have done anyway, as her legs were starting to buckle. That was nothing unusual – Mother Superior always had that effect on her.

'I have spoken to your mother on the telephone, and she is coming for you straight away,' Mother said in her precise English. 'There may be some difficulty hiring a car on a public holiday, but she promises to be here as soon as possible. In the meantime, I would rather you stayed in your room, and not mix with the other girls. As you know, some of them have not been able to go home for Christmas. It is for your own sake,' she added, and for the first time, Charlotte detected a touch of pity in her manner. 'The girls will be naturally curious, and I want to spare you any further embarrassment.'

'But what have I done? Why won't anybody tell me what I've actually *done*?'

Mother Superior seemed reluctant to answer a straight question. 'It is nothing you have done, my child. You are the unfortunate victim of circumstances. Your mother will explain everything to you . . .'

'Is that why you've sent for her?'

Mother Superior overlooked the temerity of this remark. 'She is coming to take you home. I suggest you spend the time packing your possessions.'

'But I haven't unpacked yet. The clothes I took to Moreton-in-Marsh are still in my case.'

'I am not only referring to clothes, but everything that you possess. Books . . . games . . . I will ask Sister Mary to get your trunk from the store . . .'

'I'm being expelled . . . that's it, isn't it!' Charlotte sprang to her feet. 'I want to see Sister Teresa . . . where's Sister Teresa? She'll tell me what's happening.'

'Shouting will not help the situation,' said Mother calmly. She too, rose. 'Yes, certainly you may see Sister Teresa, but later, when you have eaten. I will send her to help you pack your trunk. You are not being expelled,

Charlotte, you are being requested to leave. I have no alternative. Major Peacock was very adamant about that.'

Charlotte fled. She did not want to break down in front of Mother Superior. She started up the stairs, two at a time, and was nearly at the top when Mother called her back.

'Charlotte, that is not the way to mount a staircase. Now come back here and start again. In a ladylike manner this time.'

'I thought the reason I'm being expelled is because I'm not a lady,' Charlotte retorted recklessly.

'Are you going to tell me why I'm being sent away?' Charlotte looked up with red-rimmed eyes as Sister Teresa came into the room. 'If not, don't bother to say anything.'

Sister looked at the untouched tray, the half-filled trunk, and sighed. 'Charlotte, you must eat. You have a long journey before you.'

'Why am I being expelled?'

'You are not being expelled. You are being asked to leave for the sake of the school. Major Peacock could make things very difficult. Mother Superior is fearful that if you don't leave, many of the other girls will be taken away . . .'

'I have given up hoping that anyone will tell me what I've done.'

Sister Teresa sat on the bed beside her, and took her hand. 'The blame does not lie with you, Charlotte. It is a question of the sins of the fathers being visited on their children. Do you understand?'

'*My* father was a war hero,' said Charlotte, her eyes flashing.

'Yes, my dear, I know . . . but . . . Now, shall we continue with the packing?'

In some ways, the journey back to London was even more of an ordeal than the earlier journey with the Major. It's late, it must be tomorrow already, thought Charlotte, seeing the lights of London on the horizon. She didn't feel sleepy, but nauseous, as if she wanted to vomit.

Because there was no privacy in the hired car, there had been no opportunity to question her mother. Lottie sat tense beside her, and every now and then, Charlotte heard her swallow. At the start of the journey the driver had tried to make conversation, but had given up, discouraged by their stilted answers.

Aggie was waiting up for them. It was she who settled up with the driver and helped him to carry in the trunk. Tight-lipped and with burning eyes, Lottie went straight to her sitting-room, Maud's old room, and poured herself a glass of whisky which she drank neat. Charlotte, who had followed, felt no surprise, though it was the first time she had seen her mother touch spirits. She was beyond emotions such as surprise or shock, she told herself. All she wanted was an explanation, and she wasn't going to bed until she had one.

'Sit down,' said Lottie. 'I have something to tell you, and it's going to take some time . . .'

'Liar . . . fraud . . . hypocrite . . .' Charlotte was beside herself with fury. Her voice rose to a scream. 'Harlot . . . whore . . .'

'It's pronounced hoar – not woar,' said Lottie. In spite of her ghastly smile, her face was like a white mask. Only her eyes showed any expression and they were two black circles of despair.

'How can you joke at a time like this. You're – you're inhuman – a monster . . . You're not fit to be a mother . . .'

'I certainly haven't made a very good job of you,' conceded Lottie. She wondered how much longer this ranting would go on – how much longer she could bear it. All her past suffering seemed to have crystallised into a hard core of pain in the region of her chest. She rested her chin in her hand and stared into the fire. Christmas isn't the best of times for me, she thought. Christmas

1913, when it had all started in the little attic room at Thornmere Hall. Christmas 1916, when her mother died. Christmas 1917, when Flo had written to tell her about Henry being gassed. And now this Christmas, 1930 – perhaps the most dreadful of them all. Could this be Charlotte, her beloved daughter, screaming such obscenities?

She turned to face her once again. 'Couldn't we just discuss this in a rational manner – like two adults,' she begged.

Charlotte sat down. 'Oh yes . . . Now when it suits you, you want me to be an adult. You want me suddenly to be an understanding woman. Then why have you treated me like a child all these years! Why have you fed me on lies and deceit? Why did you give me a fictitious father . . . ?'

Lottie gave a hollow laugh. 'He was not fictitious, I can assure you. I took the best parts of two brothers and made them into someone you could look up to and admire. Your real father was a war hero, I didn't lie about that. His name was Joseph Massingham . . . Sir Joseph Massingham now.'

An odd expression crossed Charlotte's face. *Sir* Joseph Massingham. She wasn't just the bastard child of a servant girl then? Her father had connections – perhaps he even had a mother who had been the granddaughter of an earl. She felt a shudder of anguish go through her. That dream was all over now.

'And who was Henry Foster?' she said.

'Massingham, not Foster. He was Joseph's younger brother. He died of war wounds just before the war ended. He was just as much a hero as your father – in some ways more so. He hated the slaughter on the Western Front – he hated war, but that didn't stop him fighting for his country. Your father gloried in it. He was in his element out there on the battlefield. . .'

'How dare you sneer at my father. Don't you ever say anything against my father . . .'

'Charlotte – I was not saying anything against him – I was trying to explain . . .' But nothing she could say would make any difference now. Lottie realised she had lost her case. Charlotte, by her impassioned words had given judgement. Her father was her hero – but her mother was her enemy.

'Can't we discuss this further in the morning? I'm so tired. And you must be too . . .' For the first time Lottie allowed herself to make excuses. 'I only did it for you – pretended I was a married woman, I mean. I started to wear a wedding ring after you asked me why I didn't have a ring like other mummies. I did it for your sake, Charlotte . . . children can be so cruel to one another . . .'

'You didn't do it because of me – you did it to conceal the truth.' Charlotte's voice was contemptuous. 'No, don't go, mother. I want to hear more about my father . . .'

Charlotte lay on her bed, scheming how to get out of the place undetected. She no longer felt hysterical. She wished she did, because the icy emotion that racked her instead was more painful.

A brothel. She had been born in a brothel. She couldn't banish that thought from her mind. Even the discovery that her father was a baronet as well as a war hero, didn't ease her wretchedness. He would undoubtedly deny her existence, and in any case, he lived abroad, so Lottie said – but how could she believe anything her mother said, anymore? Joseph Massingham – a name completely unknown to her. And Henry Massingham – not Henry Foster. Her uncle, not her father. A web of lies – her mother in the middle – spinning deceit and hypocrisy.

Nothing but a servant girl – sneaking off to have her baby in a brothel. Surely she could have found herself an honest job – or gone to one of those places for unmarried mothers. Anything would have been better than sinking to this level.

'I was never a prostitute,' her mother protested with a

paper-white face, when Charlotte first flung that accu
sation at her. What's in a name? She lived off immoral
earnings, didn't she! In an agony of self-pity, Charlotte
buried her face in her pillow, trying to shut out the scene
at the Christmas dinner. No wonder the Major had
turned on her – who would want their grandchildren
contaminated by someone reared in a brothel?

She got down from the bed, stripped off the new silk
dress, tearing it in her haste as she did so, and flung it
across the room. She changed into something warm, and
checked the contents of her bag. Two pounds in notes,
and four shillings in loose change – plenty to go on with.
She had nearly fifty pounds in her savings account, more
than enough to live on until she found a job, and that
shouldn't take long for a bright girl with a good appearance. Her case was still unpacked.. It contained all she
would need for the time being. Tonight, or what was left
of it, she'd spend at the YWCA.

She crept down the stairs. The restaurant had closed
long ago – the staff gone home – everywhere was quiet
except for the sound of sobbing from the sitting-room,
and Aggie's muted words of comfort. She turned a deaf
ear to that. The door proved no problem. Silently, she
slipped the bolt, and stepped out into the cold night air.
How easy it had been after all. She had got away – and
nothing or nobody would force her back. She was free of
her mother – and free of Fosters forever.

NINE | *Charlotte*
1934–1939

It was starting to drizzle. Charlotte turned up the collar of her mac. She had a moment of panic, thinking she had lost her sixpence. A sixpence would buy her a bowl of soup, a roll, and a cup of tea. Or half a veal and ham pie and a roll and butter. Or poached egg on toast and a portion of chips. But why go on tormenting herself? She hadn't eaten all day, and very little the day before. Hot soup was what she needed. She dragged her eyes away from the food displayed in the window of the Lyon's tea-shop and went inside.

She was greeted by a rush of warm air and the smell of food which started her salivating. Once such a smell would have nauseated her. But once she wouldn't have known what it meant to be so hungry. She was surprised to find how full the café was, even at this late hour. There was one small table unoccupied, up against the wall at the back; she went straight to it, and presently a Nippy came along and took her order.

'Is this seat, taken?' It was an elderly man in a navy-blue striped suit and carrying an overcoat on his arm. Well, not old really, but well past forty. He spoke politely, and she shook her head. Immediately he had given his order he hid himself behind his evening paper.

'Mussolini Urges German Rearmament,' she read. She noticed that the first two fingers of the man's right hand were stained orange with nicotine, and felt unreasonably resentful. All that money going up in smoke and she was out of a job, and starving.

Her soup arrived, and she fell on it ravenously. Such a

small helping for threepence, or perhaps she had drunk it too quickly. She took longer over her roll, trying to chew each mouthful fourteen times, but she had swallowed long before she reached ten. The man's order came. Steak and kidney pudding and chips, and a cup of coffee. He stabbed the pudding with his knife and rich brown gravy leaked all over the plate. Charlotte stared at it, fascinated, and wondered why, as she was already sitting down, she should suddenly feel as if she were falling.

The face of the man opposite came floating back into focus. He looked concerned. 'Are you all right? You're not going to faint? Take a sip of your tea, quickly . . .' She was staring at his plate as if hypnotised.

He thought, My God, the kid's hungry. He was a man who acted by instinct, and he pushed his plate across to her and said, 'Eat that. It's all right, I haven't started on it. I'll order myself another.'

Charlotte gathered her tattered pride together and tried to refuse, but her hunger pains were stronger than conviction. She gabbled a few words of thanks and then set to, using her knife and fork like weapons.

The man watched with amused and kindly eyes. The waitress came and took his repeat order, and kept him waiting to show her disapproval of a man his age picking up such a young girl. While he waited he lit a cigarette. Normally, this would have put Charlotte off her food, but not tonight. She had finished her steak pudding and was mopping up the gravy with the remains of her roll, when his plate was slapped down before him. She sipped her now lukewarm tea, idly watching him eat in a slow, methodical manner, when the full force of her actions suddenly hit her. Her eyes rounded with horrified apprehension.

'I can't pay you for this. I haven't got a penny in the world. I've lost my job and my landlady has turned me out because I owe three weeks' rent. She's kept all my things too . . .' She was unable to stop the gush of tears. They poured down her cheeks and plopped on to the table. They came in floods, filling her nose and sinuses with mucus, and as fast as she wiped them away more spurted forth to take their place. She had been too weak to cry before, but now she was warm and her stomach was full and once she had started, she couldn't stop. She wept for the months and weeks she had walked the pavements of London looking unsuccessfully for work. She wept for the watch and the books and her best winter coat she had been obliged to pawn. She wept for the loss of her savings, swallowed up in just existing. But mostly she wept out of self-pity, and the awful thought that she had no alternative but to crawl ignominiously back to her mother.

The good Samaritan in the striped suit watched in embarrassed silence, knowing that every eye in the place was on their table. They might think he was the girl's father – he'd better do something quick before she got really hysterical.

'Let's get you out of here – what you need is fresh air,' he said. He helped her to her feet, and then into her macintosh. He shrugged into his overcoat, folded his paper and put it in his pocket. The Nippy who had waited on him was talking to the cashier. Both looked at him with hostile eyes when he paid the bills. Propelling Charlotte before him, he guided her to the door. It was now raining heavily.

'Let's make a run for it – my car's just round the corner.'

'You have a car in London?'

'I'm a salesman – I need a car. It's just along here, at an all-night garage.'

The road he led her to was narrow and dark and lit by one old-type lamppost. It reminded her a bit of Boot Lane which still relied on gaslight for illumination. The garage was underground and as shadowy as a barn. Her companion pointed to a corner. 'That's my old bus – that bullnose Morris. Old, but still roadworthy. Come along, let's get you on board.'

It was dry – it was somewhere to sit and she had been on her feet all day. Charlotte, unresistingly, slid into the passenger seat. It was a small car, just room for two in front and a dicky seat at the back, but it was shelter. He took a rug from the back and tucked it round her.

'Where are you taking me?'

'To my mother's.'

'*To your mother's*!' She felt weak with relief. There had been a moment or two while he was hurrying her to the garage, when all kind of fears went through her mind, including that of white slavery. There had been a lot of rumours about white slave traffic lately, though the perpetrators were more likely to be women with syringes, who preyed on unwary girls – jabbing them in cinemas and cafés and the Ladies' cloakrooms at mainline stations. She felt that if it had been an older woman who had offered her supper, she would have found the strength to refuse.

But she felt incredibly safe with this man. He was so ordinary looking and had such nice eyes – and more important, he had a mother. She could relax.

They left the City behind them and drove through a maze of unfamiliar streets hemmed in by darkened buildings; then they were out in the open, and she could see lights reflected in the oily river and the outline of Tower Bridge smudged by the rain. 'Are we going across the bridge?' she asked hopefully. South of the Thames was an unknown country – her mother would never find her there.

'No, I am taking you to Southend – Old Leigh, actually; that's where my mother's house is. It's just over an hour's drive from here. You can curl up and sleep or you can talk – tell me about yourself. Whichever you prefer . . .'

When she didn't answer, he turned and looked, and saw she was half-asleep already. He didn't mind – he had a lot to think about. He began to whistle jauntily, under his breath.

*

Charlotte stirred and tried to stretch — but her legs came up against an obstruction. She opened her eyes. It was too dark to see where she was, but she could tell she was moving. She was in a car, and the cold night air was blowing through a crack in the window. Suddenly she remembered — the café, the meal, the stranger. And now she was on the way to meet his mother. Mother? Instantly her mind was filled with thoughts of Lottie.

It was nearly three and a half years since she had walked away from Fosters. Three years, three months, and six days, actually. She kept a record in her diary. Each day she added was an extra triumph. She had not seen her mother since that time, though not for the want of trying on Lottie's part. How she had discovered where she worked or where she lived was a mystery to Charlotte, but she suspected that Lottie had paid someone to find out for her.

Her first letter arrived a month after Charlotte left home. Charlotte promptly re-addressed it and sent it back. She had lost count how many letters she had returned since then. She had never been tempted to read them. Once only had Lottie tried to contact her in person. That was when she was lodging in Clerkenwell. When she had returned from work that day her landlady accosted her.

'There's been a visitor for you,' she said, her small eyes pin-points of curiosity. 'Very smart, she was. She left this for you.'

It was an envelope with her name on it. Charlotte felt the crackle of notes inside. She didn't open it. She sent it back by registered letter.

She changed her lodgings. They were even smaller and dingier, and she had to share facilities with four other lodgers. It was sometime before her mother discovered her new address, and then the letters started to come again.

'Had a good sleep?' The voice came out of the darkness.

Charlotte jumped. Lost in her thoughts, she had become unaware of him. As his head turned in her direction, the light from his cigarette showed up an unshaven upper lip. An uncomfortable sense of her vulnerability took hold of her.

'I don't even know your name,' she said.

'It's Denis – Denis Hudson. D'you feel up to talking about yourself yet? Where you come from . . . about your family?'

No she didn't feel like telling him anything. She'd feel happier talking to a woman – his mother, perhaps. She must be a very old lady – nearly eighty. What would she think at being awakened at this time of night, and presented with a strange and homeless girl? Her doubts grew twofold. She must have been mad to let herself in for this. No, not mad – just desperately hungry and too weary to think straight.

'Are we nearly there?' She wondered if she had the nerve to borrow some money from him and get the first train back to London.

'I've just turned off the Arterial Road – not far, now,' he assured her.

'Is this the place?' She couldn't see too well as there was no street lamp on, but it appeared as if the car had stopped up against the front wall of a small terraced cottage. There was no garden. Denis Hudson produced a torch and a set of keys from his coat pocket. Grunting, he inserted the key into the street door and pushed it open. 'After you,' he said.

Always sensitive to smells, Charlotte involuntarily recoiled as she crossed the threshold. She recognised the unpleasant mixture of mildew, damp and cabbage water. Her old lodgings had smelled the same. Mr Hudson lit a match and applied it to the gas-light hanging from the ceiling, and slowly the hall came into focus as a short and narrow passage leading to a flight of stairs.

Charlotte waited for the creak of movement from

above, but the only sound she heard was the hiss and plop from the gas mantle.

'I expect you could do with a hot drink,' Denis Hudson said. 'I could do with something stronger. Come along . . . this way . . .'

There were two doors on the left-hand side of the passage, he opened the second of these and ushered Charlotte through before him. The light from the hall showed up a small, and over-furnished room dominated by a large square table. From this room led a scullery, a black and unsavoury cavern smelling faintly of fish.

Mr Hudson busied himself lighting other mantles, filling the kettle, putting cups and saucers on the table. He wouldn't let Charlotte help him. She perched uneasily on the edge of a wooden chair and watched in a state of apprehension.

'I know Mum had a bottle of whisky – I bought it for her at Christmas. She couldn't have drunk it . . .'

He searched first in the dresser and then in the larder. 'Here it is – among the pickles and chutneys – I'll have to do something about these soon . . .' he seemed to be talking to himself. He made the tea and added a generous measure of spirits to his cup. Charlotte didn't even wait to be asked before she refused.

'There's no milk, I'm afraid, but there's sugar . . .'

'I don't take sugar . . . it's all right, I can drink it without milk.' She could when it was weak, but this was the colour of stew. She swallowed it mouthful by mouthful; it was the warmth that mattered – not the taste. Her mac was still damp and the house was as cold as a mortuary.

How could anybody live here – especially an old lady. But did anybody live here? The place had the feel of an empty tomb. Her stomach began to churn. On the wall was a calendar showing the date as December 1933 – three months ago. Somebody must have lived here then.

'How are you going to explain me away to your mother?' she said.

He lit another cigarette. 'I don't quite know how to say this . . .'

'Why not something like . . . "I haven't got a mother — I tricked you." ' She rose abruptly, fumbling with the buttons of her mackintosh, hoping he wouldn't notice her agitation.

'Hold on there . . . I intended to tell you. I didn't trick you — I said I would take you to my mother's house, and I did. To tell you the truth I didn't know what to do about you. You were destitute — hysterical — I couldn't just leave you in Joey Lyons. I was coming down here anyway — I have a room here I use occasionally. I thought, after a good night's sleep, we could talk it over . . . decide what was best for you . . .' He shot her a look that seemed straightforward enough.

Her heart had stopped its painful thudding, the tightness on her chest had eased. Gingerly, she resumed her seat. 'You say this is your mother's house. Then, where is your mother?'

'She died — just after Christmas . . . She had a sudden stroke . . . I don't suppose you noticed the agent's board in the dark, but this house is up for sale.' He gave a disconsolate shrug. 'But so are hundreds of others in the area. Go along any street and you'll see a forest of estate agents' boards: "To be let or sold" in every other garden. Sign of the times. The Depression hasn't only hit the North, we feel it down here too.'

A silence fell between them. He sat forward with his head bowed and Charlotte wondered if he was thinking of his mother. She crossed and uncrossed her legs.

'The Depression is having an effect on businesses in London too,' she said. Her voice though not exactly friendly, was much less hostile and he perked up a little.

'Is that the reason you lost your job? Tell me about it. It might help you to talk. Come along, Charlotte — you can tell me.' Hearing her name spoken in that kindly fashion gave her confidence. It was ages since she had been called by her first name. At work she was known as Miss Foster.

She told him about the dreary years she had spent with the poky little firm in Gray's Inn Road. The Hawthorne Drawing and Tracing Office. She had gone after the job so gleefully, thinking it was something to do with a detective agency. But discovered that the word tracing meant just what it said. To trace with a special pen on to shining, stiff, blue tracing-linen, the plans made in pencil by one of the draughtsmen. The tracing-linen, if washed, or preferably boiled, became a limp white material which could be made into underclothes, though this chance rarely came her way. One of her duties was to take the finished tracings to the printers to have blueprints made from them, and these in turn were delivered or posted off to the firms who had commissioned them. Her starting wage was a guinea a week and she had gradually worked up to twenty-five shillings.

In her spare moments, which were very few, she said, for her other duties consisted of running errands, making the tea, (with a kettle over a smoky fire, which she had to get alight first) typing letters, shopping at Sainsbury's in Drury Lane for the boss's wife, dusting the offices (the general and the drawing office) and answering the phone, she was given small pieces of tracing-linen to practise on. She never got the hang of holding the tracing pen correctly, and in any case, she spoiled her chances of being taken seriously because instead of lettering in technical words used in the engineering profession, she printed out the names of her favourite film stars instead.

'So that's the reason you were sacked,' Denis Hudson said, much amused by this information.

'I wasn't sacked – not the way you mean it. Business is so slack they had to cut down on staff. Mr Hawthorne said the only thing to save him going bankrupt is a war. He said there would be plenty of work for draughtsmen if a war came.'

'There isn't going to be a war,' said Mr Hudson, taking the empty cups and sluicing them in the scullery.

She had drawn her ten shillings a week unemployment pay for the first few weeks, but that had stopped when she turned down a job offered to her at the Labour Exchange. It was for somebody to help with the office work in a restaurant in Boot Lane, but she didn't tell Denis Hudson that.

'This was my mother's room. There's some bedding in this cupboard, so help yourself. You should be snug enough in here.'

Like the kitchen, the room was so crowded with furniture there was barely room to squeeze round it. One side of a large iron bedstead was jammed against the wall, and on the other side was a hideous piece of furniture, a combined dressing-table and washstand with a marble top. Charlotte was suddenly gripped by a fearful thought.

'Did your mother die in that bed?'

Mr Hudson gave her a startled look. 'Of course she didn't . . . I thought I told you. She had a stroke and died a few days later in Rochford Hospital . . . Do you want me to help you make up the bed?'

'I can manage . . .'

'There's no gas up here, I'm afraid, but I'll leave you plenty of candles. Oh, by the way . . .' He cleared his throat. 'The thingummy-jig is down the garden . . . you have to go through the scullery to get to it. But . . . well . . . on a wet night like this . . . My mother kept a – um, a receptacle under the bed. It should be still there . . .'

She went rigid with embarrassment, and also indignant that he should mention such an object. She'd rather die than use what Aggie called a po.

'I'll manage,' she said coldly.

'Well, I'll say goodnight, then. And if you should need anything, give me a shout. I'm just next door.' It was this thought that was worrying her.

She waited until all was quiet, then opened her door and listened. She could hear him snoring. Not loudly, but rhythmically, like one in a deep and compelling sleep. Reassured, she held her candle aloft and felt her way carefully down the stairs. He had left his torch on the draining board, which showed he was thoughtful. He was quite a nice man really, and younger than she had thought at first. It was still raining and she ducked her head as she made a dash across the yard. The beam of the torch lighted up the wooden door, and beyond that the primitive water closet. She was relieved to see that at least it was on main drainage.

She washed at the sink in cold water – there was no hot tap, and she dabbed herself dry with her handkerchief, as the roller towel looked grubby. By the time she got back to her room, and with some difficulty had wedged a chair against the door (she was taking no chances) she was more than ready for bed. She couldn't be bothered to make it properly, but crawled in between the blankets, which smelled strongly of mothballs, but she was too tired to let that bother her. She slept in her petticoat, hugging herself to keep warm, and went to sleep almost as soon as her head touched the pillow.

'I took you up a cup of tea about eight o'clock, but I couldn't get the door open . . . it must have jammed . . . Anyway, I thought, it would do you good to let you sleep in a bit. And it gave me the chance to go up to the corner shop and get some groceries.'

'I have never slept so late before,' said Charlotte, feeling uncomfortable about the chair.

They were sitting over a late breakfast, or it could have been an early lunch. Denis Hudson had cooked bacon and eggs and fried bread. There was a loaf, still hot, from the baker's and fresh milk from the dairy. On the yellow-painted dresser was cheese and fruit and a large pork pie. And in the kitchener was a small, glowing fire.

The kitchen looked less off-putting in daylight. A fire made all the difference. There were patchwork cushions on the wooden chairs and a rag rug at the hearth. And other signs that Mrs Hudson had been a careful house wife.

Her thoughts wandered. Was there another Mrs Hudson? Mr Hudson hadn't mentioned a wife, yet most men his age were married. Perhaps he was like Mr Coe, a draughtsman at the drawing-office, a mild-mannered little man, who, someone had whispered to her, was 'one of those'. Perhaps the chair jammed against her door had been unnecessary. She felt rather foolish.

Mr Hudson said, 'I think I've found a solution to your problem. Would you like to stay on here and look after the place for me? Don't say anything . . . not until you've heard me out . . .

'I'm a salesman for a woollen mill in the West Country, near Gloucester. I'm responsible for an area in the South East and part of East Anglia. I keep a small office in Holborn as a base to work from, but usually I'm on the road. I could do with a secretary, but there isn't enough work to employ one full time. When I'm working in the London area, I come down here to sleep – I did even when my mother was alive. I didn't mind the journey and it was cheaper than staying in town. It's crossed my mind several times to close up the London office and move my stuff to this house and use it as my base for this area. There doesn't seem any likelihood of selling this place until the market picks up again, and I could save my firm a penny or two on office rent. I think you can see what I'm driving at . . . I could do with somebody to type my letters and check orders and sort out my samples. Nothing very taxing, but work that piles up if it's not done regularly . . .' He interrupted himself to take out a cigarette, light it, and inhaled as if he was in desperate need of something soothing.

'It's more than that,' he said. 'I really need somebody to be here all the time. I don't like leaving the house empty. Once the damp gets a hold it'll be hard to get rid of it. The job's yours if you want it. It means you'd be on your own a lot of the time of course, because I'll be out on the road, but they're a friendly lot around here, and Old Leigh has a character all its own. It's like stepping back into history, living here. You'll see what I mean if we go out, later. It will be something to tide you over until you find a proper job. What do you think?'

'You mean . . . I'd be a sort of caretaker?'

He was delighted that she hadn't refused outright. 'More than a caretaker. Look upon this as your home for the time being, and the little jobs you do for me, just a sideline . . .'

He saw the struggle on her face. 'I know what you're thinking, but I give you my word of honour, you have nothing to fear in that way. You don't know what a favour you'd be doing me. To come down here after two or three weeks on the road, and to find a meal waiting for me and a comfortable bed . . . a place to relax, before I set off again. Boy, that would be something . . .' He saw her frown. 'I can't pay you much – just enough to keep you in food to start with. All my mother left was this house and some unpaid bills. I can see there's going to be difficulties . . .' he admitted as she still did not answer. 'You're worrying about what people will think . . . Don't let that bother you. A place like this isn't a suburb or a village where gossip is a way of life. There'll be talk at first – but it will soon die down. I expect you're more worried about what your family will think . . .'

'I have no family,' said Charlotte – and with that remark made her commitment.

I knew it couldn't last, she thought. It had all been too good to be true. Being the chatelaine of her own little house, discovering she had a flair for housekeeping. Actually enjoying housework! She could thank the nuns for that. Every Friday afternoon, the girls were made to polish their desks and empty the inkwells and clean them out – leaving the classroom in a pristine condition ready for Monday's lessons.

There had been a freedom about her life during those first few months. She could come and go as she pleased. She could get up early or stay in bed reading, and there was nobody to question her. Her timetable was flexible, but she felt duty-bound to get Denis's work out of the way, before she took herself off to the pictures or to catch a tram at Leigh Broadway and go off to Southend to look round the stores.

She could never be quite sure of her feelings towards him at first. She was grateful to him of course. He had provided her with shelter and a job, and what she valued far more – security. And what did he ask for in return? Just the normal comforts of a well-run home and a bed and a meal for when he came back from a journey. So when did that become not enough?

It had started innocently enough with a peck on the cheek after a longer than usual absence. He always brought her a little gift such as a bunch of flowers or a half-pound block of chocolate. Then came the little hugs, which she tolerated. It was all so innocuous, until that occasion they had gone for an evening stroll along the cinder track to Chalkwell; stood for a while and watched the Jolly Boys, then walked back through the cliff gardens arm in arm, in the twilight. Huddled figures under trees or on the ground might have put ideas into Denis's head.

That night he kissed her goodnight on the lips, taking her unawares. She tried not to mind though her inclination was to push him away. His breath smelled strongly of stale cigarette smoke. She decided she would have to revise her assessment of him. He wasn't at all like Mr Coe.

As she undressed she heard movements from the next room. Denis was undressing too. She heard the creak of the bed as he sat down to unlace his shoes, and soon she knew she would hear him snoring. The walls were paper thin.

She climbed into bed and picked up the book she had borrowed from Boots in Southend that morning. Reading by candlelight strained the eyesight, but reading in bed was a habit she couldn't break. When she heard a faint scratchy noise, she took it to be a mouse. She wasn't frightened of mice. She turned a page. But when she saw the door handle slowly turning her insides went into a spasm. She was trapped in a bed jammed up against the wall. She froze.

The door opened. Denis stood on the threshold wearing only a shirt and a sheepish grin. 'Any chance of a little cuddle?' he said.

'*Get out of here*!'

His mouth fell open. He looked stupefied. 'But you let me kiss you . . . you didn't say anything. I naturally thought . . .'

'Then you thought wrong. If you don't leave . . . I'll scream . . . They'll hear next door.'

He couldn't believe she meant it. 'Charlotte, lovey – be reasonable. I'm a man – I can't help how I feel about you. I've tried to fight it. I thought . . . well, I thought you liked me. You always seem so pleased to see me. Couldn't we talk this over . . . ?'

He took her silence for consent and moved nearer to the bed. Then she screamed and threw the nearest thing she had to hand which happened to be her book. It missed him, but the effect was the same. He left.

She didn't sleep very well that night even though she had wedged the chair against the door again. She was awake the instant she heard Denis stir. She didn't get up to cook his breakfast or see him off. He kept coming up and tapping on her door and pleading with her. He grovelled verbally – he was abject with his apologies. He kept saying he didn't know what came over him – just a terrible yearning for her. He said he would put a bolt on the door for her, and when that didn't bring a response, he said he would get someone to come round that morning and do it. She didn't get up until she heard him drive off.

She wouldn't stay, she told herself. She'd just get herself

some breakfast first, then pack and leave. She lingered over her breakfast, the wireless was playing as usual. She always had the wireless on for company though she rarely listened attentively. Fred Gower, from the boat builders down the road, caught her still in her dressing-gown. He made a quick job of fitting a lock to her bedroom door, grinning to himself as he worked. This story will go the rounds of the pubs tonight, she thought.

When Fred had gone she sat down and did some serious thinking. This put a different complexion on things. Could she trust Denis anymore? Last night could have been a sudden aberration, but it could happen again. Supposing one night she forgot to lock her door, and Denis took advantage of it – what then?

A ripple of laughter shook her. Now that she had got over the initial shock, she could see the funny side of it. Denis in his shirt, those awful stick-like hairy legs and that stupid grin, conjured up an indelible image. He wasn't a bad sort really – it was a shame to laugh at him. Another man would have turned nasty and taken her by force, but Denis wasn't like that. In a way, she was very fond of him. And if she left, where would she go? She suddenly realised what the loss of a home and job would mean to her. She'd stay – but only under her own conditions. Mrs Charlotte Hudson. Yes, she liked the sound of that.

When Denis discovered that she wouldn't be twenty-one for another year, he made that an excuse to put off the wedding. She had to tell him then about Lottie and her own illegitimacy.

'Illegitimate off-spring come of age when they are eighteen. I found that out at the registry office, so there's nothing to stop us getting married straight away.'

But even that didn't seem to reassure him. 'I hope we're doing right,' he said. He was thoughtful all evening. 'Is that why you broke off with your mother – because she deceived you?' he asked.

'She lived a lie for sixteen years. She was the cause of my humiliation and suffering. Do you expect me to forgive that!'

He sighed. 'No, I can tell you're not one to forgive readily.'

It was a quiet ceremony at the Southend registry office. Two of the registrar's staff were witnesses. Afterwards they had lunch at the Palace Hotel. 'This place was bombed during the war,' he told her. 'And for a time it was used as a military hospital.'

'Do you think you could keep off the subject of war? After all it *is* our wedding day.' The headlines in the paper that morning read: 'Hindenburg Dies: Hitler is Supreme.'

After lunch, Denis was all for going straight home – even to spoiling themselves with a taxi. But Charlotte, anxious to put off what she knew was inevitable, suggested that a slow walk along the promenade would make it seem like a holiday.

She was outraged at the things that Denis was now licensed to do to her, or rather, did not do to her. She had previously mugged up the act of love in a copy of the *Woman's Home Doctor* she had found among old Mrs Hudson's small stock of books. The suggestion of dim lights and sweet music, endearments and foreplay, left her puzzled as well as feeling cheated. There was nothing playful about their first night, when Denis with a few grunts and one quick painful thrust, suddenly collapsed on top of her. Why do they think this has anything to do with love, she asked herself. It left her feeling not loved, but besmirched. And yet, some faint awareness of something more promising had begun to stir within her, but it came to nothing, for by then, Denis had finished.

Her longing for a child did not come upon her suddenly. It was born of a growing sense of frustration and the conviction that motherhood would compensate for the distasteful ordeal, which more than three years later,

Denis still referred to coyly, as a little bit of a cuddle. Loneliness was her main problem now – loneliness and lack of money. She felt as if life was passing her by and she was trapped here in this tiny house with only the wireless for company. Denis seemed to be working harder than ever, he was away for longer spells, and the pressure on him was beginning to show. He did now look like the old man she had first thought him.

So what had she really got out of this marriage? Well – a different name for a start. The stigma of illegitimacy banished forever. The right to call herself a married woman, and the feel of a gold band on her finger. But the greatest pleasure of all still evaded her. What was the good of having all this if she couldn't flaunt it at Lottie?

If she and Denis lived along Marine Parade, or better still, in one of those big houses in Chalkwell Avenue, and if Denis had been young and successful, she wouldn't have hesitated. But to introduce a husband old enough to be her father – older even than Lottie – and a home as humble as the terraced cottage. No, she couldn't face that.

But if she had a baby. Ah, that would make all the difference. To have someone of her very own to love, and cosset, and plan for. Someone to fill the gap that was missing in her marriage, and perhaps bring her that something that had eluded her nearly all her life – happiness. She wouldn't mind then about not being rich in other things. But there was one important obstacle in the fulfilment of her dream. Denis. He wouldn't even discuss the possibility with her.

The only time he came anywhere near to losing his temper was when she had gone on longer than usual about having a baby.

'No! No . . . no . . . *no*,' he cried, his voice reaching a peak of exasperation. 'I told you right from the beginning that there will be no question of a family. It's not that I've got anything against kids – I like them, but as things are at present, we can't afford them. And I'm too old to start that kind of lark – sleepless nights – making up feeds – wet nappies hanging up to dry all over the place – doctors' bills – school fees . . . there's no end to it . . .'

She stared at him. 'What do you know about sleepless nights and wet nappies . . . you've never had children.'

That foiled him.

'But I know chaps who have . . . I've heard them talk. Nothing but bills – bills – bills . . . They never have a penny to spend on themselves.'

If Denis had one fault above all others it was his meanness. It seemed to have got worse since they were married. The little gifts of chocolate and flowers stopped – even the payment for the secretarial work. Wives were expected to work for nothing, it seemed.

It was in a state of desperation that she decided to take matters into her own hands. She always felt like this just before her period. Tense – her nerves jangling – moody and weepy. It was during this time that her resentment towards Denis increased, and grudges against her mother built up like a vendetta. A baby would free her of that – for nine months at least, and perhaps longer if she was able to breast feed. She convinced herself that a baby was the answer to all her problems, might even make her a better person. It would certainly make her a member of a family. A husband and wife on their own, wasn't a family – any more than a woman with an illegitimate daughter was a family. All right. If Denis wouldn't do anything about it – she would!

She started on a systematic search for his condoms. She knew he used them, though that was another subject he refused to discuss with her. Sometimes, hearing him fiddling under the bedclothes as he fitted one on was the first indication she had that he was feeling amorous.

She found them in one of his drawers, in an opened packet, marked *Wives' Friend*. Wives' friend! . . . that was a laugh. She took them out, one by one, and pierced the ends with a darning needle. That should do the trick, she told herself. But it didn't.

I'm going about this the wrong way, she thought. I ought to show more willing. It takes two to make a baby. Her feelings towards him took an upwards turn. Poor Denis, he hadn't looked at all well lately. He had something on his mind; business matters, he told her. But perhaps it was more than that. She wondered if she should persuade him to see a doctor.

He was a dear old thing, really. Dull and quiet, but reliable. He would bring breakfast up to her when she wasn't feeling well, and he often did the ironing. I must try to be more tolerant towards him, she thought.

The sky had turned a milky colour, and the sun, blood red like an orange, was slipping, imperceptibly, nearer the sea. The days were getting shorter. The tide was full, lapping against the back of the buildings opposite, and alongside the cinder track the little boats of Leigh were bobbing about on their moorings.

When she had first come to live in Old Leigh there had been several large liners anchored in the middle of the estuary, laid up because of the Depression. One by one she had seen them go. There were no liners now – things were getting back to normal. But not quite normal. This time last week the country had been on the brink of war, then Chamberlain had returned from Munich, waving a signed agreement from Hitler. Peace in our time, he promised.

Certainly Old Leigh had never seemed more peaceful than it did on this early autumn afternoon. Time stood still. Fishermen carried baskets of cockles along to the cockle-sheds like their fathers and grandfathers before them, slung from yokes across their shoulders. A Thames barge unloaded timber at Bell Wharf. There was a sound of sawing and hammering from the boat-yard. Charlotte waved to one of the boat-builders as she walked on towards the corner shop.

She was planning a special meal for Denis tonight. Something to tempt his appetite. She had gone to the butchers in Leigh Broadway that morning to buy some best braising steak, then found she was out of mustard. She could buy that and fresh butter locally.

She was going to try cajolery where nagging had failed. There were ways of getting round a man. Denis could be stubborn, but just as easily seduced. All she knew about seduction what was she had seen at the cinema, and she didn't think she was up to that, but at least she could try. Denis must be tired of always seeing her in slacks – she'd change into her brown marocain dress, which fitted her rather tightly, and later on this evening they would walk up to the Billet for a drink.

Just before she reached the shop, she was accosted by a woman. 'I'm sorry to trouble you . . . but could you tell me what's happened to Old Leigh station?'

'Oh, that closed down some years ago – before I came to live here. It's still there – ' Charlotte pointed it out. 'Opposite the jetty, by the level-crossing – can you see it? The new station is in the other direction, near the marshes where all the house-boats are. It's quite a walk from here . . .'

'I know it is,' the woman said ruefully. 'I've just come from there. I suppose you wouldn't know where I could get a cup of tea, would you?'

She was in her late forties or early fifties, dressed in a coat years out of date, and wore a maroon hat shaped like a pancake. She looked so very tired that Charlotte was nearly tempted to invite her back to the house for tea and a rest. Commonsense prevailed. Denis had not been home for four weeks, the longest he had been on the road before, and she couldn't risk having a stranger around when he arrived. She had other plans for this evening.

'There's a café near the jetty that does a nice pot of tea. They don't close until six o'clock,' she said.

'Thank you, miss.' The woman smiled, and walked

on slowly. Charlotte noticed that her ankles were badly swollen.

On the hob the casserole was keeping warm. Potatoes in their jackets were baking in the oven. Plates were heating at the back of the stove. The table was laid for supper. As an extra touch Charlotte had added a vase of purple asters. In the scullery, keeping cool, was a fruit jelly. Poor Denis, she thought, he'll be racking his brains, trying to remember if it's my birthday or some sort of anniversary.

The doorbell rang. He had forgotten his key. Just like him!

On the doorstep was the woman in the pancake hat. Her surprise was as great as Charlotte's. More than surprise – her face registered consternation.

'You,' she said, in a whisper. In the fading-light her skin looked grey. She straightened her shoulders, and raised her voice as if to make an announcement. 'I'd better introduce myself. I'm Mrs Hudson.'

'I don't know whatever came over him. It isn't as if he's ever been a ladies' man. He was always such a good husband and a wonderful father. He always did so much for the boys – was so ambitious for them. None of them were clever enough to win a scholarship to a grammar school like he did, but they've all got on. Dick and Frank are in good jobs – both getting married soon, and Eric has nearly finished his apprenticeship at the engineering works. It's been a bit of a struggle paying young Denny's school fees, but it was worth it. I don't know how Denis could have gone on like this all these years. Deceiving me . . . deceiving you . . . I couldn't believe it at first. But I do now, of course . . .'

The homely, forgiving, uncomplaining voice went on and on. Like the wireless on occasions, it had long since ceased making sense to Charlotte. *All the time he had another wife I knew nothing about. He gave her four children and he wouldn't even give me one!*

'I didn't know of course until his firm told me – then out it all came. They had discovered that he had given up the London office four years ago, but he was still drawing the expenses for it and for a secretary's wages. And then there was the car. His own car – that old Morris. He made out he was using a company car, a much bigger car, more expensive to run – he even made a little bit out of that. "Whatever came over you," I said. "A bigamist – a thief – running two homes. Didn't you ever think you'd be found out?" Guess what he said . . . ?'

The room had turned dark. Charlotte got up and lit the gas, then wished she hadn't. The woman had been an irritating voice before, now she was a person suffering.

'He said he was sick to death of being the bread-winner. A payer of bills – gas bills – electricity bills – doctors' bills – the universal provider, he called himself. He said he earned it – we spent it. When the chance came to have a little bit of fun, he took it. He didn't mean any harm, he said. He tried to please everybody. All the way down here, I've been trying to think what possessed him. I wonder if men go through a difficult age, like women. That could account for it, I suppose. But I still think he shouldn't have done it to a nice girl like you.'

Don't you dare feel sorry for me.

'D'you know, he never told me his mother owned this house. I assumed she was a tenant. Now it's got to be sold along with everything else. The firm says it won't bring charges against him providing he makes restitution. Otherwise he goes to prison . . .'

'Won't he go to prison, anyway – for bigamy?'

'That's why I came to see you – perhaps we could think up something between us. He's going to lose everything as it is. His job – his family – his home. The boys never want to see him again. What about you? He's – he's a broken man . . .'

'I'm not as forgiving as you. You can tell him I never want to see him again, either.'

*

But she did see him just once more, less than a year later. She was living back in Boot Lane by then, in the basement flat Lottie had refurbished for her, and she was on the top deck of a 73 bus going along Park Lane.

Preparations for war were going on everywhere. So much for peace in our time, she thought. She could see sandbags piled against offices, shops and hotels. In Hyde Park, gangs of unemployed men were digging slit trenches. Her mouth went suddenly dry, and her heart lurched sickeningly.

It was Denis. She could see him among the line of unemployed, in his shirt-sleeves, wielding a pick-axe, looking older than she remembered. Her eyes welled with tears.

'Dear God, give me the grace to forgive him,' she begged.

| *Charlotte*
1939–1943

There was nothing phoney about the phoney war in Charlotte's opinion. For her it was seven months of undiluted pleasure. The black-out was a menace, causing, so it was said, more casualties to civilians than enemy action. Yet, even that had its compensations. For the first time, looking up at the night sky, she saw stars shining above London.

At first, war had been fun – a bit of a lark even, for suddenly London was crowded with soldiers. It was exciting to see the different uniforms – those of the Dominions soon mingling with the English, the Welsh and the Scottish units. And the Free Poles who had escaped the invading German armies.

Charlotte was quite bowled over by the charm and courtesy of the Polish officers. They bowed from their hips, and they kissed her hand, and only smiled politely when she showed that she was not prepared to go further than a kiss or two.

In those early days of the war, when danger seemed in abeyance, a young and attractive woman had her pick of escorts. Most evenings during that bitter winter and early spring of 1939–1940 Charlotte found herself hell-bent on a ceaseless round of pleasure, for her need for fun seemed never satisfied. It was as if she couldn't get enough of it to make up for the sterile and empty years she had spent as a so-called wife.

Lottie, for patriotic reasons, had decided to turn the whole of the ground floor of Fosters into a non-profit-making club for the forces, where food and drink was readily available, also an opportunity to dance to the music of a small swing band. The mezzanine floor, still in use as the main restaurant, was left safely in the charge of Monsieur Jacques.

Both Aggie and Jacques thought Lottie was mad to undertake this new venture. They said she would bankrupt herself before the war was over, and though Charlotte too had been against the idea at first, fearing that she might be dragooned into helping, which proved correct, she found it had its advantages. It afforded her more chances of pleasurable, transient friendships, helping to dispel from her mind the image of the broken man she had seen in Hyde Park.

When, in 1938, she returned to Fosters, broken in spirit, and keening like a wounded animal, it had been as an action born of desperation. She had no money, no shelter, nowhere to go. The one idea in her mind at the time was to get away from Old Leigh and escape the nerve-racking risk of facing Denis Hudson again.

She had arrived at Fenchurch Street station still wearing the brown marocain dress she had donned that morning, and over it a lightweight summer jacket. All she carried was a case that contained the things that had come originally from Boot Lane. Anything bought with Denis's money she had left behind.

It was getting dark and it was raining. She stood in a shelter at the station, pondering her next move. There was only one place to go really, and that was Fosters. If she had the money she would have found a cheap rooming house – but she didn't think she was likely to get a bed for two and threepence – all she had on her after she had paid her fare. She had left her post office book at the Old Leigh house, and didn't waste time looking for it. Once she made up her mind to leave, she had made a dash for the station, leaving Mrs Hudson to deal with Denis.

She had no fear that her mother would refuse to take

her in, but she did dread Lottie's forbearance or worse still – her pity. She could do without coals of fire being heaped on her head – her cup of bitterness was already flowing over. She would get no forbearance or compassion from Aggie, quite the reverse – just the sop to her pride that she needed. She could hold her own with Aggie.

The rain fell relentlessly. She was becoming hungrier and colder by the minute. Mark Lane underground station was less than ten minutes away – she'd make a dash for it.

When she got out at Tottenham Court Road, the rain had eased little. The street lamps reflected pools of light on the gleaming pavements, and miniature streams gurgled in the gutters. The rush hour was over, but the pavements seemed as busy as ever. Hurrying legs were all she could see as she walked with her eyes cast down. She was in no hurry. She walked as slowly as she could, putting off the coming encounter at Fosters.

Charing Cross Road too was crowded. It always was at this time of the evening with people on their way to the theatre or cinema, or looking for somewhere to eat. She was so hungry she was nearly tempted to turn into the nearest Lyons or ABC, mindful that this had all happened to her once before. In her mind's eye she kept an image of Fosters with its gaily striped Continental blinds, and the bay trees standing either side of its entrance, and the light from the carriage lamp on the wall, illuminating its shallow step. There was plenty of food to be had at Fosters – nobody ever went hungry there.

Suddenly she was arrested by her reflection in a shop window, highlighted by the sodium lamp behind her. She stopped and stared, aghast at the sight of herself. Her marocain dress had shrunk in the rain, and the front had risen up to her knees, revealing several inches of petticoat. Even worse, her beret looked like a sodden lid from which her hair fell in dripping rats' tails to her shoulders. Let her mother see her like this! She'd rather throw herself off Waterloo Bridge.

She was unaware that a taxi had pulled into the kerb and that a woman alighted, running towards her. She heard her name called on a rising note of excitement, and knew there was now no escape. Lottie had spotted her.

There was no recrimination in Lottie's voice, only gladness. She asked for no explanations and gave none herself though she was in evening dress. She said, smiling through her tears, 'We must get you out of those wet things straight away.' And before she knew it, Charlotte found herself bundled into the waiting taxi.

The driver was instructed to return to Boot Lane. Charlotte made a feeble protest, but it was too late. Lottie was in charge of the situation. 'This is such an incredible coincidence,' she said. 'I just happened to look out of the window – and there you were . . .'

To Charlotte it was no coincidence – just further evidence that God had deserted her. 'You're all dressed up to go somewhere,' she said flatly.

'A farewell party for the *maitre d*' at Glendennings . . . He retires this month. I'll phone and make my excuses. They'll know that your return is far more important to me. . .'

'I'm only staying long enough to get dry.'

Lottie smiled. 'Of course dear, I'm fully aware of that . . .'

Her mother looked no older, Charlotte thought. If anything, younger than she looked the last time she saw her – that disastrous Christmas in 1930. Her gown of oyster satin was cut on the bias, a flattering fashion for one with a youthful figure, and over that she wore a silver fox cape. In her ears were two diamond clips, the first time Charlotte had seen her with earrings. The contrast between her own appearance and that of her mother could not have been more marked. Her own cheap and sodden clothing – her mother's elegance. She felt like

Cinderella after the clock had struck midnight. She felt extremely chastened.

To spare her the ordeal of going through the restaurant, her mother took her by way of the basement door at the back. They picked their way through the flat that had reverted to its former use as storage rooms, and it was just bad luck that the first person they should meet as they reached the top of the stairs, was Aggie. She stopped dead and goggled at them. Charlotte felt her colour rise.

Aggie, though bereft of speech, could use her eyes, and she took in Charlotte's plight in one quick glance. Any minute now, thought Charlotte bitterly, she'll burst into one of her shouts of laughter. She turned to her mother. 'Any chance of a hot bath?'

'Just what I was going to suggest, darling. Your room is waiting for you . . . I've kept it as it was all these years . . .'

She didn't begrudge her mother the note of reproach in her voice, she just didn't want to hear it. She hurried away, knowing that once she left, Aggie would quickly recover her power of speech – bombarding Lottie with questions.

Not only was her room the same as when she left it, but in the wardrobe were all her old clothes, including the blue silk dress which Lottie had repaired. Charlotte snatched it from its hanger, rolled it up, and pushed it out of sight at the back of the wardrobe drawer. She couldn't bear to see it. It represented a period of her life too painful to recall.

The other clothes were useless too. Schoolgirl fashions – hopelessly out of date. But her nightgowns still fitted her – and with them she found the rose-patterned chintz housecoat, a sixteenth birthday present from her mother. She bathed, and showered herself with her mother's 'Evening in Paris' talc, then put on a pink rayon nightie and stepped into the housecoat, zipping it up to her throat. She towelled her hair dry, and because she had had it permed recently, it dried into a bushy frizz. But she felt much better now – more confident to face her mother.

The rain had stopped at last, and for the first time in years she listened to the sounds of London. The constant throb of traffic, the shouts of the newspaper vendors, hooting of impatient drivers, the distant whine of a tram. An unexpected surge of excitement began to stir within her. It was good to be in London again – there was always something happening in London. London would help her forget.

The door opened and Aggie stood on the threshold carrying a tray. They exchanged cautious glances. Charlotte was determined not to be the first to speak. Aggie's expression was wooden.

She slammed down the tray so fiercely the glass of milk spilled over onto the bedside table. From the covered plate came the teasing aroma of roast chicken. 'Here's your supper, and I hope it chokes you,' Aggie said.

'I'll do my best to try not to disappoint you,' Charlotte countered, feeling better by the minute. Roast potatoes, stuffing, bacon rolls and sausages – nothing had been forgotten. She set to with zest, not caring that Aggie was watching.

'I don't know what you bin up to these past eight years but something's for sure – you ain't lost your appetite. I used to see you polish off a meal that would do a navvy credit. Is that why you come back? – For the grub?'

Charlotte sent her a winning smile. 'No, I came back because I couldn't bear to be parted from you any longer, Aggie dear.'

'If I was your Ma, I'd soon wipe that smirk off your face. What you want, my girl, is a damn good hiding . . .'

'Aggie, please . . .' Lottie had appeared unnoticed. She had changed out of her evening dress into the smart black suit in which she always greeted customers. 'Aggie, I came to this place once in a very distressed condition, not knowing which way to turn. You took me in – you and

Maud, and showed me nothing but kindness. Couldn't you do the same for my daughter . . . ?'

'You deserved it, Lottie – she don't. You were grateful for everything what was done for you. She wouldn't know what gratitude was if it jumped up and bit her in the face. She'll be away as soon as she's fed and wangled some money out of you, you mark my words . . . She'll break your heart, Lottie . . .'

'It's a funny thing about broken hearts . . . they mend. Did you know that? My heart has been broken many a time, but it still goes on functioning.' Lottie smiled, a little tearfully. 'Be charitable for old times' sake, please, Aggie. You worshipped her when she was tiny. Nothing was too good for her then, don't you remember?'

'I needed my head examining . . .' Aggie took up the tray, and looked at the empty plate, then at Charlotte. 'Well, I hope you're feeling more human now you've got that lot inside you. You looked like a drowned rat when you come in.' The remark was a clumsy attempt at an olive branch, but Charlotte ignored her, glancing covertly at her mother instead.

So now they were alone together and she must somehow make it plain that she had no intention of staying. A day or two perhaps until she had found a job, but then she would be on her way again. She was determined not to reveal anything concerning Denis. If her mother questioned her she would parry with half-truths.

Lottie paced the room, her fingers interlocking nervously, trying, Charlotte thought, to find the words for the most obvious question. At last it came, but only after difficulty; 'Charlotte . . . are you in trouble?'

'If you mean am I skint, or out of a job and nowhere to go . . . yes, I'm in trouble.'

'I didn't mean that at all – and all that nonsense is just bravado. You are none of those things . . .' Lottie was beginning to lose patience, which gave Charlotte greater courage. She could deal better with an angry mother than a forgiving one.

'You mean — am I pregnant? The answer is no.'

Lottie's relief was palpable. 'But there is a man . . .'

'Was a man, mother. Was. But it's all over now — kaput — finis — finito . . . and I never want to talk about him again. Understood?'

'He must have hurt you very badly.'

Charlotte's lips were clamped together, her chest heaving. Lottie sat down on the bed beside her, but had the sense not to touch her. How she behaved now made all the difference between Charlotte staying or leaving.

'Anytime you feel like confiding in me, I'll be here ready to listen. But if you want to keep things to yourself, I'll respect your privacy. Everyone has a right to privacy. It's not your past I want to talk about, Charlotte, it's your future. You talk about finding a job . . . You don't have to look far. I'm desperately in need of an assistant who will double up as my secretary. The girls I have interviewed so far have all turned the job down because of the hours. I can't promise set hours. I might want someone here in the evening when the restaurant is at its busiest — or weekends and bank holidays. You know Fosters' watchword has always been: "We never close". That is stretching the truth a little, but it's near enough.' Lottie paused. Her hands were still now . . . She looked more relaxed.

'If you stay on and help me, I'll pay you well. That isn't a bribe. I would pay the same to anyone who could do the job. But with you, there would be an extra incentive. I'd do up the old basement flat for you. I always intended to when you left school. I'll have it completely refurbished, and you can choose your own colour scheme. You'll have your own key — your own front door — all the privacy that you could possibly need . . . What do you say . . . ?'

What could she say to that but yes, and yet she hesitated. Supposing Lottie went back on her word and in an insidious way tried to worm out of her just what had happened during the intervening years? But she had never known Lottie go back on her word.

'Charlotte, listen . . . A wise old woman once told me, when I was in much the same situation as you are now, that I knew which side my bread was buttered on. I did too, and I chose to stay on here. I think you too know which side your bread is buttered . . . Be honest.'

Charlotte knew her feelings towards her mother hadn't altered basically, but they did shift now into a slightly warmer zone. When Lottie squeezed her hand she squeezed it back, then she buried her head in her mother's shoulder and began to weep.

In the spring of 1940, Charlotte's shaky, uncertain, unreal, fun-loving time came to a sudden halt. War started in earnest.

On 9th April came the shattering news that Germany had invaded two neutral countries, Denmark and Norway. Hardly had this outrage registered on the stunned British public, before more shattering events followed. German Panzer divisions steam-rolled their way through Holland and Belgium, by-passed the heavily defended Maginot Line, and headed for the Channel ports. A new word was on everyone's lips. Blitzkrieg.

One evening Charlotte sat in the cinema and watched, transfixed, as the horrors of total war unfolded before her eyes. This was not one of Hollywood's recreated stories of the 1914–1918 war which she had watched so many times in the '30s. These straggling lines of refugees, the elderly, the sick, the children – people pushing old prams and handcarts containing all their worldly possessions, fleeing from the invading army as planes swooped down and strafed them. This was no film script being played out by actors. This was real. The drama and death she saw up there on the screen was really happening. And it was happening now.

The glorious cloudless days of May became nightmares of speculation. Rumours circulated. Lord Haw Haw was in his element crowing over the victories of his adopted country. Lottie refused to listen to him, but Aggie sat glued to the wireless every time he was on the air.

'You're just as much a traitor as he is, believing all he says,' stormed Charlotte.

Aggie was quick to defend herself. Being called a traitor by Charlotte of all people, stung her to the quick. 'You don't think I get taken in, do you! I've got two young nephews in the BEF, and I want to know what's happening to them. Haw Haw always gives the names of British soldiers what's been killed or taken prisoner. If you don't want to listen, just shove off and close the door after you.'

That evening, at the cinema, Charlotte saw on the newsreel the start of the evacuation of the British Expeditionary Force from Dunkirk. Those same eager young troops who had landed in France in 1939, confidently singing 'We're gonna hang out the washing on the Siegfried Line'. Tears stung her eyes as she watched them straggling in the water, waiting in line to be picked up by the flotilla of little boats who had gone to their rescue.

It took her mind back to the little boats of Southend and Westcliff and Leigh-on-Sea. The pleasure boats – the sixpenny trips on the Skylark type craft – the private cruisers and motor boats – the barges and cockle bawlies that used to unload at Bell Wharf in the old town. From the coastal regions of the East and South came the little boats, playing their part in the evacuation of the beleaguered forces.

She came out of the cinema that night resolved to offer her services to her country. If she were a man she would fight. She came from a long line of fighters. Her father was a war hero – her uncle had died from injuries received in battle. Her grandfather had been at Khartoum. Generations of Massinghams had fought for their country. In the past she had visited Somerset House and had written to the Records Office at Norwich and from these sources had discovered that a Massynghame had taken part in the Crusades. With illustrious ancestors like that, how could she not now play her part?

First she applied to join the WRNS, but found that the WRNS were only accepting recruits who had fathers or brothers serving in the Royal Navy. Next she tried the WRAFs but the only opening was in the cookhouse, and working in a cookhouse wasn't her idea of fighting. So it would have to be the ATS, which was as it should be. The Massinghams had all been army men.

The date of her medical was fixed for Monday, 17th June, which turned out to be the day that France surrendered. The evacuation from Dunkirk was over. Paris had been captured on the 14th. She felt it a bitter twist of fate that her date with the medical board should fall on the same day as their ally's capitulation. Later, she saw it as a bad omen.

She met the postman as she was leaving to go to her appointment. 'We're all on our Jack Jones, now,' he said cheerfully. She resented his cheerfulness. Her own mood was one of defiance, but she saw nothing to feel cheerful about. In her diary on that day she had written with bravado, 'Well, the worst has happened, France has surrendered. I wonder what will happen now? Churchill had offered us nothing but blood, toil, tears and sweat – but also victory. And we will have victory – I know we will . . .'

Her next entry was far less emotional – very muted. 'I've been turned down for the ATS – I didn't pass the medical. All because I had rheumatic fever when I was a child. How was it I caught rheumatic fever? Why didn't my mother take better care of me? Too busy with her own affairs, I suppose . . . as she always is.'

Was it then the old antagonism, never quite stilled, began to rise again? she wondered. And yet, when the blitz started in September, she felt closer towards her mother than at any time since she was a child. Everybody was everybody else's friend in that time of trouble. Living under the threat of constant death made a common bond between them.

Lottie, preparing for this emergency, had had the cellar strengthened and made into an air-raid shelter, stocking it with emergency rations. Now, for seventy-six consecutive nights it was filled with a motley crowd of shelterers. Members of the armed forces, diners from the restaurant, living-in staff, and any luckless bystander who had been caught out in the street when the air-raid warning sounded. Often a party spirit prevailed, and usually entertainment. The band would play, and though there was no room for dancing, there was nothing to stop them singing, which they did with gusto, and the most popular songs were those of the first war – the second not having produced any memorable ditties, so far. The din they raised almost drowned out the sound of the ack-ack guns – only the whine of a falling bomb or the crump as it landed could silence them. There would be a brief hush – then the merriment would start again.

'I have left a copy of *The Times* in my office,' said Lottie. Her eyes had a strained, almost defeated look in them. She's feeling the pressure of overwork, Charlotte thought. With Germany's invasion of Russia in 1941, Britain had had a much needed respite from heavy bombardment – and the long sleepless nights for Londoners had practically ceased. But work at the canteen had multiplied. By early 1943 it was 'discovered' by the Americans.

Even against the distinctive uniforms of the Free Forces, the red pom-poms of French sailors and the jaunty headwear of the Polish officers, the GIs stood out as impressive figures. Charlotte eyed them with suspicion. Had they come as Allies, or to boast that they had come to win the war for the Brits as they did the last time? They looked so smart and so well-fed that she resented their very appearance. Her countrymen by contrast, looked shabby in their rough, ill-fitting, khaki battledress.

The GIs seemed to have more of everything. Money . . .

food . . . cigarettes . . . and girls. Especially girls. They were as generous with their money as they were with gifts, and they seemed to have access to a constant supply of nylon stockings, a luxury that Charlotte had not yet encountered. And had no wish to if obtaining a pair meant doing a GI a favour, as she had been told.

'Why should I want to see *The Times*?' she asked suspiciously.

'There's an announcement – in the personal columns – that might be of interest to you.' Lottie tucked a strand of loose hair back in place. Though it was now loosely sprinkled with grey, it was as long and thick as ever. And at forty-eight, her figure still retained its girlish slimness.

Wondering how anything in the personal columns of a newspaper could have any possible significance for her, Charlotte made her way to the back of Fosters and thence to the office. There, on top of the weighty pile of government directives, and forms from the Ministries of Food and Fuel that were awaiting her attention, was a current copy of *The Times*. She picked it up, and in the column under Deaths, she saw the entry Lottie had marked.

'Massingham. Sir Joseph Massingham, Bart., M.C. of Nairobi, Kenya. On June 28th, after a short illness. Age 54.'

Nothing more. No mention of his links with Norfolk, or Thornmere Hall. Her father. The man she had, as a schoolgirl, fantasised into an heroic figure. A man who was no more than a name to her, and who had no idea of her existence. The pent-up dreams and hopes of her girlhood, never quite extinguished, suddenly turned sour. She felt cheated.

It was another example of Lottie failing her. Lottie would never discuss the man who, she claimed, had raped her. She had been ready to talk about Henry, but the slightest mention of his brother would silence her. She must have known of Joseph's whereabouts – whether he had married? Presumably not, or there would have been a mention of a widow. But were there children? Perhaps he had fathered other bastards, and somewhere out there in East Africa there could be a litter of half-brothers and half-sisters. Her longing for a family had never left her. She slumped down at the desk and cradled her head in her arms, giving way to a rush of pity for herself and an excess of rancour towards her mother.

Aggie came in and caught her.

'What's up with you?'

'Oh nothing, just a headache . . .'

'That all! That's all right then.' Charlotte knew she had long ago forfeited any feelings Aggie once had towards her. In front of Lottie they kept up a pretence of tolerance towards each other, but when alone it was a different matter. 'I came in to see if your mum was here. If she asks for me tell her I've just popped down to Stratford to see me Cousin Hilda. She phoned to say she's got some clothing coupons for us.' Aggie's family had many tentacles, spread over most of the sub-divisions of East London, and between them they ran a small black market in clothing coupons. When children were plentiful, as in their case, there were always clothing coupons for sale. The current rate was a shilling each.

Charlotte disapproved of this until such time as she needed a new coat or pair of shoes, then she stifled her conscience. But now, not even clothing coupons could rouse her interest. 'I'll tell her,' she said listlessly. 'I was just on my way to find her, anyway . . .'

Lottie, unwittingly, had borrowed some of Maud's old habits. She, too, enjoyed entertaining some favoured visitor to an aperitif in her sitting-room. But there was no question of slipping up the back stairs to keep a rendezvous in one of the little rooms afterwards. Those days had long ago passed into history, and most of the rooms had vanished too, incorporated into the mezzanine floor. Some still remained, part of the banqueting suite on the top floor.

Charlotte, entering the sitting-room hurriedly, stopped

dead on the threshold feeling as if in her memory she had suddenly been caught in a time-warp. She had a fleeting vision of Maud, a stout figure in black taffeta, holding a glass of port, and chatting amicably to a man sitting opposite. Charlotte, as a toddler, had hesitated in the doorway as she was doing now, nonplussed at the sight of a stranger. He had turned pale glassy eyes upon her, holding out a piece of chocolate as bait. She shuddered and the image shattered, and it was Lottie, not Maud, smiling at her and beckoning, and the man sitting opposite was thin and lanky, not short and rotund. At the sight of Charlotte, Lottie's visitor rose lazily to his feet.

'I'm sorry,' she said awkwardly, looking from him to her mother. 'I didn't know you had someone with you.'

'This is my daughter Charlotte, the one I was telling you about,' said Lottie eagerly. 'Charlotte – this is Lieutenant Miller of the United States Army Airforce. I've discovered that he is stationed in Norfolk, quite near to where I used to live, and he's been bringing me up to date with the latest news from Thornmere . . .'

Charlotte gave the barest acknowledgement that good manners allowed. 'I wanted to speak to you in private,' she said pointedly. 'It *is* rather urgent . . .'

The tall American ambled to the door. 'I'll leave you two to talk then.' His tone was good-humoured. 'Don't worry, ma'am, I'll see myself out. We'll finish our chat later . . . I'm sure to be around . . .'

'That was very rude. You practically asked him to leave,' said Lottie.

'I wanted to speak to you, urgently. Anyway, why should you kowtow to a bally American? They have a big enough opinion of themselves without giving them any encouragement. You seem to have time for everybody but me. Whenever I want to talk to you, you're always busy talking to someone else . . .'

Lottie sighed and sat down again. 'This is not going to be another one of your outbursts, is it?'

'I don't know what you mean by outbursts. I just want a few straight answers to questions, that's all. Why won't you talk about my father? Why did you let me read about his death in *The Times* instead of telling me, yourself? Why couldn't we have discussed it . . .'

'The last time I tried to discuss your father with you, there were painful consequences. Remember? I couldn't go through all that again. Charlotte, I do wish you would try to understand why it's not easy for me to mention your father's name.'

'And I wish you would understand how desperate I am to know more about him. He is – was – my flesh and blood. I've only got your word for what he was like, and that's probably biased. Isn't there one good thing you can bring yourself to say about him?'

She saw Lottie's hands come together in an unintentional gesture of supplication, but she steeled herself against pity. 'Haven't you heard anything of him since you left Thornmere?'

'Nothing that I haven't already told you. What more do you want of me . . . ?'

'I want to know why he didn't come back to live at Thornmere Hall when he inherited the estate, and whether he was married or had children?'

Lottie shrugged. 'I wouldn't know . . .'

'And don't care either, I can tell that.' Charlotte slumped down in the chair which the American had just vacated. It was still warm from his body. 'I always meant to get in touch with my father – I would have done so if circumstances had been different – now it's too late. Isn't there anyone else in his family who would talk to me?'

Lottie gave her a steady look, then shook her head. 'There were some maiden aunts living in Cheltenham, I believe, but they couldn't still be alive now. You're chasing after rainbows, Charlotte . . .'

In the open doorway, Charlotte had one last thing to say. 'And please don't discuss me or my business with any Tom, Dick or Harry who happens to pop in to have a drink with you. You like to keep certain things in your life private. Then please respect my privacy too. I don't like to think I'm a topic for gossip among these Yankees . . .'

He was leaning against the wall in the hallway, one leg crossed over the other. He must have heard every word that had passed between herself and her mother. He grinned. 'I said I would hang around.'

She eyed him stonily. 'Eavesdropping, you mean.'

He straightened up. 'As you didn't bother to close the door, I decided what you had to say couldn't be all that private. I waited because I hadn't finished what I was telling your mother . . .'

The hallway was narrow and he was in her way. 'May I pass, please,' she said, excessively polite.

'As you wish, ma'am, but there's one thing I'd like to get straight with you first. I'm no Yankee — I come from the South.'

She walked away with all the hauteur she could muster. All Americans were Yankees as far as she was concerned. Damn Yankee, she thought. Damn Yankee, she kept saying to herself all the way down to her own apartment. She could be private here. Her pent up tears came readily. She sat on the bed and cried noisily like a child. She wished she had the guts to run away again. But another attempt would mean cutting through such a mound of red tape, and would the effort be worth it? There would be all the business of re-registering her ration books and clothing coupons and identity card. Nobody could enjoy anonymity anymore. Damn and blast the bloody war.

The letter arrived a week later. She looked at it puzzled. It had a Norfolk postmark and the handwriting was unfamiliar. When she opened it she found it was signed, Jefferson Miller. I don't believe this, she thought, but she read it eagerly all the same.

215

'Dear Miss Foster,

At your mother's request, I have been making enquiries about your father's family. I found, during my own enquiries into my English forebears, that the fountainhead of knowledge is usually the parish priest. In this case it is a Rev Mr Francis Thomas who's been vicar of Thornmere since the 1920s. He's a bit of a local historian with a remarkable memory, and more to the point, he's writing a history of the Massingham family, so he had all the information I wanted at his fingertips. We spent a very enjoyable evening together and he brought out some parish records for me to see and advised me that if I wanted further information to apply to the Records Office in Norwich. That hasn't been necessary. I have listed below the relevant details.

Joseph Massingham inherited the Thornmere estate in 1922. He was then running a coffee plantation in the highlands near Nairobi and was heavily in debt. He had no wish to remain in England as all his interests were centred in Africa, so only stayed long enough to sell off the estate, intending to invest what he received for it, in his African farm. As he died penniless, the investment can hardly be said to be successful . . . The title lapsed with him as he left no heir . . .'

Who asked for his comments, thought Charlotte furiously. Why can't he keep his opinions to himself! She screwed up the letter and threw it in the waste-paper basket, then retrieved it, smoothed it out, and continued reading. 'Will you please tell your mother that I will be with her again next weekend, if all goes well.'

If all goes well – what did that mean? Then she reminded herself of the strategic bombing of cities and dockyards and industrial areas of Germany, being waged by the RAF in conjunction with USAAF 2nd Division.

That Lieutenant Miller was a navigator in one of the large four-engined bombers known as Liberators . . . that losses were high, especially among the American bombers who were responsible for the daylight raids. A chilling sensation came over her, and goose-pimples rose on her arms. All the same, he had no right to go saying such things about her family, and Lottie had no right to involve him in their private affairs . . . The best thing to do was to write him a polite letter of acknowledgement and then forget him.

All must have gone well with him this time, for he was back again a week later, on another of his forty-eight hour leaves, and this time laden with presents. A bottle of perfume for Lottie, cigarettes for Aggie, and nylons for herself. She had a struggle with her principles before accepting the stockings, which she was certain he was aware of, catching the sardonic glimmer in his eyes as he passed them over to her. But there was no point in cutting off her nose to spite her face. Even decent rayon stockings were hard to come by, and she'd rather stain her legs than wear lisle which made even the shapeliest legs look like beer bottles.

On another quick visit he dumped a large packet in Aggie's lap. Her green eyes bulged. 'Blimey! – cigarettes – all for me? Enough here to last me 'til the war's over . . .' She tore greedily at the wrappings, then nearly fell off her chair with uncontrollable laughter. It wasn't cigarettes at all – it was a neatly stacked pile of toilet rolls, pale pink in colour and as soft as tissue paper.

'That's the funniest present I ever had give me in my life. Not that it ain't welcome, mind you, but what made you think of it? Is it a joke?'

'It's no joke. I took pity on you. I don't know how you Brits manage with that greaseproof type toilet-paper you use over here . . .'

'Because we're not cissies like you lot over there,' retorted Aggie, still chortling. 'Here, that reminds me . . .

Did I ever tell you about the time Lottie took me to tea at Buzzards? You know, that posh caff in Regent Street ... well, afterwards, when we went to the Ladies ...'

'I'm sure Lieutenant Miller doesn't want to hear about that now,' interceded Lottie tactfully, but the lieutenant wagged an admonishing finger at her.

'I certainly do, ma'am. Go on, Aggie, tell me what happened.'

Charlotte slipped away unnoticed. Aggie's stories made her toes curl under, and the more appreciative her audience, the more embroidered they became. Charlotte couldn't understand why the quiet American encouraged her, unless he was fascinated by her Cockney accent. He wasn't a man much given to laughter, though he had a wry sense of humour which seemed to keep him in a constant state of silent amusement. It was a cliché to think of him and Lottie and Aggie getting on like a house on fire, but they did, and she, Charlotte, was the odd one out. His scrupulous politeness towards her, she felt, was only put on for Lottie's sake. Why should she care that he thought of her as some kind of prude – a wet blanket even? Damn Yankee!

Charlotte never felt so much on the fringe of things as when her mother and Jefferson Miller were discussing Norfolk. He was stationed at a camp midway between Beckton Market and Thornmere, on what, between the wars, had been a private Air Club. Listening to him, Lottie would grow animated, her pleasure lighting up her smile and eyes, and Charlotte began to suspect that she was falling a little in love with the charm and good looks of the American. There was fifteen years difference between them, but Lottie, when glowing, as she always was in his company, looked much younger. And I look older, thought Charlotte, as she stared morosely at her reflection in her wardrobe mirror one sunny day in July.

She felt that the best of her youth had been squandered

on a phoney marriage, and the war had eaten away what was left of it. Would the war ever be over so that there could be an end to killing, and rationing, and the black-out?

She thought back to last November and the glorious victory at El Alamein. The church bells all over Britain rang out, not to warn of an invasion, but to celebrate a victory. Churchill warned against undue optimism: 'Now this is not the end. It is not even the beginning of the end. But it is, perhaps, the end of the beginning.'

Promises – promises – and time was running out for her. In another month she would be twenty-nine. Another year – thirty, and she had never yet known what it was to be in love or to know real sexual fulfilment. But now she was beginning to understand what it meant to be physically attracted to someone, but whether that had anything to do with love, she wasn't qualified to judge.

And what did he see everytime he looked at her? A discontented and frustrated woman? How did she compare with the girls he had left behind in his own country? In her unsightly hose (the Americans were great ones for legs and tits she had been told. Her legs were good, but her tits were practically non-existent) and Utility clothes? Actually, the Utility dress she had on at present wasn't all that bad, and certainly value for money, which non-utility clothes were not. It conformed to regulations in that the skirt had no more than two pleats and the sleeves were narrow, but she had dressed it up with a belt she had got from a secondhand shop, which after careful washing with some of her hoarded soap flakes, had blossomed out into Oriental colours. And a pre-war silk scarf worn as a cravat was a nice touch, she thought, as she preened at her reflection in the wardrobe mirror. The nylons made all the difference to her appearance, but who was there to show them off to – who was there to care how she looked? Oh, what the hell! There were plenty of men out there ready to give her a good time.

What was stopping her – her scruples? Fat lot of comfort they were.

'You look as if you have just made up your mind to give someone a sock in the jaw. I hope it isn't intended for me . . . ?'

Charlotte stopped short, caught unawares by the sight of his lanky figure leaning over the balustrade. He looked so young – so jaunty with his hat pushed to the back of his head. He was a good deal older than the average age of a bomber crew, but now he looked just a boy. She blushed like an adolescent. 'I didn't see you there. A – actually, I was just going for a walk. I'm wearing your nylons – ' such a stupid remark, but the sight of him had dried up all inspiration.

'So I noticed. It's taken you long enough to make up your mind. Would you object if I join the nylons in a walk with you, or have you got a date already?'

She hated to admit that she had not, but on the other hand . . . 'I wasn't doing anything in particular.'

'Then as it's such a fine afternoon, what about a walk in the park and tea somewhere? I don't have to catch a train until around seven . . .'

Hyde Park was a popular venue for tired war workers, trysting couples, foreign servicemen. There were still a few nannies who had not been evacuated with their charges, and young officers on leave, cantering along Rotten Row. Except for the barrage balloons speckling the sky above, and uniforms thick on the ground, this quiet corner of the park could have been a scene from pre-war days.

They had walked from Kensington Gardens, alongside the Serpentine, and were now in a leafy spot near Marble Arch. They had been lucky enough to find two unoccupied deck chairs quite near to a small herd of grazing sheep.

Charlotte closed her eyes, listening to what could have been sounds of the deep countryside. The rustling of leaves and cooing of pigeons, and the gentle pull on short summer grass as the sheep justified their existence – growing wool and releasing human grass-cutters for war service. But when she opened her eyes again she stared straight at a public air-raid shelter, and there came unbidden an instant image of a line of unemployed men digging trenches.

She turned her head and found Jefferson staring at her. His eyes were not dark as she had once thought, but such a deep shade of blue that they looked black from a distance. 'That was a funny expression that crossed your face just then,' he queried. 'You were thinking of something unpleasant, I guess. Something you didn't want to remember.'

'I didn't, but unfortunately, we can't always control our memories. It would be much more comfortable if we could.'

He whistled reflectively to himself. 'Well now, this seems the right time to bring up why I lay in wait for you at the top of your stairs. Didn't you wonder why?'

'It wasn't to admire the nylons?' She felt confident enough to rib him a little.

He gave one of his slow smiles. 'There was that too, of course. But I'd just been talking to your mother and she was telling me about a time in your life that is a closed book to her. She said she thought some man had tricked you, caused you a great deal of pain and unhappiness – that you carried hidden scars . . .'

'She actually used those words?'

'Yep, ma'am. Scars that made you very moody at times . . .' His voice petered off. His eyes moved from her to the figure of a pregnant girl in a crimson dress walking hand in hand with a British naval rating. Their faces told of a shared and silent despair, and he guessed that a parting was imminent.

Charlotte was watching the couple too. She thought: Well, at least she is carrying his child. She's got that to see her through if he doesn't come back. She wondered if the 'hidden scars' might not have healed by now if she had had a child of her own to love.

Jefferson was saying, 'I know what it's like to carry scars, and the only good thing I can say about them is that they fade in time. I've been through a broken marriage – some time ago now, before the war. She was the girl next door, and we married too young. We remained good friends – it was all very civilised. She married again and now has two fine boys who call me uncle, which is fine for me – makes me feel one of the family. What about you? Would it help to talk about it – might get rid of that chip on your shoulder. Sometimes it is easier to talk to a stranger than to someone closely related.'

'Do you think I have a chip on my shoulder?'

'A mighty big one, honey.'

They sat talking until the shadows of the trees crept up to their feet, then Jeff looked at his watch and gave an exclamation. 'Holy mackerel. I've got half an hour to catch my train. D'you think I'll make it?'

'If we're lucky enough to find a taxi . . .'

They had five minutes to spare at Liverpool Street. Charlotte ran with him to the platform. 'You've been up and down on this line so often you must know the route by heart . . .'

'I'm on speaking terms with every bend in the track.' Black smoke belched from the engine, and hung like a pall above their heads. He opened the door of the nearest carriage and jumped in. The whistle blew, he leant out of the window, put his hands on her shoulders and kissed her full on the lips. 'Next time we meet we won't wallow in the past as we have this afternoon, we'll just enjoy the present . . .'

'Make it soon,' she begged.

'Do you know why making love to you is such a pleasure,' he said. 'Because you enjoy it so. And you also thank me. I've never been thanked before. You, my dear, are a shameless hussy . . .' One of the expressions he had filched from Aggie.

Charlotte snuggled closer to him. 'I love being a hussy with you. You make it such fun.'

'You set great store on having fun, don't you.' He traced her eyebrows, her nose, her mouth with his finger. 'You take all the fun you can, you hear. God knows, these days, it doesn't last long.'

They lay, their limbs entwined, late one Sunday morning in the bed in Charlotte's basement. It was a four-by-six divan and Jeff's feet stuck out at the bottom. Charlotte wriggled down until her feet were on the same level with his, then compared them. Hers were only half the size. She giggled, feeling extraordinarily young – she had shed years since Jeff became her lover.

The wireless was playing softly in the background. They weren't listening consciously, but suddenly both became aware at the same time of what the announcer was saying: 'The RAF by night and the US Airforce by day have poured more than ten thousand tons of bombs on Hamburg in the past eight days. Seven square miles of Germany's second city have been wiped out. A greater weight of bombs has fallen on Hamburg in this period than during the whole of the 1940–41 blitz . . .'

'Jesus Christ,' said Jeff, leaping out of bed and reaching for his clothes. 'They don't have to remind us . . .'

'You were only obeying orders . . .'

'Yes, but it's bloody awful all the same.'

She sympathised with him. She didn't rejoice either when she read of the German air-raid casualties, knowing what it was like to live through an enemy bombardment. She didn't mind how many top-ranking Nazis were splattered to death – but the innocent and the children . . . Her insides shrivelled when she thought of the suffering of little children in Europe, in occupied Russia, in the ghettos.

She longed for a child. She wanted more than anything to feel Jeff's child stirring inside her. Once a respectable marriage was her be-all and end-all in life – but that no longer mattered. Only Jeff mattered, and the child she hoped he would give her. It was Jeff who had suggested marriage. One failure hadn't put him off, he said. He knew that marriage could be good, and marriage to her would be better than good. If it were at all possible he would marry her now, but there were difficulties in the way of American serving men taking foreign wives in wartime.

'But when this war is over, there'll be nothing to stop us marrying then.' He planned to live in England. He was an architect in civil life. 'There'll be plenty of rebuilding to do in this little old country, and if your planners will accept me, I'd like to play a part in it.'

'But won't you be needed back home?'

'There's nobody left to need me now. My mother died giving birth to my kid brother, Dave. He got killed at Pearl Harbor, and Pa passed on last year.' She saw anger, grief and nostalgia warring in his expression. 'But I would like for you to see the sleepy little town where I grew up, and meet the folks there. Perhaps we'll visit on our honeymoon. Afterwards, we'll settle down in this country some place. What do you say to Norfolk? I've become very attached to Norfolk.'

'I'd like that.'

Summer stretched into autumn. Jeff's visits to London were becoming shorter with longer spaces between them. The bombing of enemy cities and heavy industrial centres went on round the clock. In September Italy signed a separate peace with the Allies. Russia advancing along the whole of the Eastern Front had recaptured Kiev. The words Second Front was in everyone's mind if not on their lips.

It was a bright November day with the first hint of winter in the air when Lottie came into the canteen to say that she was wanted on the phone. There was only one person the caller could be. Charlotte ran on winged feet to take it.

'Jeff – I haven't seen you for three weeks. What's going on?'

'Plenty, Charley . . .' He called her by that pet name when he was feeling good. 'I've got seven days' leave, but there's a proviso – I've got to stay within reach of the base. Could you join me up here in Norwich? There's a hotel near the cathedral – very romantic, all crooked walls and oak-beams and cobwebs – the sort of place we Yanks go nuts over . . .' She could hear his teasing laughter coming through the soft sweet drawl that was music to her ears. 'Could Lottie spare you for a week?'

'She'll jolly well have to.'

A whole week – not a snatched weekend pass or a day visit – but seven whole days with him in Norwich. It was a dream come true. Lottie's delight equalled hers, except that Lottie's was tinged with wistfulness.

'I expect Norwich has changed since my day,' she said. 'But send me a picture card all the same.' She lent Charlotte an embroidered blouse made out of parachute silk which Jacques, who worked a barter system on the side, had obtained for her, and Aggie, all grievances buried, gave her ten clothing coupons.

'Oh Aggie, you shouldn't . . .'

'Go on, don't be silly, take them. There was a time, years ago, when I was always buying you pretty things to wear. Well, these'll have to do instead . . .'

Even Aggie's homely, heavily made-up face, assumed for Charlotte, in her present mood of ecstasy, a picture of heavenly benevolence. She kissed her, and tried not to cough when a sudden strong whiff of perfume caught her unawares.

Jeff was waiting for her on Thorpe station. 'What's in this?' He took her case, and the paper carrier bag she'd been holding.

'Mother made you an apple pie. She thinks you're deprived of home cooking . . . It's hearing that song on the wireless all the time: "Oh Ma, I miss your apple pie . . ." '

Jeff laughed. 'There's one thing for sure, I won't be deprived of her daughter for the next three days . . .'

'Three days! You said a week.'

'Hopefully a week. But one never knows. . . Things are happening, Charlotte, but it's all hush-hush . . .'

Did Jeff mean he might be transferred to another base? To the under-belly of Europe perhaps where the Allies were advancing slowly and bloodily up the boot of Italy? Dear God, please don't send him out of the country. Please keep him here for me . . .

They had their three days of enchantment. Making love at night – exploring the city by day. The weather had changed, the wind was coming from the east. A high slate grey ceiling of unbroken cloud blotted out the stars.

But not even the weather could spoil their delight in each other. Their freedom to roam, to explore – to poke in odd corners of Norwich, to sit on a city bench, Charlotte sheltering in the lee of Jeff's well-protected body, watching as he sketched the tower of a Norman church, or part of the flintwork of the ancient Guildhall. And always the nights to look forward to. She counted them off like jewels in a crown.

And then on the fourth day she spoilt it all by plunging, suddenly, into one of her moods of depression. It started so well too, with Jeff saying he had a pleasant surprise in store for her. He went off soon after breakfast and returned with a car. Not a jeep or an army car, but one of questionable age – and more important . . . a tank full of petrol.

'Wally procured it for us,' he said.

She knew all about Wally. He was the one who could provide at a moment's notice, packets of chocolates, perfume, cigarettes, nylons, blankets, whisky . . . all had found their way to Fosters at some time or the other. 'I wish we had a Wally,' said Aggie once, tittering rudely.

Charlotte had never met Wally but she had seen a

photograph of him, a chubby man, standing as high as Jeff's shoulder, with thin hair and myopic eyes, almost invisible behind thick glasses. Wally, on the fringe of action, but everybody's buddy. If anything was wanted – a pass, an excuse, a remedy, someone's address – and in Jeff's case, a car . . . ask Wally.

'But what is his job exactly?'

'Officially, he's a radio operator – unofficially, our middle man. He's all middle actually, that's why the guys call him Tubby . . .'

Jeff was in one of his jesting moods, when she didn't know whether to take him seriously or not. He put her in the car beside him, tucked a rug around her, and after one or two false starts they headed east, out of the city.

'But where?' asked Charlotte.

'Wait and see,' he said tantalisingly.

They were out in open country, driving through winding lanes, past thickset hedges and grass verges and trees in glorious autumn colours.

'I wish you could have been here in August, before the corn was harvested. Flying low, we would look down on a patchwork of green and gold . . .'

'You're taking me to your camp,' said Charlotte, making a guess.

'Charley, I wish I could – but we'll be going quite near.'

They passed though a hamlet.

'What's that dreadful smell?'

'Hogs – pigs. There're a lot of pigs around here. Every cottager seems to keep one in his garden.'

Charlotte held her handkerchief to her nose. 'How awful. I don't know how anyone can live with that smell.'

'I bet you wouldn't refuse a plate of roast pork and apple sauce . . .'

'Well, now that you come to mention it . . .'

They laughed together. Jeff put his hand on her knee and squeezed it. 'I promise we won't keep pigs when we're married. This is Beckton Market. Did Lottie tell you about Beckton Market?'

'I don't remember.' She looked about her with interest. A few shops, some nice houses, flint cottages, an attractive old Market Cross and a church with a round tower and then more fields, stretching before them, flat and endless.

'I bet it is bleak here in the really cold weather,' she said. 'I wouldn't fancy living in a place like this. But I like Norwich . . .'

But Jeff was not paying attention. He stopped the car and switched off the ignition. 'Listen.'

It was then she heard the noise that had alerted him, the drone of aircraft engines. Her blood ran cold. It always did at the sound of aeroplanes overhead; a sound she always associated with the wail of sirens, the scream of falling bombs.

A flight of four engine bombers was flying over, low enough to be able to distinguish the white star on the underside of the wings and some of the gashes in the fuselage. Liberators with gaps in their formation, limping home 'on a song and a prayer'. If it weren't for the fact that he was on leave, Jeff might have been up there in one of the damaged planes or lying dead in some enemy field. She touched him nervously, and he closed his hand over hers.

'Don't think about it,' he said. 'Remember what we promised each other – to make the most of this time together . . .'

They turned into a lane too narrow for two vehicles to pass each other comfortably, but twice within the space of a few yards, Jeff was obliged to draw in to allow the free access of an army vehicle. Charlotte wondered if he had taken a wrong turning, this lane didn't look as if it were going anywhere, but presently a large house came into sight, and here there were more army trucks and cars parked in the drive and men in khaki coming and going, in and out of the front entrance. The sinister-looking barrels of anti-aircraft guns poked out of the trees.

'This can't be Thornmere Hall,' she said, filled with dread and disbelief.

'Charlotte, I would have spared you this if I could. You should know by now what happens when the army takes over. But don't worry, everything will be put back as it was.'

She doubted it. There were gaps in the elm tree avenue that led from the lodge to the house. Chopped down for fuel, or because they were in the way of the guns? The beautiful avenue, which, according to Lottie, had been Sir Roger's pride and joy. And the famous wrought iron gates – where were they? Requisitioned, along with railings from public parks and private gardens, in the campaign for salvage?

'When did the army take over?' she said, feeling resentful on behalf of the Massinghams.

'My informant told me in 1939.'

'And who was living there then?'

'Some guy called Harker. Made his money in the fourteen-eighteen war, and bought this place in 1922, which he left rather hurriedly when the balloon went up. He lives somewhere in Canada now, I believe. Seen all you want to see? Depressing, isn't it. Never mind, better luck next stop . . .'

She stiffened like a pointer, suddenly realising what he intended. 'Jeff stop – turn the car. I want to go back to Norwich.'

But it was already in sight – the gatehouse – an ugly yellow-brick building, isolated in a uniform landscape. Lottie's birthplace.

A bell on the wall of the house sounded, and seconds later a thin man with rounded shoulders and scanty white hair appeared, and limped towards the level-crossing gates.

'Turn round, and go back,' Charlotte whispered urgently.

'Why? Don't you want to meet with your uncle? That's your Uncle Ted, Charlotte. Your mother's eldest brother.

The rest of her folk have either passed on or emigrated, I discovered. You can't just walk away and ignore him. He's your flesh and blood, it's only right for you to introduce yourself. If you're shy, I'll come with you.'

The gates were open. In the distance they could hear the approaching train, and see its smoke snaking between the trees. While he waited, holding on to a gatepost for support, Ted turned and spat. Charlotte watched the globule of spittle fly through the air and land on a patch of nettles. She shuddered.

That man her uncle! She stared at him. A stranger . . . no collar . . . a shapeless cardigan with one elbow out . . . carpet slippers. A slouching, shabby figure – her flesh and blood? She didn't believe it. She caught the smell of pig from the sty at the end of the garden, she could hear the creature grunting. She held her breath. Nothing – nothing on earth would induce her to identify herself with that setting.

The train rattled past. The fireman lifted a hand in greeting which Ted acknowledged glumly. He turned and limped back to the house, throwing them a glance of suspicion, as if wondering what they were up to by just sitting there, waiting in a parked car.

'Now's your chance. Quick, before he goes in. Go and speak with him – hurry . . .'

'I certainly will not! I won't even accept that he is my uncle. I've only got your word for it. If you don't take me away from here at once, I'll get out of the car and walk. . .'

Jeff leant across and obligingly opened the door for her. 'Right lady, you do just that. I'll go and talk with the old guy instead . . .'

She stumbled up the lane, past the anti-aircraft unit, past two gunners who grinned at her, then looked away when they spotted her tears.

The wind cut through the thin cloth of her coat, but it dried her cheeks. She had left her handkerchief in her handbag and that was still in the car. She sniffed, then used the palms of her hands to wipe away more tears.

Jeff overtook her at the bend of the lane. 'Get in,' he said curtly. They did not speak. All the way back to the hotel they travelled in silence. She had never seen Jeff like this before. She would not have believed that such an easy-going, good-natured man could be so icy. She felt sick in her stomach at the way the day had turned out. She didn't know how to make him understand why she couldn't for the life of her speak to that man he called her uncle, because she didn't rightly know herself.

Their quarrel was bitter. They faced each other across the bed and said things neither of them would have thought possible that morning.

'You're nothing but a prissy little snob. My goodness, it makes me dizzy to think how quickly you would have run to get to him, if he'd been a Massingham . . .'

'You Americans are all the same! Arrogant . . . tactless . . . always so quick to barge in where you're not wanted. I don't suppose you got a thank-you for making yourself known to him, either. I thought not.' She could see she had scored a bull's-eye. 'Why did you have to do it – why didn't you ask me first? You just assumed it was what I wanted, didn't you?'

All at once, the fight went out of him. He gave a futile shrug. 'I guess I thought I was doing you a favour . . . You're right, I should have asked you first . . .' He threw her a wary look as if gauging her temper, then came round the bed towards her. She backed away.

'Charlotte, let's not go on like this – tearing each other to pieces. Let's scratch this morning, and start afresh. Darling, I'm sorry. Jesus . . . do I regret taking you to Thornmere . . .'

But she couldn't forget the word snob. It stuck in her mind like a barb in the flesh. The truth about oneself always hurts and she was mortally hurt. She took recourse in silence. Silence was a weapon she used against Lottie or Aggie, but they knew her well enough to leave her alone until she felt like talking. Jeff didn't. He tried to laugh her out of it, tried cajolery until finally he lapsed into silence himself, utterly baffled.

That afternoon he walked her through the bomb damaged parts of the city, to show her where graceful Georgian buildings or historic Medieval treasures had once stood. 'Demolished during the Baedeker raids on Norwich,' he said. 'We're not in any sort of position to condemn this sort of thing, we're doing plenty of it ourselves right now, and we'll go on doing it until this bloody war is over . . .'

It should have been so easy then to slip her hand into his and to say she was sorry for her pettiness. She *was* sorry, desperately sorry. She wanted him to know how much she loved him, but by now she was just as much a victim of her silence as he was. It had got such a hold on her she didn't know how to break it.

She left him in the bar drinking when she went up to bed. Curled up and lying on the extreme edge with her back to the door, she waited. But he didn't come.

She awoke with a start. Daylight was streaming through the window. A city clock was chiming. Nine o'clock. She must have gone to sleep eventually, but she couldn't remember when. There was no sound of breathing beside her. She turned and saw that Jeff's side of the bed hadn't been slept in. Her heart plummeted, then started racing until she saw the note on the pillow.

'I've been recalled to base. I came up to tell you, but you were sound asleep and I hadn't the heart to disturb you. Darling, wait for me – don't go. I love you . . .'

She sat, with her legs curled under her, on a chintz-covered sofa in the entrance hall where she had an uninterrupted view of the revolving door. When her legs went dead, she straightened them out, but she didn't shift her position. Jeff had asked her to wait, and she was waiting.

She was completely oblivious to the curious glances thrown in her direction. The foyer began to fill – by lunch-time it was crowded. She was obliged to share the sofa with two others, a man and a woman who tried to draw her into conversation, but gave up when they realised by her glassy stare that she was hardly aware of them.

The long empty hours passed. A waiter came to enquire whether there was anything she wanted. Coffee? A drink? A sandwich, perhaps? She shook her head. Everytime she saw someone enter wearing the uniform of an American airman, her heart lurched. Every time the wearer turned out to be a stranger, she died a little. She tried not to think of the gaps in the formation of Liberators they had seen yesterday. The losses must have been heavy. Was that why Jeff had been recalled? Was he over there now on another deadly mission? What was it he had once said to her: 'We can replace the aircraft – replacing the crews takes longer.'

Dear God, send him back to me. Give me this one chance to tell him how sorry I am – how much I love him. I'll go with him to Thornmere. I'll go and see the level-crossing keeper. I'll do anything Jeff wants me to if you'll only bring him safely back. Please God, have pity on me . . .

The door revolved. She saw an American airman cross the floor, then hesitate. A small tubby man with glasses, and the expression of a worried cherub, peering about him short-sightedly. She stood up. There was only one reason Wally had come instead of Jeff. Her mouth opened on a silent scream, and across the floor her eyes met the eyes of the American. He came to her, but even before he was close she saw the tears behind the pebble glasses.

He had gone. Poor Wally. At least he had found relief in tears; 'Jeff was the greatest guy I ever met – he hadn't got an enemy in the world.' She could not cry. Her senses were numb – she felt and acted like an automaton. One day she would be able to take this in – know it was too late to make her peace with Jeff – but not yet. She stood outside herself, as if watching a stranger, pack and order a taxi and catch the train to Liverpool Street, behaving so cool and rationally, that she marvelled at her self-control. Don't let her wake up, she thought, don't let her come back to life again and know the agony.

Mercifully, it was Lottie who opened the door to her. Not Aggie or one of the staff – but Lottie, her mother – the only one she had to turn to now.

'Darling – why didn't you let me know you were coming? Why didn't you phone me?' Lottie's smile faded as she saw Charlotte's pale face go even paler, then as she reeled, she caught her.

Aggie came hurrying up. 'What's happened?'

'Charlotte – she's fainted. Help me with her, Aggie. Get her into my room – it's nearer.'

Charlotte felt herself drifting in and out of consciousness, heard herself babbling Jeff's name, calling out for him. When she fully came to it was to the sound of voices, muted at first, then growing louder. A man's and a woman's. It's Jeff, she thought. I didn't wait, and he's come after me. Then memory came back to her and she wished she was dead, for death was more merciful.

'There's no need to shiver like that. Cover yourself up, woman.' It was young Dr Harvey, not young anymore, but called that to distinguish him from his father, recently retired, who had brought her into the world. Would that I had died then, she thought. She stared at the doctor with burning eyes, hating him for his insensitivity, then remembering that during the blitz his wife had been killed by falling masonry. 'That won't do any good,' she told him dully.

'When did you last eat?'

She couldn't remember – nothing today – very little yesterday – what did it matter?

'While your mother is preparing something for you, I'd like to give you a thorough overhaul. That was more than just a faint you had. When did I last take your blood pressure?'

He examined her chest, percussed her rib-cage, took her blood pressure, pursing his lips over his findings. It crossed her mind that he was being over-zealous, but she was in too deep a depression to wonder why. Why couldn't they just let her die?

He sat on the bed beside her. 'When did you last have a period?'

She stared at him in apathy. 'I don't remember – I'm never very regular. Sometimes, I miss a month. . .'

'Yes, I can tell you're anaemic – we'll have to do something about that.' He got up, squeezed her shoulder, walked to the door, turned and said, 'Chin up, Charlotte, you may find you have quite a lot to live for, after all. Stay in bed for a day or two, then come and see me at the surgery.'

Lottie brought her scrambled eggs and coffee, and thin bread spread with butter – not margarine. She thought the food would choke her, but it didn't. After the first forced mouthful she ate quickly, and soon finished. Lottie sat and watched her. She had been crying, for her eye-lids were red and swollen, but there was something about her expression that negated total sadness. She drew her chair up to the bed and took Charlotte's hand.

'Charlotte – darling – I know things look too black at the moment to make sense to you, but there is hope as well. Dr Harvey thinks you may well be pregnant . . .'

Charlotte stared incredulously. This couldn't be – she would have known. Was it a conspiracy between the doctor and her mother to stop her doing anything silly? Was this a plot between them? Could they – would they play such a trick on her? She looked searchingly into Lottie's eyes and saw something there that made her grasp at hope.

'But he didn't give me that kind of an examination . . .'

'Dr Harvey has dealt with enough expectant mothers to know how to recognise other signs – but he wants you for a more detailed examination as soon as you feel well enough.' Lottie was suddenly off her chair and on her knees beside the bed. 'Oh Charlotte, do you realise what this means – Jeff will still go on living through you – through his baby . . .'

Charlotte had a sudden vision of Jefferson looking at her with a hint of a smile in his dark blue eyes, as he always did before producing a surprise. She began to sob – great gulping sobs washed down by copious tears. The tears came readily enough now – she couldn't stop them. She didn't want to stop them – they were her comfort and her relief. Her safety valve.

Lottie climbed into the bed with her, rocking her in her arms. 'That's what you need, a jolly good howl. Scream if you want to, Charlotte – swear at life and the bloody awful things it can do to us, but don't give in.'

'You never gave in?'

'Sometimes I wanted to – but I always had you. I couldn't have done it without you.'

Charlotte fell silent, shaken every other second by a shuddering sob. Presently, calmer, she said, 'If only I had had the chance to say goodbye to him. I wanted to tell him I didn't mean all those awful things I said. I wanted to tell him how much I loved him . . .'

'He knows, darling.'

'I wish I could believe like that . . .'

'Mother – *mummy* . . .'

'I'm still here, Charlotte.'

'I thought you'd gone. Will you stay here, with me, tonight?'

'Of course, darling. You were too young to remember, but we've slept in this bed together before . . . when you had rheumatic fever. Maud gave up her room to us.'

'There's something else playing on my mind. I don't want my baby born here – not in this – this place.

Promise not to make me have it here. I don't mean I want you to give up the business – but if we could afford to have a house as well . . . somewhere to live . . .'

Lottie held her a little tighter. 'Darling . . . I'll start house-hunting tomorrow.'

It had to be somewhere not too far from central London, yet far enough away to escape the worst of the bombing. Lottie studied a map of Essex and drew a circle around the area that included Epping Forest – the residue of a vast primeval forest, called, not without reason, the lungs of East London. Woodford and Chingford and Loughton – there were plenty of places to choose from, all within easy reach of Boot Lane.

But the task that looked so easy on paper proved more difficult in practice. Charlotte and Lottie went out house-hunting whenever Lottie could be spared from the restaurant. Charlotte knew exactly what she wanted and it wasn't a house on an estate or in a street. She had a morbid fear of neighbours.

'They'll be curious – me all on my own with a baby. They'll think I've lost my husband – they'll want to help. They'd always be dropping in to see how I am. I'll never be alone . . .'

'I don't want you to be alone. I shall be there with you whenever I can, and when I'm not, it would be a great relief to know someone is keeping an eye on you . . .'

'I don't want anybody else at all. I just want to be alone with my baby.'

Dr Harvey said, 'Humour her. She's still suffering from the effects of shock – her mind at the moment is precariously balanced. Once she feels the baby quicken, she'll calm down. And her blood pressure is still too high. This constant house-hunting isn't doing her any good. Apart from being exhausting for her, it's playing havoc with her nerves.'

Aggie took Charlotte's place, and now the outings became fun. Christmas was rapidly approaching and they took advantage at the same time to do a little Christmas shopping.

An agent at Woodford told them about the Wenley house. 'It's a bit isolated – along an unadopted road. There are other properties around, but all in very, very large gardens. It's a mixed road – cottages too. Mind you, the house will need some money spent on it, but it's still a bargain. The owners abandoned it when we had the invasion scare, and have settled now permanently in Torquay. They want to sell, very badly, but are frightened to advertise in case the house gets requisitioned. How they've managed to keep it empty as long as this is a mystery to me, unless they have friends in high places. It would be a good investment. Properties in Wenley will be in great demand once the line from Liverpool Street is electrified. It would've been done before this but for the war.'

'It sounds just what we're looking for,' said Lottie.

The bus took them from Woodford Green to Wenley. They got out at the station, and following the agent's directions, started up the hill, passing a handful of shops which included a post-office stores. Large houses screened by high brick walls or quickthorn hedges passed them by, and then a village green, lined on one side by a group of weatherboarded cottages. Lottie could imagine, in pre-war summers, old ladies in black aprons, serving set teas in their parlours at ninepence a time. Then came a long, low, gabled inn and a church with a wooden steeple, and at last, the turning into Back Lane.

'Blimey,' said Aggie, out of breath. 'How much further?'

'Just half a mile along here,' the agent said. 'We can't miss it. It's called Laburnum Lodge.'

They did miss it – they couldn't see it for the trees. They retraced their steps, and saw a weathervane sticking up between two poplars. The name of the house was painted on the gate.

'It could do with a lick of paint,' said Aggie.

'I expect we'll find that it will need more than a lick of paint inside. It's much too big and it's a long walk from the station, and I'm sick to death of looking over houses – but Aggie, if the roof is still intact – this will have to be it.'

The roof was intact, and really all that needed to be done were some minor repairs, and painting and decoration. The rooms were large and airy, and when they stood in the hallway, a pale December sun, shining through the stained glass panel in the front door, made a mosaic of coloured patterns on the parquet floor.

'I think,' said Lottie, 'this will make a very suitable nest for Charlotte's baby.'

ELEVEN

*Charley
The Early Sixties*

From an early age Charley Foster knew that there was something very distinctive about the place where she had been born. It was an air-raid shelter. Not many girls her age could boast of that, said Aunt Aggie. 'And what was more – not one of your tuppenny 'appenny Anderson shelters either, half buried in the ground, and as sure as fate with two inches of rain water in the bottom.' No, she had been born in an indoor shelter – a Morrison shelter that looked like an enormous steel table with chicken wire sides.

It was a story that Aggie never tired of telling, and one that Charley knew so well, that should Aggie stumble over her words, or forget her place, she could prompt her.

'There we was, listening to a play on the wireless, and eating oranges what your Gran brought back from London that very day when the sireen went.' Siren to Aggie, was always sireen. 'We hadn't had any bad raids since early in the year – the "little blitz", it was called. It wasn't near as bad as the blitz of 1940, but it was bad enough, so we weren't taking any chances. This time, it was only a nuisance raid, but we wasn't to know that, and we all got into the shelter. It was always a bit of a squeeze, what with me and your mother being – but anyway, we managed. We'd hardly got ourselves settled down, before out you p – '

'*Aggie!*'

'All right, Charlotte – keep your hair on. I was only going to say – that along come this bl – blooming big stork and pops you in on us. That was a carry on, I can tell you, as the stork should really have taken you to a nursing home in Woodford. Not that we minded. You were the loveliest little bombshell that had ever landed in our laps. A darling little peach of a baby, you was, and all covered in down. Mind you,' she added, on a more solemn note, 'a month later when the flying bombs started to come over, we were in that shelter nearly every blessed night. We didn't think it so much fun then. But we gave up going to the shelter altogether when the V2s started. What was the point – they were over before anyone knew it. London was getting the brunt of it as usual. Your Gran, she still went up there, back and forth every day. Not getting home till after midnight, up early again the next morning. She never give in once, not even when she'd been up half the night nursing you when you had teething troubles.'

Charlotte put down her book and rose. 'Charley, sweetheart, collect your toys. It's time for bed.'

'But Mummy . . . it's still light outside . . .'

'It's eight o'clock, pet. Hurry, otherwise I won't have time to read to you.'

Charley knew by her mother's tone there was no wheedling an extra half-hour's grace out of her that evening. And she soon discovered the reason why. It always happened – Charlotte's face going stiff with pain, and her voice changing whenever Lottie's name was linked favourably with her own. She had learnt quite early on, that it was most unwise to show she preferred her grandmother to give her a bath, or dress her, or wash her hair, for it always ended up with her mother in tears. There was nothing she hated more than her mother's tears, except perhaps her kisses. 'You are mine – you are mine,' Charlotte would sometimes say in a breathy, desperate voice. 'And she's not going to take you from me. You love me, don't you, darling? Show me how much you love me . . .'

And of course she loved her mother, but she wished

she didn't have to prove it to her so often. Lottie seemed to know she was loved without being told.

When she was about six years old, Charley decided it was time to put Aunt Aggie right about the matter of the stork. The story started as usual. 'It was just before D-Day – you won't know what that means yet, but you will one day. A lovely evening – it kept light until late in them days because of double summer time . . . then suddenly the sireen went. We made a dash for the shelter, getting your mother in first, and was just getting ourselves settled when along comes this whacking great stork . . .'

'Aunt Aggie, storks don't bring babies . . .'

Aggie, stopped in full flow, recovered quickly. 'Oh? I suppose you think the doctor brings them in his little black bag?'

'No – nothing like that – that's baby stuff! Mummies and Daddies rub their botties together, and then the mummy lays an egg in her tummy . . .'

Aggie's eyes, normally like pale, shrivelled gooseberries, grew twice their size. 'And who told you that cock and bull story. . . ?'

'A girl at school – Wendy Simms. Her mummy told her, and mummies don't tell lies . . .'

'Oh, don't they!' said Aggie wrathfully. 'And some mummies haven't got the sense they're born with, trying to explain things what little kids are too young to cotton on to. Come and sit on my lap, precious. That's right, and give poor old Aggie a kiss – it'll help soothe her ruffled feelings.'

Charley liked sitting on Aggie's lap, it was like cuddling up to a bolster. She was soft and cushiony and smelled of violets. She always kept a tin of cachous in her pocket which she said she took to when she gave up smoking. She popped one into Charley's mouth with the instructions to suck, not crunch.

'Aunt Aggie . . .'

'Yes, my poppet?'

'Why aren't there any men in this house? Why haven't

I got a daddy or granddad or uncles or brothers? Why are we all girls? Wendy Simms said her mummy says it's a pecu'lar set-up. What's a pecu'lar set-up? Is it a kind of porch? Wendy Simms' house hasn't got a porch.'

'You tell little Miss Wendy Simms that if I hear any more of what she says or what her precious mother says, I'll come down to the school and box her ears. I didn't go to a posh school or wear a fancy uniform – I only went to the board school and though I didn't learn much, I did learn not to pass remarks about me elders, which is more than little Miss Smarty Pants seems to know. You can tell her that from me, and you can tell her if I ever meet her mother, she'll look like a peculiar set-up herself by the time I've finished with her.'

Charlotte appeared like a whirlwind. She snatched Charley from Aggie's lap and went off at a run with her. Charley affronted at being carried like a baby wriggled to get down, but her mother's grip on her was too strong. Up the stairs, across the hallway, and into Charlotte's bedroom. Only then was she put on her feet.

For the first time in her life Charley felt frightened of her mother. Her face was white and her eyes had a wild, frenzied look in them. She looked, thought Charley, as if she was going to smack her. She, who had never been smacked in her life, backed away.

Charlotte advanced towards her, but not to chastise her daughter. She fell on her knees and clasped the small resisting body to hers, and kissed her with such urgent, desperate kisses that they hurt just as much as being smacked.

'What did I do, Mummy?' she whispered.

'You did nothing, precious. It was Aunt Aggie. Don't talk about your school-friends to her anymore – she doesn't understand them. I didn't hear all she was saying to you, but I heard enough, and I want you to promise me that you won't repeat what she said about Wendy Simms and her mother. She didn't mean it – it's only her funny way, but that sort of talk could cause trouble, and we don't want that.'

Charlotte rose to her feet and lifted Charley up on the bed beside her. She held her close, but gently this time, and began to play with her hair – lifting it strand by strand, and letting it pour through her fingers like water. The feel of it seemed to give her comfort.

'I shouldn't have much to do with Wendy in future,' she suggested. 'Find some other little friend to play with, and if any of the girls at school ask about your father you tell them that he was killed in the war. Your father was a war hero, Charley, and so was my father, and that makes us kind of special. Your father gave his life to help make this country safe for you, and for other little girls like Wendy. He was a fine, good-looking man with chestnut brown hair just like yours and the deepest of deep blue eyes, and he looked so handsome in his uniform. Lieutenant Jefferson Miller, United States Army Air Force. Never forget that, Charley.'

This wasn't the time, thought Charley, to ask why her name was different from her father's.

On 5th April 1955, Churchill resigned as Prime Minister. Charley couldn't understand why this should make her mother cry; it wasn't as if he were dead. Even Lottie seemed rather cast down, and Charley who had been looking forward to this day so much felt rather cross with Sir Winston. Why couldn't he have waited just one more day before announcing his retirement? Her mother had an appointment for a perm, and would be gone about two hours – with luck, perhaps three, which meant that she and Lottie would have all that time together. But one never knew with her mother. Perhaps now she would break her appointment, and stay at home and sit about moping. Anything remotely connected with the war brought on a sudden change of mood.

But the day was not lost, after all. Later that morning, Charlotte drove off in their newly-acquired Ford Popular, telling them not to keep lunch for her, as she might have something at the Copper Kettle. The two left behind exchanged stealthy laughing glances. The lack of constraint made Charley feel quite giddy. She had been away from school with a chesty cough, and Charlotte's mothering had overwhelmed her. At night, she had done her coughing under the blankets so that her mother wouldn't hear and come running in and fuss around her.

But Lottie would appear with a glass of cough mixture mixed with hot water, which soon soothed her throat and stopped the coughing. When Charley asked her how was it she heard the coughing and Charlotte didn't, Lottie said she had her own built-in radar system.

'And now,' said Lottie. 'What shall we do with our time, my pet?'

Anything that she and Lottie did together was enjoyable. The most unimportant occurrence Lottie made into fun. There was no sudden moodiness with Lottie, no storms of tears or frightening silences. No angry outbursts or smothering kisses either. Lottie, thank goodness, was always predictable.

'Could we have a picnic?'

'Why not, and being out of doors will do you good. Let's have a picnic in the garden. I don't want to go far from the phone.'

There was an outside bell, that when it rang sounded like a fire alarm, and acted like a bird scarer. It could be heard from the furthest corner of the garden.

A month ago Aggie had suffered a stroke which had paralysed her right side and impaired her speech. Though she was still in hospital, the outlook was hopeful. Her doctors said there was a good chance of improvement – not a hundred per cent, but enough to get her on her feet again. Lottie visited her every evening and kept vigil by the phone during the day.

'Could I have cheese and apple sandwiches, and could I have coffee instead of milk?'

'I don't know what your mother would say about you missing your milk. What about a milky coffee?'

'That's disgusting, Lottie – that's neither one thing or the other. No, I like coffee the way you have it, without milk or sugar. You can taste the coffee then.'

'Well, I must say, for an eleven-year-old you have very discerning taste-buds,' said Lottie putting on her *maitre d'* voice, as Aggie used to call it. Then she smiled. 'Come along child, help me make the sandwiches, or your mother will be back before we know it.'

They took deck chairs and a picnic table to the back of the house, leaving the conservatory door open so, should the telephone ring, Lottie could make a quick dash indoors. Though the wind was chill, the sun was warm for early April, and in a sheltered spot, seemed even warmer. A friendly blackbird hopped around their feet searching for stray breadcrumbs. Every year, blackbirds nested in the honeysuckle growing against the boundary wall. The daffodils were over, but now in the edges of the flower beds primroses were burgeoning, and tulips would soon be in flower. It was Lottie's favourite time of the year, and though she knew it was far too early yet, she hopefully kept one ear alert for the cuckoo.

Charlie contentedly chewed her sandwiches. Everything tasted better out of doors, she thought. She listened to the birds that sang all around them, trying to distinguish a thrush from a blackbird or a great-tit from a chaffinch. Lottie could tell her, but she wanted to find out for herself.

'Lottie,' she said, airing a thought that often struck her. 'Have I always called you Lottie? The girls at school think it strange I call you by your first name instead of grandma or granny. I can't really think of you as a granny. You don't look old enough.'

'Darling, you flatter me – I'm old enough to be a great-grandmother, let alone a grandmother.'

Charley laughed, clapping her hands together. 'You a great-grandmother! – that sounds so *ancient*. Will you still be called Lottie then, I wonder. But isn't Lottie a hard word for a baby to say? When did I first call you Lottie?'

'I suppose when you were about two.' Lottie put up her hand and pushed a loose strand of hair back into place. The years dissolved. The tall slender girl beside her was again the delightful toddler, her dancing feet beating a rapid tattoo on the parquet flooring. She was never still – she was like a ripple on the water – or wind in the corn – she was constant movement.

She was the sunshine in Lottie's life. She would pretend she was Charley's mother, and she called her 'my child' – and in return, Charley called her mama.

Mama was the first word she had spoken. Mummy, for Charlotte had come a little later. It was her way of distinguishing between them. It was a way that caused Charlotte great pain.

'She will grow up thinking you are her mother. Even now, when we're out together, people are puzzled. They look from one to the other of us, wondering who's the mother.' They were often taken for sisters, a bitter pill for Charlotte to swallow. 'You're trying to take her from me . . . You've come between us since the day she was born.'

'What nonsense, Charlotte. I love her the way I love you. I look upon you as my children.'

'There you are,' Charlotte's voice rose in agitation. 'You admit it. But she is not your child – *she is my child*. You are only her grandmother.'

It was the word only that hurt. Only – such a derogatory word the way Charlotte said it. 'Can't you see,' Lottie said, though when Charlotte was in one of these moods it was hard to make her see anything. 'I love her so much because she *is* your child. She's a child of your flesh just as you are a child of my flesh . . .'

'She's a child of *my* body,' said Charlotte cuttingly. 'You had no part in it, but that's beside the point. You're trying to take my place – you have too much influence over her.'

'If Charley calling me Grandma instead of mama will make you happy, then I'll start teaching her as soon as she wakes up,' Lottie promised.

Aggie, much to Charlotte's annoyance had recently given Charley a kitten, a tabby with a little white bib which had earned her the name of Bibba. Charley could say Bibba very plainly. Lottie saw no difficulty in getting her to say Grandma.

Charley came down from her morning nap with her cheeks rosy from sleep. 'Darling,' said Lottie, kneeling before her. 'This is Grandma.' She pointed to her chest. 'Say Grandma – Grandma – say Grandma . . . say it.'

Charley, thinking it was a game gurgled with laughter – then she was off, chasing the kitten. Lottie caught her and went through the pantomime all over again. She patted her chest, and with every pat she said the word 'Grandma' determined to go on until Charley understood.

Suddenly light dawned, and Charley's face lit up like a sun-burst. 'Grandma,' she shrieked excitedly. 'Grandma – Grandma – Grandma.'

Triumphantly, Lottie went into the kitchen to tell Charlotte of her success. 'You won't hear her calling me mama anymore,' she said. 'She's learnt to say Grandma quite plainly.' She tried, for Charlotte's sake, to sound pleased about it.

It was hot in the kitchen. Charlotte had just stoked up the boiler. Lottie unbuttoned her cardigan and dropped it on the seat of the wickerwork chair by the window. She donned an apron and took out her pastry-making things. Bibba came streaking in and jumped for safety on to the chair – Charley close behind her. There was a sudden silence as the twinkling feet ceased their pattering, then Lottie felt a tug at her apron.

'Mama – Mama, look,' said Charley solemnly. 'Bibba's on your grandma.'

The only thing that stopped Lottie from laughing outright was the look of anguish and despair that settled on Charlotte's face. It was then she decided to teach Charley to call her Lottie.

Charley listened to this story with great earnestness. 'I suppose I was about four when I suspected that Mother was jealous of you,' she said reflectively. 'As soon as I realised, I tried not to show how much you meant to me . . .'

A spasm of pain crossed Lottie's face. 'It's a terrible thing for a four-year-old to be put into that kind of situation. It makes me feel very guilty to hear you say that. Is that when you stopped coming into my bed? I did so miss our early morning cuddles.'

'And I miss the stories you used to tell me about Thornmere. You remember . . . the pig-killing – and the Empire Day celebrations – and how you and your sisters used to help make the Christmas puddings . . . chopping the suet and rubbing bread-crumbs, grating the nutmeg, and cutting up the candied peel. It sounded such fun . . .'

Lottie was lost again in the past, remembering the time when she was Charley's age. They had been a happy and united family then. Her dark eyes clouded over and she smothered a deep and troubled sigh. Charley was watching her.

'Do you remember that cut-out paper doll with several changes of clothes you bought me one Christmas?'

'Good gracious, child, I can't remember every present I've given you . . .' Lottie paused. 'Is that the Christmas when you were four?'

'Yes, that Christmas. It was only a small present from the tree, but it was the one I liked the best. Your real present was a dress you had made for me. Mother gave me a hideous baby doll . . .'

'Charley!'

'It *was* hideous. It was bald and it wasn't a bit like a baby. It was hard and cold, not soft and warm and cuddly. It didn't smell like a baby and it didn't goo like a baby, and it had this horrible hole in its mouth . . .'

Lottie laughed. 'Oh Charley, you are funny. What kind of hole in its mouth?'

'Where the dummy should have been, but Mother had taken it out before she gave the doll to me. She didn't believe in dummies, she said. I couldn't bear to look at it let alone play with it, and I spent most of Christmas Day dressing and undressing the paper doll. Next day that had gone. I looked everywhere for it, then Mother said it might have been thrown away with the wrapping paper. She burnt it, Lottie, I know she did. When I cried you said you would buy me another one to take its place, but Mother said I already had a proper doll to play with, and she said something else about you putting ideas into my head . . . I didn't know what she meant by that, but I did learn not to make a fuss over anything you bought me in future. I can't understand how she can be jealous of you, Lottie . . . her own mother.'

Lottie bit her lip. It was a tricky moment, and she had to choose her words carefully.

'Not exactly jealous, Charley, that's something you must put out of your mind right away. She's very frightened of losing you . . . She hasn't got a lot of confidence in herself, and she sees me as a rival. If anything, I'm the jealous one.'

'Lottie! – you're just saying that . . .'

'I mean it. Your mother had a few blissful and happy months with the man she loved. I've always envied her that . . .'

'Envy isn't the same as being jealous. I envy my friends who are allowed to wear teenage clothes . . . Mother makes me dress too young. And another thing, she bears grudges. . .'

'That's quite enough mother-bashing for one day, my pet. I think your mother dresses you very sensibly. And I may as well tell you that I can do a pretty good line in holding grudges, myself . . .'

'I don't believe it . . . I know you too well. . .'

'There's also a lot you don't know about me, young miss.'

Lottie as always, looked elegant in a black edge-to-edge coat. Charlotte looked fashionable in a navy blue two-piece, and Charley felt a drag in her school blazer. It was the only black garment she possessed, and her mother insisted she wore it.

'But people don't wear black at funerals these days, and Aggie wouldn't have minded. She loved bright colours and Lottie said she would have been tickled pink if I had worn the dress she gave me for Christmas.'

'Your grandmother must be out of her mind! Electric blue for a funeral – what would the neighbours think! You look very nice, and that blazer is more suitable for your age.'

'Mother – I'm nearly seventeen . . .'

'Nevertheless, you are still a school-girl.' But in saying that, Charlotte knew it was only half the truth. It never ceased to astonish her, that her daughter, from being a delightful but untidy and lively child, had in her teens, blossomed into this amazingly beautiful creature who moved with the lissom grace of a dancer, and looked, even in school clothes, as if she had just stepped out of a bandbox.

She watched Charley now as she followed Lottie out to the garden where the undertaker waited to escort them to the leading car, herself staying behind just long enough to give last minute instructions to Mrs Baker. The threat of rain had passed, fortunately. There was nothing more dreary than a wet funeral. Charlotte dreaded the ordeal before them. The gloomy drive through mean streets to the Victorian cemetery where Aggie was to be buried with her mother – the service in the chapel – the clergyman's unctious address – the solemn procession to the graveside afterwards, and the likelihood of Aggie's many relatives and friends descending on them for refreshments.

Charlotte looked anxiously at her mother. She hadn't

cried since Aggie's death, but she knew it would have to come sometime. Please God, not at the graveside – not in front of all that rabble. But Lottie sat dry-eyed throughout the tedious journey, and throughout the committal service. She was paler than usual, and except for the way she kept clutching at Charley's hand, showed no emotion.

As Charlotte had feared, most of the mourners followed them back to Laburnum Lodge. They packed into private cars, or in taxis, or cadged lifts. They filled the house – eating and drinking – rapidly turning the occasion into a wake. Lottie looked on benevolently. 'It's the least I can do for Aggie,' she said. 'Giving her a decent send-off.'

'They'll be doing Knees up Mother Brown, next,' retorted Charlotte, escaping upstairs.

Waking suddenly, Charley heard the sound of muffled sobbing. She slipped out of bed, padded across the room, opened her door and listened. It came from Lottie's room across the landing.

Outside, the sound of gentle rain pattered against the window panes. Was it loud enough to muffle her footsteps if she risked going to Lottie? For if her mother heard there would be reddened eyes and reproaches in the morning.

She cautiously turned the handle. The bedside light was on. When her eyes became accustomed to the glare, she saw a movement in the bed, then Lottie emerged, blinking, from beneath the bedclothes. 'Charley, is that you?' She struggled into a sitting position, tossing her long grey rope of hair over her shoulder. Charley moved swiftly towards her.

'Lottie, may I get in with you? . . . like I used to when I was little?'

The high double bed had belonged to Maud. Charley remembered playing tents in it, tying the bedspread to the bed knobs by its tassels. Climbing into it was like sinking into a cloud. She got in, and warmed her feet on Lottie's warm patch. 'I heard you crying, Lottie. I had to come.'

'I didn't mean to wake you – I couldn't keep it back any longer. I'm glad you're here though, I felt so lonely.' Lottie took Charley's arm and placed it through the crook of hers. 'I couldn't sleep. I've been trying to read, but all I could see was Aggie's face on the page. As it used to be before she had her stroke. She was such a good friend to me. We went through two wars together. Now she's gone and I feel that part of my life has been buried with her. There . . . I'm just being morbid . . . giving way to foolishness. I should be ashamed of myself for saying I'm lonely. I've got you – and your mother . . .' Lottie wiped her nose and tucked her handkerchief under the pillow. 'But dear old Aggie . . . I'm going to miss her. There's only me left now to remember Maud . . .'

'I shall remember Maud for you. I remember all the things you and Aggie told me about Maudie's and Fosters and the old days . . .'

'As long as your mother doesn't know you know . . .'

'Oh Lottie, what am I going to do about Mother? I sometimes feel that she's eating me alive. Doesn't she realise she's driving me away with her possessiveness . . . She's so unfair . . . and the way she talks to you, some-times. You, her mother! How can you put up with it?'

'She doesn't mean it. Half the time she doesn't know what she's saying. Underneath it all, I know she loves me. . .'

'Then she's got a funny way of showing it.'

'That's her way.' Lottie sighed. 'Goodness knows it's difficult enough for us to live together at times, but it would be impossible for us to live apart. We've grown too used to each other. And Charley, you may not think so, but your mother really has your good at heart.'

'I know – that's what makes me feel so guilty. Lottie, I've been thinking . . . there's no way I can get to college. I'll never pass my A levels for a start . . .' Charley stopped, and listened. 'I thought I heard someone moving . . .'

'It's just your mother turning in her sleep. She's a

restless sleeper. What would you like to do instead of going to college?'

'I'd like to learn shorthand and typing. I'd like to be a journalist, and if not that – at least work for a woman's magazine – a fashion magazine if possible. I love clothes – and I want to learn more about them, and even write about them. To get any sort of job with a publishing firm I'd have to know shorthand and typing.'

'It would help even more if you had a degree.'

'But Lottie – I'd never get to college. I know my limitations, but I daren't breathe a word of this to Mother. She's got her own ideas about what she wants me to do. Would you have a word with her?'

'You know that would only make matters worse, my dear.'

'What has Mother got against you? I've never been able to understand. You tried to explain to me once, some years back, but I didn't really understand then, and I can't understand now. Is it jealousy, Lottie? You said it wasn't, but I can't see what else it can be . . .'

'It's more a sense of injustice I think. I'm much to blame. I've kept her tied to me, dependent on me. I was so fearful of losing you if she left.' Lottie fell silent, plucking at the sheet, pleating it between her restless fingers. 'Your mother told me once that the happiest time of her life, with one exception, was when you were a baby and a toddler. I was very much tied up with Fosters at the time, and Aggie came up most days to give me a hand. Your mother was left here alone with you. She had a freedom then that she hasn't had since, and she had you all to herself. Just the two of you in this big house, and no-one to interfere. Then I decided to appoint a manager at Fosters, and I retired. She told me later, that was the time her days of happiness ended. That was a terrible indictment on me, Charley. She accused me of stealing your affections. I never intended that, but I did see you as Charlotte all over again, and I wanted to recapture that time. As I've said, Charley, when it comes to possessiveness there's nothing to choose between us.'

'But you wouldn't stand in my way if I had set my heart on doing something I really wanted?'

'No, I wouldn't do that, but I wouldn't encourage you to leave school either. Think it over carefully.'

'I have, and I still come up with the same answer.'

'Then discuss it with your mother. Don't shut her out.'

Lottie's voice was fading. Perhaps she would sleep now. Charley reached across and switched off the light, then slipping out of bed, tip-toed across to the door.

She didn't expect the landing light to be on but it was, highlighting a figure standing in an open doorway, her face in shadow.

Charlotte's voice was void of expression as she said, 'Get to bed now Charley, or you won't be able to get up in time for school. You've missed enough days already . . .'

'Mother, that's something I want to discuss with you . . .'

She heard a sharp intake of breath, then Charlotte said, 'It will have to wait until tomorrow.'

Lottie, lying with her eyes closed, listening to their voices, was unable to distinguish the words, but could guess what passed between them. She heard Charley's door shut behind her, and she heard Charlotte going downstairs. Off to make herself a cup of tea, which Charlotte often did when she couldn't sleep. Lottie was tempted to join her. She knew she wasn't going to sleep tonight either. Though her body was physically tired her mind was too active.

Her thoughts wandered back over the years to when Charlotte was a baby. Just as pretty as her daughter, but more stolid in her movements and so solemn. Sometimes, the only way to get a smile out of her was with a sweet. Lottie sighed to herself. Oh dear, how they had spoilt her, the three of them, Maud and Aggie and herself. They treated her like a little doll. They dressed her up and encouraged her to show off, laughing themselves silly at her antics. If there was anything lacking in Charlotte's character, she had only herself to blame.

What Charlotte lacked even more was the steadying influence of a father. There were several candidates willing to take that place, Lottie had not been without her chances. Someone in particular she remembered with tenderness. But nothing came of it – he was already married. And even if he had been free, given the choice of going away with him or staying at Fosters, she would have stayed.

Marriage for her was out of the question. She was the breadwinner. She had Charlotte and Aggie and Maud to think of. More than that she had Fosters – and she had plans.

'Make a go of Fosters,' Maud had once said to her, and make a go of Fosters she did. There were times when the load seemed unbearable, when she longed to shed her yoke. To be free from having to think and act for others. To be a wife and someone else's responsibility. To have children and live a quiet family life, seemed at such times, to be the pinnacle of success.

Then she would remember the promise she made to Maud and the vow she had made on Armistice Day. Duty, she found, was a powerful motivator. Only once had she reneged on her duty and she had paid for that with a troubled conscience. She gave up all thoughts of a life of her own. She had Charlotte, and one day Charlotte would marry and have children – and they would be her children too. Charlotte and she would share them, as Charlotte and she would one day share the business. Partners in all things. All her energy – all her suppressed unsatisfied longings were channelled into planning for the future. Fosters became the centre of her world.

There were structural changes. Most of the little rooms on the first floor were incorporated into the mezzanine floor, and that became the main restaurant. The ground floor was used mainly for lunches and *thé dansant*. The top floor, converted from the old garrets, was turned into banqueting rooms for private receptions.

And there were other changes. Waiters replaced the waitresses. Waitresses, she felt, were too reminiscent of the 'bad old days'. In any case, with so many men out of work and many with families to keep, it seemed wrong to employ women at a lower wage. Just after the First World War was a hard time for married women. They had to give up paid work and go back to their kitchens. No married women teachers or nurses. No married female bank employees or civil servants. No married women in many private businesses or shops unless they were unfortunate enough to be widows.

Aggie fumed. 'They took us quick enough in wartime – now they've given us the boot.'

'Aggie, there's more than enough for you to do here . . .'

'I'm not talking about myself, I'm thinking of me sister-in-law. My brother works for a firm of carriers earning three quid a week. They can't bring up a family on that. What is Sylvie doing? Going out cleaning offices. During the war she was working a machine lathe.'

Yes, it was very unfair, but it was also traditional for customers in restaurants to be waited on by men. Seeing all these strange young men about, Maud became suspicious. Maud was becoming senile. Most of the time she wasn't aware of what was going on around her, but at other times she was too sharp for their peace of mind.

'Lottie, I have something to say to you. Close the door. Now what's all this – what's going on here?'

'Just a change of staff, Maud. They are waiters . . . they mostly come from around here. Don't you remember the Italian and the French children we used to see playing in Soho Gardens? Some of these waiters may well be their older brothers.'

'Not a change of heart on your part then? Not going back to the old ways? I was just getting to like it as it is now. It's more peaceful. And I like that pretty music. Where does it come from?'

'From a small orchestra on the mezzanine floor.' But Maud's face had fallen vacant, her eyes dull. She would sleep now, and remember nothing of this conversation. Which was just as well thought Lottie, wondering how on earth she could explain what a mezzanine floor was.

The late twenties and early thirties had been the peak years of her career. It was then she started to wear the tailored black suits in which she greeted her customers. Severe in cut, but always relieved with a touch of white. A lace jabot, or white chiffon cravat, or a high-necked satin blouse. Except for the casual diner, she knew all her customers by name, and always had time for a word with them, enquiring about their families when they were alone, or their holidays or their plans if they were dining *en famille*. She made everyone feel welcome. More than that, she made them feel like guests in her home. It was this gift she had of putting her customers at ease that more than anything else contributed to the growing success of Fosters.

The Depression did not hit her as hard as it did so many other businesses. Of course there was a dip in trade, and the sight of the lengthening dole queues and the homeless sleeping on the Embankment gave her sleepless nights. She instigated a form of soup kitchen, and here Aggie, in her element, was in charge. The basement flat was made available and the door that led into the cobbled alley-way was thrown open at ten o'clock. News soon spread that there was food to be had at the back of Fosters.

'Rich people's leavings,' muttered the more disgruntled, but hunger got the better of their scruples.

The winding queue attracted attention. Some of her customers were offended by it. They didn't want other people's distress to impinge on their enjoyment of a good meal, and a night out. But the majority were generous, perhaps they too had consciences to salve. Lottie's fund for the down and outs became part of the menu.

Then the war years. In their way, they had been good too. She enjoyed running the canteen. It had brought, temporarily, a closer relationship with Charlotte. It was after the war that things had begun to go wrong.

She had retired too young, she could see that now. If Charlotte had come into the business as the partner she had once envisaged, she would have carried on. But Charlotte had no interest in Fosters. She seemed to overlook, thought Lottie sadly, that it was the income from the restaurant that kept them all in comfort. She had made a mistake giving up her restaurant life in order to live full-time at Wenley, hoping to fill in her time looking after Charlotte's baby. It hadn't crossed her mind that Charlotte might not want her there. It was hard to accept the fact that Charlotte had no intention of sharing Charley.

They had given a retirement party for her at Fosters. All her loyal staff who were staying on, doing her work for her, clubbed together to arrange the party. It was all hush-hush, but of course she had guessed, it was hard to keep a secret in that claustrophobic setting. When Jacques, elderly and white-haired now, but as spry as ever, had asked her to come to the blue banqueting room as there was something he wanted to show her, she had played along. But she was still surprised. Surprised and overwhelmed by the size of the crowd awaiting her. Staff and customers shoulder to shoulder . . . Old friends from years back. As she entered the room the applause was deafening, and she struggled hard to fight back tears, because everybody else was laughing.

But the thing that stayed in her mind, the thing that touched her heart more than anything else, was that someone had remembered she loved sweetpeas. A small vase of them stood on the table with the cake and champagne.

Fosters had gone on making money for her. All through the post war years and up to the end of the fifties it had prospered. One of her regular customers was a successful stockbroker and he had shown her how to invest her money. Money for money's sake was of no interest to her. She was investing for the future and security of her family. For Charlotte and Charley and Charley's children. She wanted to make sure they would never go short.

Now their future was doubly insured. The area around Boot Lane was due for redevelopment. As the leases of the little shops and businesses expired, construction firms gobbled them up. Concrete and glass edifices took their place. Maud had bequeathed her the freehold of Fosters, she could hold out against progress, she could even use her premises as a bargaining point, and what was the point of hanging on any longer. All the other old places had disappeared. The future had caught up with Fosters.

It was hard to let go. Fortunately, she could leave that side of it to Edward Lincoln. As a young solicitor he had handled the buying of the house at Wenley and had looked after her affairs ever since. She was unprepared for the sum of money finally agreed upon for the sale of Fosters. It took the wind out of her sails.

'But they didn't even buy it as a going concern. They only wanted the land. It's worth as much as that?'

'You've been a very astute woman, if you don't mind me saying so, Miss Foster. You hung on – you were an obstacle in the way of them fulfilling their plans for Boot Lane. That whole area is scheduled to be one huge office block.'

'I didn't hang on in order to wangle more money out of them. It was because I couldn't bear to part with Fosters.'

'They weren't to know that.'

She could hear Charlotte coming back upstairs. She listened as she went into her room and shut the door. She heard the creak as Charlotte got back into bed. She imagined her daughter lying sleepless, despairing, thinking of the coming confrontation with Charley.

Lottie turned over and composed herself for sleep.

260

There was no question in her mind as to who would win that particular battle. Poor Charlotte was a natural loser.

Charley could hear the blackbird singing again as she went down the steps into Farringdon Street. That was two days running she had heard the same blackbird. Lottie couldn't believe it. 'A blackbird singing on Holborn Viaduct! Are you sure it wasn't someone whistling?'

'Lottie! You're the one who taught me all I know about birds. I do recognise a blackbird when I hear one.'

She took the short-cut through Smithfield market, passed the shop where she bought her lunchtime sandwiches, and along the street where, in summer, rosebay willow herb clothed the scars of an old bomb-site. She reached the imposing entrance to Clifford House, named after the founder of Clifford Publications, and pushed her way through the massive mahogany doors. Crossing the patterned marble floor, she flashed a good-morning smile at the hall porter, ignored the lift, and took the stairs to the third floor two at a time.

She'd been doing this for eighteen months. The first six months as a junior on *Weekly Garden*, and the last twelve as a trainee sub-editor on Clifford's newly-launched glossy – *Trend*. It was a leg-up for Charley – a step in the right direction towards becoming a journalist.

Miss Leigh, a senior sub-editor was already at her desk. She liked to come in early to have the cloakroom to herself while she applied her make-up. Now she was sitting down to a cigarette and the first cup of coffee of the morning. There was always work waiting. This morning a pile of galley proofs. Miss Leigh pushed them across the desk she shared with Charley. 'These have just come from the printers. D'you want to make a start on the corrections, or have a coffee first?'

At thirty-five, Mary Leigh was the oldest member of the staff, except for Antonia Warner, the editor-in-chief who looked twenty-five, but, it was rumoured, had a married daughter. Charley saw little of her as she mostly stayed in her inner sanctum and used her own door into the corridor. Sometimes she walked through the department leaving a scented trail of Chanel No 5 and looking like a film star. However, and taking Miss Leigh's word for it, behind those long-lashed hazel eyes and exquisitely moulded features was an intellect as sharp as a needle.

Miss Leigh liked to talk in metaphors. 'Think of us as a newly-launched ship on our maiden run. If we hit the rocks, we'll all go down together. If the circulation figures begin to fall that means there's rocks ahead, and then we'll get the Friday afternoon call to scuttle. That, my child, means we cease publication on the Monday. So it's up to all of us to pull together and make for the shore. In other words – make sure the bloody thing sells. You may think Miss Warner is the boss, but she's only the skipper. The Admiral of the Fleet is the real boss. It used to be Sir Hubert Clifford, but since he died, his son has taken over command – and a right bastard he is!'

It amused Charley to see how the importance of individual editors was judged by the size of the carpet on their office floor or the quality of the curtains at the windows. The rooms and corridors of the executors and editors of the highly valued glossies, were close carpeted. The carpets became less lush and disappeared entirely as one came down-market. Right at the back of the building, with windows looking out on the fire escape, was a small office with just one small rug and paper blinds. This was where a two-man team struggled to keep a religious weekly going. 'They're due for the three o'clock chop,' prophesied Miss Leigh. 'Keep your fingers crossed, Charley. It could happen to anybody.'

'What do you do exactly?' her mother asked after her first week with *Trend*.

'Well, I'm still doing some secretarial work, but I've got the status of a sub-editor. A very junior sub-editor – Miss Leigh is teaching me the editorial side of things.'

'What is the point of having a status if you don't get paid for it?'

'I get a terry towel instead of a huckaback one,' said Charley, which made Lottie laugh. Charlotte looked annoyed.

'Are you poking fun at me?'

'No Mum, it's true. The juniors and the messengers are issued with huckaback towels, but everyone on the editorial side gets one made of terry towelling.'

Lottie broke in. 'I can remember,' she said musingly. 'The first lot of nappies I bought for you, Charlotte, were made of huckaback. Terry towelling napkins didn't come in until years later. They were a great improvement.'

Charlotte, conscious that Charley was convulsed with laughter, glared at her mother.

'I can't see the purpose of that remark,' she said angrily.

'I was only trying to bring a little levity into the conversation.'

'I don't see the need for levity. I asked a perfectly straightforward question. Charley! Stop that stupid sniggering.'

'Sorry Mum, I couldn't help it. And I will get a rise of course, as well as a terry towel, I mean.' She was afraid to catch Lottie's eye – afraid of the laughter welling up inside her. It would be better to get off the subject of towels. 'And the job is so much more interesting. I'm learning a lot – about correcting proofs and lay-out and line drawings and design. Gosh, there's so much to know. I love the art side of it – the studios are fascinating. They are on the top floor under a glass roof. And there's always something going on up there. They're a jolly bunch the artists – not a bit how you'd expect artists to be – no artistic temperament, I mean. They're mostly middle-aged men and they have to work to a deadline, just like journalists. We're all ruled by Press Day. D'you know what one of them said to me the other day? That I should be a model. He said with my legs I could get a modelling job any day. We've also got photographic studios on the ground floor, but the doors are always closed and I haven't seen inside yet. I've seen one of the photographers though – I took him for a beatnik. He turned and had a good look at me, but perhaps he was just studying my legs professionally.'

Charlotte showed her disdain. 'For goodness sake behave yourself, Charley. You're acting like a schoolgirl.' This recalled old grievances. 'A pity you didn't stay on at school and get your A-levels. You could have been at university now. I understand that Wendy Simms is doing very well at Bristol . . .'

Charley bent over and planted a kiss on her mother's cheek.

'Mummy dear, we had all this out years ago and you promised me you would never bring the subject up again. And you do appreciate all the free magazines I bring home, don't you? And you do like to hear the latest buzz on autumn fashions? I think there's something new in the air, and if I hear anymore about it, I'll let you know.' Over her mother's head, Charley winked at Lottie. Anything to keep Charlotte sweet.

That morning, over breakfast, a headline in the paper caught Charley's eye: 'Beeching's axe falls on BR branch lines.' Lottie, by the cooker, was slicing bread for toast.

'Lottie, have you seen this? Do you think it will affect the Thornmere line?'

Through the kitchen window Lottie could see a bush of golden forsythia shining in the sun. She remembered when she planted it. In 1946, to commemorate Victory Day. There had been sixteen springs since then, and now spring had come again, and even someone her age could feel the sap rising. Poor Charlotte on the other hand was prostrate with a migraine. The attacks which had started soon after Charley left school against her mother's wishes, were becoming more frequent.

'What did you say, dear?'

'Read this and tell me if it means any threat to Thornmere.'

Lottie searched for her reading glasses, put them on, and read the paragraph Charley pointed out to her. 'I don't think Thornmere will be affected – I hope not. I wonder what will become of the gatehouse if the line is closed.' She thought of Ted. He'd be seventy-something now. Was the cottage still his home? She had tried to contact him years ago, but he hadn't answered her letter. They'd be strangers now, anyway. Sadly, she turned to the job in hand – switched on the grill, and placed the bread ready on the grill pan. Charley who had a train to catch, swallowed the last of her coffee, and kissed Lottie goodbye.

She usually felt good, but today as she walked to the station there seemed an extra special something in the air that went to her head like wine. She was conscious that the dress she was wearing suited her, clinging to her slim young body in a most flattering way. It was made from some new man-made material that felt like silk and needed no ironing. 27th March, 1963. What was so auspicious about this day that she should feel like this? It was a day she was to remember for the rest of her life.

In the middle of the morning, she was sent to the studios to collect a cover. It was for a summer issue of *Trend* – a picture of a girl in a white bikini. She was brown, and glowing with health, and held in one hand a pair of heart-shaped sunglasses. It had originally been designed for a Spanish periodical, and like all covers that came out of Spain, the colours were bright and powerful. Most of the covers used by *Trend*, Charley discovered, originally came out as illustrations in continental magazines. *Trend* only bought second rights to them.

It intrigued her to see how the covers were doctored by the art department to fit a different set of requirements. The original painting was protected by a plastic sheet and any additions were made on that. The name of the magazine lettered across the top – the issue number – the date.

Sometimes the colour of the model's hair was altered to fit a story line or a different background painted in. In this case, the heart-shaped sunglasses had been made to look round, in case the fashion changed by the summer. When photographed for the printers, the alterations blended in with the original. The seams didn't show.

That morning she stopped at the art editor's desk to ask why they went to all this trouble. Why didn't they commission a cover from a British artist instead?

'Because no British painter can produce such strong colours. The covers we have commissioned in the past look anaemic by contrast. See what I mean . . . ?' Matt Daly tapped the rough of an illustration with his pencil. 'It's something to do with our climate, I think – all these grey skies and washed-out colours.'

'Rubbish,' a voice boomed behind them. A bulky figure of medium height approached the desk, walking with the rolling gait of a sailor. He had an engaging smile and piercing blue eyes which swept briefly over Charley. Something seemed to happen to her then. A kind of madness . . . a spark . . . a tremor . . . a sense of floating in space. He carried an artist's portfolio which he plonked down on the desk.

'Look through that, sonny – and tell me what's wrong with my colours.' Like many deep-chested men he had a low-pitched carrying voice. He flicked the folder open and took out an unfinished painting. Though it was upsidedown to her, Charley could see that the work was skilfully executed – an illustration showing a partly-dressed girl looking sideways into a mirror. 'That's the rough for the story you're running in your July number. The rough, mark you – not the finished article. What's wrong with that?'

'Nothing – nothing. We've got no criticisms of your work, Larry – you always give us what we ask for . . .'

'I give you what I'm paid for! I won't let you fob me off with peanuts, like you do some of those other poor blighters. If I ever again hear you querying the quality of the corpuscles of my fellow artists, I'll pin your ears back.'

Matt grinned. 'What's this? Patriotic Week?' He looked at his watch. 'It's nearly lunchtime. Coming out for a quick bite?' He stood up, and took his jacket from the back of his chair and put it on. 'The Steak House or the Mitre?'

'Introduce us.' The man called Larry was leaning on his hands on the desk top. Charley caught his eye and blushed.

'Miss Foster meet Laurence Marsh. Larry — meet Charley. She's our latest acquisition and marked fragile. Coming . . . ?'

Larry ignored him. His eyes had not left Charley's face. 'Would you sit for me? I'll paint you in colours that will make baby face here eat his words . . .'

Behind the artist's back, Matt made a face at her. 'Do not trust him, gentle maiden,' he warbled. This time, they both ignored him. He looked from one to the other. 'I'll be at the Mitre,' he called over his shoulder, but they didn't hear.

'Yes.'

'Yes what?'

'I'll sit for you.'

'Ah . . . good. Will this evening do?'

Charley hesitated. 'No, not this evening . . .' Charlotte worked herself up into a state of nerves if Charley wasn't home the time she said she would be and the next day had a migraine. 'But I could manage tomorrow . . .'

'Tomorrow then.' He produced a card. 'Could you make it about seven? I hate to admit this, but I won't be able to pay you much — only a percentage of what I'll get.'

She squirmed with embarrassment. 'But I don't expect payment . . .'

'In that case I must feed you first. I'll pick you up here at six o'clock sharp.

*

267

'Lottie – I'm in love.'

Lottie put down her knitting with a sigh of relief. Charley who had brought a rug out of the conservatory and spread it on the ground beside her, lowered herself on to it in one graceful movement.

'Thank goodness it's only that – I was beginning to think all manner of things. All these late nights . . . Your poor mother has been out of her mind . . .'

She too had been imagining all sorts of things, making herself wretched over Charley's evasiveness. Never before had there been a lack of openness between herself and her granddaughter.

Charlotte made herself ill with worry. 'I hope to God it's not a repeat of the Denis Hudson story,' she said one day, in a burst of despondency.

Lottie stared at her. 'Denis Hudson? Who's Denis Hudson?'

Charlotte went brick red, turning her face from her mother. 'It was a name I hoped never to say again. It – it just slipped out . . .'

Lottie took a chair near her daughter. 'Is it to do with that time . . .' She saw Charlotte wince. By common consent those lost years were never mentioned – a mutual desire to forget them. 'Is that the name of the man who wronged you? Charlotte, don't get so distressed. If you don't want to talk about it, forget it . . .'

Charlotte shrugged. 'It doesn't matter now – I've been through too much already. It's just that worrying about Charley brought it all back to me. He was a married man, and he cheated on me. I get sick at heart thinking that Charley might be embroiled with a married man.' Charlotte suddenly lost patience. 'This wouldn't have happened if she had only done what I wanted and stayed at school, and gone to college. She was so anxious to get out and earn her living.'

Lottie tried to pour oil on troubled waters. 'From what I read in the papers, the parents of students are having greater problems. All this talk about drugs . . .'

'For God's sake, Mother! Even to think such a thing . . .'

'I only meant to say, at least we have her safe at home with us.'

'And not knowing where she is half the time.'

That argument had just gone round and round. Charlotte refused to be comforted. Lottie looked wistfully at the cause of all the trouble.

'Why the secrecy, Charley?' she said. 'You've always told me everything before.'

'I didn't think you would approve.'

Charley's eyes were guileless, as clear as crystal, yet there was something in their dark depths which caused Lottie some misgiving. She had spoken to Charley lightly, hiding the fact that she was not unaware of the change in her. She had watched her turn from an inexperienced girl into a woman so sexually awakened that her senses had taken on a heightened perception. Charley knew the heights of rapture and suffered the depths of despair with equal passion. Lottie rejoiced and agonised with her. And kept silent, waiting until her confidence was required. That moment had come.

'Why should I not approve?' she said, not bearing to look at Charley — not wanting to see the light go out of her eyes. 'Is he married?'

'No — nothing like that. He hasn't got time for marriage.'

'A lot of young boys go through that phase. Their ideas change once they have had their fling and are ready to settle down. If he is serious though . . . ?'

'He's not a boy, Lottie. He's nearly forty.'

'Child, do you know what you're doing . . . ?'

It was another fine April . . . warm enough to sit out in the garden. The conservatory that got the full force of the westerly sun was like an oven. Spring passed so quickly, Lottie would not waste a moment of it by staying indoors. She was reaching her three score years and ten and every spring could be her last, so she felt she had to make the most of it. The laburnums were breaking into flower, and the flowering cherry was in full bloom already. There was birdsong all around her, so she should have been happy, but she wasn't. She was too concerned for Charley.

'Darling . . . tell me more about him . . .'

'His name is Laurence Marsh – I call him Larry. He's a commercial artist. He illustrates children's books and women's magazines – anything that will bring in money. But his heart isn't in it. He calls that his bread and butter job, but he really wants to be a serious painter. He's done some wonderful work – work that can stir you to the very depths of your being. One day he'll make a name for himself, I'm sure of that.'

'He's left it rather late, hasn't he?'

'There were reasons – mainly his father, who died last year. He had to care for him. Then Larry gave up his job in an advertising agency and went freelance. As soon as he's got enough money behind him he says he's going to give up commercial work altogether and concentrate on serious art. I want to help him, Lottie. I want to protect him against the world – to keep the nuisances away and give him a chance to get on with his real work.'

Lottie looked into Charley's earnest and beautiful face, and the inclination to smile, faded. 'I worry so much for you . . . there's something so vulnerable about you. I've got a tough streak in me and so has your mother – something we must have inherited from our peasant stock – but it's passed you by. Sometimes it seems to me you're nothing but spirit.' Lottie shifted uneasily in her chair. 'I hope this Laurence Marsh appreciates the way you feel about him. I hope he isn't just using you. You haven't given me a very good impression of him, but perhaps I'm biased, nobody in my opinion is good enough for you. Perhaps, if I knew a little more about him. . .'

Charley jumped to her feet. 'I have something to show you – don't move.'

'Child, I have no intention of moving.'

She was back again in a matter of minutes, her feet flying over the newly-mown grass. She was wearing shorts and sandals that she called flip-flops. Her legs and arms were the colour of toffee, her face pale cream in contrast. She dropped down on the rug again and undid the package she was holding.

'Mother's stirring. I daren't let her see this – she'd ask questions. I keep it hidden in the bottom of my wardrobe. It's a painting Larry did of me. In a way, that picture is responsible for everything. Larry had intended to sell it – but afterwards . . . he couldn't. He gave it to me . . . Well, Lottie – what d'you think?'

She was in Larry's studio-cum-bedsitter, at the top of a tall Victorian semi in Fulham, stiff with posing. If she moved her head just a fraction or so it was possible to catch a glimpse of the river between the opposite buildings. Larry threw down his brush and came to her. 'It's finished – now you may look.'

She looked, was silent, and then burst into tears. 'You have made me so beautiful – I'm not a bit like that. . .'

'I paint what I see.' He began to kiss her and she responded without restraint. She had loved him unequivocally and intensely since their first meeting, nursing her secret as if it were some small timid animal frightened of the light. She thought if Larry knew, he would laugh – but now she knew he would not. He undressed her expertly. It was the first time any man had seen her without her clothes – it was the first time any man had caressed her – his fingers and his lips giving her such erotic pleasure that she felt the drawstrings of her sensations tightening. He was an experienced lover and she was a novice, but the earth obligingly moved. Later – glorious hours later – Larry added a title to the painting.

And now Lottie was gloating over it, holding it with both hands as if reluctant to let go, and Charley could see the moisture rise in her eyes.

'He's caught you . . . your Laurence Marsh – he's caught the very core of you. "A Girl in Love" – yes, very apt. He must be in love himself, I think, to see you like this. I admire your Laurence Marsh as an artist, Charley. I would like to meet him . . . but first . . . you must tell your mother.'

As if on cue, Charlotte appeared at the conservatory door, looking wanly suspicious. 'What are you two up to?' she said, walking towards them. She saw the painting on Lottie's lap and changed colour. She snatched it up. 'What's this – where did it come from? Have you given this to your grandmother? Charley, why wasn't I told?'

Lottie eased herself out of the garden chair. 'I'm going in to make tea. Haven't you something to discuss with your mother, Charley . . . ?'

'And how did she take it?' Larry knew all about her mother – the uneasy truce that existed between her and Lottie – the migraine attacks if she was crossed or made upset.

'She accepted it – eventually. Please don't make me say more than that. Now she wants to meet you. I have to take you to be inspected on Sunday. I think she will ask you about your intentions . . .'

'Which are distinctly dishonourable. Haven't you told her . . . ?'

Charley sighed. A last flicker of hope died. 'I haven't the stamina – not yet. One step at a time, please.'

Larry drew her down on to his lap which he often did when he wanted to talk seriously. She felt safe there, her head resting against his broad shoulder. Feeling like this, she could face anything. Even Sunday.

'What would you say to coming to Cornwall with me?'

She sat up and stared at him. 'For a holiday?'

'For as long as the money lasts. It's no good me going on as I am here – I'm getting nowhere. I've been thinking for sometime about giving up the commercial work and concentrating on what I really want to do. I've given myself a goal. If I haven't made even the smallest dent in the art world by the time I'm forty, I'll come back to

London and work nine to five in an advertising job. I've got two years to prove I can do it. Now this opportunity to rent a place in St Denys has come along. It's made up my mind for me. Come with me, Charley . . .'

She hesitated, stunned by his announcement. She thought of her mother spring cleaning the house from top to bottom in readiness for his visit – of Lottie, baking all day.

He would not plead. He said, without making excuses, 'I want you there when things go wrong. I want your encouragement and your faith in me – and yes, I want your youth. I can feed on that. I'm a bloodsucker, Charley, a parasite, but as far as it is in me to love anybody – I love you. That's all I can offer.'

She slipped down from his lap and went over to the window. It was too misty to see across the road. She could hear nothing but the hooting of a tug, and inside her, the thudding of her heart. She knew if she turned down his offer she would never see him again. He would go to Cornwall and find someone to replace her. He loved her yes, but if he had to choose between her and his objective – his objective would win every time.

And did she love him enough to give up her all for him? To devote her life to his wishes – to be his housewife, his carer, his mistress and more than these . . . his disciple? There was no question about it. Yes, she did. But what would they live on in Cornwall with no money coming in? Perhaps she could get a job, and there was still some of Aggie's legacy left, and Larry could sell the lease of the studio. That should keep them going for a while.

They would live like the friends Larry admired. A colony of painters – writers – sculptors – potters – she knew of them all. He talked about them – had spent holidays with them. They lived like Bohemians, according to Larry, sharing their property – their successes and their failures. But would her sheltered upbringing fit her for that? Would she not end up a millstone round his neck?

He came up behind her and whispered in her ear.

'Come with me.' He slipped his hands under her shirt and began to fondle her breasts. He knew she could never hold out against that, and it saddened her to think that he felt he had to entice her. Just asking her was sufficient.

The visit to Laburnum Lodge was a disaster. Charley had not expected it to be a success, but had hoped they would get through it in as civilised a way as possible. But all hope died, and her spirit quelled when she saw the expression that crossed Charlotte's face when Larry was introduced to her.

She had begged him to put on a suit and wear a tie, but he possessed neither, and she saw his point that to buy new clothes to be worn possibly just that once would be an unnecessary expenditure. However, she thought he looked very presentable in a turtle-necked mustard-coloured sweater under a corduroy jacket, and his jeans were clean. For the occasion he had had his hair trimmed, but not enough to please Charlotte obviously. She lapsed into one of her awesome silences.

Lottie had made one of her raised duck pies, a speciality of `Fosters, served with an orange salad. She had also made a walnut gateau, and another speciality from one of Jacques' recipes. Jacques, with fruit and cream and eggs and liqueurs as his basic ingredients, concocted delicacies that were as much a delight to the eye as to the palate. Larry had two helpings of everything.

He was the only one with an appetite. He seemed unaware that the other three were only toying with their food. Charley, torn between amusement and despair, kept her eyes on her plate, praying silently and incessantly that they would get through the rest of the afternoon unscathed. She was fearful that her mother would have one of her emotional storms. She could feel the tension rising.

The storm broke just as Lottie served coffee. Larry provoked her mother into breaking her silence. 'Has

Charley told you of our plans?' he said, spooning sugar into his coffee.

'What are your plans, Mr Marsh?' her mother said frigidly.

'Larry please.' He grinned. 'And I'll call you Charlotte. It sounds more chummy. About us living in Cornwall.'

Charley recognised the calculating gleam in Larry's eye. He's doing this on purpose she thought. If he loved me he would spare me this. She was hoping to introduce the subject of Cornwall when the time was ripe. He had chosen the worst possible moment. His very manner was a challenge. She saw her mother go white and compress her lips together. She looked across at her, ignoring Larry.

'What's this nonsense about Cornwall?' she said.

Larry answered for her. 'Charley and I are going to join a commune at St Denys. That's a beauty spot on the south Cornish coast. It'll be a free and easy life – no worries – no responsibilities. It'll be the making of your daughter, Charlotte.'

Oh Larry, why are you doing this to me. She felt she was bleeding inwardly.

Charlotte's face was suffused with angry colour. 'A commune? Another word for a hippy colony, I think. I suppose none of them are married.'

'Is that important? A lot of people get by without being married.'

Fireworks!

'Did you have to make that dig about not being married? It was so cruel . . .'

'Honest to God, Charley, I had clean forgotten that neither of those respectable women were married. It doesn't matter a hoot to me, anyway.'

That bit she could well believe. She was walking Larry to the station, still shattered by her mother's outburst. Charlotte had been beside herself, screaming hysterically, showering abuse on Larry, and finally dissolving into a child-like weeping. Lottie led her away, taking her upstairs to rest.

'I never want to see you again,' said Charley, and at that moment meaning it.

'What did I say?'

'Oh Larry, if you don't know that, what's the good of my trying to tell you . . .'

'Darling, I wouldn't do that to you on purpose. But my God, how is one expected to react when a woman sits there like a block of ice, not saying a word? I was bloody nervous, Charley – I didn't know what I was saying. I was only trying to make conversation.'

She desperately wanted to believe him.

'Your appetite wasn't affected by your nerves, I noticed.'

He laughed at that. 'It's not often I get the chance of a good nosh-up like that. And if I hadn't eaten, I would have insulted your Lottie by implication. Now there's a woman I wouldn't like to cross.'

'*Lottie!*'

'Yes, Lottie. Your mother is all noise and fuss – but that's not Lottie's style. I saw the warning look she gave me across the table. It said very plainly, "You do any harm to my granddaughter and I'll fight you tooth and nail." Charley, I'm telling you, she's the one who could come between us – not your mother.'

Charley didn't believe a word of this, but she did notice a difference in Lottie when she rejoined them. There was a graveness about her manner, and a studied look in her eyes that Charley had never seen before. Even so, she was still the perfect hostess.

'I'm afraid your coffee has got cold, Mr Marsh. Could I make you another?'

Charley noticed he didn't tease her into calling him Larry. With Lottie he was on his best behaviour. 'I think I had better go,' he said. 'I feel I may have outstayed my welcome.'

He waited, but she made no answer. He said, 'May I borrow your granddaughter as far as the station?'

This quip brought on a faint replica of her customary smile. 'I think Charley is quite capable of making her own decisions.'

As they left the house, Larry whispered in her ear. 'How does that line go – "The smile on the face of a tiger"?'

'Please Larry, for goodness sake grow up!'

They had twenty minutes to wait for a train. The trains didn't run so frequently on Sundays. Apart from a porter with a broom, the platform was empty. Charley sensed that beneath his bravado, Larry was shaken by the events of the afternoon.

'I made a fool of myself, didn't I?'

'You certainly did.'

'I honestly didn't intend to. Things just got out of hand. I'm not used to lunching out in polite society.'

'You knew just what you were doing, Larry.'

He cupped her face in his hands. 'I can't hide anything from you, can I. I apologise for spoiling your day. I will write an abject apology to both your mother and to Lottie if that would help?'

'I think it best if we just forgot that today ever happened.'

He accepted that. He bit his lip, staring intently into her troubled eyes. 'But you will still come with me to Cornwall? Charley, say you will come to Cornwall.'

Her heart ached with love for him. She couldn't keep away from him if she tried. 'Of course I'll come to Cornwall,' she said.

TWELVE | *Charley*
The Swinging Sixties

If she sat here, on Tony's rock, an outcrop of granite embedded in sea-thrift and overlooking the creek, she'd be able to see Larry approaching whichever way he decided to come.

He had two choices. Either to catch the bus from Truro to St Denys, and walk from the bus-stop to the other side of the creek, a matter of a mile, then whistle for someone to row over and fetch him. Or he could hitch a lift from Truro to Penbridge and walk the three miles over downs and woodland, coming in by the back way as they called it. It depended whether he had good news or not. If it was disappointing he'd delay his arrival for as long as possible, hating to face them all. He might even continue by train to Falmouth and spend the evening drinking himself insensible. He'd done that before. Then Tony and Derek would have to get out the dinghy and row across to St Denys where Derek garaged his car, and then drive on to Falmouth in search of him. It was all done with good humour and understanding. They had trodden the same path themselves.

Paradise, she had dubbed this place back in the spring when she first arrived, and paradise it still was in many respects. Its position was unique. Tony's place (it had another name⁻ but she'd forgotten it) had been built in the mid-nineteenth century as a summer retreat for a retired industrialist. He had modelled it on a Swiss chalet, but at some later date another storey had been added which gave it a top-heavy appearance. Time had weathered it, and ivy had smoothed over the unsightly joins.

Wooded heights sloped down to within a few yards of the back walls, and a narrow spit of sand and shingle separated the front of the chalet from the waters of the creek. Two boats were beached just beyond the verandah. A clinker-built dinghy, and a fibre glass sailing boat. This was their only means of transport, apart from Shanks's pony, until they crossed over to the St Denys side. It was virtually an island, with an added advantage of having one link with the mainland.

Nothing had been done to improve the chalet for more than twenty years. Tony bought it with the money he won on the pools – not as an investment though the land was worth more than the house, but as a retreat. He had opted out of society long before it became fashionable.

He made his keep by letting out rooms, and of these Larry and Charley rented a large studio/bedroom on the ground floor. From the studio, a door led out onto Charley's vegetable patch, made with help from Tony, in a small clearing amidst the trees. Because it got so little sun, nothing grew satisfactorily, but Charley persisted, as it made her feel less inadequate among all these motivated people.

She heard the sound of someone approaching through the wood, not from Penbridge, but from behind her. It was Tony, bringing sustenance, his hair floating around his head like a halo of dandelion floss. Dear thoughtful Tony. He lowered himself on the ground, and out of his knapsack produced a Thermos flask, mugs and a parcel of sandwiches.

'I made them myself, so don't expect too much. You've missed lunch – Liz made a huge pot of borscht, but there's none left, I'm afraid. How much longer are you keeping up this vigil, Charley? Larry might not arrive until the last train.'

She picked up the topmost sandwich, and bit into it. She felt more at home with Tony than with any of the others. Nobody knew much about his private life, other than that he had given up a hated job in a bank as soon as he received his windfall. If he ever had a wife, which seemed unlikely, he made no reference to her, or to any other relatives. Yet he was never lonely. He liked solitude. Sometimes he would take a sleeping bag and go off and sleep out in the woods to get away from them all.

'He's either catching the ten-thirty-five or the twelve-thirty from Paddington,' she said.

'He couldn't have caught the ten-thirty, he would have been here long since. And even if he'd caught the latter train . . .' But Tony didn't follow this up. He could see she had already thought it out herself. He said, 'Perhaps there's been a hold-up on the line. Perhaps the engine ran out of steam, I've heard of that before . . .'

'You think so?' Her relief was enormous. 'Of course, that's what must have happened. Stupid of me not to have thought of it — I was frightened that . . . well, you know what Larry was like the last time he had a dis-appointing trip to London.' She changed the subject. 'How's the book coming along, Tony?'

Tony had been writing a book ever since he gave up his job, but so far had only got as far as chapter five.

He grinned self-consciously. 'Now who was it, who when asked that same question, answered: "I've spent all the morning putting in a comma and all the afternoon taking it out again"? That's about where I've got to at present. Mind you, I'm pretty good at commas.'

They lapsed into a comfortable silence. It was September and warmer than it had been in June. In the spring, when Charley first arrived the woods had been carpeted with blue and white bluebells. She had picked a bunch and arranged them, as she thought, artistically in one of Poppy's reject vases, and placed them in the hall. Only later, when everyone was running around holding their noses or ostentatiously fanning the air did she realise that what she had taken for white bluebells was in fact, wild garlic. She wasn't allowed to forget that in a hurry, but her mistake had broken the ice. Until then she had felt on the outside of the magic circle which encompassed Larry.

The mug holding her coffee was another of Poppy's rejects. Poppy, Derek's wife, was using a large outhouse out in the trees as a pottery, working often in bra and panties when the heat from the kiln became too much. Her products were becoming known, and she supplied most of the gift shops in St Denys and Penbridge with her wares. She was the mother of three-year-old twins who frolicked about the place like a pair of unchecked puppies, naked, and as brown as berries.

Squinting into the sun Charley was surprised to see a barge approaching. The creek was never without craft of some kind, but a barge was unusual. It was coming under power, its red sails furled. She wondered if it was the same Thames Barge that had been moored in Carrick Roads for the past two weeks. Larry had looked on it with covetous eyes, saying he would give an arm and a leg for the chance to paint it. Such hyperbole had once made her laugh, but not any longer. It was too near the bone. She had learnt, that apart from mutilating himself, there was little Larry wouldn't do for the sake of his art – nothing or nobody he wouldn't sacrifice.

Tony lay sprawling on his back beside her with his eyes closed. 'I could spend the rest of my life just lying here listening to the cooing of pigeons and hum of insects and the sound of the wind in the trees,' he said. 'Give me all this, and a pint of bitter, a crusty loaf and a wedge of mature cheddar, and to hell with the rest . . .'

'You are the most contented person I've ever met.'

'There's a very thin line between contentment and indolence,' he said, self-mockingly. She didn't answer and he opened his eyes and saw that her attention was riveted on the creek. Suddenly she got to her feet, nearly toppled over, regained her balance and jumped down. Running to the water's edge, she began to wave her arms, shouting at the same time. Tony raised himself on one elbow, and saw that she was trying to attract the attention of someone standing in the bows of an oncoming barge.

It was Larry, who saw them and waved back. A young man he'd never seen before was steering the barge expertly through the shallow waters. Tony got to his feet. 'They'll be heading for the landing stage . . . it's a tricky manoeuvre when the tide's as low as this . . .'

He was alone. Charley was off like a deer. He saw the flash of her red skirt as she disappeared round the side of the chalet. He lumbered after her, arriving at the landing a few seconds later. The others from the group were already assembled – Liz and Jerry, the Bailey sisters, Sebastian, and Poppy and Derek with the boys – for once silent – watching with fascinated eyes, the progress of the big black boat.

Larry's new friend was an experienced sailor. He adroitly avoided the rotten planking below water-level and drew as near as he could to the landing without running aground. Larry leant over the side of the barge, his grin broad enough to split his face. It could only mean good news.

'Can anybody give a landlubber advice on how to get off this thing?' he shouted.

There were many ribald suggestions from the watchers. 'Jump' was the politest, so he did, lost his balance and landed half in and half out of the water.

'Idiot,' said Tony. 'Couldn't you have waited? It'll only take a minute to fix up some sort of gang-plank.'

Laughing, water streaming from his hair, the suit he had bought for his trips to London splattered with mud, Larry in tremendous spirits splashed out on to dry land amid cries of Encore. Charley ran into his arms.

'You could have broken your leg,' she scolded.

'I could have broken my arm which would have been more inconvenient – but I didn't.' He kissed her with an equal amount of zeal and passion.

'I've done it, kiddo,' he said, taking her by her shoulders and smiling at her with gleaming, triumphant eyes. 'I've been taken up by the Brownlow Galleries – and with an option on further work.'

'They took all three of your paintings!' This was better than even she had hoped.

'As good as – they have a customer in mind. A wealthy American – who else! They'll take their carve-off, of course, but they've given me a handy little retainer to be going on with.' He beamed an exultant look on the others. 'Barbecue tonight folks – roast pork and fizz.'

'Hi!' came a voice from the barge. 'Hurry up with that gang-plank – I can't wait to be introduced.'

His name was Hilary Parton. Larry had met him on the train, they had got talking, then when Hilary heard that Larry's destination was the St Denys creek, he suggested he came on to Falmouth with him and he would take him the rest of the way in his barge. It was moored in the bay – he lived on board, and had just spent two days in London on business.

He had a proprietorial manner which Charley considered patronising. He was dressed, she thought, as if he had just come off a millionaire's yacht, and perhaps saw them as a band of gypsies. She was prejudiced – he had stolen the hours Larry could have been with her. When she was introduced, their eyes met with equal animosity.

She fretted inwardly, longing to get Larry away to herself, but the others detained him, besieging him with eager questions. His success enheartened them – he was the trail blazer – perhaps they could follow. They were avid for further details. By the time she did get him alone his clothes had dried on him. But even so, she made him strip them off and she rubbed him down with the beach towel. Normally this would have led straight to bed, but now Larry seemed anxious to get back to the others. Adulation meant a lot to him.

'But I haven't had a chance to ask you any questions myself yet. What did the people at the gallery say? What did they think of your treatment? I want to know what was said in their exact words . . .'

He was both amused and flattered by her fervour. He put on pants and jeans and pulled the sweater she handed him, over his head. It ruffed up his hair, which when left to grow longer than he normally wore it as now, was inclined to curl. He sat on the bed to lace up his shoes.

'I can't remember the exact words, except that they were extremely complimentary. I could kick myself for not having gone to a top gallery like Brownlow's in the first place ... Wasting my time on those piddling little back street places. Too depressing was their main complaint about my work. Mr Barter said nothing about it being depressing. He said I painted living photographs, though God knows what that's supposed to mean! I just paint what I see.'

Charley thought she knew. She would not have chosen those exact words herself, but both she and the gallery owner had recognised the same quality in Larry's work that made it outstanding. He painted dereliction – not depression. A disused tin mine, a wrecked trawler, an abandoned chapel – so skilfully drawn that they could pass for photographs, but photographs with a misty effect as if taken through a filter. He had worked hours to get just that right effect, snapping at anyone who interrupted him, going without food or rest until he was too weary to stand at the easel any longer.

When money ran short, rather than worry him, Charley would get Tony to row her over to St Denys to work part time in one of the gift shops or cafés. There were plenty of jobs for casual workers in the holiday season, and Larry didn't even miss her.

But now it was all right. No more worrying about how to find the rent. They were always short of ready cash, and Charley couldn't understand why. Larry hadn't owned his studio flat in Fulham as she had supposed, he was only renting it, and was still owing a quarter's rent when he left. They had paid that debt off, but there were others outstanding. Larry wasn't very good with money. He spent it as fast as he made it. He loved to give parties, and he was giving a party tonight by way of celebration. A beach barbecue and fizz. Champagne? Who put that idea into his head? His new friend? Yes – he looked as if he had expensive tastes.

Larry was rummaging in a drawer for a clean handkerchief. She found one for him. 'What else do you know about this Hilary Parton?'

'He's quite an amiable chap, really. Well-heeled, as you can see. He dabs a bit with paints himself. He showed me some of his work on the barge, and it's not at all bad. In the talented amateur class, I'd put it.'

Of anyone else Larry might have said, 'Roughly WI standard.' She felt ashamed of her cynicism. She felt ashamed of her sudden illogical idea of Hilary Parton as a serpent in Paradise.

Larry was saying, 'He's rolling in money. His father's something big in the city and the barge was a twenty-first birthday present. His old man works on the principle that if he lets his son get the painting bug out of his system, then he'll be ready to settle down and join the family firm of merchant bankers.'

'Is Hilary only twenty-one? He looks older.'

Larry gave one of his rumbling laughs. 'He is older – much older. He's stretched his birthday out a bit. He's been sailing that old barge round the coast of Britain, staying off at any place that takes his fancy. Quite a feat when you think about it, but then, he's an experienced sailor – it's always been his hobby. He's spent the summer in the Scillies, and he's off to the Greek Islands for the winter.'

'On his own?'

'He'll find someone to crew for him. There's always someone anxious for that kind of holiday. Well, I'd better show willing. I can't let my guests do all the preparations . . .'

She pulled him back, capturing him within her arms, her eyes expressive with longing. 'It's been two days, Larry. Aren't you glad to be back with me again?'

He kissed her ardently, but she felt, with a somewhat detached ardour. Gently, he disentangled himself. 'Sweetie, what's the hurry? We've got all night . . .'

'But these beach parties sometimes go on all night – and then someone will be sure to suggest a midnight swim . . .'

'Thanks for reminding me. I'll take my trunks. Bring your costume too – or are we swimming in the buff as usual?'

'It gets cold this time of year . . .'

'But the water's warm.' He gave her another, more hasty kiss. 'Don't be long. It's a jack and roasting-spit job tonight – the real McCoy. I brought a great chunk of pork back from Falmouth.'

'And champagne . . . ?' It was a pity her voice sounded censorious when she hadn't meant it to be. She saw Larry stiffen, and cringed at the look he shot at her.

'Yes, and champagne,' he said. 'A whole bloody case of it. Do you begrudge me having a celebration? Perhaps you think I haven't got anything to celebrate?'

She clung to him in misery. 'Of course I do, Larry. Oh darling, of course I do. I just got all worked up waiting for you – thinking all sorts of things. Oh Larry – Larry – please – please, don't be like that. I can't stand it when you're angry.'

He relented. 'I'm all worked up too, as you put it. I'm knackered actually. I didn't get any sleep last night thinking of my appointment with the gallery this morning.' He paused at the door, looking back at her. 'Get changed and join us as soon as possible, it'll be dark soon. And Charley, please don't start acting the wife with me.'

She stripped and looked at herself critically in the mirror, sideways on. She didn't show yet, but why should she? She was only two months, though she had read somewhere that thin girls showed up more quickly than their well-covered sisters. Some fat women had even been able to hide their pregnancies until they went into labour.

She didn't want to have to tell Larry — not now — not after what he just said. He might think he'd be obliged to marry her — that she had set a trap for him. He always left her to take precautions. She hadn't meant it to happen, but now it had she was glad. She couldn't imagine Larry being glad. All that mattered to him at present was that his work was at last being acknowledged. That's all that had ever mattered to him really. She couldn't kid herself about that. She had always dreaded the thought of being a burden to him. How much more of a burden would a baby be?

Well, there was no need to say anything for another month or so. No need to face the problem until she came to it. She spread her hands, finger tips touching, across her belly. It felt as smooth and as flat as always. She could hide the swelling, when it started, with a crêpe bandage. Wear it like a cummerbund beneath her clothes.

It was on such a night as this, with a sky like black velvet and the stars white with brilliance, that she and Larry had swum to the upper reaches of the creek. Then, because the tide was running out fast, and the water was no longer deep enough to swim in, Larry had picked her up and waded with her to a sandy bar where shore birds roosted.

Their coming disturbed the sleeping birds, who showed their disapproval by making weird, low cries that were completely unrecognisable as bird sounds. A startled curlew gave a long-drawn haunting cry before taking off in the dark. They made love on the sands, fell asleep, awakened and made love again. The tide had turned. They had waded out into deep waters and swum against the current, back to the landing, crept through the sleeping house and fallen exhausted into bed. Charley liked to think that was the night her baby was conceived.

She ached with trying to keep awake. The fire had died down, and the light from its glowing embers played on the recumbent bodies who lolled in its proximity. An owl hooted, water lapped gently against the sides of the barge, and as a plaintive accompaniment to the sounds of the night, Beverley played softly on her oboe. Bev was one of two sisters who shared the attic. Between them they had created an exquisite book for children, written by Christine, illustrated by Beverley, but so far no publisher had shown interest. They had thin clever faces and both were musical.

In his sleep, one of the twins began to whimper. He and his brother lay curled up together between their parents underneath a car rug. Poppy sat up. 'I'd better get them to bed. Coming Derek?'

'I think I'll stay on for a bit. D'you want a hand?'

'No, I can manage.' Poppy was a big woman, bigger than her husband. She threw the rug over one shoulder, then hoisted a sleeping child under each arm. Derek stirred himself at last, hauled himself to his feet, and stumbled after her.

'He's taken on too much ballast,' said Tony with a chuckle. 'If he attempted to swim with that load, he'd sink. Who suggested this swim anyway?'

The plaintive notes of 'The Swan of Tuonela' had acted like a soporific.

Only the two sisters showed any willingness. They undressed and ran into the water, their pale bodies gleaming whitely in the starlight. Sebastian followed more slowly, wearing his underpants in lieu of swimming trunks. The three of them glided smoothly and silently through the black water, throwing up spray which shone with phosphorescence.

'Is it obligatory?' said Hilary lazily. 'I feel too comfortable to move.'

'What about you, Charley?' Larry asked.

'I'd like to go to bed.'

'Yes, you do that – you seem tired. I'll be along in a minute . . .'

'What about all this mess?'

'Leave it till the morning,' said Tony. 'We can all muck in and do it then.'

'He gave me a week to make up my mind. Did I want to go with him to Greece or not? Of course I want to go – it's a chance in a lifetime. But I'm not going without you. Yes or no, Charley. I can't keep him waiting much longer.'

They faced each other across the studio, Larry baffled by her silence. He knew she didn't like Hilary – in a twisted sort of way was jealous of him, but he couldn't understand why she hesitated at such an offer. A few months ago she would have jumped at it.

'You won't be the only woman on board. The two Bailey girls are coming, and that means Sebastian as well. You know he follows wherever they go. Milos, Ikaria, Naxos – doesn't the sheer magic of those words set your blood on fire?'

She knew she had never looked less like being on fire. Physically she felt a wreck. Lately, everything she ate came up again. Everybody in the house knew about it except Larry, who spent most of the daylight hours in Falmouth working on his painting of Hilary's barge. When he was absorbed in work, as he was now, the rest of the world could pass him by without him knowing.

'I thought a cruise around the Greek islands would buck you up. You haven't been looking yourself for weeks . . .'

She must look the picture of misery for Larry even to notice that much.

'I'm pregnant,' she said.

He was pacing up and down the room, whistling impatiently through closed lips. He stopped and stared at her.

'You're *what*?'

'I said I'm pregnant.' If just one hint of pleasure showed on his face, she'd run to him, go with him anywhere he wanted. But all he registered was consternation.

'My God! How long have you known?'

'Two months for sure. I'm about four months gone . . .'

'Then why the hell didn't you warn me before this!'

Warn him! With difficulty she kept her voice from trembling. 'Because I dreaded the way you'd take it.'

'Ye gods, Charley, if you felt like that, why didn't you do something about it?'

Her eyes were swimming. She didn't want to cry, she'd tried her best not to because he hated women who cried. But now that she had started she couldn't stop, and when she found his arms around her, the crying got out of control.

He soothed her, making comforting noises, wiped her tears away and kissed her wet eyelids.

'You poor kid – keeping it to yourself like that. Are you so frightened of me? Am I so much of an ogre . . . ?'

'Oh Larry, I want this baby. But I want you to want it too . . .'

She heard his sigh, deep and troubled. 'Darling, I told you once I'd make a lousy husband, but I'll make an even lousier father. I don't even like kids.'

'You seem fond enough of the twins . . .'

'That's because they're someone else's responsibility. Can you imagine me trying to work with a baby bawling in the next room?'

No, she couldn't. 'What are we going to do?' she said nervously.

'You won't consider an abortion? We can afford it.' She shook her head. 'Then I'll see what Hilary says. I don't see why you can't still come along. Goodness knows the barge is big enough. And there are some good doctors in Greece. That's where medicine all started, isn't it?' He tried to sound jocular and failed.

She moved away from him, going over to the window, leaning with her hands on the sill, and stared bleakly at the barrier of trees. A few dried leaves clung precipitously to upper branches, but most of the trees were bare, stripped in a recent gale. It was a typical grey November day.

Earlier in the month it had been sunny with blue skies, but since the gale, the weather had become unsettled. How menacing the trees looked without their leaves, like something out of a Walt Disney. What a stupid thought – as if a tree could harm her. It was her own despair that menaced her.

She knew her news couldn't have come at a worse time for Larry. Just as he had gained a foothold in the art world. The three paintings were sold, and commissions were coming in for others. One for a painting of the Acropolis. That's what had put the final seal on her fate. Nothing could keep him away from Greece now.

He came up behind her, swung her round to face him, and searched her face with a shrewd blue gaze. 'You would like me to give up the whole idea, stay here with you until the baby comes. Isn't that it?'

She gave him look for look. 'Yes, that's what I'd like – but I know it's impossible, just as I know it's impossible for me to come with you. I'd only be in the way, not able to work my passage – a burden to everybody. It's not only that. I want to be with my mother and Lottie when my time comes . . .' That little lie was for his benefit, and she saw, with pain, the relief that came to his eyes.

'Then what about you joining us later – when you're well enough to travel, I mean. You could fly out – I'll send the cash to cover expenses . . .'

With or without the baby? But it would be too cruel to say that. Oh Larry darling, what's the good of pretending? Once we part it'll be for good. She knew it, and knew he knew it, but would never admit it. His was a love that couldn't sustain a parting.

He looked wretched. Her news had shattered him, his cheeks sagged, deep grooves had appeared in his forehead. The idea of fatherhood appalled him, but she couldn't hold that against him. He had warned her that his art was more important than anything else in his life.

'Let's just see how things work out,' she said.

She heard him swallow. 'I'll keep these rooms on, just in case. I'll pay Tony in advance, so if you ever want to make use of them . . .' His voice dropped on a dying fall. He would miss her until he found someone else to fend for him – to keep the world at bay – to be his house-keeper, his mistress, his apostle. She knew he would never want for volunteers.

She took his two hands in hers and kissed the backs of each in turn. 'I have one last favour to ask of you, Larry. Don't ask me to watch you sail away. I could face anything but that. Let me be the first to leave.'

His face contorted with pain. 'Don't make me feel more of a bastard than I do already,' he said gruffly.

She stood on the St Denys side of the creek and looked across to Tony's place. It seemed uninhabited, or at least there was no-one about that she could see. Not even the twins – no small, familiar, golden figures playing on the sands. Surely someone was at home, the house was rarely left unoccupied. The sailing boat was missing, but the dinghy was in its usual place – that looked hopeful. How could she attract attention? She couldn't whistle. She cupped her hands and shouted, but there was no response.

She could wait – someone would spot her eventually. It was good to be back – to fill her lungs with that invigorating smell of salt air and the gently teasing fra-grance of pines and thrift and samphire that for her would always recall nostalgic memories of Cornwall.

It was July, and though it had rained throughout most of her journey, here it was dry, the sky shining with that translucent evening light that again she always connected with Cornwall. She hadn't warned Tony of her coming, wanting to surprise him, but perhaps her surprise had backfired.

She was content to wait, feasting her eyes on well-remembered places. It seemed to her now that she had been away longer than eight months. She had last seen St Denys in November when the trees were bare and rain had flailed her horizontally as Larry rowed her across the creek to the taxi that was to take her to Truro. Only her eyes remained dry. She'd been too numb for tears, even when saying goodbye.

She remained in a sleep-like trance throughout the journey to Paddington, but when alighting from the train, she had been jerked back to wakefulness by the headlines on the billboards: 'Kennedy shot – in critical condition.'

'My God, see that . . . ?' she heard another passenger say. There was a rush for the news-stand. She exchanged shocked and disbelieving looks with those around her. She heard a rising tide of horrified exclamations. Her immediate thought was to make for a phone booth and break the news that she would soon be home. Home? She had stopped thinking of Laburnum Lodge as home six months ago.

Lottie answered.

'Charley, darling, what a lovely surprise . . . Have you heard about President Kennedy? We heard it on the six o'clock news. Isn't it dreadful? Can you believe that anything like that could happen these days?'

Her surprise phone call took second place to the tragic news from America. Lottie hadn't even enquired where she was phoning from. Or how she was.

'Lottie, I'm speaking from Paddington. I should be home within the hour.'

Lottie's voice immediately changed. She sounded no longer shocked but anxious; 'Charley, is anything wrong?'

'I can't stop now, someone's waiting for the phone. I'll tell you everything when I get home.'

There was no-one waiting for the phone, but she couldn't say what she had to say over a length of impersonal wire.

She walked up from Wenley station. She could have phoned for a taxi for she was tired after her long journey and her case was heavy, but she was delaying, for as long as possible, coming back.

The headlights of a car picked her out as she was

nearing the top of the hill. The car drew over to her side of the road and stopped beside her.

It was her mother.

'I was hoping to save you the walk. I've been down to the station once already, then went home to see if you had phoned again. I should have stayed.' Charlotte took the case from her and put it in the boot.

Charley had not known what sort of welcome to expect – hostile even, remembering her mother's wrath when she left for Cornwall. But though Charlotte did not offer to kiss her, or say hallo even, she was not unfriendly. It was just as if I've never been away, Charley thought. As if I'd just come back from a day's shopping in London. She was not unaware, however, of her mother's sideways anxious glances.

'Is there any further news of Mr Kennedy?' she asked.

'I'm afraid he died on the operating table.'

'Oh no . . . Oh, no I can't believe it. But why? He gave us all such hope . . .'

They sat in silence for the rest of the short journey as if they were too stunned to speak. But it wasn't solely because of the news. Charley suspected her mother was storing up what she had to say until they got in. She dreaded the expected words; 'I told you so . . .'

But when they reached Laburnum Lodge, all that Charlotte said was, 'I'll take your case upstairs – then I'll get you something to eat. Mother, help Charley off with her coat. She looks worn out.'

Lottie's arms were round her, Lottie's face pressed against her own. Lottie brimming over with love and comfort and security. Lottie, her safe harbour. The tears pent up too long, began to flow. She couldn't stop them – she hadn't the will to stop them. 'Lottie,' she sobbed. 'Mother didn't even kiss me . . .'

'Is that why you are crying?'

'Yes . . . no . . . I don't know . . . Oh, Lottie, I'm so tired . . .'

Lottie sighed. It was happening all over again – the

old old story. History repeating itself. What sort of trap had she set her girls – what legacy had she handed down to them? She was filled with bitter self-reproach as she saw the result of what her example had done to Charley.

'Did *you* offer to kiss your mother?' she said.

'N-no . . . I didn't . . .'

Lottie gave a shaky laugh. 'Then how can you complain? Now come by the fire and get warm. Your hands are frozen.'

Charlotte reappeared. From her eyes they could tell she had been weeping too. Mother and daughter exchanged wan smiles – a look of sympathy for each other passing between them.

'There's some casserole left over from lunch,' she said. 'Would you like me to warm it up for you?'

'No thank you, Mother. I couldn't manage anything heavy. Just a hot milky drink and some toast would be lovely.'

Lottie switched on the television. 'Just to see if there's anything more about the assassination,' she said.

The atmosphere as Charley ate her supper was muted. The news from Dallas acted like a damper on their spirits. She had the feeling that Lottie and her mother were relieved in a way to have an excuse to postpone, for the time being, more personal discussions. Perhaps they thought she looked too exhausted, perhaps they dreaded having their suspicions confirmed. She was wondering how best to broach the subject, for she knew she must get it over with before she went to bed, or she would lie awake all night worrying. It was Charlotte who put a sudden end to her torment.

'I can't bear this suspense any longer,' she cried. 'I've got to know for certain. Charley, have you got something to tell us?'

'Yes Mother, I have . . . I'm pregnant.'

'And is that – that bounder going to marry you?'

'No.'

'Thank God for that!'

*

An ear-splitting whistle roused her from her memories. It was Tony, semaphoring to her from the opposite bank. She waved back, overjoyed to see him. He disappeared – to get the oars, she thought. But no, he reappeared carrying an outboard motor, and soon the silence was peppered with the sound of its engine as he came splashing across the water to her.

She flung herself into his arms, delighted to see him. He held her at arm's-length, searching her face with thoughtful eyes. 'Motherhood suits you,' he said. 'You're more beautiful than ever.'

'And you haven't lost any of your old blarney . . .'

She still radiated liveliness, her laughter was as effervescent as ever, yet Tony thought he detected a brittle undertone that had not been noticeable before.

'It looks as if nothing's changed,' she cried, as they neared the other side. 'I was dreading changes.' Yet there were differences. The landing stage had been repaired, and someone had made a narrow flower bed in front by the verandah, and planted fuchsias. And someone, perhaps the same person, had pulled down most of the ivy from the walls of the chalet, and painted them white.

'You've got a new lodger,' she guessed. 'Another artist?'

'You could say that. He's a useful chap with a paintbrush anyway.' Tony grinned. 'He's a painter and decorator by profession, but can turn his hand to anything. He mended the landing stage – he bought the outboard – painted the place up a bit. You should see inside.'

She preferred it as it was. Its run-down air of raffishness was part of the chalet's charm. She had had enough of order and organisation at Laburnum Lodge. 'You told me you wouldn't let your rooms to anyone who wasn't arty,' she chided him.

'Unfortunately the arty ones can't always afford the rent, and I must eat. Anyway, don't pass judgement until you've met Brian. He fits in with the rest of us very well.'

'I can't wait to meet him. Where is he?'

'On Saturdays he goes to visit his mother – anyway

that's his story. He usually arrives back about midnight, completely blotto, yelling at the top of his voice for someone to go over and fetch him. You'll be sure to hear him tonight. You are staying . . . ?'

'Of course I am. But where's everybody? They haven't all left you, have they?'

'No, the others are still here. Poppy and Derek and the twins are spending a few days with Poppy's people in Bristol, and Liz and Jerry have gone on an evening sail to Malpas, taking sleeping bags and blankets, intending to stay the night if it doesn't rain. I'm afraid there's only poor old me to entertain you tonight, and all I can offer in the way of sustenance is the heel of a Stilton cheese and some cold rabbit pie.'

'Manna from heaven.' She forced herself to ask the question that had been trembling on her tongue. 'What about the Bailey sisters and Sebastian? Are they back from Greece?'

Tony looked surprised. 'You mean . . . you haven't heard?' She didn't have to answer that. He sighed. 'Let's get supper over with first, then we can talk,' he said.

They had coffee on the verandah. It was good coffee, Tony's one indulgence. He sent away for it from a place in Old Compton Street.

'Before we get on to – to other things – tell me more about Carla,' he said, putting off the subject that both were reluctant to discuss.

'She's three months old now, and already trying to pull herself up. She's very forward. She's got eyes the colour of violets and blonde hair, which Lottie tells me will grow darker as she gets older, because my mother's did. Naturally, I think she's the most beautiful baby that ever was . . . but sometimes I worry . . .'

'About that?'

Charley shrugged. 'Having too many mothers. I had two, but Carla will have three. I expect she'll survive . . .'

'If she inherits your sunny nature, she's sure to survive.'

'Not so sunny these days, Tony.'

Their eyes met. The time had come to bring out into the open what was on both their minds.

'And what about Larry, Charley? What does he think of his daughter? Have you sent him a photo?'

A look of despair crossed Charley's face. 'I didn't send him one. I waited to see if he would ask, but he didn't. It was what I wanted, I told myself. It's what I told him I wanted – a clean break, but I didn't think he would take me at my word.'

She took a deep breath, knowing that sometimes helped her to control her voice, but this time it didn't. 'It was the most sensible thing, in the circumstances. I couldn't have him coming back into my life and disrupting it as he had once before. I couldn't go through another parting. But I went on hoping – hoping against hope, that he would come back to me – that he would want to see his little daughter. Actually, it was Lottie who wrote and told him about Carla and then he cabled me some money for her. That really got up my nose, Tony. I didn't want his *money*! I returned it and said my daughter would never be in want – that she had a grandmother and great-grandmother to provide for her, and that I intended to go back to work.'

'I don't see Larry taking that lying down,' put in Tony quietly.

'He didn't. He sent the money back to me, this time doubled. I didn't see the sense of this tit for tat, so I banked the money for Carla's coming of age. But I did write again. I told Larry that if he ever sent me any more money I'd give it to a charity for unmarried mothers. I said receiving money from him made me feel like a prostitute. I didn't hear from him again after that . . .'

Tony gave a little grunt that could have meant either approval or disapproval. 'My word, Charley, when you do decide to stir things up, you don't do it by halves,' he said dryly. 'Whatever made you say such a thing – knowing how Larry would take it?'

'I don't know – well, yes I do. I was ill after Carla was born . . .'

Her doctors called it post-natal depression, but all she could remember was floating away in a world that had no reason. Sights and sounds were alien to her, she didn't know what was going on half the time, she suspected everyone of treason.

Later she was told that Lottie and her mother were so concerned that she might take her life that they took it in turns to guard her. They had engaged a nurse for Carla, for she had rejected her baby. She couldn't believe she had ever rejected Carla – it hurt to think she could be such an unnatural mother.

'But you were ill, my pet,' Lottie assured her. 'You weren't responsible for your actions. You made up for it when you were well again. Nobody could love their baby more than you do . . .'

It was while she was keeping vigil that Lottie wrote to Larry. She told Charley later, but was vague about its contents.

'Did you tell him about Carla?'

'Yes, and that you had been ill . . .'

'Did he answer?'

'No – but then I didn't expect him to.'

He cabled some money to Charley instead.

'I've regretted what I said in my letter to him,' she told Tony. 'Lord, how I regretted that letter. We are never given a second chance in this life, are we?'

This was Charley with her defences down, more vulnerable than he had ever seen her. She gave him a wan smile. 'Did you know I had a card from Hilary Parton?'

This surprised him. 'No I didn't – from Greece, you mean?'

'From Paxos. I got it about a month ago – it just said, "Just to let you know we're still in the land of the living – painting, boozing and wenching. Give our regards to the old crowd if you see anything of them."'

'The smarmy little blighter – just the sort of remark

I'd expect from him! I always suspected he was a trouble-maker.' Tony gave Charley a questioning look. 'So you knew Larry was still in Greece?'

'I would have known anyway – I saw his painting of the Acropolis on show at the Royal Academy.' She didn't say how she had scanned the papers for news of him, and was finally rewarded with a small piece about one of his paintings being on the line at Burlington House.

'I wouldn't have thought the Royal Academy his style. I thought he'd be the sort to prefer the alternative exhibition on the Embankment.'

'You never thought much of Larry, did you, Tony?'

He obviously wouldn't commit himself. 'I thought highly of him as a painter.'

'And what about Sebastian and the Bailey girls?' she asked. 'You started to say something about them earlier on . . .'

'They got lucky in the end. They sold their book to a New York publisher and flew off to the States as soon as they heard. Needless to say, Sebastian went with them. I haven't heard anything since, but if I don't hear soon, I shall have to let the attic. I've had several enquiries. I've a feeling I'll be going legit. No more beach parties, or midnight swims, or sleeping out in the woods . . .'

'It was all so harmless,' said Charley reflectively.

'There's some who wouldn't think so.' Tony eased himself out of his chair and went indoors. He came out again with drinks – a gin and tonic for Charley and a glass of bitter for himself. 'Sorry I couldn't offer you a choice – the cellar is rather low at present. Here's to you, Charley. Here's to you and Carla.' He raised his glass. 'What are your plans for the future? Any chance of coming back here? The rooms are paid for until November.'

She acknowledged his toast. 'The one thing Larry's taught me was that if you want anything badly enough, you have to go out and grab it. It won't just drop in your lap. There was a time I wanted to be a model. It was put in my mind when I worked for Clifford Publications –

so many of them there said I would make a good model. I'd always loved dressing up. Lottie kept a chest of cast-off clothes for me to play with on rainy days, when I couldn't get out in the garden . . .'

'Why didn't you take up modelling then, when you had the chance . . . ?'

She said simply, 'I met Larry . . .'

Of course there was a scene with Charlotte when she said she wanted to go back to work. 'Go to work! Leave your baby! You must be mad – you've barely got over your illness.' When she saw that Charley was adamant, Charlotte changed her tactics, trying persuasion.

'It's so nice having you here, Charley. It's good to have someone young about the house. It's cosy, just the three of us, and baby. You don't have to go to work – you won't want for money.'

Charley saw her life stretching on and on as grand-daughter and daughter. Family ties robbing her of an identity. She knew Charlotte chafed about her own position – yet that was just what she wanted to impose on her daughter. Charley turned to Lottie for advice.

'I want to go back to work. I want to pick up the threads of the life I had before I met Larry. But mother is getting fussed and I don't want to hurt her again. I defied her when she wanted me to stay on at school. I defied her again when I went off with Larry, and she was so decent to me when I came home again. But now it's all starting up again – the old clash of wills. What shall I do, Lottie?'

'Do you have to ask me that? Haven't you already made up your mind?'

'Yes, I have. But I don't only want a job – I want a career. And I want to make a success of it – not only for my own satisfaction, but for Carla too. She's my responsibility, and I want to provide a home for her.'

'But until you've made that home, Charley, where do you propose to live?'

Charley put her head on one side, and looked at Lottie

appealingly from beneath her lashes. 'Would you mind having a lodger for as long as it takes?'

Lottie laughed and lightly touched her cheek. 'In some ways, you're still that little rascal who used to wheedle pennies out of me. Get on with you – my lodger indeed! But seriously, darling, if you want to make a career for yourself I won't stand in your way, and don't worry about your mother – leave her to me.'

All the time she had worked for *Trend*, Charley had not once been inside Antonia Warner's office. Now she had the temerity not only to make an appointment to see her, but to ask her a favour. Motherhood she found, had given her that little extra bit of confidence.

'So you want me to put in a word for you,' Miss Warner said, her lovely eyes obscured by tinted glasses. She took her glasses off, and to her relief Charley saw that the eyes were friendly. So Miss Warner was not holding it against her, her sudden departure in the spring. 'And if you don't make it as a model, we'd like to have you back here. Miss Leigh thinks highly of you.'

Charley had the impression that Miss Warner also had a high opinion of Miss Leigh's judgement. Whatever it was – influence or good fortune – the next thing she knew she was in the studio having her photograph taken from every angle.

'That was a month ago,' she said. 'I think somebody must have been impressed, because I'm off on my first assignment next week.'

Tony drained his glass. 'I'm genuinely pleased for you, but bally disappointed for myself. I was banking on you coming back here to live, but I can see there's no chance of that now. Has this visit anything to do with Larry? Did you think he might have returned?'

'I knew he hadn't, but I did think you might have some up-to-date news of him. But that wasn't the only reason I came back. Tony, I wanted to see you again – see the old place once more. To say goodbye properly. I went off in rather a hurry last time, remember?'

He conceded that. 'Well, if you ever do want to escape from the rat-race, you know where to come.'

She intended to stay for a few days at least, but one night in the bed she had once shared with Larry was all she could stand. The room was full of memories. Everywhere she looked she saw images of Larry – heard echoes of his voice. Her dreams were sensual and unsatisfying, and she woke up aching for him.

She left the next morning without seeing anyone other than Tony. The new lodger had come in after she had gone to bed, and was still asleep when she left. Tony motored her across the creek, and borrowing a car from an acquaintance at a boatyard, drove her on to Truro.

'Keep in touch,' he said, as they waited for the London train. 'Come and visit again soon. Bring Carla next time.' She promised.

The train came in. Tony opened a door for her, kissed her briefly. 'I shall look out for you on the covers of every glossy magazine in future,' he said.

She smiled. 'You may have a long wait, but I'll do my best.'

She waved until she could see him no longer. He was the only man she could trust, she thought, and he was old enough to be her father. If she'd known a father, would she have been able to manage Larry any better? Not knowing a father – or brothers – had for her, given men a mystique that was both unknown and exciting. They seemed to her to be on a higher mental and intellectual plane than women. She must make sure her daughter did not grow up with such outlandish ideas.

London was swinging. London was great. A fun city to work and to live in. Each day was too short to cram into it the new chances and experiences that came her way. Though she was no longer in her teens, she felt and looked a part of the youth explosion.

Fashion designers pandered to the young, and the clothes they created only the young could wear with success. London was now the centre of the fashion world – not Paris or New York. Charley haunted the boutiques that mushroomed in Carnaby Street and the King's Road, looking for anything that was way-out enough to wear.

Mini skirts were in, and fun furs, chunky knitwear in exciting new colours, sexy-looking knee-high boots – and new words to go with them. Pop art, pop music, pop culture; they seemed to express to Charley new attitudes to life. Pop – short and explosive, like some of her experiences. Love – not very successful. Drugs – not for her, except for an occasional escape with marijuana. Work was a better means of escape, she discovered. Tony did not have to wait long before seeing her on the covers of magazines like *Trend*.

Larry's success paralleled her own. His style had changed, jumping from modern day pre-Raphaelitism to his own style of Impressionism. Now immense canvases painted in the bright hot colours of the Mediterranean came from the small island where he had settled. She attended every exhibition where his work was shown. It was easy now that she lived in London. She rented a basement flat in Earl's Court, among a colony of friendly Australians. She was sometimes sent on an assignment at short notice, and Wenley was too far away from where it was all happening.

Whenever she could get away, she went to Laburnum Lodge to see Carla, and though her daughter was always pleased to see her, she didn't seem to mind when it was time for her mother to leave. But why should she, Charley asked herself. Carla had two other mothers who stayed with her all the time. They didn't disappear for days on end . . . They gave her the security she needed.

It was Lottie, Charley noticed, who Carla turned to whenever she fell and hurt herself – or wanted a drink – or needed to go to the toilet. With a little ache in her heart she realised at last what her mother must have felt when she, at the same age, had shown her preference for Lottie. That revelation determined her to do something about it. She had talked glibly about making a home for Carla. Now she must act before the gap between Carla and herself widened. That was the penalty, she thought, for putting a career before motherhood. She would find a place – not too far from Wenley for there was no point in upsetting the two Grans. Then she would engage a nanny.

The photographic crew left London for Norfolk in the early afternoon of a chilly November day. Ben had gone ahead in his Vitesse, closely followed by the rest of the gang in the wagon. Ben was fast proving himself one of the best fashion photographers of his generation, and her name was becoming linked with his in the fashion world. Their relationship was purely professional; he was not that kind of a man. Tony and now Ben, she thought – I get on well with men like them. She liked Ben for his gentle toughness, his morbid sense of humour.

She broke her journey when they neared Wenley, coming off the A11 to make her way to Laburnum Lodge. She had not yet broken the news of this exciting new assignment, and arrived just as her mother, back from shopping, was pulling up on the driveway. Charley drew up behind her.

Charlotte stepped out of the Singer and stared at Charley's Mini as if she couldn't believe her eyes.

'What on earth have you done to your car!'

'Painted it in psychedelic colours. It's all the rage now. What do you think of the daisy on the roof? That's my masterpiece.'

'You must be mad, taking it on the road looking like that. It's a wonder you're not arrested for obstructing the traffic.'

'Haven't you heard of flower power, mother? Well, this is flower power on wheels.'

Charlotte had no patience with the zany type of humour Charley indulged in lately. She thought it artificial. The girl had changed – for the worse in Charlotte's opinion. The rot had set in when she went off with that charlatan, of course. Then she got in with that arty crowd down in Cornwall. Now she was in with an equally disreputable set in London. The permissive society – the swinging sixties – the generation gap – men aping women. Whenever she saw men with hair down to their shoulders she thought back to the clean-cut lines of the young American servicemen with their crew cuts, and wondered what the world was coming to. The world that she and Jeff and thousands like them had sacrificed their youth for.

She was uncomfortably aware that Charley was watching her intently, and wondered what was going through her mind. She wasn't as close to her daughter as she would like to be. She thought, unjustly, that since Charley had joined the sophisticated world of fashion, she looked down on her mother as an old-fashioned fuddy-duddy.

What Charley actually felt was pity. She could see how discontent and a deep-rooted unhappiness had gnawed away at her mother's looks. I must take care she thought, that I don't fall into the same trap myself. I don't want to look old before my time. She wasn't sure how her mother would take the news of her assignment in Norfolk, knowing how she felt about the gatehouse. Lottie, she knew would be delighted. She waited until her mother had gone off to prepare tea, before telling her.

Lottie stared with mouth open. 'Not the *Thornmere* gatehouse – not my old home? What a strange coincidence!'

'Not really. I saw it listed in a recent advertisement in the *Daily Telegraph*. British Railways are selling off redundant gatehouses and stations in Norfolk, at give-away prices – some as low as six hundred pounds. There's no water or electricity of course, but just think – a week-end cottage for the price of a car! Anyway, I knew that Miss Warner was looking for an unusual venue for the spring number of *Trend*, so I showed her the advert. She wasn't very interested at first — she had set her sights on some National Trust property, but there was some mix-up over dates, and now it's all settled. It's the gatehouse. We're going up to Norfolk tonight, and starting work first light tomorrow.'

'Where will you stay?'

'I thought perhaps the hotel where mother stayed during the war. I'd like to stay two nights if possible, so that I'll have time to see something of Norwich while I'm up there. What was the name of that hotel?'

They were sitting close to the fire which was enclosed by a fireguard for Carla's protection. Carla had climbed onto Lottie's lap, and was regarding her mother with alert violet-blue eyes, waiting for a present to put in an appearance. Presents and Charley, she knew, always arrived together.

'I shouldn't mention Norfolk — not tonight. This time of the year is always difficult for your mother. Today is the anniversary of your father's death. I'll tell her about your assignment tomorrow . . .'

Charley's expression clouded. 'Poor Mother, after all this time — she still feels it, doesn't she. I used to dread this day when I was young, she was always so depressed. I'll try not to say anything untoward — I'll be on my best behaviour, Lottie, I promise.'

'You always are, my dear. Now I'd better go and help Charlotte with the tea.'

She stood Carla down, and Charley alone with her daughter and anxious for a cuddle, beckoned to her. 'Come and sit on my lap, darling. Carla, come to mummy.'

But Carla held back, shyly sucking one finger. It wasn't until Charley produced a parcel that she ran forward, her face all eagerness. It was a colouring book and crayons. Nothing delighted Carla more than a book to colour or scribble in. She immediately squatted down on the hearth-rug and got to work.

'Do your colouring on my lap, Carla. Then I can watch you. Come along darling, let me see . . .'

Carla looked up at her and grinned, reminding Charley with a stab of pain, of Larry. She bent down and tried to hoist her bodily, but Carla struggled, and Charley then discovered how heavy an uncooperative child could be.

'Carla, sweetheart, don't be so difficult – mummy only wants a little cuddle.'

Charlotte arrived with the tea-trolley. 'What's going on?'

'I was only trying to get Carla to sit on my lap, but she doesn't appear to want to . . .'

'What else do you expect? You're practically a stranger to her.'

Charley forgave her mother that remark, taking into consideration the day it was.

They had tea at the fireside, Carla in her own small chair. She had fastidious table manners and the air of a miniature adult, which for the first time, Charley found worrying. It was unnatural in a child of that age to be so well-behaved. Four generations, she thought – four generations of Charlottes. Three generations of unmarried mothers, and possibly a fourth if history repeated itself. And all presenting to the world a picture of middle-class respectability.

A sudden thought came to her. A house of women – a nunnery – a house of birds, that's what they were, nothing but a house of birds. *A House of Birds*. It struck her as funny, and though she tried to hold it back, laughter exploded from her. The suddenness of the noise so startled Charlotte she upset her tea, and with black looks went off to deal with the stain on her blouse.

'You promised me,' said Lottie reproachfully.

'I'm sorry Lottie, I couldn't help it. I've had such a silly idea. I suddenly thought of this house as a house of birds. Birds – females – get it . . . ?'

'I do, and I don't think it at all funny – in fact it's vulgar. And for goodness sake, don't repeat such nonsense in front of your mother . . . Good gracious, whatever's the matter with Carla . . .'

Carla, drumming her heels on the legs of her chair, her face as red as a beetroot, her mouth wide open, was shrieking with laughter. 'She's only trying to out-do me,' said Charley, amused.

'She's hysterical! See what your foolishness has triggered off . . . You'd better calm her down before Charlotte comes back . . .'

What Charley could see, with painful clarity, was that Carla was laughing in a way she had never laughed before. Laughing like any normal excited child – making as much noise as she could, and thoroughly enjoying it. She had every care that money and love could provide, but she was deprived of the one thing that was every child's birthright – fun. Laughter was missing in that house – along with the company of other children.

No more procrastination. As soon as she got back from Norfolk, she would arrange for Carla to start at nursery school or join a playgroup. Then she would start looking for a home for the two of them. She couldn't blame Charlotte or Lottie – they had done their duty by Carla as they saw it. It was she who had failed in hers.

She lifted Carla from her chair, and this time Carla didn't resist her when she sat her on her lap. She held her close, stroking her hair, kissing her unashamedly in the way that her mother used to kiss her. She remembered one of the games Lottie used to play with her when she was a toddler. 'This is the church, and there's the steeple.' Carla loved it . . . she couldn't have enough of it.

'More,' she said, every time Charley stopped.

Sitting there, watching fondly, Lottie said, 'Children never outgrow those old nursery games. You should do this more often, Charley.'

'I will in future . . .'

When it came time to say goodbye, Carla clung to her and for the first time ever, burst into tears.

'Don't go, Mummy, don't go . . . stay with me.' Her arms tightened round Charley's neck.

Carla wanted *her*. Not Charlotte – not Lottie – but her – her mother. Torn between grief and happiness, Charley hugged her daughter.

'I don't want to go, either, darling, but it's the last time.' She wiped away Carla's tears and then her own. 'When I come back we'll be together always and always . . .'

'Come along – let's get cracking while the light's still good.' Ben stood chafing his hands together. He was wearing nothing over his velvet jacket which was designed for style rather than warmth. The wind blew his hair across his face and his eyes were watering. 'Ye Gods – what a place. Charley, whatever possessed you to wish this on us? What on earth have we done to deserve it?'

Poor Ben. He hadn't much flesh on his bones, and now he looked shrivelled. Some places did not inspire him, and it was obvious the gatehouse was one. She had been disappointed at first sight too, but that disappointment soon wore off. It was no good expecting the gatehouse to look as it did in Lottie's time. More than half a century had passed since then.

It had been empty for six months, and no house left empty looks inviting, especially on a November's day when the clouds hang low and the wind bears down from the north-east. The windows of the old house had been boarded up, but some vandal had prised one of the shutters loose and that kept up a constant banging.

They had had a vociferous audience for the first half hour – the men harvesting the beet in the field alongside the line. Then, just as the equipment was in place and they were all set to start, a throaty bray like that of an aging donkey heralded the approach of one of the diesel trains that still carried freight along that line. Charley, shivering in a diaphanous kaftan was treated to a series of wolf whistles from both driver and guard.

Silence once more. The harvesters had moved on. There wasn't another train due until three o'clock. Work could commence.

At last Ben was satisfied. He had taken some good shots of Charley. One in a sleeveless white wool gaberdine with knee-length socks; in another kaftan, this time made of synthetic silk; a red plastic raincoat with matching hat, and finally a bolero-suit and a nylon boa wound round her throat, its ends trailing down her back.

She changed back into her own clothes in the van which was used, when not acting as a chuck-wagon, as a dressing-room. They had been offered the key to the gatehouse by the station master at Beckton Market, to whom they had had to show the written permission to use the premises, and were now sorry they hadn't taken him up on the offer. At least they could have sheltered inside out of the wind, and perhaps got a fire started. The earth closet at the end of the garden came in useful.

'I wish there was a pub nearer than the Ferry Inn,' Ben grumbled. His pocket flask was empty and there was no more coffee left.

'That place we passed up the lane looked promising,' said one of the crew. 'D'you think there's any chance of getting a drink there?'

'No chance, buddy. Didn't you read the notice – Thornmere Hall School for Girls. Of course they might, out of the kindness of their hearts, offer to make you a cup of cocoa.'

'Get lost!'

Ben strolled over to Charley, sitting in her car, and waiting. 'The lads are anxious to hit the road. What about you? What do you say to a drink and something to eat at the village inn first?'

'I'd like a drink, and I could certainly do with something to eat, I'm starving . . .'

'You're not in a hurry to get back then?'

'No, I thought I told you. I'm staying an extra night.'

There was a piece of waste land next to the inn that

served as a car-park. They pulled up, facing the river. As Charley switched off her engine she noticed a Broad's cruiser moored up at the staithe, and heard voices coming from it, then a girl's laughter.

In summer the inn was crowded out with boaters, but out of season it relied on the locals and occasional travelling salesmen. Workers from boatyards in the district, or men working on the land, often called in for their lunchtime pints. All this they learnt from the station master who was eager to impart any information he thought might be useful. Ben led the way into the bar parlour where the first thing they spotted was a blazing fire. Charley went to it like a homing pigeon.

Three men who were propping up the bar, looked them over, docketing them in their minds, she thought, as a couple of London freaks, or more likely, foreigners. They must get used to all sorts coming to the Broads, though what they made of Ben, with his velvet jacket and silk shirt, and thin narrow face framed in long wavy hair, she couldn't guess. She saw one old local, seated at a nearby table, make voluble use of a convenient spittoon.

Ben came back from the bar with red wine for her and Scotch for himself.

'The landlady said she could do us cold beef sandwiches and coffee. Okay with you, darling?'

Warming herself by the fire, listening dreamily to the Norfolk voices, Charley felt a sense of well-being steal over her. Had Lottie ever been in this old bar-parlour, she wondered. She doubted it – women of her generation didn't frequent pubs. This one was really old. Its smoke-grimed walls leaned inwards, its beams were genuine. It must have been a feature of the landscape generations before Lottie was born. The sandwiches arrived, and not just sandwiches. Three varieties of pickles and a tossed salad was served with them.

By the time they had finished their meal, and they didn't hurry, the small room was crowded, and hazy with cigarette smoke. Sleepily, Charley rested her head against the wall and closed her eyes. She drifted effortlessly. Voices raised in good-humoured ribaldry, waxed and waned about her. One Norfolk voice, louder than the rest, aroused her to full consciousness.

'I know my missus wouldn't think much to a honeymoon in one of them leaky ole tubs of Percy Brown's,' she heard.

'Your missus wouldn't know a honeymoon from a Saturday night out, you mean old bugger,' came a retort which brought forth knowing gales of laughter. One laugh, full-voiced and booming, hit Charley like a douche of ice water.

She felt the blood drain from her face. She looked desperately towards the knot of men at the counter, and shivered.

'What's the matter?' said Ben. 'You can't still be cold.'

'Somebody just walked over my grave.'

The coincidence was too incredible. She must be mistaken. She must be dreaming! It could not possibly be Larry. He was in Greece, wasn't he? When she thought of the implication behind the remark about honeymooning on the Broads, she felt sick.

'I'm going to get you a brandy. I don't want you passing out on me...' Ben got up and walked over to the bar. The knot of men made way for him, and it was then Charley saw a girl with Larry's arm lightly resting on her shoulders. She was talking rapidly, her voice unintelligible against the hubbub, but whatever she said was met with admiring laughter. She had, Charley could see, her audience eating out of her hand, and that included Larry. She was dark, and years younger than he, and she bubbled over with an effervescence that Charley found woundingly familiar. The girl reminded her of herself as she used to be.

She stumbled to her feet, unintentionally scraping her chair on the bare floorboards as she did so. Larry looked round, and across the smoke-filled room, their eyes met. She saw the shock of recognition in his, the sudden surprised delight that suffused his face. She saw him push his way through the crowd to get to her, and she turned and fled.

Outside, the cold air took her breath away, but it cleared her head. She heard Larry crunching over the loose stones in pursuit of her, shouting her name. She dodged round the back of the inn and ran for her car knowing once there she would be safe. He wouldn't be able to follow. His car would be parked in the garage of the boatyard from which he had hired the cruiser.

His last angry bellow was cut short as she revved the engine. She crashed the gears, started with a kangaroo leap, stalled, started again, took off smoothly, and shot away at sixty miles an hour. Larry dropped away behind her. She reached the bridge – rocketed over. She began to laugh.

Her laughter increased when she thought of Ben coming back to the table with the brandy, and finding her missing. How long would he wait before it dawned on him she wasn't in the Ladies?' He was magic with his camera but when faced with the unpredictable, he was lost. Suddenly, she found she wasn't laughing anymore, but crying.

'Lottie?'

'Darling! What a lovely surprise. Where are you speaking from? The hotel. Well, how's everything going? How's Norfolk? Yes, dear, of course, I'll hear all about it when you get home. Carla's fine – yes, fine. Keeps asking when you'll be back, of course. Charlotte has taken her down to the shops in the push-chair. Charley dear, are you crying?'

'Lottie, I've seen Larry again – yes, just now – at the Ferry Inn. He came in . . . he came in with his wife – I said *wife*, Lottie . . . I know it was his wife, I saw her wedding ring. They're on their honeymoon. Yes . . . I'm sure. I can't stay here any longer – I've settled up, and I'm coming straight home now – yes now. I want to see Carla . . . Oh, Lottie – I'm so unhappy – I thought I had got him out of my system but I haven't – I love him as much as ever. Oh, Lottie, what shall I do . . . I feel so desperate . . .'

It had started to drizzle as she left Norwich, and now, half-way on her journey home the rain was pelting down, closing around her like a thick grey curtain. It was not yet four, but daylight was fading, and her headlights cut two bright swathes through the gloom, highlighting the shining surface of the road.

Fortunately, there was little traffic, and what there was was coming from London. The road ahead was clear. Impatiently, she brushed away the tears that would keep spurting. Stupidly, they seemed to come of their own accord. She didn't feel like crying anymore – she felt more like screaming obscenities at a quirk of fate which had brought Larry back into her life.

What a fool she was to have run off like that. She should have kept her cool, introduced Ben. Ben, with his malicious wit, would soon have put Larry in his place. Larry had wanted to speak to her – had shown pleasure at seeing her, not embarrassment. Perhaps he had wanted to ask about Carla. It could have all been so civilised – except there was nothing civilised about her feelings for Larry. They were raw, and raging inside her. Her tears came in earnest. Oh Larry, you bastard, why did you have to reject me? Why did you marry her – why not me? Didn't you love me enough for that? Oh Carla – you're all I've got now. Little precious, you'll help me forget . . .

She leant forward to wipe the condensation from the windscreen, and then saw the tree . . . but too late to avoid it.

THIRTEEN | *Carla*
Present Day

It was July, and the barley in the field alongside the cottage rustled fitfully, ripe for harvesting in the drying wind. Carla, barricaded in the cottage against a plague of harvest mites, prayed earnestly for rain. These tiny, black living creatures, no bigger than grains of pepper, were driving her mad. Living in the country, she was discovering, was not all honeysuckle and roses. It had its drawbacks.

She had just returned from London where she had been to attend Mr Lincoln's funeral, that kindly man who had steered her through the first difficult weeks following Lottie's death, and had taken the headache out of the business of disposing of the Wenley house and its contents.

She had spent the night at the home of an old school friend, and the following day had driven past Laburnum Lodge on her way to call on Mrs Baker. It was strange to think of that substantial Victorian house now belonging to someone else. It had been part of her life for twenty-five years, and one couldn't just wipe out a quarter of a century without a pang of regret. Yet, if she had her time again, she would not undo her hasty decision to sell up and move to Norfolk. City life wasn't for her any more. She enjoyed a shopping expedition to the West End, but returned to Anne's house exasperated by crowded pavements and even more crowded streets. She longed for the wide open spaces of Norfolk.

But even in Norfolk problems awaited her. There was all the business of having the cottage wired for electricity, and then the wait until the electricity board got around to erecting the necessary poles to carry the cables to the cottage. The final bill for all this was staggering, but it was either that or relying on a generator, which she knew she couldn't cope with. Well, now she had electricity, but there was still no water. A date had not yet been fixed for the digging of a deep bore well, and until then, she still relied on Jessie for bed and breakfast.

She locked the cottage door behind her with a sense of achievement. With the exception of the well, the cottage was now complete. The summer days had passed happily, as she had fitted out and furnished her gatehouse, using only the choicest and smallest pieces from the Wenley house. She had supplemented these with articles from craft fairs and the antique shops of Norwich.

To her delight, the house martins had returned in May. At first they were frustrated by their unsuccessful attempts to gain access to the house. She had been warned by Mr Cartwright to keep all the windows closed until they had found alternative sites, which they did, settling down to nest under the eaves. The twittering of the fledglings was a continuous accompaniment as she went about her job of unpacking, and sorting out, and making room.

She spent her nights at Thornmere Lodge and her days at the gatehouse, and unless she had something heavy to transport, she normally walked the short distance between the two places. During her walks she had observed, with the eye of an artist, how the colours and pattern of the countryside changed with the seasons. Now, in high summer, with the corn ripe and the trees heavy with leaf, there was a dreamy, tired and rather dusty look about the landscape. There were poppies among the barley, and honeysuckle in the hedgerows, and the grass verges were afroth with cow-parsley. Yes, it was very pleasant, here in Lottie's land, she thought. And just over three miles away, her father lived.

She had played a game with herself all summer. Such as, I'll wait until the decorating is finished and then contact him. Then, I'll leave it until the place is furnished. And now, I'll wait until the well has been dug. She knew these were all excuses, and that she would go on making excuses until something jolted her out of her uncertainty. But why did she hesitate? Was it fear of being rejected? No, worse than that. Fear of being accepted with indifference.

The lodge was empty. Jessie was not yet back from the churchyard where she had gone to put flowers on her parents' grave. Carla ran a bath and soaked herself free of the dust that had blown off the fields. She washed the mites out of her hair, and now sat in a towelling bathrobe, drying it in the open air. Jessie returned, carrying an old-type zinc bucket which she dumped on the tiles outside the kitchen door. Her face was streaked with perspiration.

'The churchyard was like an oven,' she said, blowing out her lips as if expiring for air. 'There's not a scrap of shade since all the diseased elms had to come down. Have you had supper? I left it ready in the fridge.'

'I waited for you. No, I'll get it. You sit down, you look worn out. Have you been pestered with these horrible little mites or harvest blight or bugs, whatever you call them? They've tormented me all day. They even got into my fridge.'

'They'll be gone as soon as the barley is harvested, and that won't be long now,' said Jessie with the complacency of one who accepted such things as a fact of life. 'They've already made a start on the field next to the church.'

They sat over their meal until dusk had gathered and bats swooped overhead, hawking for moths. It was as warm as midday, and they ate crab salad from trays on their laps. Crab freshly caught at Cromer, according to Jessie.

'Do you know how I spent most of my time up at the churchyard?' she said, aggrieved. 'Scrubbing the headstone. It was covered in some kind of slimy green weed, and it took me ages to get it off. I won't let it get such a hold again.'

'I hope it wasn't some rare lichen you scrubbed off, Jessie. You'll have the conservationists after you.'

'Blow that for a lark,' said Jessie impatiently. 'I didn't pay out good money to put up a headstone to my mother and father, and then not be able to read it. By the way, old Tom Butcher came and had a word with me. He was the sexton before he retired – the last of a dying breed, I think. He asked after you – you've caused a lot of interest in the village. There isn't anybody in Thornmere now who doesn't know of your connections with the gatehouse. He pointed out to me where the Fosters are buried. It's in a corner of the churchyard waist-high with nettles. I thought if we took a bill-hook over there one day, per-haps between us, we could tidy it up a bit – make it look as if it's being cared for . . .'

Carla, who had fallen into a state of torpor under the influence of Jessie's somnolent voice, was suddenly wide awake. 'Graves? Did you say Foster graves? I didn't know anything about that. What graves?'

'Only two as far as he knew. The one where Lottie's mother and father and baby brother were buried, and next to them, the one belonging to the youngest Foster girl, Violet. Ted Foster was cremated. It's impossible to see the graves, it's too overgrown . . .'

'But the headstones. It must be possible to see the headstones, surely?'

'Carla, my dear, working class people in those times didn't have money for headstones. Many of them didn't have graves of their own, even. They were buried by the parish in common graves.'

Carla thoughtfully digested this information. 'I wonder if it's too late to do anything about headstones now,' she said.

The well was finished. It had taken five days, and for that five days the gatehouse became a focal point for most of the men and lads of the village. Carla was kept on the trot, serving refreshments to the well-diggers, and wondered if she should extend hospitality to the thirsty spectators also, for the heat-wave still went on. When she consulted Jessie who had come up to help her, the reply was brief and emphatic, 'You start that lark, my girl, and you won't know when to stop.'

The men had arrived, early one morning, and parked their lorry just inside the garden. They then erected a tripod within working distance of the generator fixed in the back of the lorry which would, in turn, supply power to hoist the pile driver and hammer it into the unyielding ground. Having all this explained to her in words one would use to a five-year-old, Carla found rather funny.

'But how do you know that you will find water in the exact spot you've chosen?' she asked the more senior of the two men. 'Don't you have to employ a water diviner to tell you whereabouts to sink a well?'

The man eyed her with amused contempt. 'Anywhere you drill in Norfolk, you'll come to water,' he said.

They came to water around midday, on the third day, and spent all the afternoon pumping it out. Carla watched the milky-coloured liquid flowing freely along the lane, and rejoiced to think that her days of carrying cans of water up from the lodge were numbered. The well diggers came again on Thursday and spent that day pumping too, and just before five o'clock, the time they normally knocked off, the water ran clear. They said they would come the following morning to collect their equipment, and thanked her for the way she had looked after them.

So what now was stopping her from making herself known to her father? She'd just wait until the electrician had fitted an automatic pump to the well head, which when switched on would pump water to the storage tanks in the gatehouse, then she would see about it. When that was done she could think of no further excuses.

The Thatched House, Beckton Market was easy enough

to find, as it was the only house with a thatched roof in Station Road; an unadopted tree-lined avenue that swept down to a defunct station, now being used as a timber yard.

Carla turned the car in the station approach and drove slowly back along the avenue, still putting off an occasion which she dreaded and desired in equal measure. Most of the houses were late Edwardian, standing in one acre plots originally, but many had since been infilled with modern houses. Not the Thatched House however. It stood freely amidst an orderly wilderness of trees and shrubs and lawns sprinkled profusely with buttercups and daisies. Carla fell in love with it on sight. Nothing put her off a garden more than geometrical ranks of brightly coloured annuals.

The drive led in a wide sweep to the side of the house, where the main entrance was situated. And here, running at right angles to the double hedge that separated the garden from its neighbours, was a trellis work screen entwined with climbing roses and sweetpeas, the only cultivated flowers in the garden.

She stood for a while, contemplating the sweetpeas, remembering they were one of Lottie's favourite flowers and felt a sudden urge to paint them.

The house itself was a charming architectural fraud. For though it was designed to look like a Tudor manor house, it was undoubtedly Edwardian. She could tell that by the width and height of its casement windows with their large clear panes of glass, instead of the tiny diamond panes usually associated with Elizabethan houses. As with the garden, she fell instantly in love with it.

Well now, all she had to do was to knock on the door and introduce herself. She had dressed well for this occasion, in a new classic two-piece she had purchased while in London, and an Italian blue silk blouse which did not quite match the violet of her eyes. She wore the medallion containing Henry Massingham's photo pinned to the lapel of her jacket, and her hair, newly cut and styled in Norwich, framed her face in a medieval page's bob. She looked, she knew, the epitome of chic and confidence, but the palms of her hands were wet with perspiration as she rang the bell.

It was opened, after a long wait, by a good-looking, black-haired woman wearing a linen overall. She took in Carla's appearance with a studied look from heavy-lidded, very dark eyes, in which Carla fancied she saw a hint of cynicism.

She started to speak, then swallowed. Her mouth was extremely dry. She tried again. 'Is Mr Laurence Marsh at home?'

She was disconcerted to see a look of amused exasperation come and go in the woman's face. Had she come at an inopportune time? Would any time be opportune?

'Mr Marsh is rather busy just now,' the woman said, with a slight foreign-sounding inflection.

'I see . . . I – I wouldn't take up much of his time.' Only twenty-five years of reminiscences in which he had not the slightest interest! She suddenly thought of a valid reason for her visit. One that would get her past the door, anyway. 'A few months ago I saw a painting by Laurence Marsh of the old gatehouse at Thornmere. It was on display in Bentall's Gallery and I tried to buy it then, but Mr Bentall said it was not for sale. I wondered if Mr Marsh had changed his mind since then?'

The woman invited her in. 'In that case, you had better ask him yourself,' she said with a thin-lipped smile.

She led Carla through a hall furnished like a sitting-room, and used as one by the look of its comfortable disorder. Down three steps into a barn-sized kitchen, where an enormous Welsh dresser and an Aga cooker flanked two opposing walls, and bunches of herbs and onions hung from superimposed beams. Then through a stable-type door into a smaller more modern kitchen, where, on an electric stove, jam was bubbling in a preserving-pan. From here, a glazed door led into the rear part of the garden.

This was a repetition, only larger, of the one at the front and side of the house. Lawns and shrubs and trees, and a patch of rough grass left as a children's play area, with a swing, and slide, and see-saw. At the far end, was a very superior garden chalet, and before this, a heavily built, grey-haired man was playing rough and tumble with two small, shrieking boys.

'I'll leave you to introduce yourself,' the woman said, with another thin-lipped smile. 'I must return to my jam.'

Could this possibly be Laurence Marsh, this elderly man, on whose broad back the smaller of the boys was straddling, and from whose underparts the older boy hung like a spider monkey to its mother! Her image of the Shelley-type person she had nurtured for over twenty years suddenly faded, making her feel defrauded.

Her approach made no sound on the moss-ridden lawn, and as she drew closer she saw that the two little boys were in fact, two little girls in cotton shorts. Their likeness to the woman who had opened the door was unmistakable.

Her nervous 'Good afternoon' was drowned by excited yells from the children. She gave an apologetic cough, but without effect. She moved until she stood right in the line of Laurence Marsh's vision, should he look up, which he did, staring fixedly at her legs. He raised his head and a grin spread broadly across his face, then he got smartly to his feet, shedding the two small girls like unwanted pieces of clothing. They immediately clamped themselves, one to each of his legs, protesting vociferously. He shook them off.

'Enough is enough,' he boomed in a voice of authority. 'I have a visitor, and I wish to be left in peace. Will you please go into the house and ask your mother if she could make us coffee?'

To Carla's surprise, the girls dutifully trotted off but not before beaming in her direction, accusing and baleful glances.

'Your housekeeper told me you were busy,' she said uncomfortably.

'I was busy – minding her children while she was busy making my jam. And by the way, to avoid misunderstanding, Irina is my wife – not my housekeeper,' he said, watching her closely.

She had a stomach-churning conviction that he had guessed her identity. There was something of a small boy caught out in mischief in that sheepish grin. She smouldered with resentment.

'I really don't want coffee,' she said. 'And it's hardly fair to ask your wife to stop her jam-making just to get it for me.'

'And for me, too. My mouth is very dry, which is not a sign of nervousness, I hasten to add, but a sign that I want my coffee. Don't you think a stimulant is in order as we talk? We may need it.'

His casual reference to what was uppermost in their minds filled her with panic. It was, as she had dreaded, to be an indifferent acceptance after all, and she had prayed for something more meaningful. All right, then. She could play that game too.

Her mind was in a turmoil over dates and ages, which seemed to her to be all wrong. If only, instead of sparing Lottie's feelings, she had pestered her for more information about her father. She would, she felt, have been less put off balance by discovering that he was old enough to be her grandfather. She had been brought up to respect her elders, but respect was the last thing she felt towards Laurence Marsh at the moment.

'So Carla', he said, as he seated himself the other side of a wickerwork table. 'You have come to see me at last.'

Hearing her name on his lips brought a sudden rush of tears. She blinked them away, hoping he hadn't noticed. 'You knew who I was. You knew who I was the minute you clapped eyes on me,' she charged him.

'Clapped eyes on your legs, more like it. I couldn't fail to recognise your mother's legs.' His smile faded. He stared with arresting blue eyes beneath shaggy white brows. 'I have been awaiting your arrival since Bob Bentall told me about your interest in my painting of the Thornmere gatehouse. He also told me that you are now its present owner. You're not exactly unknown around here, Carla. Your builder, Fred Cartwright, is an old drinking pal of mine. He's kept me informed of his progress.'

Irina arrived bearing coffee on a tray which she put on the table between them. 'Coffee for two,' she said in her throaty voice.

'You're not joining us?' Larry queried.

'If I don't get my jam into pots right away, the pots will go cold, and the jam will set in the pan.'

'Irina. This is Carla.'

Immediately, the woman's veiled antagonism vanished. She looked at Carla with startled eyes, and then her face broke into laughter, turning its severe lines into becoming curves.

'*Carla*! You are Carla! Oh, I wish I'd known that sooner. I wouldn't have greeted you so starchily. I took you to be another deluded female admirer of my husband – your father, I mean. He attracts them like bees to a honey-pot. They come as disciples and stay as slaves. I feed them and wait on them, and clean up after them, while they sit at Larry's feet and silently worship him. They think he is a romantic figure. He is hailed as the most romantic painter of modern times. Romantic! They should hear him snore. They should see him without his body belt.'

'My wife exaggerates,' said Larry, taking a piece of shortbread and biting into it. 'They are not deluded creatures, though I grant they are all female. They come in all ages and sizes, with one thing in common. To become accomplished artists. Some are good, but more often than not, they are hopeless. I encourage the good and I tell the hopeless to go away and take up cooking instead. My wife cooks extremely well. She is also a great comforter and provider. She mops up the tears of those I have offended, and sends them on their way, if not rejoicing, at least in better spirits. Irina, my dear, please do join us. This coffee is excellent.'

'I said no, darling. I really must get back to my jam. Besides, you two must have so much to say to each other. See you later, Carla. Larry, you must persuade her to stay for supper.'

'You will have noticed Irina's slight accent,' said Larry, when she had gone. 'Very sexy I thought it, when she first came to work for me. You were right, she was my housekeeper for a time then she became my mistress, and then, my wife. Her mother was Spanish and her father Hungarian, and she was reared in England. All my wives were or are foreign . . .'

'Wives!' said Carla, jolted out of her morbid silence. 'Did you say *wives*?'

'Three actually. My first was a girl from a remote Greek isle with eyes like pools of ink. She died when my eldest son, Andrew, was born. Then I was married for ten years to an attractive American lady, who left me eventually because, she said, she couldn't put up with my arrogance any longer. She married again, and now lives happily in a very lush house in Philadelphia. Actually, we were on our honeymoon on the Broads, when I first saw the Thornmere gatehouse, and it was she who suggested I painted it. She thought I was real mean not to give it to her, but I had in mind someone else to give it to.' He lost the thread of his narrative, then with a sigh, resumed. 'I bear no ill-will towards Alison for leaving me. Our marriage was good while it lasted, and she allowed me to keep the children. They always spend summer holidays and New Year with their mother.'

'How many children do you have altogether?' said Carla, tensing herself for his answer.

'Five. Andrew, who is at his final year at Cambridge, but in Africa with the VSO at present. Timothy, a sixth-former at Beckton High School, and hoping to follow his half-brother to Cambridge. And Victoria, who has no ambitions but to be good, and last year at the age of fourteen, after going to a revival meeting in Norwich, became a born-again Christian. And Irina's two youngsters, of course. There you have it.'

'I see,' said Carla, feeling the pain of his omission like a stab from a knife. She tried to quell her jealousy of the generous-hearted Irina, of her two beautiful daughters, of the other, as yet, unknown half-siblings, but suppression only increased her pain. She was an outsider. She didn't belong.

Blissfully unaware of her feelings, Larry was saying, 'My one regret is that none of my children appear to have taken after me, which is just as well, as art, in any form, is a demanding mistress. I can't speak yet of the little ones, but if the graffiti on the walls on their bedroom is anything to go by, it shows a lamentable lack of talent.' He paused. 'You are not drinking your coffee. Perhaps tea would have been more to your taste? My wives weaned me from the ubiquitous English habit of drinking tea.' Absentmindedly, he helped himself to the remaining piece of shortbread. 'Irina will make you tea if you prefer it. Just give her a shout.'

Carla thought of the portfolio of drawings she had left on the back seat of her car, hoping that an opportunity would arise for her to show them to her father. She had imagined in her more sanguine moments, a conciliation over a pot of tea. But it had turned out to be coffee, and as bitter as the occasion.

'*I* take after you,' she said passionately. 'But then, I suppose, it goes against the grain for you to admit that I am also one of your offspring.'

They looked at each other like two opponents in a ring. 'I had no idea you wished to be considered one of my offspring. I thought, just the reverse,' he said irritably. Then his voice softened, his expression turned to one of appeasement. 'Did you bring any samples of your work to show me?'

'No,' she said, intent on goading him. 'I didn't think you'd be interested.'

'Regrettably, I recognise traits in you I remember in your grandmother.'

'If you mean Lottie, she was my great-grandmother.'

'I mean your grandmother. I met her the one and only time I went to Laburnum Lodge, just before I took your mother to Cornwall. It was a devastating experience for all of us. Lottie seemed to like me, I think, at first anyway. She welcomed me warmly, unlike your grandmother who showed her disapproval the minute I set foot in the door. She disapproved of everything about me. My age, the way I dressed, the way I lived. Most of all, she disapproved of the fact that marriage between me and Charley was not on the agenda.'

'And why not?' Carla hurled at him in outrage. His seeming heartlessness put her teeth on edge. 'What did you have against marriage to my mother? I understood you weren't the marrying kind – yet you went on later to marry not once, but three times. Doesn't that prove that it wasn't marriage as such that you objected to, but only marriage to my mother? Why? Didn't you love her sufficiently?'

'On the contrary,' he said. 'I loved your mother more than I loved or love any one of my wives.'

'A funny way you had of showing it – going off and leaving her just when she needed you most!'

The effect of her barbs was beginning to show on him. In the way the lines in his face deepened, the almost desperate note in his voice. 'Let's put it this way – that once I tried marriage, I rather liked it. I was a child of a broken marriage at a time when divorce wasn't condoned as it is now, and it left its mark on me. Little Marie cured that. Marriage was rather forced on me by her two brothers who came looking for me with knives. I know that sounds like a tall story, but it's absolutely true. I discovered to my delight that marriage was not the trap I once thought it, and I was devastated when it came to an end so tragically.'

'It's a pity my mother didn't have two brothers with knives,' Carla said sourly, and had the satisfaction of seeing him wince.

'That remark isn't worthy of Charley's daughter,' he said.

'No, but it's the sort of remark you'd expect from the daughter of Laurence Marsh,' she retorted.

He did not answer, and a welcome diversion came from the direction of the house. The sound of banging doors and raised voices. 'School's out,' he said quietly. 'Are you staying for supper?'

They exchanged noncommittal glances, and she did not see behind the smokescreen of his indifference, a man touched on the raw.

'I don't think so. I will tell your wife.' She walked away from him, quickly putting distance between them, and went into the house. The utility room was empty, but filled with the lingering smell of boiling strawberries. A dozen jars of jam lined up on the work surface, reflected rosy patches of light on the white-washed walls. A tall youth with his father's blue eyes appeared in the open doorway, grinning self-consciously, and behind him in the main kitchen, Carla could see the hovering figure of a younger girl.

'Hi there, you must be my new sister. I'm Tim – have a paw,' he said, extending his hand. 'Happy to have you join the club.' He behaved as if the sudden appearance of an unknown sister was an everyday event. 'This is my kid sister, Victoria, lurking behind me. She wants to say a quick hallo before she disappears upstairs to say her prayers. She always feels religion coming over her whenever there are chores to be done. Such as washing up or preparing vegetables . . .'

Victoria burst into stormy tears. 'You rotten beast – you're always saying that, and you know it's not true.' She lacked her brother's robustness and seemed also to lack his roguish sense of humour. Her eyes met Carla's shyly, then flooded with tears again. 'I wanted to show you my collection of foreign dolls. I've been collecting them since I was six years old, but now he's spoilt it, the beast!' They heard her drumming up the stairs, and a door banged.

'Timothy,' said Irina sharply. 'That joke of yours is wearing very thin, and I don't want to hear it ever again. Now go up and make peace with your sister, and offer to help her with her homework. That should dry her tears. Then you can peel the potatoes for me. I've left them ready in the sink.'

Irina, Carla could see, had got Larry's children well in hand, but the reins she held were slack. Her own two, completely indifferent to the hubbub around them, sat at the kitchen table, happily absorbed in cutting up runner beans with safety scissors.

Irina turned her attention to Carla. 'These little storms are frequent, but not long-lasting. Victoria's emotionalism is only skin deep.' A peal of girlish laughter, floating down the stairs at that moment, gave point to this observation. 'Now, would you like to visit the bathroom before we eat?'

'If you don't mind, I won't stay for supper,' said Carla awkwardly. 'I have several jobs awaiting me at home.'

'I hope my manner, when you first arrived, hasn't put you off. I'm afraid I am rather on the defensive where Larry is concerned. I feel I've got to protect him against himself. People are inclined to take advantage of him.'

We can't be thinking of the same man, thought Carla. They walked to the front door together. 'I'll come as far as my herb garden, I want some rosemary for the lamb.' Irina stepped out onto the drive with her. 'Where did you leave your car?'

'In the lane.' Carla looked back at the house, its pale pink walls stippled now with shadows. Through the trellis work she could see Larry sitting on the verandah of the garden chalet, with his arms dangling between his knees and his head bent. He could be sleeping or he could be sulking.

Was this how Lottie felt when she was rejected by *her* father – this painful mix of anguish and anger? Rejection – such an ugly word, as ugly-sounding as its meaning. An on-going tragedy for all the Foster women. Lottie . . . Charlotte – for death in a way was a rejection . . . Charley and now herself . . . both rejected by the same man. She gritted her teeth, staring fiercely at the sweet peas as they swam in and out of focus, willing herself not to cry.

'I see you're admiring the sweet peas. They are lovely, aren't they?' said Irina.

'Beautiful . . .'

'We've had a good show of them this year, but they're nearly over now. Would you like some to take with you? I could pick you a bunch . . .'

'Oh no,' said Carla hastily, intent on escaping. 'I must go – I fear I've been too much of a nuisance, already.'

'You a nuisance!' Irina laughed. 'We've been waiting for you, Larry and I, expecting every day for you to call. I don't know why – but I had in mind . . . let us say, I didn't expect such a very chic and sophisticated young lady.'

'I'm far from sophisticated,' said Carla with desolation. 'I'm full of qualms at present.'

Irina's warm black eyes expressed her sympathy. 'Don't think too harshly of your father,' she said. 'Don't mind the things he says. He is not one to carry his heart on his sleeve – his feelings go too deep for that.'

'So deep he's probably forgotten where he's buried them,' Carla said. She forced a smile. 'Thank you for being so nice to me. I'm glad I've met you and – and the others. You are a lovely family, and I love your house. I'll be able to picture you all now.'

'Don't just picture us – come and see us. Come any time. The children would love to get to know you better.'

But by now Carla was wishing she hadn't come.

Nothing had been resolved. Sleeping dogs are best left undisturbed.

Her floral arrangement was coming along nicely, she thought, stepping back to admire her work. She had started near the painting of her mother, which she had hung, to follow a precedent, facing the bed, and was now working her way towards the window. A scattering of sweetpeas, delicate and decorative against the ivory-painted walls of her bedroom.

Painting, she found was a tonic, as well as a solace. Helping to cure her of the bitterness and disappointment that had convulsed her as she had driven away from the Thatched House. The visit had thrown her into a state of depression that lasted until she had a sudden remembered image of the sweet peas in Laurence Marsh's garden. Those delicate, pastel shaded flowers, balancing like butterflies on the tips of slender stalks had left a lasting impression on her. Her urge to paint them resurfaced, and she went off to seek out her painting materials which she had not touched since Lottie's death.

She had made a start on a humid day of dull skies and a still atmosphere, oblivious to the twittering of the housemartins, or the combine harvester chomping its way around a nearby field. With joy in her heart, she had become reacquainted with her muse, and in three days, working without pause, she had completed ten little bunches of flowers, catching with her brush, the delicate, almost transparent texture of sweet pea petals. She had also expunged the hurt stemming from her visit to the Thatched House.

Absorbed in her work, she did not hear a car draw up outside the gatehouse She did not hear the fruity — 'Anyone at home' — bawled through the open kitchen door. She did not know she had a visitor until someone behind her said, 'Very good. Very good, indeed. I see I won't have to tell you to take up cooking.'

She was pleased to find that she could greet her father

without any rush of blood to her head or sweaty palms. She said: 'I happen to know how to cook. Lottie taught me at a very early age.'

He grinned. 'That's as it should be.' He looked over her shoulder at the wall. 'But what have we here? Painted wallpaper?' He moved to examine it more closely, but instead his attention was caught by the old painting of her mother. He froze in his tracks, then she heard a sharply-drawn intake of breath. 'I had forgotten that,' he said. 'Completely forgotten it.'

She was gratified to see his eyes go moist. A week ago, she might have said something about the painting, for him, having more commercial than sentimental value. But not now. The wish to score points off her father had gone.

'That is my most valued possession,' she said. 'It brings my mother alive in a way that none of her photos do.'

He smiled at her with a whimsicality that sat oddly on his heavy features. 'That, I think, is the nicest compliment I have ever had paid me.' There was a pause in which their embarrassed, emotional glances slid off each other. 'Let's see if I can repay the compliment.'

Now indeed, her palms did feel wet. She waited with hammering heart as he went from sample to sample of her work, scrutinising carefully each posy of sweet peas in turn.

'They're damn good,' he said finally. 'I can't fault them. A bit too pretty-pretty for my tastes, but then I could be saying that out of envy.' He winked at her. 'My touch isn't delicate enough for this kind of work. Do you intend to repeat this sweet pea motif on all of the walls? If so, it's going to take a helluva time.'

'It's only a small room. It's the one where Lottie slept.'

He ignored that piece of information as if it were of no consequence. 'But you can't flog a wall to a dealer,' he said. 'You can't put a wall in an exhibition. You want your work to be recognised, don't you? For goodness sake girl, get your paintings down on paper. If you want to decorate your bedroom, buy wallpaper.'

'This was just a whim,' she said.

'Have you any other, hopefully portable, whims I can take a look at?'

'I brought a portfolio of my work to show you, last week. I got the impression you weren't interested, so I brought it away again.'

He looked shamefaced, but not for long. 'Yes, we did rather get off on the wrong foot,' he admitted. 'A pity, but never mind that now. I tried to phone you, but you're not on the phone, you exasperating girl, and I'm no bloody good at writing letters. I decided it was up to me to return your call.'

'I'm glad you did,' she said sincerely.

'But why aren't you on the phone? A phone these days is a necessity of life . . .'

'It's also a distraction, and in any case, I don't need a phone. I can't think of anybody I want to phone.'

He stared at her. 'I can't believe this. No boyfriends for you to call or have call you? Don't tell me a girl with your eyes and those legs doesn't have a list of callers.'

'No boyfriends,' she said firmly.

'What about your sex-life?'

Though embarrassed by his bluntness, she couldn't repress a laugh. 'I can take it or leave it.'

'*I can take it or leave it*,' he mimicked. 'What sort of answer is that?' With a grunt he squared his shoulders. 'Show me some more of your work. At least, there's a sense of realism in that.'

She took him to the room next door, the main bedroom. 'I'm using this as a studio, until I have a proper one built. Down the garden, where the old outhouse used to be. Mr Cartwright says the foundations are still good.'

'You're not intending to settle here permanently? I'm surprised. I thought you intended it as a holiday home.' She didn't answer, for she had no answer to that yet. She put her portfolio of paintings into his hands and waited, anxious and expectant, for his verdict.

The wait was not long. She saw interest dawn in his face which increased to enthusiasm. He went through them all again, studying each one more closely. When he had finished, he gave a deep and satisfactory (to Carla) sigh.

'They're damn good,' he said. 'Some of them lack style, and your technique is a bit dodgy, but practise and experience will put that right. Carla, you have talent. I'm proud of you.'

He singled out two canvases, her first attempts in oils, though oil she had found was an easier medium to paint with than water colours. She recalled driving out into rural Essex to catch the effect of sunshine on a field of ripe mustard. And another time, she had been emotionally aroused by the surprising blueness of a field of borage.

'Your Van Gogh period, I presume,' he scoffed teasingly. 'I like them, Carla, but your colours are not bold enough. The rape should be more yellow, and the lavender, purple.'

'That's just the point,' she said hesitantly. 'It's mustard not rape, and borage not lavender. I suppose I should have titled them.'

He gave a howl of laughter. 'Pardon my ignorance. I don't suppose I've seen a field of borage in my life, though I believe Irina grows some in her herb garden. But seriously, Carla, what are these paintings doing shut away in a portfolio? They should be on display. Don't be selfish. Give someone else a chance to enjoy them.'

'You think they are as good as that?' She couldn't believe he meant it. He was a tease, like his son, Timothy.

'Of course I mean it. There's room for improvement, but the talent is there. Work on it, Carla.'

She kept her miniatures until last, because they were important to her, and she wanted to spring them on him as her *piéce de resistance*. 'My Hilliard phase,' she said lightly. But he only mildly liked them, saying they were not up to the standard of her other work. He saw her disappointment.

'You can't be good at everything, my girl, and still-life is your métier. Still-life – and in water colours. I think, if you stick to it, you could become a brilliant water-colourist.'

'You're thinking of the sweet peas?'

'I'm thinking of what you're best at. But yes, I'd like to take another look at your sweet peas . . .'

But what he really wanted was to take another look at her mother's portrait. 'I remember her looking just like that,' he said reflectively. 'She laughed such a lot. Do you laugh much, Charley's daughter?'

'Not much – but I smile quite frequently.'

He grinned. 'You've always got an answer pat, haven't you. Presumably, you get that from me.' He fell serious. 'I'm never going to make you understand how I felt about Charley.'

'You could try.'

'I'd be using a weary old cliché to say I loved her too much to marry her, but that's how it was really. She would have subjugated herself to me, and that enviable unquenchable spirit would have been quenched in time by my infidelities. I couldn't keep faithful to any one woman, Carla, not then. I can now, because I'm a burnt out old man, though Irina does manage to bring me up to scratch at times.

'I sent her some money for you. That was a mistake too. A bloody, stupid, crass thing to do. I wasn't trying to ease my conscience, or to make a point. I was trying to make a contribution. Your mother wrote and told me she had put it by for your twenty-first birthday.' He gave Carla a cautious, sideways look. 'I hope it came in useful?'

'I bought a car with it. My first car – an old banger – and I spent the rest on a weekend in Paris. I went especially to see the Mona Lisa, but couldn't get near it because of the security at the Louvre, and because of all those Japanese trying to view it with periscopes. I came away disheartened, and spent the rest of the morning in W.H. Smith's, buying up English paperbacks I could have got cheaper in London.'

Larry laughed. 'Put it down to experience, kid. No experience is wasted. It will come out in your painting sooner or later. Did you know Lottie wrote to tell me about your mother's illness?'

'I didn't know my mother was ill. When was that?'

'When you were a few weeks old. Lottie wrote to say that Charley had had a serious breakdown, that she was recovering, and taking an interest in her baby again, but the doctors feared that the slightest upset could have serious consequences. I think she was hinting at suicide. She begged me to stay out of Charley's life. She said it would be the kindest thing I could do for her now. Her letter was full of concern for your mother, she appealed to my better nature, and I thought there was a touch of irony in her choice of that particular phrase. For Charley's sake, she said, please don't come back and disrupt our lives again.

'I did what Lottie asked, but there were times though, when I wanted to chuck everything up and go back for Charley . . .' That deep strong voice faltered for a moment, but quickly recovered. 'It was just as well I didn't. Your mother went on to make a good life for herself, though God knows why it had to end the way it did. And it was better for you, being brought up by those two cosy old dames, than leading a vagabond life with me.'

'It wasn't all that cosy at times,' said Carla, remembering certain events in the past. 'I could have done with a father sometimes.'

'And now? Could you do with a father now – or is it too late? Carla, look at me. Tell me it's not too late.'

She hesitated, then smiled cautiously at him through her tears. 'I don't quite know how to answer that,' she said.

'What about – "Hiya Dad, how about a drink?" '

His face had the crumpled look of a man on the verge of tears, but at the same trying his best not to show it. He put his arms around her, awkwardly at first, because such actions did not come naturally to him, then as tension between them eased, he hugged her fiercely.

'I meant that about a drink,' he said huskily. 'Oh boy – I need a drink right now.'

It was his suggestion that they continued their talk out-of-doors. He didn't say so, but he felt uncomfortable in what he thought of as her doll's house. He was frightened of knocking over some piece of Beatrix Potter china, or leaving marks on the Laura Ashley chair covers. Besides, he badly needed to smoke, and there wasn't an ash-tray in sight.

They strolled about the cottage garden amid knee-high grass. Carla was wearing the old clothes she used when painting, but her father had dressed specially for this occasion, as she had when calling on him, in a white linen jacket and lightweight trousers.

'This is not doing your trousers any good,' she pointed out. 'You've got grass stains on the bottoms of them.'

'Irina will wash them.' He flicked his cigarette end over the fence, where they had come to rest, looking over the field of stubble where a cock pheasant was pecking among the straw with the sun glinting on its scarlet face feathers.

He had a sudden immense desire to paint Carla, in this setting, just as she looked now with her chestnut hair scooped up at the back and tied with a rainbow-coloured shoe-lace, wearing crumpled jeans turned up to her calves, and a sleeveless top like a man's singlet. Her face was partly turned towards him and there was just a glimpse of her amazing violet eyes partly obscured by long golden lashes. He hadn't felt such an urge to paint in years, and couldn't wait to get a brush in his hands.

'I brought a present for you,' he said. 'A sort of house-warming, peace-making present. It's in the car. I think you'll like it.'

'If it's what I think it is,' she said, charged with emotion, 'I'll more than like it. Oh damn, I think I'm going to cry again.'

'No, don't do that. I want to talk to you, and I can't talk to a crying female . . .'

She wiped her eyes. 'I've coveted that painting since I saw it in Bentall's Gallery. How can I thank you enough . . .' she paused. 'I would like to say, "Thank you father", but the word father doesn't come easily to me. Would it be okay to call you Larry?'

'You can call me anything you like as long as it is in that tone of voice.' He took her by her shoulders. 'Now I have something else for you. A piece of advice – from an old man who's been through it all himself.'

They went slowly back to his car arm in arm. 'Your work is good – extremely good,' he said. 'But there's room for improvement, and you won't get it by shutting yourself away here . . .'.

'I intend to travel when I'm finished with all the things that still need doing . . .'

'What things? What else is there to do?'

'I want to have the garden laid out, and then there's the studio. I'd like to supervise the building of that. And I must do something about the Foster graves in the churchyard. I want to tidy them up and have a headstone erected with all their names on it, and Lottie's too. It will be like reuniting her with her family. Don't you understand?'

'The only thing I can't understand is your morbid obsession with the past. Carla, it's time for you to let Lottie go.'

She smiled. 'It's funny you should say that. When I first came to the gatehouse, back in November, I always felt she was near me. I actually thought I saw her once. But not anymore. She's gone, or else I've lost the power to recall her. Perhaps, because I've rebuilt her home for her, her spirit is now at rest.'

'I can't believe I'm hearing this,' her father said impatiently. 'So this is what comes of being brought up by two batty old women, and having your head stuffed with superstitious rubbish. Get away from here, Carla. For God's sake get away.' He paused. 'But, perhaps not just yet. I'd like to paint you first.'

'Larry – you're priceless!'

But he returned to the theme again when it was time to say goodbye. 'I haven't felt the urge to paint for years. Prints of my paintings are still bringing in a good income, so I haven't got the incentive to make money anymore. But this is different – this is something personal.'

'To pair up with the painting of my mother, you mean?'

'No, I want to keep this one for myself – to hang on my wall. I haven't got any pictures of you, Carla. Not even a photograph.'

'I'll put that right when I've unpacked my albums.' She stood by his car, hugging the painting of the gatehouse. His gift to her. She felt renewed and full of promise, for her father had pointed the way for her.

'It would suit my purpose to have you stay on at this old gatehouse,' he said. 'Where I could see you every day, and get to know you better. But I'm not the same selfish bastard your mother fell in love with. I've matured since then. I'm telling you, Carla, for your own good, to get out of here. There's a different world waiting for you out there. You've done your duty by Lottie, now what about the duty to yourself? You have a gift – a talent – don't bury it here in this remote corner of Norfolk, take it out and air it.

'Go abroad to serve your apprenticeship,' he went on. 'Not by first-class travel though I know you can afford it. Go by banana boat or by train, travel third-class. Go and meet the people of other lands – not just the tourists. Find out how other people live. You're far too insular at present. Go to the beautiful cities of Europe and study their art treasures. Not just paintings, but sculptures and architecture too. Go to Rome and Florence and Dresden and Prague for starters. Visit India and Japan – don't confine yourself to Western art. Then when you think you've ingested enough to last a lifetime, find a good master and study under him. Your technique needs brushing up.'

'Would you be my master?' she asked artlessly.

He laughed at that, but looked flattered. 'I couldn't teach you anything. I'm only a painter who happens to be in fashion at the present. Nobody will remember me in forty years hence. I want better things for you.'

His face in this short time had become very dear to her. A crumpled, lived-in, well-used face, lit up by a pair of still remarkable blue eyes, in which there lurked at all times, a hint of self-mockery.

'And fall in love while you're about it,' he said. 'Sex is good for art. It enhances the depth of emotion you put into it. No more of this – "I can take it or leave it" – nonsense.'

'I'll see what I can do,' she promised, smiling.

He arranged to come over the next day to start his portrait of her. He would come in the afternoons and leave the mornings free for her to work on her sweetpeas. 'And once we have both finished our allotted tasks – off you go,' he said.

'This plan you have mapped out for me will take years . . .'

'And you've got years to spare. Don't worry about the gatehouse. We'll camp out here once a week to keep the place aired. We'll arrange for the garden to be landscaped, and we'll see that the studio is built satisfactorily. I'll personally supervise that. I like the idea of a studio in your garden. I could make use of it myself.'

'And the graves . . . you won't forget Lottie's name on the headstone.'

He heaved a reluctant sigh. 'That too, though it goes

against the grain. Who is there to impress after all this time?'

'They are my family, Larry.'

'They *were* not *are*. Your family is alive and kicking, now this minute – not in the past – but at the Thatched House, Carla. Waiting at the Thatched House!'

He had gone, her father, driving off she knew, with his mind working on plans for her itinerary. He was as excited as if it were he and not her, who was starting out on this journey of self-discovery. She went into the gatehouse and looked round for a picture hook on which to hang his painting. Not in her bedroom. This was to hang in state over the mantelpiece in the sitting-room. The sun was low now, sending shafts of light in dappled patches on the carpet. This was the home she had built for Lottie, and in so doing had nearly made a prison for herself. A pretty and cosy prison, but a prison nevertheless, and her father had rescued her. A most unlikely knight errant.

She went upstairs. There was still light enough for another hour or two's work. She took up her brush, wiped it clean, and dipped it in a blob of paint, and with a sure hand touched in a few pale green curling tendrils. She felt at peace with herself. She felt happier than at any time she could remember.

Lottie was gone – and yet she was everywhere. She could not look out onto the lane without conjuring up a picture of Lottie, in her borrowed finery, walking off to her fate in the grounds of Thornmere Hall. She could not look at her mother's portrait without thinking of Lottie's love for her – for all her children. Charlotte, Charley, and herself Carla, had to all intents and purposes, been Lottie's children.

Smiling now, she outlined with careful brush strokes another delicately tinted flower.

The sweet peas were her farewell gift to Lottie.

A Selected List of Fiction Available from Mandarin

While every effort is made to keep prices low, it is sometimes necessary to increase prices at short notice. Mandarin Paperbacks reserves the right to show new retail prices on covers which may differ from those previously advertised in the text or elsewhere.

The prices shown below were correct at the time of going to press.

☐	7493 1352 8	**The Queen and I**	Sue Townsend	£4.99
☐	7493 0540 1	**The Liar**	Stephen Fry	£4.99
☐	7493 1132 0	**Arrivals and Departures**	Lesley Thomas	£4.99
☐	7493 0381 6	**Loves and Journeys of Revolving Jones**	Leslie Thomas	£4.99
☐	7493 0942 3	**Silence of the Lambs**	Thomas Harris	£4.99
☐	7493 0946 6	**The Godfather**	Mario Puzo	£4.99
☐	7493 1561 X	**Fear of Flying**	Erica Jong	£4.99
☐	7493 1221 1	**The Power of One**	Bryce Courtney	£4.99
☐	7493 0576 2	**Tandia**	Bryce Courtney	£5.99
☐	7493 0563 0	**Kill the Lights**	Simon Williams	£4.99
☐	7493 1319 6	**Air and Angels**	Susan Hill	£4.99
☐	7493 1477 X	**The Name of the Rose**	Umberto Eco	£4.99
☐	7493 0896 6	**The Stand-in**	Deborah Moggach	£4.99
☐	7493 0581 9	**Daddy's Girls**	Zoe Fairbairns	£4.99

All these books are available at your bookshop or newsagent, or can be ordered direct from the address below. Just tick the titles you want and fill in the form below.

Cash Sales Department, PO Box 5, Rushden, Northants NN10 6YX.
Fax: 0933 410321 : Phone 0933 410511.

Please send cheque, payable to 'Reed Book Services Ltd.', or postal order for purchase price quoted and allow the following for postage and packing:

£1.00 for the first book, 50p for the second; **FREE POSTAGE AND PACKING FOR THREE BOOKS OR MORE PER ORDER.**

NAME (Block letters) ....

ADDRESS ....

....

☐ I enclose my remittance for ....

☐ I wish to pay by Access/Visa Card Number | | | | | | | | | | | | | | | | |

Expiry Date | | | | |

Signature ....

Please quote our reference: MAND